THE CHRISTMAS TRAP

L. STEELE

For the girls who never miss a deadline,
never let anything slip,
but still ache for the one man
who can undo them with a single command.
You don't have to hold it all together here.
Welcome home.

Now turn the page

LARK'S HOLIDAY PLAYLIST

Ariana Grande – "Santa Tell Me"
Mariah Carey – "All I Want for Christmas Is You"
Michael Bublé – "It's Beginning to Look a Lot Like Christmas"
Taylor Swift – "Christmas Tree Farm" (Old Timey Version)
Sabrina Carpenter – "santa doesn't know you like i do"
Love Actually – Darlene Love – "All Alone on Christmas"
Sabrina Claudio & The Weeknd – "Christmas Blues"
Justin Bieber – "Mistletoe"
Kelly Clarkson – "Underneath the Tree"
Olivia Rodrigo – "All I Want"
Pentatonix – "Mary, Did You Know?"
Sam Smith – "Night Before Christmas"
Norah Jones – "Christmas Calling (Jolly Jones)"

FROM LARK'S DIARY

My Life Plan

Things I want to check off by the time I'm thirty.
(AKA: proof I'm not a disappointment.)

1. Pay off my student loans so my parents can stop worrying.

2. Help my sister cover her living costs while she's a student, because she deserves to dream without limits.

3. Retire my parents even if they insist they're "fine."

4. Make CEO. *Because I'm ambitious. And if I don't get to the top, then what was all this for?*

5. Get married in a picture-perfect wedding. *This. So much this.*

6. Have two kids, spaced right, who wear matching Christmas pajamas on Christmas morning. *Oh, wouldn't that be cute?*

7. Make my parents proud, properly proud, not just "oh, she's doing okay" proud.

8. Be the sister who always shows up. (No matter if I'm running on empty.)

9. Be the wife who listens and the mother who never yells (I'm going to try my best to do this without ever losing patience.)

10. Celebrate Christmas every year like it's my job. Because I love the tree, lights, and traditions.

1

Lark

"Happy thirty days to Christmas." My voice is so upbeat, the words seem to chirp back at me. I wince.

I've officially turned into one of those irritating people who treats the holiday countdown like a national emergency wrapped in tinsel.

But how can I *not* be cheerful? It's almost Christmas. *Ch-r-iiii-stmas.* My fave time of the year.

I'm in the front office of Davenport Capital on the executive floor, which is also the top floor of the building they own.

The receptionist lifts her gaze. The expression on her face implies my intrusion is unwelcome.

Undeterred, I flash my brightest smile. "Don't you love this season?"

She grimaces. Some of the color fades from her features.

"Are you okay?" I scan her face, concerned.

"Yes. Of course. Thanks for asking." She winces, then presses a hand to her stomach.

I lean forward. "Are you sure you're alright? You don't look well."

"I'm fine. Period pains." She pinches her lips. "Nothing some ibuprofen won't cure. Only I seem to have run out."

"Oh, I have some." I dig through my bag and pull out the mini bottle I always carry.

Her face brightens. "You sure?"

"Of course. Go ahead, take it."

"Thank you, so much." She takes the bottle from me, shakes out two in her palm, then swallows them down with water. "Thanks again. I appreciate it."

"You're welcome." I slip the bottle back in my handbag. "I'm Lark. Lark Monroe." I hold out my hand.

"Evelyn Rainer." She shakes my hand and smiles.

"I'm here to interview with Mr. Brody Davenport."

The smile vanishes. There's a flicker of—*pity?*—in her eyes.

She recovers quickly, smoothing her expression into a practiced neutral one. Her eyes, however, stay soft.

"You're here to interview for the assistant role?"

"*Executive* assistant."

Because that's what it is. On paper, sure, it's EA. But in reality? This job is the equivalent of the Chief of Staff to the CEO.

It's access. Power. Money. Enough to pay off my student loans, help support my sister's tuition, and provide a more comfortable life for my parents.

Not to mention, it's a once-in-a-lifetime break. A monster item to check off my list. It's right up there with getting married. Which, for the record, I *am*. Engaged that is.

I'm deep in seating charts and dress fittings. I have an excel sheet to track the deliverables from vendors.

Soon, the life I've always wanted, with the perfect job and the perfect husband, will be a reality.

"Of course." The receptionist checks her screen then looks at me again. "Mr. Davenport isn't in."

"He...isn't?" My smile falters. "But the meeting's at ten, right?" I check my phone.

"It is." Her tone is apologetic. "He'll be back shortly. He asked that you wait in his office."

Right. So, my prospective boss is the kind of CEO who schedules an interview, then ghosts the first ten minutes.

My chest tightens.

This job is supposed to be *the* opportunity; the one that changes everything. But now, it feels like I'm chasing someone who can't be bothered to show up on time.

I clamp down on the rising doubt. Nothing ruins my festive spirit. Not even being stood up by my could-be boss.

On the other hand, it shows he needs an EA to make sure he turns up to appointments on time.

And I'm the woman for the job. *I hope.*

"This way, please." Evelyn rises and leads me down a hallway dotted with glass-fronted offices. People are glued to their phones or buried in their screens. Senior management, I assume.

In between them, a scatter of cubicles hums with keyboard tapping, and meeting rooms brim with polished tables and serious faces.

The whole place is a study in minimalist white desks, aluminum fittings, and brushed chrome. Exactly the kind of fast-growing, billion-dollar company I want to work for.

What it doesn't have? A single hint that Christmas is less than a month away. No garland. No sparkle. Not even a lonely string of tinsel.

Tragic. That'll be the first thing I'll fix when I get the job.

I trail Evelyn across the gray carpet toward the double doors tucked away at the far end of the office.

Just before she opens them, she pauses.

"Good luck."

Her voice is concerned.

That borderline-pitying look is back in her eyes. Just like that, the butterflies in my stomach start breakdancing. Why do I get the feeling I'm walking into the lion's den?

I researched my ass off; I pulled together a whole personality profile on Brody Davenport. But now? When faced with his receptionist's reaction, I wonder if my ambition has bitten off more than it can chew.

I shuffle forward, then stop in the middle of the large room.

It's a corner office and has floor-to-ceiling windows with a view of the Thames and the boats that ply on it, leaving white foam in their wake. The view feels too curated to be real.

The kind which money—or a surname like Davenport—can buy.

The office is situated in a heritage Victorian building and is located on prime real estate in the center of London on the Southbank.

From the outside, it's four stories of weathered red brick, crowned with ornate cornices and a black wrought iron balcony that curves like a sneer above the main entrance.

Inside, it's a shrine to futuristic design.

Mr. Davenport's office is a masterclass in masculine minimalism: cold-toned chrome and brushed steel. All sharp lines and angles.

The space hums with the kind of tension that makes me want to stand straighter and breathe a little shallower. It's built for power plays, not pleasantries. For raising empires. For issuing orders and expecting to be obeyed.

His desk dominates the room. It's large yet sleek, immaculate yet intimidating. It tells me a lot about the man whose office this is.

It's the kind of desk I envision for my own office one day. Sitting behind that polished surface is everything I dream of.

It's also uncluttered.

Except for a pair of glasses, a sleek computer screen, a keyboard and… *What is that?*

I take in what looks like a length of black rope.

It looks strong. Probably military grade. And it's twisted into intricate knots. Huh? It's so out of place in the room.

I walk toward it then reach out and run my fingers over the pleated coil. It's deceptively soft, silken to the touch. *Strange.* Wonder what he uses it for?

I draw in a deep breath, and the scent of something dark and peppery, with underlying notes of pine and sandalwood, fills my lungs. I know instinctively that it's *his* scent. It feels like I'm wrapped up in a very masculine embrace.

A shiver grips me.

I'm simultaneously turned on and left with this aching need to feel what it would be like to be in the shoes of my possible would-be boss.

Without stopping to overanalyze my actions, I round the desk for his big armchair, then sink into it.

That scent deepens; it's as if he's right here in this room with me. My skin prickles. My toes curls. A sense of power fills me. *So, this is what it feels like to be the CEO?*

I let my gaze leisurely flicker around the room. On my left is a wet bar. In front of it is a comfortable settee and two armchairs with a coffee table between them.

Then there's the bookcase opposite the desk. It's filled with hard-backs and paperbacks. Books, which seem well-used. They're not the kind of leather-bound tomes designers put on shelves which scream that they're for show.

Hmm. Apparently, Mr. Davenport has read them.

What a surprise. Now I'm curious about what kinds of books they are.

I slip off the chair and approach the bookcase. That's when I hear panting.

I turn to the doorway, in time to see a massive Great Dane amble in. The mutt is so tall, its head comes up to my chest. It's tail waves in the air like a flag. It's the last thing I expected.

The big dog makes a beeline for me, his tongue lolling, his face wearing what can be described as a smile.

I find my lips curve in response.

"Where did you come from?" I hold out my hand.

The dog sniffs my fingers, then licks them.

"Good boy." I give in to the cuteness overload and rub the space between his eyes. He makes a purring sound in his throat.

"Tiny, sit."

The command slices through the silence, low and clipped.

I look up, and my breath catches.

A man stalks into the office like he owns it. Because, judging by the authority which radiates from him, *he does*.

The very air seems to contract around him, charged and alert, as if the room itself recognizes him as a threat, or a king. *Maybe both.*

Holy North Pole. He's tall. Imposingly so. Broad shoulders that block out the door behind him, a perfectly cut black jacket clinging to every hard line of his body. His chest strains against the lapels, sleeves clinging enough to suggest the kind of arms that don't come from leisure, but labor, precision, control.

Then there's his face. Harsh angles, sharp jaw, and a scowl carved so deeply between his brows; it could be chiseled in stone. Disapproving. Intense. Almost devastating in its precision.

And that heavy-duty watch with the worn front plate on his wrist. It's not the kind I'd expect on a billionaire CEO. Too hard-edged. Too tough. But it matches the manly, dangerous energy he exudes.

I should look away. I *try* to look away.

But an awareness detonates between us. Hot. Immediate. My lungs constrict. My skin prickles. My pulse drops, then surges; like my body can't decide if it wants to run or leap into his arms.

I recognize Brody Davenport from his pictures. But those photos didn't convey how commanding he is in real life. How lethal. How *beautiful*.

How inappropriate that I'm gawking at my possible future boss like he's some kind of buff gingerbread man, and I'm dying to lick the icing off. And how deeply, catastrophically unfortunate that I'm attracted to him. I'm engaged. *Engaged*. Ugh.

This is wrong on so many levels.

I should not be ogling him. But apparently, being almost married doesn't make me blind, because my eyes are too busy notifying my brain—loudly—that the man in front of me is a prime male specimen radiating pheromones the way a pine tree sheds needles.

Enough. I need to get a grip.

I manage to rein in my hormones, and school my features into a professional expression. *I hope.*

He stops behind Tiny, who is now seated and, clearly, less affected than I am, and levels that scowl directly at me.

His icy gaze slides down to my chest. The furrow between his brows deepens like he's staring at a crime scene.

"What are you wearing?"

"Excuse me?" I blink, then glance down at myself.

He tilts his chin, like he can't believe he has to spell it out. "That. On your jumper."

I look down at my merino wool *pullover*. I'm not used to how the Brits call it a jumper. It has a festive design…but it's discreet.

It looks understated. *Classy*, in my opinion.

I paired it with a sleek pencil skirt and my one pair of red-soled heels. This is my version of the 'please hire me, I'm festive and fierce' combo.

In my head, I looked like the executive version of a Vogue Christmas cover. But taking in the distaste on my maybe boss's face, I'm worried I resemble a malfunctioning elf from the discount store. Ugh.

I was hoping to make a positive impression on him, too.

Suspicion filters into my mind.

Surely not. He can't hate Christmas, can he? Nah. *Who hates Christmas?* But, given how he stares at the reindeer like it dropped a turd on his plate of Christmas cookies, I'm beginning to think otherwise.

I resist the urge to cover it with my handbag. Instead, I point to my chest. "In case you were wondering, that's a subtle reindeer motif." I sniff like I'm describing museum art.

"Hmm." He grunts.

That's not a nice hmm. In fact, it's a very worrying hmm. Also, I should not have pointed to my chest because now his attention is locked there. I flush, then tell myself sternly to stop.

Note to self: Never try to win over a man who looks like he could have Christmas arrested.

"Do you…" I shudder not wanting to ask the question but having to do so because that suspicion has grown until it clogs my brain like poisonous fungi. "Do you not like the festive season?"

He jerks his gaze up to my face, and his own features are hard. "I detest Christmas."

That fizzy feeling I harbor in my chest during the festive season wilts. *How can I work for someone who hates Christmas?* I swallow.

But I do want this position. And there aren't many EA jobs on the market.

Of all the offices in the world, I walked into this one. Unless… He's saying it to test me.

"Yeah, right." I chuckle.

Not a crack in his façade. If anything, his features grow more thunderous. He glares at me like it's a forgone conclusion that he's never going to say anything in jest.

"You're serious." My shoulders slump.

It's just my luck to be stuck with a Grinch for my boss in my dream job. Assuming he's going to make me his EA, that is.

"Very." He eyes me with a disgusted look. "You, on the other hand, are a—"

"Christmas groupie." It's best to rip this off like a Band-Aid. "I love everything to do with Christmas."

He opens his mouth to, no doubt, retort with something scathing, when Tiny thumps his tail on the floor. He whines, then looks up at Mr. Davenport with what I can classify as a pleading expression.

"Fine," Mr. Davenport grumbles, like he and the dog had some kind of unspoken conversation.

A thought strikes me. "You were walking the Great Dane; is that why you were late?"

He nods.

Anyone who brings his dog to work and takes the time to walk the pooch instead of tasking one of his team with it can't be too bad, right? Never mind that he hates Christmas, which, in my books, is almost irredeemable. *Almost.*

"Let's start over again, shall we?" He's pushed aside whatever his aversion is to Christmas and is wearing an emotionless expression. One which is very difficult to interpret. I almost prefer the one that screamed his loathing of the festive season instead. "You must be Lark Monroe."

His hard voice pronouncing my name does weird things to my insides. My scalp tingles. My throat dries. Vibrations gather at the base of my spine. *What in the name of tinsel-coated trouble is happening to me?*

I shouldn't be this turned on by the sound of his voice. He might become my boss. Also, I'm engaged. *Engaged.*

This is not how a woman who's going to be married in less than a month behaves.

I should be thinking of my fiancé instead. And my wedding preparations. And how thrilled I will be to walk down that aisle and tick another item off my life list.

Unfortunately, none of my admonishments help when my possible boss's blue-gray eyes turn a dark indigo. Like the deepest, most unforgiving depths of the Atlantic. Where the waters are the coldest and light goes to die. I could dive into them and die happy. *Filled with guilt.* But very, very happy.

A-n-d. Time out.

Get yourself together, woman.

I shake off these unwarranted, and very wrong, emotions that this hot as Hades man seems to elicit in me.

Instead, I hold out my hand and take a step in his direction.

He ignores my attempt at a handshake and firms his lips. "Why do you want to work for me?"

2

Brody

"I… I…" she stammers, then squares her shoulders. "You were voted one of the top forty CEOs under forty by a major business publication. I could learn from you."

I stare at her, the flicker of disappointment sharper than I expected.

Not sure what I was hoping for, but *this*, a recycled line about my profile she came across, isn't it.

I created this new EA position because I need someone who can take over a large share of my day-to-day.

Someone competent enough to run a meeting if I can't be there, and confident enough to lead in my place.

It's part of my succession plan. I want the person in this role to eventually step into mine. I need an EA who can steady the chaos I'm pulled into every day. I want this person to grow into my replacement so I can move on to other things.

I've had applicants with impressive résumés and years of experience. But they felt jaded. Safe. Predictable.

Lark Monroe's cover letter stood out. I saw ambition and hunger. And between the lines, I sensed a vulnerability that she didn't try to hide.

She acknowledged she didn't have the same experience as the others, but promised that if given an interview, she would prove she was the right choice.

So far, she hasn't.

Maybe she needs a minute to warm up. To find her rhythm.

I cross my arms over my chest and wait.

She swallows then composes herself. "Davenport Capital is part of the Davenport Group, which is one of the most prestigious family-run companies in the world." Her voice is smoother, but her nerves show in the way her fingers dig into the leather of her bag.

That's when I notice the curve of her mouth. Pink. Full. The kind of lips that distract a man like me. Her chin tilts with stubborn grace. Her neckline is elegant, skin smooth like cream, exposed enough to tempt. Except for that irritating reindeer motif. But I don't want to judge her abilities based on something as superficial as that.

My gaze trails lower.

Tiny waist. Hips that flare in a way that piques my interest. Legs that go on forever, framed by a tailored skirt that should look professional, but doesn't. Not on her.

Heat pulses up my spine, low and sudden.

How long has it been since a woman caught my attention, *really* caught it? Since anything besides boardrooms and bottom lines held my focus. The next deal, the next merger, the next acquisition... It's all starting to feel like white noise. Meaningless. And now I'm getting philosophical about it.

Since when did I wish I had something more in my life to look forward to than the next meeting? Something more personal. Something that resembles this curvy woman who I can't take my eyes off. *Great.* This is an interview. I cannot be thinking such unprofessional thoughts about a woman I'm going to potentially employ as my EA.

And the very fact that I'd allow feelings to creep into my thoughts in the middle of a working day? That's a red flag.

She clears her throat, snapping me out of my thoughts. I drag my gaze to her face and attempt to keep it there. Which turns out to be a mistake. Because those eyes—massive, green, impossible to ignore—pull me right back under. Her blonde hair is swept up into a sleek twist, but it doesn't stop the rebellious tendrils curling at her temples. There's a flush high on her cheekbones. It shouldn't be distracting, but it is.

She looks like sin wrapped in merino wool and tied up with a Christmas bow. And that's the problem.

This time of year? I loathe it. Tinsel, carols, fake snow, gift wrap, false cheer—it's all a farce. Bah, bloody humbug.

The fact that she admitted to being a full-blown Christmas junkie? It should've disqualified her on the spot. It required gumption to waltz into *my* office wearing a Christmas jumper. For that, I should give her a chance.

I give her the full force of my most no-nonsense CEO stare.

"You've got one minute. Convince me you're the person for the job."

She stiffens, then rolls her shoulders back. A calm, resolute expression comes over her features.

"You are an important man. You make high-stakes decisions on a daily, even hourly, basis. You need someone to back you up, no matter how stressful it gets. You can count on me to show up. To deliver. And I don't drop the ball, no matter how much pressure I'm under."

She straightens further, pushing back her shoulders. Her Christmas jumper tightens across her bust. It draws my attention to her hourglass figure; to her nipped in waist and the shape of her curvy hips.

I've never been this distracted. Have never spent so much time thinking about what lies under a woman's clothes as I have with her.

"I don't flinch when people yell. I don't crumble when things go wrong. I keep my head, I fix the problem, and I make sure my boss never has to ask me for something twice."

There's a thread of steeliness running through her words, telling me she means business. Not bad. I tilt my head, indicating she should continue.

"I have an MBA, yes. But I've also paid my way through college the hard way. I've served champagne at weddings, temped in freezing offices, and stacked warehouses on weekends. I'm resilient. I'm persistent. I know how to win."

She draws a breath; her voice is cool and clear.

"Once I set my eyes on my goal, nothing can distract me. You need a right hand. I'm the whole damn arm."

Her eyes meet mine. She doesn't flinch.

Not even when I narrow my gaze, lower my eyebrows and paste on my most fierce expression. She doesn't back down. I'll give her that much. And despite being decked out like a Christmas sale, it's clear she's serious about this role.

The longer our gazes hold, the more something shifts between us. The air thrums. A buzzing sound fills my mind. The heat expands out from my spine to my extremities. I feel alive. Expectant. On the verge of something monumental. Alarm bells go off in my head.

I can't remember the last time I felt this attracted to a woman. And it's not because she's gorgeous, or that she has an incredible hourglass figure, *which I wasn't aware I favored, until now.* Or that she's as ambitious, as focused, and as intelligent as her cover letter hinted. No, it's the complete package.

Her enthusiasm is like a jolt to a system that's running on fumes. She stands out because she wants this, not only for the title, or for the proximity to power, but because she intends to deliver.

My instincts say she'll put in the hours, fight to prove herself, and rise fast if given the chance.

That should be the only thing I'm noticing.

But it isn't.

The chemistry between us hums, low and constant, crawling under my skin in a way I have no business acknowledging. It's distracting… Annoyingly so. But her potential outweighs all of that. Enough for me to set the rest aside. For now.

I turn away, walk to my desk, and take my seat. Then I nod to one of the chairs across from me.

Time to be professional.

"Take a seat."

The tension drains from her shoulders. She swallows audibly, then walks toward the chair.

Those luscious hips of hers sway as she walks toward me. Her thighs stretch the tight material of her skirt, making me want to rip it off her and bury my face between them and— *Whoa. Stop that train of thought right now.*

I am not the kind to feel so powerfully drawn to a woman. This has never happened before. It's a complication. And I've long resolved not to have those in my life.

I've worked toward becoming CEO of Davenport Capital since I left the Royal Marines.

Money and power are everything. That's what my grandfather taught me. And I intend to live up to Gramps' expectations.

I might allow a woman into my life by getting married like he wants, but I will not complicate my life by allowing her into my heart, like my brothers have.

The reminder helps me shove the unwanted attraction I feel for the woman sitting opposite me to a corner of my mind.

There's a woof, and Tiny pads over to her. He parks his butt next to her chair and looks up at her with his tongue lolling and what looks like hearts in his eyes. It irritates me for some reason. I can't be jealous of a mutt. *Can I?*

I snap my fingers. "Tiny, to your place, boy." I pull out a chew toy from my drawer and toss it over to the rug at the side of my desk.

For a few seconds, he doesn't move. Then, as I wonder if I'm going to have to lead him by his collar, he heaves a sigh.

He lumbers up to his feet and, with a last toss doleful look in the direction of the gorgeous woman in the chair, he pads over to the rug and collapses with another sigh. Instead of playing with his toy, he slides his head between his paws and blinks up at Lark.

"He's so cute." She smiles at him.

It's unusual for me to conduct an interview with a mutt in attendance. I'm taking care of him so my grandfather can enjoy some time off.

It's singularly irregular that the sight of the Great Dane mooning over her fans the kernel of jealousy in my chest into full-blown fire.

It makes me want to get the pooch out of the room.

With a last scowl at him, I turn my attention back on the woman seated opposite me.

"I have had more than a thousand applicants for this role."

"A thousand?" She pales.

"What sets you apart?" I tap my fingertips together and survey her.

The seconds stretch as she shuffles through her thoughts, then she firms her lips. "I don't just want to impress you. I want to *anticipate* you."

I arch an eyebrow. *Not bad.*

She presses on, gaining confidence. "The others are probably more polished. They're definitely more qualified than me. But I'll try my best to be ten steps ahead. I'll anticipate what you need from me. You'll never have to tell me twice. You'll barely have to tell me once."

Interesting. And audacious. *Definitely courageous.*

She knows she has me hooked. A small smile curves her lips.

"You can trust me to be ahead of the curve every single time."

I still. "That's a tall claim."

"It's true."

"Prove it."

She looks askance, then recovers admirably. "I know that you fire fast but reward loyalty. And that you don't just want an executive assistant, you want a shield. Someone who can manage the day-to-day problems which crop up and put out fires without having them intrude."

Good answer. I lean back in my seat. "What makes you think I don't want to know what's happening day-to-day in my own company?"

She doesn't hesitate. "You need perspective to be effective. You're a big picture man." She levels a shrewd gaze at me. "You want to focus on strategy without being pulled into the minutiae of business. That's where I come in."

She's saying all the right things. I'm almost convinced. *Almost.* But I need someone who can deliver. There's no room for failure. There's also a lot at stake.

It's why I thought long and hard before creating this position. *It's why I decide to test her further.*

"You think you can streamline my workflow?" I scoff.

She leans forward. "I'll not only streamline it, I'll own it."

I lean forward, mirroring her posture.

"I'll make the running of the business smoother," she says with complete confidence.

Woman has guts. And assurance. Something I find hugely appealing. I run my thumb under my lip. Her gaze is drawn there, and she flushes. But she quickly recovers herself and squares her shoulders.

"I don't want to be just your EA, Mr. Davenport. I want to be your advantage."

"Is that right?"

She sets her jaw. "Absolutely. If you give me the position, you won't regret it."

3

Lark

He regards me with skepticism. A sinking sensation opens in my belly, and I push it aside. I was sure I'd convinced him. *Maybe he's testing me one last time before making up his mind?*

"You don't believe me?" I lift my chin, daring him to say it.

He pauses. Long enough to make it sting.

"I admire your confidence. And your initiative. Your belief in your abilities is…impressive."

I can't let myself relax. There's a 'but' coming. I can feel it.

"But —"

There it is.

I cut in. "You don't think I can actually deliver."

His gaze narrows.

"I don't blame you. You don't know me at all. But you can check my references. My last line manager will happily attest to my capabilities. In fact, it was he who insisted I apply for this job."

His focus sharpens. Then he picks up the pair of glasses on the desk and plants them on his nose.

Sweet sleigh bells. As if he wasn't sinfully good-looking. Now, he's giving billionaire Christian Grey hotness. It's so unfair.

Not to mention, it's wrong that I'm objectifying Mr. Davenport in my head. I'm engaged. I need to think about my fiancé. *My. Fiancé.* Guilt squeezes my chest.

I drag my mind out of the gutter and decide to interpret his move as having piqued his interest.

My theory is confirmed when he tilts his head. "Why did you leave your last position?"

I choose my words carefully, trying to push home my advantage. "Unfortunately, the company went out of business."

He takes in my words then sets his jaw. "What's your plan?"

"Excuse me?" I frown.

"Your long-term plan. I assume you do have one?" He fixes me with an impatient expression.

Once again, I compose my answer in my head before speaking. My instinct is, it's best to be upfront with this man. He's busy. He meets people who want something from him every day.

The only way to impress him is if I stand out. My window of opportunity to do so is closing.

"I want to be CEO of a company someday. There's no reason that I can't lead a team and be at the head of a company like this one if I work smart and put in the hours, and I'm consistent."

I firm my lips.

"I don't take things lying down. I give as good as I get. A trait that will hold me in good stead."

He places the tips of his fingers together. "You talk a good talk. But you haven't told me why you want to specifically work for *me*?"

With that, I realize, he's considering me for the role. It feels like I've passed some kind of test he's set me. I release my grip on my bag and set it on the seat next to mine.

I force myself to remain calm, composed. *Confident. I am confident. I* will *get this role.* Think positively. I must convince him that I'm the person for this role.

"You're a master strategist. You're known to be exacting, but you've turned this company around in less than two years. That's an achievement, by any standards. I want to learn from the best. And the best is you."

One side of his lips ticks up. "You trying to blow smoke up my arse, Monroe?"

"Nah." I lift my shoulder. "Maybe, a little." I hold up my thumb and forefinger with a little space between them, then smile.

He laughs. A full, from the belly chuckle, which is masculine and gravelly and so hot. Little Christmas crackers go off inside my chest. *Happy Festive Season to me.* Hearing my sexy maybe boss laugh and seeing his features lit up like Trafalgar Square during the festive season make me feel like I've received an early Christmas gift.

My heart swells. *So does my pussy.* Until I remember that I'm engaged. Guilt churns my guts. My smile wilts a bit.

It's wrong to feel so turned on by a man who's not my fiancé. So why can't I stop myself?

How much trouble am I going to be in, if his every action adds to his appeal?

Can I handle this attraction to him, which deepens with every second I spend with him? I won't cheat on my fiancé. That much, I know about myself. It's that which gives me the confidence to realize that if I get this job, I'm not walking away either. I can handle this pull toward him. I can do this. I can treat him as my boss, and nothing more. I can be professional about our relationship. *Right?*

I square my shoulders, gather my wits, and focus my mind.

"It's not an exaggeration that you're known for your problem-solving skills in the business world. You see angles to an issue no one else notices. You take on impossible challenges and resolve them. Being in your orbit would force me to level up every single day. I want to learn from you because excellence feels natural around you. It feels…achievable."

There. That's a good answer, right?

But when he stays impassive, my heart sinks.

Was that too much?

Ambition is a tricky thing when you're a woman. Show too little,

you're forgettable. Show too much, you're 'aggressive.' I thought
Brody Davenport might appreciate my being honest. He invited me
to interview, didn't he?

But maybe, I crossed the line?

Maybe, I came across as too pushy? Maybe, I've bulldozed
straight past professional and landed in 'dear God, someone stop her'
territory. Ugh. My spirits plummet. I fight the urge to hunch my
shoulders.

I can't help but wonder if my determination to get the job landed
me on the CEO's naughty list.

4

Lark

Finalize the holiday playlist before I get served with All I Want for Christmas Is You for the 187th time.
— From Lark's Christmas to-do list

"You got the job?" My sister's eyes widen on the phone screen.

After the interview, I walked over to the HR manager and completed the paperwork needed so I could be put on the payroll. *Tomorrow.* Which will be my first day at work as executive assistant to the CEO.

Then I walked out in a daze and sat in the nearby public park. I stared at the scenery trying to process everything. *I got the job. OMG. I got my dream job.* It feels like a dream.

When Raya called, I automatically answered the phone.

"Apparently, I did." I take in the people sitting on the nearby benches. Most are enjoying their lunch break and taking advantage of the rare sunshine. As it gets closer to Christmas, we'll begin to lose light earlier.

"You sound...surprised?"

"I am...bemused. I didn't think I would get the role. Not after I wore my new Christmas pullover to the interview."

There's silence, then she screeches, "You did not."

"Now, you sound like my new boss." I roll my eyes.

"He wasn't a fan of your Christmas look?" She chuckles.

"Worse. He hates Christmas." I slump a little.

"Oh no." Her eyebrows draw together. "But you *love* the festive season."

"I do. Also, I must insist that my sweater is very tasteful. You can hardly see the Christmas motif." I angle the phone so she can take in the front of my pullover.

"It is...very discreet," she concedes.

"Right?" I roll my neck, getting rid of the last vestiges of tension left over from the interview. "Now that I have the role, I'll have to find a way to change his mind about the holiday season."

"Ooh, that sounds smart. I'm sure your boss will love your campaign to change his opinion about Christmas."

I frown. "When you put it like that...yeah...maybe it's not a great idea. But I've gotta try. It's Ch-r-iiii-stmas after all."

"For someone so practical, you go full delulu the moment you smell those first holiday lattes brewing." She rolls her eyes. "The grumphole aside, you're excited about this position?"

I brighten. "You should see my office; it has an amazing view."

Especially since it adjoins Brody Davenport's, and I can see him through the glass wall that separates his office from mine. It's a distraction. But that's nothing I can't handle, *right?*

I'm going to be so busy, I probably won't have any time to notice him.

Also, I'm totally engaged, and I'm totally planning a wedding so, like, why would I look at my boss?

"I can pay off my student loans and credit card debts, and help mom and dad with theirs too. I could support you with your living expenses."

"No. Absolutely not." She scowls. "I make enough from my part-time job to cover my living expenses."

I'm sure she's right. But it's only the two of us in this country, and I *am* the older sister. *And really, because I can afford to do so,* I feel duty bound to help her.

"This new job pays five times what I used to earn," I coax her.

"Five times?" Her gaze widens. "What kind of a job is this?"

"It's with Davenport Capital."

"*The* Davenports?" Her gaze widens. "Skylar Davenport owns The Fearless Kitten. She's married to one of the Davenport brothers."

The Fearless Kitten is the boutique coffee shop where Raya works as a barista. When she's not studying at the Royal Drawing School, where she got a scholarship to attend, she works there to pay for her living expenses.

"Right. My boss is Broody—I mean, Brody Davenport."

"Broody?" She chuckles.

I roll my eyes. "He is the Grinch personified. I've never met someone who hates Christmas so much. Unfortunately, he's also my boss. My very sexy, very annoyingly macho boss."

"Ooh." Her eyes grow wide. "He's a hottie?"

"Verrry." My lips curve before I can stop myself.

Her answering smile is wicked. "Oh, oh, is there trouble in paradise?"

I blink. "What do you mean?"

"You do not sound like a woman who's engaged to be married soon." Her tone softens.

Guilt pinches the back of my throat. She's right. I shouldn't be reacting to my bosshole at all. I shouldn't notice the way he fills a doorway or how his voice feels like being dragged into a warm bath I didn't ask for.

I definitely shouldn't feel my stomach flip every time he looks at me like I'm some kind of puzzle he intends to solve.

I swallow hard and lift a shoulder.

"It's nothing like that. I'm his employee. And I'm keeping things strictly professional. I'm not screwing this up. This is my chance, Raya. The job I've worked toward since my MBA."

Her expression softens. "I know how you push yourself." Her eyes shine with pride. "You deserve this, Lark. Truly."

"Thank you." My heart warms at her words.

"Bet Keith's excited too?"

I hesitate.

I want to say, yes, he is. That he was the first person I called after getting the job. But I didn't even tell him I was applying for this job. I didn't want to disturb him. Which is strange. He *is* my fiancé after all.

I firm my lips.

"I haven't had a chance to catch up with him. He's been traveling for work for the last three weeks." *I tamp down the rising disquiet.*

He wants to be with me. I mean, he proposed, didn't he? So what if he makes me feel two feet tall? He's marrying me. That must count for something, right?

Is it odd that I don't miss him?

"Gosh, must be tough with him traveling so much, and so close to the wedding." There's curiosity in her voice, but her eyes are soft.

I rub at my forehead. "It hasn't been easy. But I'm organized, and that helps me deal with the chaos of wedding planning."

She scoffs. "That's putting it lightly. You love your to-do lists, and your organizational skills are unmatched. I bet you have a dozen spreadsheets to help you track everything."

I flush. "It helps me stay on top of things."

She chuckles. "He'll be back soon, and we can pick a new date for a family catch-up with him and our parents on video call."

"I'm sorry he canceled the last one." I wince.

Only because he was called away on a business emergency.

And then, he emailed my parents and my sister to apologize. He shared how happy he was to be marrying me and becoming part of the family.

My parents were impressed.

My sister was noncommittal. I get the impression she isn't too impressed with him. Of course, she's only met him once. And briefly, at that.

"I realize, he's been elusive, but that's because of the demands of his job," I feel compelled to add.

"Hey, you don't have to defend him." She raises a shoulder. Then her expression turns wicked again. "Of course, with a name like Keith…" She shrugs. "I don't know. I'm not sure I can get past that."

"You're going to hold his name against him?" I throw up my hand.

She bursts out laughing. "Damn woman, I was kidding."

"Raya, seriously? You're so annoying," I huff.

"Comes with the territory of being the little sister." She sobers. "I didn't mean to be unkind. I want you to be happy."

"I *am* happy," I say firmly.

But am I? Since I agreed to marry him, my fiancé seems to have become MIA.

He's spending more time on work trips. He hasn't even paid for any of the wedding arrangements.

Sure, when he suggested that, instead, he could provide the down payment for the apartment we want to buy, I jumped at the chance.

And he did negotiate the reception at the pub. Still, it would have been reassuring if he'd offered to, at least, share the costs.

Besides, it's tradition for the bride's family to pay for the wedding. Only I have no intention of asking my parents to do so.

They worked hard to make sure we didn't lack for anything. We weren't poor. But we also weren't rolling in money.

Instead, on top of my student loans, I've maxed out my credit cards to pay for the wedding arrangements. *But with this new job. I'll be able to pay it off in no time.*

"It'd be easier if Keith showed a little more interest in the wedding planning," I admit.

She lifts a shoulder. "I suppose, it's normal for men not to care about these organizational details."

Which is true. Many men are that way. Right? I've been with Keith for two years, which should be more than enough time to commit to marriage.

Only, I'm beginning to wonder how well I know him.

"What I don't get is why you asked Tiffany to be one of your bridesmaids. Now Harper, I understand. She's one of your true friends. But Tiffany?" Raya snorts. "She's a fair-weather friend, and you know it. Sometimes, I want you to put your foot down and demand more from your relationships."

I stiffen. "Are you saying I settled when I agreed to marry Keith?"

"No, not at all." She exhales slowly. "I wasn't even talking about him."

Why did my brain immediately go to him when she suggested I should demand more?

She sighs. "You're a perfectionist, Lark. You hold yourself to impossible standards."

"What's wrong with that?" I ask, genuinely puzzled.

"You don't hold anyone else to the standards you hold yourself to. You forgive too easily because you want everything to stay perfect."

Her expression turns serious.

"You give so much of yourself. You're so busy being amazing that you don't give people a chance to be amazing for you. Then you end up surrounded by people who don't step up for you."

The words hit harder than I expect.

I think about Keith. About the way I let his absence slide. I never call him out for not messaging or calling me back. I've been so understanding that he's missed venue visits, or the menu tastings. I told myself it was because of his job. That he was busy.

But deep down, maybe it's because I didn't want to face the answer.

I lower my chin. "You're not wrong."

"I'm not?" She looks flabbergasted.

"I am ambitious at work, but in my personal life... I give in too easily. I say yes when it might be in my best interest to say no."

Is that what I did with Keith? No, I'm not going there.

"I want to be a good friend. And I want our parents to be proud of me. To do that, I often avoid conflict. I'm always chasing the best version of myself, no matter if it seems impossible."

She groans. "Great. Now I feel like a terrible sister. I wasn't trying to send you on some soul-searching, self-flagellation spiral."

"You're not. And you totally did." I laugh.

She winces. "Because I care. You know that, right?"

I nod. "I know you've always got my back."

"Even if I sometimes want to shake a little sense into you," she says, crossing her eyes and sticking out her tongue like she's five again.

I burst into laughter. Some of the tension loosens in my shoulders.

Someone calls to her from off-screen.

"I gotta go, Sis." She wiggles her eyebrows. "And do not let the broody hottie get in your head, okay?"

Before I can reply, she disconnects.

I huff, half-amused, half-exasperated. She is far too cheeky for her own good.

I drop my phone in my handbag and rise to my feet. I turn and gasp. Racing straight toward me, is a very familiar, larger-than-life dog.

"Tiny?" I blink.

5

Lark

Tiny's big ears flop behind him. His large, mastiff-like tail stretches out. Each time the Great Dane's big paws hit the ground, it feels like the earth trembles. I'm sure I'm having a flashback to a few hours ago when he almost ran me over.

The difference is that he's straining at his leash which is held by a very tall, broad-shouldered man with his now-familiar thunderous features.

"Tiny, sit," my boss snaps.

Instantly, Tiny lumbers to a stop and parks his big butt down on the ground a few feet in front of me.

"Hello?" I ask warily.

"I wasn't following you. But this dog"—my new boss glares at the mutt—"had different ideas."

"Oh." I look down at the happily panting Tiny, and honest-to-God, the pooch seems to be wearing a big joyful smile.

"He got absolutely restless after you left. I barely got any work done. Then he began pacing my office with his leash in his mouth, whining, and would not let up, until I brought him to the park. At which point"—he gestures to the dog who woofs happily—"he made a run for you."

"Hey boy." I eye the panting Tiny.

He has that permanent please-love-me look, with his big soulful eyes and those wobbling jowls. And then his eyebrows, which tilt in ways that make him look like he's mildly concerned about his life choices. I love it when dogs have discernible eyebrows.

The mutt is so adorable, I can't help but smile. Some of that tightness in my chest unravels. Instantly, I feel better. *Thank you, Tiny!* I think I might be in love with a dog for the first time in my life.

I move toward him. Except for his panting, he stays completely still. I tickle him behind his ear, and he makes a purring sound.

I laugh. "You're adorable."

"He made sure I couldn't get any work done this morning." My boss glowers at the dog. "I should have realized when I offered to dog sit that this was a possibility."

"He's not your dog?"

"He belongs to Arthur, my grandfather, who's on a short break with his girlfriend. He asked me to take care of Tiny. I couldn't refuse. The pooch does have a regular dog sitter, who's sick today. I had no choice but to bring him in to work."

My boss tugs on Tiny's leash.

"Up, Tiny."

Tiny doesn't budge.

"You dragged me out. Might as well do your business now," Brody snaps.

I sense my boss's growing irritation.

Tiny, on the other hand, doesn't seem to care. He continues to stare up at me.

"Tiny," Brody warns.

No response from the Great Dane.

"Tiny, up boy," I croon.

Instantly, he pops up to a standing position.

"What the—" My boss's jaw firms. He glares at the mutt.

I laugh. "Well, he's up now. I'm sure he'll follow your orders from now on.

His brow grows even more thunderous. He looks less than thrilled. Then he squares his shoulders and stalks forward. Tiny follows.

"Bye then. I'll see you tomorrow," I call out.

Tiny turns back toward me, hesitating as if he expects me to follow. Instead, I wave at the departing man and dog.

My grumpy boss doesn't bother to wave back. Big surprise.

And now, I need to call my parents. I've been putting it off for days because there's never a perfect moment. But I've landed the perfect job, so I finally have a good reason to pick up the phone.

I can't wait to hear how proud they are of me, but I don't want to do it in a public park. My mother will complain about the background noise, and I don't want any distracting questions about the weather. I want this to be as perfect as possible.

So, I head to the tube station and take a train home. Stopping to pick up some groceries on the way, I'm in my one-bedroom apartment in the leafy borough of West Hampsted in less than an hour.

I head inside, unpack my bags, then pull out my phone and call my parents. As the ringtone sounds, I picture them in Sunnyvale, California, where my father works in construction and my mother teaches at the local school.

I get my ethos of hard work from them. The being an overachieving, people-pleasing, perfectionist thing, though? That's all me. Ever since I can remember, I've wanted to make them proud. It's what led to my excelling at school and in my undergrad years. And when I won the scholarship to study for an MBA at the London School of Economics, no one was prouder than them.

"Lark, honey how are you?" My mom answers the phone.

It's seven a.m. for them.

"I'm good, are you guys having breakfast?"

"I am." She balances the phone on the table in the kitchen where I remember having rushed breakfasts before dashing to school. "Your father had to leave early. The new construction site he's working at is two hours away. So, he leaves before dawn most days."

My father's a construction worker, who's worked his way up to being construction foreman. I remember him as always being on site, sometimes even picking up weekend shifts.

"Does he have to work so hard?"

"The more he works, the more he makes. You know that." She butters a piece of toast.

"I wish he'd slow down a little." I firm my lips.

"We have a few more years' work left in us." She laughs.

"Both of you could retire early."

She sighs. "We're not *that* old, and we're both perfectly capable of continuing to work."

"I can send you what you need. With my new job, I'll be making more than enough to help."

Her forehead furrows. "You have a new job?"

"It's with Davenport Capital. And I'm the executive assistant to the CEO. Which means, I'm on track to possibly make CEO myself, at some point in the future."

It feels so good to be able to say that. I'm practically glowing. I wait for my mother to acknowledge my accomplishment and tell me she's proud of me.

But all I get is: "That sounds interesting." She bites into her toast and crunches through the mouthful. "But remember, you're about to get married, so you may need to readjust your focus. Your husband should be able to take care of you while you start a family. And if you need extra money, once the kids get a little older, you could always be a teacher. Teaching is the perfect career for moms."

I deflate a little.

Sure, I understand the importance of a balanced life. And I do want to get married and have a family.

But I want to carve out my own identity and not follow in the footsteps of my mom.

I don't think she means to be hurtful when she glosses over my career achievements, but sometimes, I wish she'd take them seriously.

While she's never overtly expressed her expectations for me, they've always loomed in the background. Sometimes, I think that if

I don't marry and have kids, she'll think I'm rejecting her life choices.

It's why I'm obsessed with leading the perfect life. I want to please myself by having a career that'll make me proud. But I also want my mom to approve of the person I'm marrying. And, I'd love to give her grandchildren. Eventually. For now, I want to build a solid career.

I want to have it all. So, I've built my life around checklists and achievements.

My need to get everything right—the job, the fiancé, the perfect life—is really about proving I can have it all. The dream career. The dream marriage. And the dream family. On my terms.

I want her to see that I can follow my own path and be happy and provide a good life for my children.

On the other hand, I can't forget how hard my parents worked to give my sister and me a comfortable life.

I don't want my mom to ever feel like I think her choices are inferior to the ones I'm making. And because I want to show my appreciation, I feel this constant need to make things easier for them now.

"I'm making a lot more. I can help you to afford a few luxuries here and there."

"Oh, we don't need luxuries, Lark. You know that."

"Really, Mom. Let me do this."

She purses her lips, looking uncertain.

"You know, if you agree to it, so will Dad. Then he won't have to take on additional jobs. That'll help with his ulcers."

Her features soften.

"You're a good daughter, Lark."

Warmth squeezes my chest. I've spent so much of my adult life striving to gain my parents' approval. It feels good to have my mother acknowledge as much.

"I am so proud of you. You've always been so ambitious, I was worried you might turn out to be one of those women who'd focus on her career to the exclusion of everything else. But thankfully, that's not the case. I'm so looking forward to attending your wedding and meeting your fiancé. You're going to make a beautiful bride."

I curve my lips, unable to muster up a real smile this time. I wish she were happy for me because I met someone who I think I'll be happy to spend the rest of my life with. And not because she's relieved that I'm settling down.

I suppose…it's, in part, her belief that a woman is incomplete unless she gets married that made me accept Keith's proposal.

It's also because he's a good man. *He's boring.* Safe. I mean, he's safe. Nothing like the brooding alpha male I met this morning. *Uh-oh, what if the reason I can't muster a smile is because I'm not actually excited about my upcoming nuptials?*

"Lark, are you listening?"

"Yes." I shake out of my reverie. Why are my thoughts veering to Brody? He's my boss. I don't know him at all. And I need to keep our relationship strictly professional, too. "I can't wait to see you here too."

"We booked a red-eye into Heathrow." Her expression is giddy. "I can't wait to finally visit you in London. I am so excited."

I can't help but smile at that. It's nice to see my mom so looking forward to the trip. They work so hard, they do deserve a great holiday.

"Oh my, look at the time. I'm going to be late. See you in a few weeks, Sweetie."

"Bye." I hang up the call and place the phone aside, feeling deflated.

I was so excited to share my triumph with my mom. I was thrilled about landing the perfect job and embarking on the next stage of my perfect career. I wanted to share that with her but some-how, the focus shifted to my future as a wife and mother.

The conversation with my mother was another version of her 'I'm never going to be successful until I'm married' lecture. It's something she and I have never seen eye to eye on.

And now, I'm even more stressed about this wedding.

My phone vibrates with an incoming call.

It's the pub where Keith and I are having a reception after the wedding.

It had crossed my mind to have the reception somewhere a little more memorable. But it made more sense to save the money for buying our perfect apartment. Naturally, he agreed.

Keith is as practical as me. It's one of the reasons we are so well suited.

Only, I didn't realize that I *do* have a romantic streak in me. It would have been nice to have a ring. And have the reception at a more memorable venue. But hey, I'm getting married. I'm not going to end up an ambitious spinster who has her career and nothing else, as my mother often warned me. Everyone is happy, right?

I'd be happier if Keith were more present and involved in the details of the wedding planning.

I shove aside my misgivings and answer the call. It's to confirm the details of the menu for the lunch. They ask me to confirm the number of guests. So, I check the RSVPs of the friends I invited to the wedding.

It's my closest girlfriends, and my family.

Keith said he'd invite his family and friends. But he hasn't confirmed numbers to me. I call him, get his voice mail—*big surprise*—and leave him a message.

———

The next morning, I bounce out of bed at dawn. I've put the call with my mother, and the stress related to the wedding organizing, out of my mind.

It's my first day of work at my dream job. And it's another day closer to Ch-r-iiii-stmas. That's enough reason to be happy, right?

I dress carefully and make it to the tube station an hour early, but the tube trains are running late. Then the train gets stuck in a tunnel. And a pregnant woman faints. I jump in to help her, because there's no way I can sit by and not. When she insists that I stay with her until the paramedics arrive, of course, I do. I don't have the heart to leave until they check her out and confirm that she's fine.

I'm hyperventilating at the thought of not being, at least, an hour early for my first day on the job. But her effusive thanks once the medics check her out and confirm she's fine, makes me feel guilty at being so selfish.

By the time I make it to the office and knock on his door, I'm exactly on time. I gulp a few breaths and tell myself it's going to be okay.

When my boss growls, "Come in," he doesn't sound okay. In fact, he sounds even grumpier than yesterday. *Ugh.*

I steel myself and enter his den—I mean, domain—and am instantly struck by the clouds of anger which seem to emanate from him.

He's seated behind his big desk, and he seems pissed off.

The perfectionist in me hates that I am not early on the job on my first day. But no way I could have left that pregnant woman upset and alone.

Only, I'm facing the consequences of my actions.

My boss's thunderous expression confirms that I have not made a good impression on my first day at all.

I take a step forward, pasting a smile on my face.

A nerve pops at his temple. The very air between us thrums with the force of his disapproval. It presses down on my chest, making it difficult to breathe.

"I'm sorry, the tube was delayed and then I helped this pregnant woman who was not feeling well, that's why I wasn't early." The words come out in a rush.

The grooves in his forehead deepen. He seems to forget whatever he was about to say. "You stopped to help a stranger on the train, that's why you're"—he glances at his watch—"on time?"

I nod. "I was hoping to get in an hour earlier, to be honest. It's my first day, after all. I wanted to get in and orient myself, to get in the zone, you know? But I couldn't leave when she, clearly, needed help."

A strange expression crosses his face. Then he squares his shoulders. "Get me the revised financials for this quarter in the next fifteen minutes. Cancel my morning schedule. Reschedule every meeting for tomorrow."

6

Brody

She flinches, and her smile drops.

I pretend not to notice it. Nor the flicker of hurt on her face. The way she folds into herself for half a second before straightening her spine.

I know I've gone too far. Her first fifteen minutes in the office, and I've unleashed my temper on her.

When really, I'm upset at myself.

I expected her to walk in half an hour, even an hour, before her official reporting time. She impressed me as someone who wanted this job enough to go that extra mile.

I was so keen on seeing her, I too got in an hour before my normal starting time.

The truth is, I barely slept last night. I spent far too long thinking about her. About the way she looked when she smiled upon finding out she had the job. About the delight on her face when she saw me with Tiny in the park. And then I began to wonder how she'd smell first thing in the morning. About how her voice would sound if I woke her up with my hands on her skin.

So, when the clock ticked toward her start time, and she didn't walk through that door, my mind went places it shouldn't have.

What if she'd changed her mind? What if she'd decided the job wasn't worth it?

I hated that the thought sent a rush of something like fear through me. That I wanted her here so badly. That I missed her before the day had even begun. And I don't even know her.

I let my fears get to me, and fuck, if that didn't frustrate me. I told myself that I made a mistake hiring her. That she's unreliable. That she's playing games. That she *wanted* me to worry. That I should have known better than to let myself care.

I'm pissed off at her for making me feel so much.

I'm *more* pissed off at myself for needing her in the first place.

And I'm both taken aback and affected by her choice to help someone in need. She knew it might make her late on her first day of a job that clearly matters to her. But she chose kindness.

That kind of instinct matters to me. It is why I became a Marine.

Seeing that facet of her stirs something deep in me, something I'm not ready to examine closely.

I shove those strange, unwelcome feelings aside and focus on the irritation I felt when she didn't show up early. It is easier to hold onto anger than admit I already rely on her.

I bite out, "While you're at it, you can explain to the board why I had to move the board meeting from this Friday to next week."

"But I don't know the reason," she protests.

"I'm sure you'll think of something."

I catch the flicker of tension in her jaw.

Without waiting for her acquiescence, I continue, "Push it back to next week. Then bring me a coffee. Black. Scalding hot. Try not to spill it."

She stills, enough for me to know I hit a nerve. She won't let it show, but I see the impact.

My demands are unreasonable, and the way I've thrown them at her is downright rude. I've been a complete arse, even by my standards. Short-fused. Sharper than I meant to be.

She doesn't say a word, but the darkening of her eyes tells me she's hurt.

I shove aside the regret that blooms in my chest.

I know I sound like a bastard.

Regret flickers through me. A quick, unwelcome tightening in my chest. I shouldn't have snapped. Not at her.

For a moment, I consider softening, offering something that resembles an apology. Something human.

I shut the thought down.

I pay her enough to keep up. I hold her to a high standard because I need someone who can keep pace with me. Someone exceptional.

So, I push. I pile on the pressure. I throw her into the deep end. If she's as good as I believe she is, she'll swim.

I'm testing her to make sure I didn't make a mistake in hiring her over the other more qualified candidates.

If she passes, I can finally let go of this constant micro-managing. I can shift my attention to the big picture. The things only I can do.

So yeah, it's a trial. For her. Also for me.

I need her to prove my confidence in her isn't misplaced.

Because if I made a mistake? I don't know what that says about me either.

I expect her to get flustered by the barrage of tasks I throw her way. Instead, she taps into her device.

When she's done, she looks up. "Anything else?" Her tone is placid. Her gaze steady. I'd have thought her calm but for the telltale flutter of the pulse at the base of her neck.

"Draft the press release about the new takeover. Details are in your inbox. I expect to see it within the hour."

She firms her lips, but when she speaks, her voice is serene. "Of course."

"Get a hold of the Madison's latest press releases and tell me what they're not saying. I want it before the end of the day. Keep on HR until they push through the contracts I signed yesterday."

She draws in a sharp breath and continues tapping into her device.

Damn, she's unshakeable.

"Find me the number of that journalist who keeps poking around about the new startup I'm funding. I'll handle them myself."

She nods.

"Order new cuff links from Harrods and have them couriered here before lunch."

She frowns. "What kind of cuff links?"

"Figure it out." I smirk.

That should push her over the limit.

She purses her lips. "I think the Christmas tree ones are your vibe."

"Excuse me?" I blink.

"Or m-a-y-b-e—" She taps her chin, like she's auditioning for one of those ridiculously stupid holiday rom-coms women seem to find funny, but which are pathetic. Finding love while getting marooned in a snowstorm? Bah. How lame.

"Yes, I have it." She snaps her fingers. "The Santa's hat cuff links are more you."

I open my mouth to tell her off, then take in the sparkle in her eyes. Huh. Is she winding me up? *She is winding me up.* Too bad I don't find it funny at all.

I gnash my teeth, ignoring her attempt at levity. No doubt, she thinks I'm a miserable sod who can't take a joke. *Which I can't.* Might as well lean into it.

"Get IT up here. My system lagged for three seconds this morning. Unacceptable," I bark.

"It's 7:10 a.m.; IT won't be in yet."

I stare at her.

She flushes. "Right. I'll figure it out."

I pick up my phone, scanning the stock market updates on the screen.

"Book me a dinner reservation for three at The Edge for eight tonight."

She stills.

For a few seconds, I stay focused on my phone. When there's no reaction or movement from her, I drawl without looking up, "Problem?"

"Chef James Hamilton received his third Michelin star for The Edge. It's bound to be booked out for the next twelve months."

"So?"

She closes her eyes, blows out a breath, then slowly nods. "I'll work out a way." She turns to leave.

"Don't forget my coffee."

She glances back at me over her shoulder, and that flash of quiet defiance on her features spears straight through my bloodstream. Lust curls low in my gut.

I love that she follows my orders the moment I give them. It's more than the efficiency of a good executive assistant. It's a jolt of power that edges into territory I've always kept far from my professional life.

And yet, I can't stop. I push her, knowing she'll push back. Knowing she'll meet my stare without flinching. Knowing she'll stand her ground even as she does exactly what I tell her to do.

It's intoxicating. It's dangerous. And it makes me want her in ways I have no business wanting.

"I also haven't dismissed you yet," I drawl.

She turns slowly to face. "I am your *executive* assistant."

"Next, you're going to tell me that you're not my 'assistant,' hence, you're not going to get my coffee." My voice comes out more belligerent than normal.

Damn, I'm trying to rile her, but I'm losing my cool instead.

"That's not what I was going to say." Her eyes gleam.

Well, hell. It's my turn to be surprised. I fix her with a gaze that has reduced my management team to nervous wrecks. But not her, apparently.

She lifts her chin. "I'll get you your coffee. However, my time is better spent functioning in the capacity of your *executive* assistant. Which means, putting my brain power to use behind executing your strategy and not wasting my time on tasks which could be performed by anyone else."

That's true. There are certain tasks which I'd like you to perform. No one else will do for that. I don't say that aloud. I also am aware that these thoughts are taking me down the wrong path. I do respect this woman. She hasn't lost her nerve, despite my having given her a long list of difficult jobs to carry out. And she's my employee... And I have never mistreated anyone on my team. And I don't plan to start with her. Doesn't mean I won't challenge her. Besides, she makes a good point.

"Good negotiating tactic." I jerk my chin. "Have HR hire an intern who'll report to you and will carry out the activities that don't require thinking time."

She stiffens. Surprise slackens her face, then she nods. "You're making the right decision."

Once more, I'm filled with admiration. She knows how to make it seem like this was my idea, when it was her who hinted at it.

Unwilling to concede this point to her, I lean back in my seat. "Let's see if *you* made the right decision by accepting this role."

Her eyes spark with the light of fight in them. My pulse thrums in response. The blood races through my veins. I can't remember feeling this alive before in someone else's presence. She's livened up the prospect of another working day.

I should be more excited with the thought of the upcoming merger I've been working on, but of late, the thrill from closing another acquisition or pitting wits with an opponent in the board-room has been fading.

I find myself increasingly drawn to helping veterans rebuild their lives after leaving the forces.

I hire former service men and women whose skills fit my company's needs. I also cover the cost of their retraining so they can transition smoothly into the corporate world.

But it's not enough. I want to do more. I want to make a real impact.

The problem is that my job takes up nearly all my time. I don't have the bandwidth to do more for veterans, and that frustrates me. Especially when my day-to-day work feels repetitive, almost meaningless by comparison.

It doesn't give me the rush of adrenaline it used to. Not until Lark, that is. Pitting wits with her is like a breath of fresh air.

The enthusiasm in her eyes, and her eagerness to prove herself are infectious.

She seems like she's about to bite back a response, one I'd have enjoyed. Instead, she firms her lips, settles for another brisk nod, then pivots and begins to head out.

"Oh, Ms. Monroe?"

She pauses.

Because I can't let her leave without getting one last rise out of her, I call out, "You have two hours to finish everything I gave you."

I have the satisfaction of hearing her gasp.

"What do you mean?" She spins around.

"You'll shadow me afterward, to familiarize yourself with what crosses my desk."

A frown mars her perfect forehead. "I need time to get through everything you asked me to do."

"Not my problem. It's your fault that you're not organized."

"Excuse me?" Color rises on her cheeks.

I'm finally getting to her. Good. Seeing her begin to simmer is the most satisfying experience ever. It lights a fire in my chest and squeezes my groin—enough that I have to part my thighs to accommodate my growing erection.

If seeing her angry turns me on so much, would watching her respond to my ministrations make me come in my pants?

I park the question and tap my fingers on the desk. "I sent you an email to that effect last night. Didn't you read it?"

"You didn't send me an email…" Her forehead furrows. She pulls up her device and scrolls down the screen.

Her shoulders tighten. "Apparently, you *did* send me an email. But I missed it."

She bites down on her lower lip. And fuck me, that turns my cock to stone. I manage to stop the groan that rumbles up my throat and lower my chin with my best 'I'm your boss from hell' glare.

She pales. Her throat moves as she swallows.

I know I've rattled her.

I was testing her, and she held up well. That last part about the email was my ego refusing to accept that she got the better of me. I couldn't resist pushing my advantage as her boss and being in a position of power. Only, the satisfaction I expected doesn't come.

Instead, when her pupils widen, an unmistakable sign of her arousal, lust punches straight into my gut.

She likes me taking charge. She likes the way I press her. And I like her reaction far too much.

It feels like I've stepped into uncharted territory. I've developed a taste for her responsiveness. One hit was enough. Now, I can't go back.

There's an inevitability to this that unsettles me, a pull I can't reason away.

I lock that chaos down, masking it with a cool, unreadable stare.

"I suggest you read your emails carefully from now on, Ms. Monroe. We wouldn't want you missing important information, would we?"

7

Lark

"Dismissed." He waves his hand.

My jaw drops. *Oh no, he didn't.* But apparently, he did. And he had the last word. With a smirk on those sinfully delicious looking lips, he turns back to his phone.

Also, why does he have to wear glasses? It's not fair that he looks even more delicious with them perched on his nose. Could the man get any sexier? It makes me want to lean in close enough until I fog them up. Then take them off and... *Ugh! Stop.*

So, my new boss is the most sinfully handsome man I've ever met. And he's tall and dark and broad shouldered and has the kind of hair that begs me to run my fingers through it. And those cheekbones of his could cut glass, and his nose is aristocratic and adds a certain haughtiness, an unapproachableness, to his image, which makes me want to climb him like a tree. *A-n-d, stop. I need to pull back on my runaway thoughts.*

Guilt consumes me. How can I have such unfiltered, carnal thoughts about my boss? And why haven't I felt these erotic sensations with the man I'm engaged to?

My head spins. This is so confusing. Despite warning myself not to, I can't stop myself from being attracted to my boss.

It's best I put distance between us and get on with the Titanic-sized list of tasks he's dumped on my plate.

I hurry out, making sure to bang the door behind me, to let him know I'm not impressed with how he's treated me so far.

He may be my boss, but he doesn't get to blow hot and cold.

He doesn't get to order me around like I'm dumb. Good thing, I'm able to think on my feet and had the presence of mind to hold my own.

It's something I've had to learn. Something which, hasn't expanded to my personal life. Still, I'm glad I've learned to assert myself in the workplace. I'd be doing myself a disservice if I didn't ensure my time is used for more of the thinking stuff.

In fact, with a little training and on the job experience, I could stand in for him if he can't attend a meeting. Hopefully, that's why he asked me to shadow him. Though he could have given me a little more time to acclimatize to my position.

Not that I expected any level of empathy from Sir Barks-a-lot. Haha! Cheered up by my silly name for my boss, I make it to my desk.

First thing, I email the board of directors, introducing myself and telling them the board meeting has been postponed.

In seconds, my phone rings. It's a member of the board telling me off for changing the date of the meeting.

I introduce myself, soothe their temper and explain it was due to Mr. Davenport having to attend to other business, which I'm guessing is kind of the truth. I mean, he can't make the meeting because he's doing something else, right?

I follow up with calls to each board member to let them know that the meeting date has changed.

I'm unable to reach one of them and leave him a message.

When I speak to the senior-most member, he's rude and slaps down the phone. Anger squeezes my guts.

Internally, I blame Mr. Oogie-Boogie-In-A-Tailored-Suit for people yelling at me. Then remind myself that this is the job... *Kind of.*

There really didn't seem to be any reason to postpone the meeting. Of course, I don't know what he's doing instead. Might be something of great importance. *Like jerking off?*

The thought of the big guy, with his big hand around his big cock, twists my belly with heat. I reach for my bottle of water and chug down on it. *Ugh, what is wrong with me?* I need to stay professional, remember?

I shove aside the familiar twang of guilt and confusion and tap open my Christmas playlist. I slip in my wireless buds, and the first notes of my favorite holiday track fill my ears. My shoulders drop an inch. Suddenly, the world feels a whole lot less catastrophic.

Fueled by the festive spirit, I call Evelyn at reception to ask who organizes the annual office holiday party. The silence on the line is my first hint. Her answer is the second.

There has never been a party to celebrate the festive season.

Not once.

I am horrified.

My boss might be Ebenezer Scrooge, brought to life and stuffed into a tailored suit, but that is no reason for the rest of the staff to live devoid of glitter, cookies, and joy. Someone has to restore festive balance to this office.

Apparently, that someone is me. *It's the kind of challenge I relish.*

I jot down a reminder to bring it up with Mr. Seasonal-Apathy himself, then dive headfirst into answering all five hundred of my emails.

Correction. Most are *his* emails which have been routed to me. And I'm grateful for the experience.

It's an immersion in the business of Davenport Capital. Which is the investment arm of Davenport Group. The company backs emerging businesses and innovative ventures around the world. I'm riveted.

I soak up the information, managing to reply to most emails with a combination of logic and experience, as well as searching online for gaps in my knowledge. I become aware of a figure standing over me.

"You must be the new secretary." He smiles a megawatt smile. The kind which, combined with his high cheekbones, square jaw, and a suit that must cost more than my entire month's salary, marks him out as a privileged prat. The kind born with money raining down on him. The kind very similar to my boss.

"I'm Mr. Davenport's executive assistant." I keep my tone pleasant.

"My apologies." He presses his hand to his chest, a contrite expression on his face. "I was wondering why the board meeting was moved."

"And you are?"

"Whittington. I'm one of the board members."

Ah, he's the one I left a message for earlier.

"Hello, Mr. Whittington." I nod. "I'm Lark Monroe. Mr. Davenport was pulled into something unavoidable and thus, had to reschedule the board meeting."

"Something unavoidable?" His tone indicates he's not buying the excuse I mentioned earlier.

"I'm afraid, I don't know more."

"Surely, you have access to your boss's agenda. You could tell me what he's doing in its stead, couldn't you?" He flashes me a smile, which I admit *is* charismatic. Instinctively, I know, it's nowhere as magnetic as how it would be if Count Crankypants were to smile.

It does soften his attitude, *somewhat.*

I lean back in my seat and curve my lips. "I'm really sorry, but that is not information I can give out."

He doesn't seem surprised. "Damn." He snaps his fingers. "And here I hoped my charm would buy me that information."

"Nope." I chuckle, his playful attitude beginning to thaw my wariness.

"How about I take you to dinner and you could, perhaps, tell me then?" His eyes are hopeful. His tone confident.

"No. Sorry." I laugh, not at all put off by his open flirtation. If anything, it's refreshing after my boss's sullen attitude.

"Why not?" He seems genuinely taken aback. "Right, you don't know my name yet." He holds out his hand. "Kingly."

"Kingly?" I almost snort but stop myself in time.

He must notice my expression though, for he chuckles. "My mother was hopeful. I do think I haven't turned out too badly." He strikes a pose. "What do you think?"

I pretend to study him, then shake my head. "Nope. Sorry. Not my type."

He pretends to be crushed. "Tough audience. Cut me some slack, will ya?"

I laugh, then lean in and beckon to him. He lowers his head.

"I have a fiancé."

"You do?" Thankfully, he doesn't glance at my ringless left hand. He does look genuinely put out though. "Damn, why are the good ones always taken?"

"You're good for my ego, though. Thank you."

"You're welcome." He dips his head. "Kingly Whittington at your service."

I take his hand. "Pleased to meet—"

"If you're done with the list I gave you, I have a lot more to add to it." My boss stalks toward us, spine straight, head held high. I have a glimpse of a tightly held jaw. Of a nerve popping at his temple. Damn, he looks ready to blow another gasket.

I pull my hand back like a kid caught with her hand in the cookie jar. This pang of unease running through me like I've done something wrong is so strange.

"Not yet. I'm…working my way through it." I wonder what's got him all worked up.

Kingly looks from me to my boss. "Ol' chap, I was asking Lark why the board meeting was postponed?"

"Have a meeting with Arthur instead," Brody says in a brusque voice.

"Ah." Kingly nods slowly. "Of course. And how is he?"

Brody ignores his question. "I need *Ms. Monroe* to sit in on a conference call."

That's rude. But Kingly doesn't seem to notice. "Certainly. Don't let me keep you." He steps aside, and when I rise to my feet, half bows to me. "Good to meet you, *Lark*."

I frown. If I didn't know better, I'd say he called me Lark to rile up my boss. His next words confirm it to me.

Kingly flashes me a flirtatious smile. "Your presence promises to liven up the proceedings of this otherwise boring office."

Next to me, my boss bristles. With a half-smile at Kingly, so as not to ignite my boss's ire further, I follow him into his office.

"Sit." He gestures to one of the chairs at the conference table. Then takes his seat on the opposite side. "Kingly's a player. You should keep your distance from him." His jaw twitches.

I frown. "I barely spoke to him. Besides, if anyone was flirting, it was him, not me."

He clenches his jaw. A muscle throbs at his cheekbone. He glares at me for a few seconds, then jerks his chin. "The upcoming video conference is with our Tokyo office. They want to discuss an expansion which will put us amongst the top ten companies in Asia."

The screen on the wall signals an incoming call. He answers it. Over the next half an hour, I listen in as he listens to the proposal, analyzes the projections, and asks questions.

By the time the call is over, my head is whirling with excitement at the scope of the company's business affairs, admiration for how insightful his questions were, and how clear his thinking was.

Now, he turns to me. "What do you think?"

I tamp down the panic that evokes. He's asking for my opinion. *It's an opportunity to make an impression on my boss.*

I gather my thoughts. "Their projections are aggressive. But your questions cut straight to the risks they didn't address. Especially around local regulatory hurdles and talent acquisition. If we move forward, we'll need a strategic partner on the ground."

He studies me, one brow raised. "Anything else?"

I hesitate, then add. "It's bold. And exactly the kind of move that could make us industry leaders. But if we're willing to invest in more than capital. It'll need vision. And leadership. Which you proved you have."

His mouth curves. "I want *you* to be in charge of the project."

"Me?" I widen my gaze. "You want to put a project potentially worth a billion dollars into the hands of a new, as yet untried, and basically unknown employee?"

8

Lark

"Does that bother you?" His lips curve in the makings of a smirk.

I realize, he's testing me.

I did tell him I wanted to be CEO, and now he wants to find out if I can rise to the challenge.

Only it *is* a billion freakin' dollars. My stomach ties itself in knots.

I am qualified to lead such a project. I studied for it. And I have experience in leading similar operations. Just not one of such a high value.

On the other hand, there's always a first time. If I don't start, I'll never know if I can do it or not.

I can do this. I can.

I take a few deep breaths and regain my composure. "It is the kind of scope that I'd expect a Davenport-related project to have."

"Good." He rises to his feet and heads back to his desk, where he begins to scroll through his phone.

"Uh, there is one more thing." I dawdle by his desk.

He grunts without looking up from his phone.

I take that as permission to keep speaking. "It's less than a month to Christmas and... I was thinking." I hesitate. "I was thinking it'd be good to have a Christmas tree up, have Christmas decorations around the office and... We should definitely organize a Secret Santa. And no way can we *not* have an office holiday party, and—"

"No." He turns to his computer and begins to read something on the screen.

"No?" I blink

"Abso-fucking-lutely not."

Wow. It's as if I asked him to wear matching Christmas pajamas with Tiny *and* pose for a company holiday card.

I'm not the type to give up easily.

"This initiative is as important as a potential billion-dollar project. Maybe more so, because it shows employees that they matter."

He raises his gaze from his phone, and a thinking expression crosses his features.

Oh good. Maybe I'm getting through?

Then he shakes his head.

Ugh. That was a show. A way to pretend he was considering my suggestion, to have the pleasure of vetoing it. His next words confirm it.

"Not happening. This is an office, Ms. Monroe, not Santa's grotto."

"More like the Grinch's panic room," I mumble.

I don't think I expected him to hear it. Or maybe I did.

For his head snaps back. "Excuse me?"

That got his attention, eh? I allow myself a small smirk.

"I mean... It's Christmas. The one time that people get taken in by the spirit of joy and giving."

He glowers at me.

Apparently, it passed him by.

"It will help with employee morale and retention if there's more of a Christmas spirit evident—"

His brows grow thunderous.

"—in the office building." I complete my statement without losing courage.

"It's a distraction." A muscle jumps at his jawline. It's as if the very mention of the season of sharing is pulling every possible ounce of joy out of his body.

"What do you have against Christmas, anyway?"

"Nothing."

His shoulders are so tight, they seem to be pulled up to his ears.

"Absolutely nothing." He narrows his gaze. "I don't care for people being nauseatingly happy, or spending all their time trying to figure out which gifts to buy, or playing that silly countdown calendar—"

"It's called the Christmas Advent calendar."

He snorts. "What-fucking-ever. My point is, it's a waste of time. I need my employees focused. Not getting all distracted, too busy planning their Christmas lunch."

Hmm. That didn't go as planned. But I'm not giving up yet. I paste a bright smile on my face. "It might be worth considering a half day for everyone on Christmas Eve. That will give the employees a chance to finish their last-minute Christmas shopping. I bet that'll buy management a stocking full of goodwill."

His features harden. A flush creeps over his cheeks. It's as if I told him I replaced the company logo with a Santa hat emoji.

Now *that* I'd try, to see what happens.

He'd probably have a cardiac. And that wouldn't be fun. I don't wish him any kind of ill health. In fact, I like him as is. Healthy, larger-than-life, and ripped. Sweet candy canes. He's so alpha male, it makes my teeth hurt to look at him.

No. No. No. Don't go there. Need to think of my fiancé. *Engaged. Fiancé. Engaged. Fiancé. Keep it professional.* I chant to myself and manage to find my focus.

Just in time for my boss chuckles, only the smile doesn't reach his eyes. "Your résumé didn't indicate you also have a sense of humor." The smile vanishes. In its place is his cold, hard, forbidding visage.

"Is there anything else?" he asks in a voice which clearly indicates that I'm wasting his time.

But I'm persistent. I'd have to be to get this far in the corporate world in such a short time. So, I square my shoulders, smooth out my features, and fix him with my best steely gaze. "Celebrating the lead up to Christmas is an opportunity not to be wasted."

"Oh?"

"People want to celebrate the holidays, but not being able to openly do so causes stress levels to spike. If we let them express their happiness, it makes them feel appreciated, increases motivation, and hence, productivity levels. It helps boost morale and provides enough momentum for the troops to weather the dreaded January slump."

"Hmph." He continues to frown but, at least, he's listening.

"Look, no one wants to hit Q4 targets while silently crying into a spreadsheet. A little Christmas cheer is a strategic investment."

"Is that right?" His tone is half sarcastic.

I nod. "Decorating a tree is cheaper than the team having to take time off due to post-holiday burnout."

"Oh?" He seems intrigued. "I assume you have research to back up these observations?"

"Absolutely." It's true.

I did get my facts from an article written by an academic in a very well-regarded business magazine.

He drums his fingers on the table. His expression tells me he's not dismissing *everything* I said.

"Besides, even the most forbidding executives are twenty-three percent less terrifying when wearing a paper crown and holding a mince pie," I say, half-jokingly. "It definitely breaks barriers and fosters better communication within teams."

He tilts his head, a considering light in his eyes. "You really believe in all this Christmas shit, don't you?"

Anger coils in my stomach. Did he call my favorite time of the year Christmas *shit?* Argh. I draw in a few deep, sharp breaths. Losing my temper is not going to help at all. And I did get him to, at least, listen to my reasoning. That's a win, right?

"Of course, I do. I've seen these strategies work before. It might seem trivial, but a little festive warmth and holiday spirit directly impacts employee productivity which, in turn, feeds the bottom line."

He seems skeptical again.

"I mean, you won't know until you try it, right?"

He rubs at his jaw where his beard is beginning to show, and its only midday. Good God.

Is this man so virile that the only way his body can cope with all that excess masculinity is by extra fast hair growth on his face? I shove the thought aside.

He's my boss. I can't have such carnal thoughts about him. I can't. *I'm engaged. I have a fiancé.*

"You make some good points"—he leans back in his seat—"but no."

"No?"

"Not happening. Everything you said is a distraction."

I set my teeth, and swallow back the insults hovering at the tip of my tongue. Calm. Cool. Collected. You don't want to lose your job on the first day, do you? "At least, think about it."

"I'll think about thinking about it." He turns back to his computer screen. "Dismissed."

Grrr. I'm starting to hate it when he uses that tone. Like he's royalty and I'm his lowly subject.

And my lurking around here isn't going to change anything. At least, I got my points across. That's got to count for something.

I pivot and head toward the connecting door which leads to my office.

I've found out the reason he has that strip of rope on his desk. Mr. Broody McNasty likes to untie then re-tie the knots as he talks on the phone. Some kind of relaxation thing, I gather.

I feel like I've been afforded an intimate glimpse into his habits.

Unfortunately, working with him this closely, I also know that he can often be a Grinch. *I'm going to call him Mr. Bah Hum-bro-dy, from now on.*

I chuckle.

"What's that?" His low, dark voice reaches me.

Damn, did I say that aloud? "Oh, just thinking out loud. I need to get back to work and plan for the upcoming board meeting." I shoot him a saccharine sweet smile over my shoulder.

Not that it matters, for he's focused on his screen. "I sent you a few more things to add to your to-do list."

Oh cool, cool.

If he thinks I'm put off by a never-ending task list, he's wrong. I have no doubt all of this is part of his way of testing me. He wants to see if I have the mettle to stick with it without giving up. Well, he chose the wrong person to challenge. I can match him task for task.

———

Or not.

It's been three days since that conversation about Christmas festivities.

It's also the end of my first work week. It's been exacting, *and* exhilarating.

My boss has set a brutal pace; I'm thriving. He's led endless back-to-back meetings, many of which I've sat in on. He's also asked my opinions on many work-related matters, some of which have led to the most intellectually stimulating exchanges I've had with anyone. We seem to bounce off each other's ideas. Enough for me to realize we make a good team.

He must also realize it too because, after the first couple of days, I notice him pushing more of the detailed work to me.

I'm loving the additional responsibilities. Every time he challenges me, I rise to it. I feel myself stretching and growing. It's been thrilling. I am so happy I took this role.

I've also begun to respect my boss more. He's proved to be as hard a worker as he is a task master.

When I come into work, he's in a conference.

When I leave, he's on yet another call. The man is relentless. And has enough energy to make me feel like I'm not doing enough. And I'm pulling twelve-hour days myself.

The constant stream of things-to-do keeps adding to my list, and that motivates me further.

Of course, my perfectionist streak wants to cross everything off before I leave at the end of the day, but I'm practical enough to realize that's not going to happen.

Instead, I make a fresh list before I leave work so it's there waiting for me when I get in the next day. Heaven!

My one complaint is that my dreams are occupied by blue-gray eyes, and images of a tall, dark, moody, holiday hater. That, and my guilt at thinking about him so much, and my consternation at why I don't dream about my fiancé instead, means I haven't slept well this entire week.

I yawn and take a sip of my coffee, trying to stop my eyes from closing, when my phone buzzes.

I stare at the person who's calling. Keith? I frown.

It's a testament to how stretched I am by this job that it takes a few seconds to register that this is Keith. *My fiancé.*

The man I'm going to marry in a little over three weeks.

The man for whom I've been leaving messages over the past ten days. Finally, he's calling me back. A mixture of relief then anger fills me. *He finally found some time for me, huh?*

I snatch it up and answer the phone. "Keith, where have you been? Why haven't you answered my messages and my voice mails?"

"Hi Lark, how's it going?" His cheerful voice comes down the line.

Ugh, how can he sound so relaxed when I'm juggling so many balls in the air—trying to get everything done at work *and* organizing *our* wedding. I swallow my frustration and make sure to keep my voice even.

"I'm good. A little tired but good. Where are you?"

"In Texas. I'm here for a conference. But I expect to be home soon."

"How soon? I need you to give me your opinion on the menu choices for the reception and the names of everyone who's coming to attend the wedding from your side."

"Is that all?" he asks breezily.

Anger simmers up my spine. "I've been working my tail off trying to get everything in order for the wedding, along with managing my new job. And you? You disappear in the lead up to the wedding."

He hesitates. "I've been busy."

"Seriously, Keith? So have I!" I grit my teeth. "You leave all the wedding arrangements to me. And don't even bother to reply to my messages."

"I'm sorry if I've been busy meeting deadlines so I can spend Christmas and New Year's with *you* in London without having to travel."

"Oh." My anger cools, a little.

"I want to make salesman of the year, so I can put the bonus toward our dream home." He sniffs.

Ugh, now I feel like a bridezilla who's been haranguing her fiancé while he's been working hard to get work out of the way so he can focus on me.

Just then, a man in a courier's uniform walks into my office with a bouquet of holiday-themed flowers: a mix of amaryllis, white roses, and eucalyptus, accentuated with holly sprigs. "Lark Monroe?"

"One second, Keith." I look up. "That's me."

He places the vase carefully on one side of my desk, then slides his device under my nose. "Sign here, please."

I oblige.

He leaves.

"What is it?" Keith asks impatiently.

"It's a delivery of flowers."

"Did you see who the card is from?" His voice carries suppressed excitement.

I open the card and see his name signed on it. I frown. "They're from you?"

"Do you like them?"

I flatten my lips. I should be flattered that he thought of me. But after ignoring me for weeks, it feels like he's trying to buy my forgiveness.

Why does it seem like he's manipulating me?

"I wanted to apologize for being away so much," he adds.

There's something in his tone that implies he's waiting for me to thank him.

Because he sent me flowers. Because he's never done so before. Because after not talking to me for days and days, now he's trying to show me that he's thinking of me?

I rub at my temple, not completely convinced about the intentions behind his actions. He's saying all the right words and doing the right things. Like calling me and apologizing for ignoring me and sending me flowers. But somehow, the very fact that he's doing this sends a whisper of unease up my spine.

He's being thoughtful. He's trying to make amends. I should be happy that he thought of me.

The gesture tugs at something in me I don't want to look at too closely. I smooth away the feeling like brushing lint off my sleeve.

The connecting door between our offices swings open.

Brody steps in and comes to an abrupt halt, his expression thunderous. "Who sent you flowers?"

9

Brody

I take one look at the ridiculously cheerful bouquet on my executive assistant's desk, and something like acid eats away at my inside.

"Who are you talking to?" I snap.

"I gotta go, thanks for the flowers." She disconnects the call, sets the phone aside, then begins to tap into her keyboard.

I prowl forward. "I asked you a question."

"I work for you. But my personal life is out of bounds." She sniffs.

"And you shouldn't conduct your personal business in company time."

She scoffs. "I spend almost all my waking hours at work. Of course, I'm going to have a couple of personal conversations during that time. As long as I get my work done, it shouldn't matter."

The cheek of this woman. I want to bark at her for talking to me in that tone, but she has a point.

She's a grown woman; she knows her responsibilities. And knows what the deadlines on the job are. And so far, she's delivered on them. So, I can't refute her observation. The logic sharpens the edge of my anger.

I glare at her, though it's wasted because she's focused on her damn screen. And the fact that she most certainly was talking to the person who likely sent her those flowers twists my guts. I want to shove those flowers off her desk, then track down whoever was on the other end of the phone line and demand they back off from her forever.

Fuck, where has this possessiveness come from?

Even on a mission, when I was faced with flying bullets and brothers-in-arms being hit, having to carry them out of range of the enemy's reach, I was cool. So much so that my nickname was Ghost.

I was stealthy enough to get in and out of enemy territory without being spotted. And could also disappear emotionally. I was calm under pressure. I never put a foot wrong. Then this curvy, feisty, ambitious woman walks into my life, and everything turns topsy-turvy.

A-n-d, she's right. It's none of my concern who she was talking to or who sent her those flowers. She's my employee. My EA. And my demands on her can only extend to the work part of her life.

She studiously continues to avoid me, and that pisses me off somehow.

Damn, if I don't want her complete attention on me. Which is a complete contradiction of how I want my employees to behave at work. I need them to focus on their jobs and not waste their time on idle chitchat. With Ms. Lark Monroe, though, my expectations are beginning to feel different. Which is…ridiculous.

Why did I come into her office anyway? I've forgotten about the task I had for her. That's how distracting being in her presence is.

I'm about to spin around and leave when something else on her desk catches my eye.

"What's that?"

She glances at what caught my attention and reddens. She snatches up what looks like a soft toy and opens her drawer and shoves it in. "It was nothing."

I lower my chin, "Was that a...unicorn?"

Her flush deepens further.

"No," she says too quickly. "That's Mr. Twinkle my...horned productivity mascot."

I have another horn that could increase both your productivity and mine. I wince inwardly. That was cringeworthy. I'm glad I didn't say it aloud.

Instead, I scowl. "You have a productivity mascot? Whom you've named?" I scowl.

"It's standard practice in glitter-powered management theory." Her tone is bland.

I stare at her. She stares back.

Her lips twitch, and she breaks into a laugh that lights up the damn room.

I find my lips curving into a reluctant smile, because who can resist the sunshine that she seems to bring to every interaction of ours?

Less than a week of working together, and I'm charmed.

Ms. Lark Monroe might be sharp and driven and focused when it comes to work, but there's also this girly side of her.

A contradiction someone else also appreciates, I remind myself, tearing my gaze from the flowers again.

"He's my emotional comfort plush. I've had him since university." She waves a finger at me. "Don't judge."

"You need an emotional comfort plush at work?" I frown.

She blows out a breath. "I'm ambitious. I expect a cutthroat work environment. But this place it's corporate frostbite." She glances around her office.

I follow her gaze. And see the space through her eyes.

Chrome furniture. Steel cabinet handles. A minimalist, charcoal desk that reflects nothing back. Floor-to-ceiling glass on one side offers a prime view of the skyline, clean, cold, expansive. The other walls are a tasteful but soulless white.

Even the carpet is gray. Not soft-gray. Not warm-gray. Just... gray. Corporate. Lifeless.

The kind of space that screams productivity and precision but never once says: *Welcome. You belong here.*

Outside, the office doesn't fare much better. An expanse of frosted glass, polished steel, and uniform desks. No plants. No personality. Not a splash of color. Definitely no sign of human warmth.

No wonder, she needs a rainbow-maned unicorn to survive it. Something softens in my chest. *Don't do it. Don't.* I firm my lips. "Let's do it."

"Do what?"

"That…decoration thing you mentioned. Let's do it."

She brightens. "You mean, the Christmas decorations?"

I wince. Fucking hell. Am I agreeing to bring that complication into my office? Je-s-us. I straighten my spine. "Yes, put up holiday decorations. No Christmas tree, though."

Her face falls.

And my heart tightens in my chest. Fuck, that is an unexpected reaction. Why do I care if my EA is disappointed? Besides, I did agree to festive decorations, didn't I?

I step into her office to discuss next year's sales projections and demand that she reforecast them, as I'm unhappy with the number. Instead, I end up agreeing to *blech*, holiday decorations. Bloody hell. I'm going soft in my old age. This woman is dangerous. I find myself doing things which are totally not in character for me.

I best get back to my office before I agree to something I don't mean to.

I spin around and make tracks to my office. Before I can step through the door she calls out, "And the Holiday party?"

"Don't push your luck," I growl over my shoulder as I shut the door behind me.

I walk to my desk faster than necessary, irritated with myself.

I don't like being caught off guard, especially not, by someone who's only been in the role a few days. And definitely not by someone whose desk drawer contains a rainbow unicorn.

I have to concede Lark has a point. Morale drives productivity.

Productivity drives performance. And performance leads to profits and helps to retain employees.

If letting her string up a few fairy lights buys me a more motivated team, then I can live with that.

I bury myself in the next item on my schedule, but a part of me is annoyingly aware of her across the glass wall. I can't help but glance out of the corner of my eye to see her on the phone. I bet she's setting the entire thing into motion with admin. Decorations. Carols. Tinsel.

God help us all.

At least, I drew the line at the Christmas tree. As for Secret Santa? Not to mention, an employee Christmas party. I shudder. Not a chance.

She'll probably make the most of it. There's something oddly efficient about her brand of glitter-coated optimism wrapped in MBA-level precision. I don't trust it. But I can't ignore it either.

By five p.m., I've knocked out three major business expansion proposals and wrapped up a video call with our New York office.

I decided not to invite her to that. I need some space from Ms. Curvy-figure-wearing-a-skirt-that-outlines-her-luscious-arse. *Bet she wore it to taunt me,* I think bitterly.

My cock perks up in interest as images of her sweet tush crowd my mind. I push away from my desk in disgust.

I'd prefer to go to the gym and work out my frustrations but, sadly, there's one more appointment left for the day. It makes sense to have Lark accompany me to this one.

I step inside her office again, and she looks up, eyes bright.

"I'm headed over to see my grandfather. I need you to come with me."

"Your grandfather?" A cute furrow appears between her eyebrows.

Cute? I didn't know that word existed in my vocabulary. At this rate, she'll have me humming Christmas carols and believing in Santa Claus.

I shut the thought down and scowl at her. "Arthur Davenport, the chairman of the Davenport Group is my grandfather. I'm meeting him. And you need to be there for it."

"When Arthur asked to meet me today, the timing clashed with the board meeting. I didn't have any choice but to agree. It's why I asked you to postpone the board meeting. What Arthur says takes precedence."

"Right." She nods slowly.

I'm not apologizing that I didn't give her enough notice about coming with me to meet Arthur.

Or that I had previously asked her to postpone the board meeting without telling her why. But I'm the boss. And what I say goes. Right?

My conscience tells me I didn't have to be a jerk about it.

We're in my chauffeur-driven car, going through details of the year-ending financials for most of the journey. She brought my attention to an error in the reporting which the finance team missed.

It confirms to me I made the right decision by taking her on. So far, she's delivered on everything I've asked of her, and more. It's made her go up in my esteem even more. Enough that I feel she warrants an apology for having made her take the brunt of the board's ire at having pushed back the meeting.

She looks out the window, digesting what I said. When she looks at me again, her features are more relaxed. "Thanks for sharing that with me."

For a few moments more, we ride in silence.

Then, she shoots me a sideways glance. "Can I ask a question?"

I nod.

"Does Arthur have veto power over the board's decisions?" There's curiosity in her eyes.

"No veto power. But he has the casting vote in a tie. He also holds majority voting shares."

"So, he can overrule the board?"

"He controls who sits on the board. So yeah, the old man's power is absolute."

She thinks through the ramifications of what I said. "He influences the decisions you make?"

"He does. And he's not subtle about it. He claims to have taken a back seat since he was diagnosed with the big C a few years ago. What that translates to is my keeping him abreast of the happenings in the company."

"Hence, the in-person meeting with him?"

She has access to my calendar, so she's aware of that.

I drum my fingers on the seat. "It would serve his health better if he weren't involved with the day-to-day, but he's been involved with the company for over fifty years. His habits are not going to change overnight."

I notice her staring at me and arch an eyebrow. "What?"

"Nothing." She shakes her head.

"Go on, hit me." I lean back in the seat.

She hesitates then gives in, "I suppose, I'm surprised by your understanding and patience with your grandfather."

"You mean, especially because I've been so erratic with you?" I smirk.

"Umm, that's not what I meant."

"You implied it."

She seems horrified. "I didn't, really—"

I hold up my hand. "Relax, I owe you an apology for making your start so challenging. I was testing you."

She doesn't seem surprised. "You were putting me through my paces, until I proved myself." A shrewd look comes into her eyes. "What's the verdict?"

It's my turn to fix her with a hard stare. "The jury's still out."

She scowls.

"But—"

"But?" she asks cautiously.

"But I think you've handled the challenges that've come your way admirably."

I didn't intend to say that. But instinct had me praise her without thinking. *A first for someone who thrives on control.* And the flush of pleasure on her features is more than satisfying. It ignites that part deep inside of me. The part I prefer to keep hidden at work. The part which gets satisfaction from rewarding someone for putting their trust in me. Damn. When it comes to my EA, my personal life is encroaching into the professional. Another first.

But it's worth it. For my words seem to put her more at ease.

"And is this part of the test?" She inclines her head.

"You mean, meeting Arthur?" I sigh and run my fingers under my collar. I don't mind wearing a tie, but by the end of the day, I'm itching to take it off. "Yeah, every meeting with him is a test, for me."

"Even though he's your grandfather?"

"Especially, because he's my grandfather. Canny goat wants to be sure I won't fail him."

There's a considering look in her eyes. "He must trust you, given he asked you to take care of his dog while he was away."

"He does." I let my features soften. "Arthur has a soft spot for the damn pooch."

She gives me an amused look. "He's not the only one."

"Yeah." The back of my neck heats a little. "Tiny has a personality all his own." I shrug. "It's difficult to make him do anything he doesn't want to. He seems to believe he knows best. He's a lot like Arthur in that way. Imelda, his partner, is the only one who can make the old man unbend a little. Especially since he's an ace at saddling the rest of us with asks we're unable to refuse."

"He sounds like a real character," she offers.

"He can be. Comes with living a hard life. He built the Davenport Group of companies almost single-handedly. He's also the one who took care of us after our parents passed."

"I'm sorry." Her eyes mirror the regret in her voice.

"It was a long time ago." I shrug.

"It was good of Arthur to step in."

"Progeny is important to him. There no question he wouldn't. Not that he's the most paternal in his approach. But he did his best."

"Sounds like you guys are close."

"In the way that family is. You're close until you aren't." I chuckle. "Arthur loves meddling in the lives of my brothers and me. The rest of them like to keep their distance from him. I don't blame them. I, however, feel a sense of responsibility toward the old man."

"It's why you keep him updated so often," she says on a sudden flash of insight. "That, and it's probably the only way to keep him at arm's length, so he doesn't get involved in the day-to-day."

"You…are perceptive." I tilt my head.

"I have to be to keep pace with you."

Our gazes lock. The air crackles between us, thick with something unspoken. A pulse of heat coils low in my belly, even as a strange ache tightens my chest. It's like my body's responding before my brain can catch up. Goddamn, this woman. There's something about her that calls to me. This awareness, which has buzzed between us from the start, ignites into something more potent.

I lean in toward her. She leans in too, and licks her lips. My eyes lock on the pink flesh. My cock lengthens. I want this woman. And I don't care if she's my employee. I want to push her down onto the seat and cover her body with mine and —

The chauffeur's voice comes over the speaker in the partition between the driver's seat and ours. "We're here, sir."

10

Lark

3.Figure out how to wrap presents without using an entire roll of tape per box.
—From Lark's Christmas to-do list

I draw in a sharp breath and straighten.

Talk about bad timing. Or maybe, that was *good* timing?

What was that about?

From the moment we got into the car, I was so aware of him. The feel of the soft leather against my thighs, the dark, masculine scent of his which enveloped me, the larger-than-life presence of his which seemed to suck out all the oxygen in that enclosed space. God. I was wet instantly. I had to stop myself from squirming around and squeezing my thighs together. Not that it would have helped fill that aching void in my core.

And when our gazes locked, I was overcome with this surge of lust that made me want to crawl into his lap and kiss him. Argh. I almost kissed my boss.

So unprofessional. So bad. *This is very bad.*

I need to get control of my lust. I'm engaged, not blind. Of course, I find my boss attractive. That doesn't mean I need to act on it. *Right?*

I feel terrible that, I haven't spared a single thought for my fiancé this entire time. And he did send flowers to apologize for being distant. I wish I could accept the gesture for what it is...but something in me wonders if there's more behind it than simple remorse.

The door on my side is pulled open. I step out and try not to notice how big he is. And how he towers over me. How his gaze seems to follow me as I approach the handsome period house in Primrose Hill.

Christmas lights illuminate the windows. More lights encircle the trees and shrubs that surround the short driveway.

To the side, I spot the waters of the Regent's Canal.

We're in the heart of the city and yet, it's so quiet. The sun has set. I take in a deep breath and smell pinecones.

"It smells like Christmas." I sigh.

"Arthur has a thicket of pine trees on his property."

I follow Brody's line of sight and spot the small woodland in the distance.

"He bought this place fifty years ago. My brothers and many of my friends live nearby."

"That's wonderful. It's a community, huh?" I want to ask him if he lives close by but decide that would give away my interest in him. *Strictly professional. Remember?*

Brody doesn't reply. I glance at his face to find a preoccupied expression. His mind must be on the meeting ahead. His grandfather must be formidable, if the tension in Brody's shoulders is any indication. He guides me forward with an impersonal hand to the small of my back.

We walk up the steps to the front door.

A beautiful Christmas wreath hangs on it. It's classic pine with gold ribbon and cinnamon sticks woven through. The scent spikes the air and makes me sigh again.

Christmas, ah!

I love that the entire place feels this festive. Apparently, unlike Brody, his grandfather appreciates the Christmas spirit. I find myself re-evaluating the picture of Arthur Brody painted for me. The fact he is happy to express his Christmas spirit is, surely, a positive sign.

Every year, I put up my Christmas tree on the last day of November. This year, I've been so wrapped up in job interviews, then proving myself in this new role, not to mention taking on all the wedding planning, I haven't had the mind space to put up a single string of lights.

I haven't lit a peppermint candle. I haven't even bought the ingredients to bake my annual "12 days of cookies" sampler, though I have the recipes memorized.

These are traditions I created. Someday, I'll have a family of my own to share them. Meanwhile, I cherish how the festive season brings color into almost all aspects of everyday life. I truly believe it gives us the opportunity to build better relationships with the people we encounter every day, and yes, also with ourselves.

It's a chance to press pause and lean into something joyful.

And yet, here I am…no gingerbread-scented kitchen, no twinkle lights in the window. Just a planner full of deadlines, and a fiancé who's AWOL, and a boss who doesn't like carols.

The door swings open to reveal a man in suit and tie. That, along with a indefinably patient look on his face, declares he's a butler. He half bows, confirming my guess.

"Otis." Brody nods. "This is Lark Monroe, my executive assistant."

"Sir, ma'am." He turns to me. "May I take your coat?"

"Of course." I look around for a place to put down my purse.

Brody takes it from me. I blink, surprised because it's a strangely intimate gesture. But he's being polite, that's all it is.

Putting it out of my mind, I take in my surroundings.

The foyer of the house is lined with dark wood panels that stretch at least two stories high and gleam under the soft glow of sconces. A staircase sweeps up in a graceful curve, its polished banister catching the light. Shadows pool between the carved panels of the wall, giving the space a solemn gravity.

In the corner, a towering Christmas tree strains toward the high ceiling, its decorations glittering like precious stones under watchful eyes. The evergreen, while a festive touch, also seems to proclaim beauty, power and tradition.

It's arranged to impress. And it does. It reflects the Davenports' wealth and status. Good for them.

Personally, I'm more of a cozy, homemade, shabby-chic Christmas decorations kinda gal.

Three doorways open from the foyer: to the right is the living room with its velvet drapes and firelight; to the left, a cloakroom lined with hooks and boot racks; and directly ahead, is a hallway leading to a study.

"There you are," a man's voice calls out.

We look up to find a guy wearing jeans and an elbow patch sweater approaching us. He's as tall as Brody, with broad shoulders and biceps that stretch the sweater sleeves.

The two shake hands.

He looks from Brody to me. His eyes light up with interest. "You are —"

"Lark Monroe." I hold out my hand.

"She's my executive assistant." Brody's voice is cool.

The man takes my palm. "James Hamilton."

"I know." I politely incline my head.

He has a well-known cooking show, and the media can't seem to get enough of him.

"We have a friend in common. Harper Richie. She's one of my BFFs."

"Right." A peculiar look comes over his features. Huh? I get the feeling there's something between him and Harper. Damn, I really need to catch up with her and my other friends.

Brody steps forward between us.

It forces James to release my hand and move back.

Brody hands my bag over to me.

"What are you doing here?" Brody inclines his head.

"I assume, I'm here for the same reason you are?"

"This is my update meeting with Gramps."

"Which he asked me to sit in on." James raises a shoulder.

"Eh?" Brody seems taken aback. "He asked you to sit in on this meeting?"

James shrugs. "I told him it was highly unusual, considering this is a business meeting, but he insisted. And when Arthur gets like that—"

"No one can change his mind." Brody firms his lips.

"This way." Otis leads us to the closed door and pushes it open. Rows of books on the wall reveal it to be the library.

I follow the men inside and step into warmth. A massive fireplace burns brightly, taking up a good portion of the wall opposite me.

The flames throw light over the man who occupies the throne-like armchair in front. A blanket covers his legs.

A cane leans against the chair but seems almost incongruous with the ruddy cheeks and the full head of steel-gray hair that the older man sports. This must be the infamous Arthur.

He nods his chin in the direction of the men. The imperious gesture reminds me of my boss. "Brody, come closer, boy."

I stifle my chuckle at my boss being referred to as 'boy.'

Said 'boy' leads me a few steps forward. I know the exact moment the elder Davenport notices me for his eyes gleam.

"You must be Lark Monroe."

I nod. "I'm his executive assistant." My voice comes out thinner than I intended.

There's something about being under the full force of Arthur Davenport's gaze that makes my spine straighten and my palms go clammy. His eyes are sharp, assessing, like he's measured me and debating whether I pass muster.

I can see where Brody gets his domineering attitude.

"Arthur Davenport." He bows that full head of hair.

"Pleased to meet you, sir." Pretending a confidence I don't feel, I straighten my spine, smooth my skirt, and flash him a polished smile as I approach the couch opposite him.

"May I?"

"Please." His eyes narrow, then gleam. "It's nice to meet someone who's not afraid of me."

"Well, sir." I smooth down the back of my skirt, then sit. "I've met scarier men. One of them signs my paychecks."

He chortles.

I smile.

Brody glowers at both of us.

I realize, having fun at my boss's expense is a lot of fun.

I sink into the couch, ensuring I sit straight. I know instinctively that getting too comfortable would be a mistake.

Arthur turns to Brody. "Finally, you made a hire who's going to add value to the company."

"Wouldn't want my brothers to hear you say that." Brody stalks over to the straight-backed chair between Arthur and the couch. He drops into it.

"Oh, your brothers know how much I appreciate their efforts in growing the company. They were also wise enough to take my advice when it came to getting married."

"You mean, they realized your machinations had worked out in their favor?" Brody smirks.

I draw in a sharp breath at the rudeness, but Arthur merely waves his hand. "The ends justify the means."

"I agree with you." Brody stretches out his long legs. "But of late, I've begun to wonder if the journey is not as important as the goal?"

Arthur's gaze sharpens.

Then he turns to me. "And you, Ms. Monroe, do you agree?"

I take my time forming my answer. For some reason, this philosophical debate seems to be one of importance to Arthur. "Moving from America to come here and study on my own made me resilient. I could only do it because I decided when I was very young to aim high. That way, wherever I land it'll be better than where I started. But also, what kept me going in the darkest days, when everything felt so uphill, was that I had the ability to look around and appreciate how far I've come."

"It gave you perspective." Brody leans forward. There's interest in his eyes.

"And that's what kept me going. It meant, I was able to laugh at myself, and marvel at where I was, and appreciate all the positives in my life."

"You get what you want the moment you stop needing it, but never stop showing up for it," he murmurs.

Something warm squeezes my chest. "A poet, huh? Never would have guessed that."

His gaze heats. Once more, our eyes meet, and everyone else in the room vanishes. There's only Brody, and the way he looks at me like he wishes we were alone.

That inevitable chemistry between us surges to the surface. He only has to look at me, and all my defenses seem to melt. I seem to forget that I'm an engaged woman. That I'm getting married in a few weeks. I should look away, but I can't. My body reacts despite myself.

I feel seen by Brody. The way I never have been by my fiancé. Brody makes me feel desirable. He's sneered at me, challenged me, apologized to me... He's never ignored me. And when he looks at me, it's like he's touching something deep inside. I feel his interest in me ignite in a deeper way. Damn. This is getting complicated. All I want is do my job and do it well, but this…connection with Brody is not something that's going away anytime soon.

The silence in the room stretches.

It's Brody who gathers his emotions first. A mask drops on his face. It's as if he turned off whatever he was feeling. He wrenches his gaze away from mine and glances at Arthur. "Why is James here?"

Arthur's features soften. He even nods at me. I can't help but feel that Arthur tested me. And I passed it. I'm relieved.

But a part of me wonders about the real significance of it. For now, I relax back in my cushion, glad not to be under the scrutiny of both Davenports.

"He's here as an observer." Arthur places his fingertips together.

"Observer?" Brody furrows his forehead. "For what?"

"For the fact that you're committing to get married."

Wait, what? My heart rate ratchets up, and I turn on Brody. "You're getting married?"

11

Brody

"It's the condition for Arthur giving me access to my inheritance." I shrug.

Old man likes the drama, so I keep my face like stone. I knew he was going to bring this up, though why he picked today of all days to do so, I'm not sure.

"You said you'd be happy to marry the woman I chose for you." Arthur curls his lips.

Unlike my brothers, I've never bothered to fight my grandfather's maniacal pursuit to marry us off. Since I never intend to fall in love, marrying a woman of my own choosing didn't seem a possibility. It seemed simpler to marry a woman he chose for me.

It has the added advantage of making Gramps happy.

I'm the only one of my brothers who seems to genuinely care enough to want to make Gramps happy. I'd be lying if I said I don't hope it'll pay off with Arthur being benevolent with me on the business side of things. Ultimately, the marriage, itself, is a transaction to help me access my inheritance.

So why would I care who he chooses?

"I did," I agree with him.

Lark's eyes widen in surprise. She seems like she's going to ask me about it but stops herself.

"James is here to witness that I'm doing my part of the job, as well as when you refuse to accept my choice." Arthur's expression is one of satisfaction and anticipation.

I flick James a sideways glance. He seems as bemused as I feel.

"How do you know I'm going to refuse you, when I don't even know who your choice is?" I incline my head.

"You do now." Arthur turns his stare on Lark.

I reel back.

What's he talking about? Surely, he's not implying what I think he is?

Lark, too, must realize what he's implying, for she draws in a breath.

"Is this some kind of joke?" I growl.

James looks between us, then at Arthur. He seems gobsmacked. *Welcome to my life—the one Arthur keeps turning upside down.*

And I let him, because I respect him too much to say otherwise.

My grandfather sighs. "As I predicted, you don't seem agreeable to this wedding."

No shit.

I committed to marry whoever he chose for me. But Lark? I flatten my lips. I didn't see that coming. I bite off the retort which hovers at the tip of my tongue. I don't want to be rude to my grandfather.

She's my employee. My executive assistant, who I've identified as a possible next in line for my role as CEO. Our relationship is strictly professional. I don't want to unsettle her, and Arthur, with his very insensitive declaration, has done just that.

In fact, thanks to him, we're in breach of half a dozen HR rules. We've left ourselves open to potential lawsuits which could hurt us.

Not that he cares. Gramps makes his own rules. One of the reasons my brothers and I restrict his interactions with the office.

Also…Lark as my future wife? My muscles coil with tension.

Lark, who'd wear my ring. And walk down the aisle in a white dress. And who'd sleep in my bed. And wake up next to me? Lark, who I'd fuck until she couldn't walk straight? Fuck. Lust tightens my groin. I'm going to be sporting a very uncomfortable chub, in front of my grandfather, my employee, and my friend, if I'm not careful.

Now that the initial shock of Arthur's words is wearing off, I can't help but admit that this might have possibilities. Not least of all because of the explosive chemistry between us.

"Umm, I thought this was supposed to be a work meeting." Lark's expression is one of disbelief.

"It is." Arthur smiles. "This concerns Brody's future and a sum of money that he can't access unless he does what I ask of him."

She stares closely at him. "You're serious?"

"He is," I cut off whatever Arthur is going to say.

She turns on me. She seems to be struggling with her thoughts. "This is a surprise," she finally blurts out

"For me too," I say honestly.

"Me too." James holds up his hand.

I scowl at him. He shrugs with a 'don't-mind-me-I'm-the-innocent-bystander watching-the-fun' expression.

Typical of Arthur to ensure there's a spectator to my being completely blindsided.

As for Lark? Her features reflect first disbelief, then wariness, then some deeper emotion I can't name.

When she has a grip on her emotions, she turns to Arthur. "I… Uh… I'd say I'm flattered. Except, I'm afraid what you're suggesting is impossible."

Arthur looks taken aback. "Explain," he says in a brusque manner.

He's not used to being contradicted or anyone telling him off. I smother a chuckle at the shock on his face. Not too many people can claim to have taken Arthur by surprise.

"I understand you want to see your grandson settle down, but I can't be the person he marries because I have a fiancé."

"A fiancé?" Arthur's bushy eyebrows draw down.

What the—? My jaw drops. "You're engaged?"

"I am..." A flicker of something crosses her features.

She doesn't seem exactly happy about this. In fact, she doesn't fit the image of a blushing bride to-be. Where's the excitement? The anticipation? The— I glance down at her left hand.

"You don't have a ring!" I'm aware my voice comes out in an accusing tone, but I can't stop myself.

"It's, uh... At the jewelers, being resized." She looks away as she says it, and I know without a doubt, she's lying.

Likely, the bastard she's marrying did not give her a ring. What kind of a loser is she tying herself to? Is she aware of how gorgeous she is? How perfect. How deserving she is of all the best things in the world. Things that make her happy, like an emerald engagement ring that would complement her eyes and look incredible on her finger. Not that she needs jewelry to amplify her beauty. She's ravishing as is.

Arthur, who's seemed at a loss for words, finally splutters. "That's not possible."

I wince. That's the wrong thing to say.

Sure enough, Lark straightens her spine. "Pardon me?"

Arthur seems to realize his mistake. "I don't mean it's not possible that you're engaged. You're beautiful and intelligent. Of course, you have a beau." His gaze clouds. "Unfortunately, my enquiries didn't reveal that."

"You had me investigated?" She stiffens.

"Every employee who joins the company undergoes a background check." I try to mollify her. "It was in the employee contract you signed when you joined."

She relaxes a little, but the cautious look in her eyes doesn't fade.

"For the record, I'm sure you made the right decision." Arthur folds his arms across his chest.

"In which case, I'm off the hook." I lean back in my seat.

Arthur scowls. "What do you mean?"

"Ms. Monroe is engaged, and we should respect that."

He sets his jaw.

"The one time your grandson was ready to abide by your choice, you got it wrong." I allow myself a small smirk.

I love Gramps, and respect him, but goddamn, I can't let up on this opportunity to have a little fun at his expense.

I turn to James. "You're witness to seeing the mighty Arthur Davenport stumble."

Arthur's brow darkens. "Be that as it may, it doesn't mean you can get out of this. You need to get married, and before the end of the year."

12

Lark

Test all Christmas cookie recipes twice. (Only for quality control of course.)
— From Lark's Christmas to-do list

"Drop me off at the office then take Ms. Monroe to wherever she wants to go." He tells the chauffeur before raising the separation between the front and passenger seat.

We're on our way home after that disastrous meeting with Arthur.

"Uh, actually, I'd prefer to get dropped off at the nearest tube station." I place my bag in my lap.

He shoots me a disbelieving look. "Just have the chauffeur drop you off, will you?"

"I—" I want to protest again, mainly so I don't have to spend the trip to the office with him. But I take in his granite hard features and realize, it's best not to debate this.

So, I subside and pretend to look out the window.

I am shaken, to be honest. So, it will be nice to get dropped off, rather than try to navigate the trains.

It was so embarrassing to have to tell them I was engaged and then lie about my lack of a ring. And of course, my fiancé is absent. And when he sends me flowers, I'm sure it's to cover up something he's done, something which he knows is going to upset me.

I've been so focused on creating my perfect life, I didn't realize I don't give off the vibes of an engaged woman.

I glance at my boss and, finding him engrossed in his phone, I pull mine out. I pull up Keith's social media handles.

There are pics of him at a hotel gym, by a hotel pool, at an airline lounge, in a meeting room, of him in different cities around the world. They show off his traveling lifestyle. There are no pics of me. Or of us. Or of him showing off his fiancée.

I tighten my lips; pull up my social media. In contrast, mine have no pictures at all. I've been too busy working to share anything about myself online.

There is nothing tying the two of us together in the virtual space.

As for in real life? I glance at the bare ring finger on my left hand. It seems to mock me back.

I don't have an engagement ring. Or spend evenings with my fiancé. We don't live together. In fact, I haven't even been in the same city as him for months.

I don't remember the last time he took me out on a date. *Or* made love to me. *I cringe.* Worse, he's never made me orgasm. There. I've acknowledged it to myself for the first time.

I had convinced myself it didn't matter, but in light of Arthur's, no-doubt, thorough investigation concluding that I was single. Unwanted. Unclaimed. Definitely not engaged. I'm beginning to wonder if I really am?

I glance at my messages in the hope that Keith has texted me since our phone call, but nope, there's nothing.

I need to do something to convince myself I'm doing the right thing. That I'm getting married. And I have a fiancé. That the perfect life I was headed for is within reach.

So, I message Keith.

Me: Don't forget to send me your RSVP list

Pathetic. That the best I can do? Where's the passion? The heat. The messages declaring how much I miss him. And that I can't wait to marry him.

I've been reduced to the role of a wedding planner in my own wedding.

No worse. Because of course, the message remains unread.

That familiar hurt tightens my guts. I slide the phone back into my purse and lock my fingers together. I'm trying so hard to manage the wedding, and this new job, and keep my spirits up in this festive season. I'm trying so hard to believe in *us*.

Why can't my fiancé make half the effort to be the kind of person I want him to be? He must, surely, want me if he proposed to me. Right?

I'm not unwanted. Or unclaimed. Contrary to Arthur's team's findings. I am engaged. *I am.*

And if my fiancé is missing? Well, I'm going to try my best to track him down.

I'm not a quitter.

I need to kick up my wedding planning and do better on the job. I need to ignore my attraction to Brody because that gives off the wrong vibe. I need to recommit to my fiancé and my upcoming marriage.

Yes, that's the best way forward.

Mind made up, and because I need a diversion from my own problems, I decide to focus on my boss's issues instead. He pulled me into this situation which, I'm sure, gives me permission to ask him a personal question.

I turn to him. "What I don't understand is how you'd leave such an important decision to your grandfather."

Brody loosens the tie around his neck. "Getting married didn't feel like a big enough deal for me to take time out of my busy schedule to focus on it. And when Arthur said he'd find me a bride, I figured, why not? It kept the old man off my back. And gave him something to do. Which meant, he wouldn't have the time to meddle in my work."

I pick up my jaw from where it's dropped. Is this guy for real? "Marrying someone who could be your life partner, who you'll see every morning and last thing at night, someone who could influence the course of your life, does not seem important?" I manage.

He shoots me a sideways glance filled with pity. "Our definition of marriage must differ."

"Please, tell me how you see it." No sooner are the words out of my mouth than I grimace.

What does it matter to me how this man views marriage? He's my boss. I work for him. I should restrict my discussions with him to the job. That's it.

"You know what, forget I asked. It's of no importance to me."

"On the contrary." He fixes me with those steely eyes. "Since you asked, and since my grandfather, for some reason, seems very taken with you, you should know that I intend to marry to claim my inheritance."

"So, the marriage will be in name only?"

He hesitates. "This will be the only time I get married. And I want children. I assume I'll come to feel something for my wife over a period of time."

I rub at my temple. "That seems cold."

"As opposed to?"

"As opposed to finding someone who you love and appreciate, and marrying her? That, after all, is the reason for the condition Arthur has imposed, isn't it?"

And is that why I'm pushing through with marrying my fiancé? I mean, I think I love him. And I think he loves me, in his own way.

Yet based on how he's treated me, does he really love and appreciate me?

Somehow, I'm not quite able to convince myself of it. A disquiet squeezes my chest, but I shove it aside and focus on my boss.

He looks incredulous. Like falling in love is up there with finding out Santa Claus is real and double-parked outside.

"It has been known to happen," I murmur.

He sneers. "I don't believe in love. I'd rather keep my life clear of such entanglements."

"And what about when you have kids? Are you planning to steer clear of entanglements when it comes to them too?"

"Of course, not. That's different."

I shake my head, trying to make sense of what he's saying. "So, you'll marry for the wrong reasons?"

"They're the right reasons for me. Whoever marries me will not want for anything."

"Except love."

He gives me a disbelieving look. "The money will more than make up for it."

"Money *is* important. But a marriage without love? You realize how pitiful that sounds?"

He reels back. "What do you mean?"

I realize, I'm lashing out at him. It's more to do with how I'm feeling about my own engagement right now. And how emotionally upset I am that I don't have the answers to the very questions I'm asking him. Yet I can't stop myself.

"You've ruled out all the important experiences that make you human."

"It holds no value for me." His features are set. His voice is hard. Yet there's something in his eyes.

Doesn't take a shrink to figure out that this man had something happen to him which resulted in him withdrawing from the idea of love.

"Who hurt you?" The words are out before I can stop myself.

I immediately regret it.

His features close. The vein popping at his temple seems ready to burst.

I slide further toward my door, as much as my seat belt will allow me. "Forget I asked. It's none of my business."

"You're right, it isn't." His voice is remote. "And for the record, I decided a long time ago there was no place for love in my life. It's why I trusted Gramps to pick the right woman for me to marry. Only, he seems to have picked wrong."

"It does seem that way." I lower my chin.

Until I met Brody, I was perfectly happy marrying my absentee fiancé. I was confident everything in my life was as I had planned it.

I'm confident that marrying my fiancé is what I want. I am. *Right?*

Keith loves me. He will make me happy. He's the one who proposed to me, after all. And he does desire me.

So does Brody. I know that, based on the chemistry that hums between us.

And I?

It's only after I met Brody that I realize how it feels to be truly drawn to someone. To want to physically be with someone with an urgency that makes my chest hurt and my pussy quiver.

An intensity that I haven't felt with my fiancé.

Not in the way that a mere glare from Brody makes me want to drop my clothes and climb him like he's a sturdy pine tree.

Am I making a mistake marrying someone who doesn't make me feel desired?

I was insecure, thinking that if I turned him down, I might not find someone else to marry. So, I said yes to his proposal.

My motivations might be different, but my willingness to marry someone I don't truly love is not that different from Brody's.

Ugh. Enough. Remove Brody from your mind. Focus on anything else. A thought strikes me.

"If you don't marry, you won't inherit," I feel compelled to point out.

"That's true."

"You don't seem concerned." I turn to face him.

"I'm sure, I'll be able to find a woman who can marry me. Better yet, I could shortlist a few and have Gramps choose from them. It's only a matter of time before I come into my inheritance."

Of course, he'll find another way. The man is resourceful. And when he makes it known he's looking for a wife, there'll be a list of

women a mile long waiting to marry him. My stomach sinks. My
heart wilts. Damn, why does that make me feel depressed?

Speaking of… "I hope I can keep my job after this debacle."

He seems taken aback. "What do you mean?"

"Your Gramps thinks I'm the woman you should marry. But
clearly, that can't happen now. In a sense, we are going against his
wishes, and Arthur seems like the kind who doesn't take kindly to
being disobeyed."

"Arthur shouldn't have involved you with this discussion about
my marriage. Of course, your job is safe." He looks at me intently for
a few seconds. There's a struggle going on in his eyes. Then, as if he's
unable to stop himself, he asks, "The flowers you received that day,
were they from—"

"My fiancé, yes." I tip up my chin.

His throat moves as he swallows. "And the wedding is—"

"In three weeks."

His jaw hardens. "In. Three. Weeks?"

I eye him with curiosity. The skin stretches across his cheekbones; his jaw seems so tight, he must, surely, have a tension
headache. I wonder what's making him this angry? Did I say or do
anything to warrant that reaction? I don't think so.

I need to distract him from talking about my upcoming nuptials.
"The Christmas decorations will be up later tonight. There's a team
coming in to put them up around the office."

He winces. And predictably, he seems to mentally check out as
soon as Christmas is mentioned. I have never met someone who has
such a lack of festive cheer.

He picks up his phone and begins to scroll through it.

Guess our conversation is over. It was an entertaining evening, at
least. *Sort of.*

I, too, pick up my phone and start replying to my emails. I mean
his emails which continue to be forwarded to my inbox.

When we reach the office, he's about to open the door to exit the
car, then pauses. "By the way, you'll be leading the board meeting."

"Me?" I gape at him. "You want me to lead the board meeting?"

"Yes."

What? *What?* What's he talking about "You're referring to the one n-next week?" I sputter.

"Is there another?" he asks politely.

I shake my head. "But…that's so soon."

He arches an eyebrow. "Do you have a problem with that?"

I shake my head. "No. I mean. Yes. I mean   " I rub at my forehead, feeling like I've stepped into an alternative reality.

Stay calm. It's fine. You can work this out.

"I'm new. And I'm your executive assistant."

"And part of your job description is to lead meetings in my absence."

"Yes. But—"

"Are you saying you can't deliver on the demands of this role?"

I frown. "Of course not, that's not what I mean."

"Then what is it?"

"It's a board meeting. All senior management will be there. And I've never lead one of these before."

"This would be a good way to start."

I narrow my gaze on him. Is he being deliberately obtuse?

"I don't have the kind of experience needed to lead a meeting of this importance."

He scans my face. I'm sure he's about to say something cutting. But whatever he sees on my face seems to strike a chord with him. His features soften.

"I wouldn't be asking you to lead the meeting if I didn't believe in you."

"Oh." Warmth coils in my chest. I feel like I've been ejected from my seat and am flying through the stratosphere. I realize, I'm staring at him with what must be a flabbergasted expression, for he frowns.

"You all right?"

"No." I clear my throat. "I mean, yes. Thank you for this opportunity. You won't regret it."

He looks at me closely. Whatever he sees on my face must convince him this time, for he nods. "Don't screw it up, Monroe."

13

Brody

"No, I cannot meet you. I have a conference call at midnight." I take off my glasses and squeeze the bridge of my nose.

Gramps isn't budging from this insane end of the year deadline for me to get married. Which means, it's my responsibility to find a wife.

I've never had to actively date before because women threw themselves at me. I had my pick and didn't have to woo them before I had sex. I fit the cliché of the wham-bam-thank-you-ma'am man and gave two shits about it.

It fit my lifestyle and provided a way to satisfy my urges without having to wade into the quagmire of emotions that comes with trying to have a relationship.

But given the insane timelines I'm working with, I engaged a matchmaker. Who lined me up with a string of dates over the past week.

It took only a few minutes on the first one to realize that I'm not cut out for this bullshit. You have to pretend interest in what the other person is saying. What the — ?

Then you have to give the women gifts. And pretend to like them. Apparently, there's a blueprint to this dating with a view to finding someone to marry game. Before I propose to a woman, I actually have to win her over. A shudder scrolls up my spine.

It's been a week since we met my grandfather. I've taken out a different woman every night for dinner for the last five days. Oh, and I've walked out mid-date on all of them. And yes, of course, I paid for the meals.

Far from being intrigued by the lives of the women I've tried to spend time with since that meeting with my grandfather, I've found most of them boring. Some downright repulsive. And if I'm being truthful, none of them are as interesting as my EA. *There*. That's the crux of the matter.

Thoughts of Lark have crowded my mind since that fateful meeting with Arthur.

I'd be lying if I said I haven't imagined a scenario where I could be married to her — to have her in my bed, and make love to her, and wake up next to her, and discuss work challenges with her.

It's the first time I've met someone who I like spending time with…no, who I look forward spending time with.

Too bad, she's engaged. She still doesn't have a ring on her finger though.

Surely, it doesn't take that long to have a ring resized. Which means, I was right thinking she was lying. Her loser fiancé didn't buy her a ring in the first place.

So why the hell is she marrying him?

She should be marrying me.

Whoa, hold on. I can't be seriously thinking this?

"Hello, are you there?" asks the woman on the line. *What's her name again?* I've forgotten it despite being on a date with her last night.

"I'm not interested." I hang up and place the device on my desk.

That's when the door to my office opens. My EA walks in. "The sales reports you asked for are in your inbox. Marketing has put in their expense forecast, which is too high, and—"

"Is everything okay?" I take in the harried expression on her features.

She's handled every challenge I've sent her way. Never once, has she backed down.

The more I hand over to her, the more she seems to thrive. In fact, it's occurred to me that she could well fill in for me as CEO on the occasions I'd rather be off working on initiatives related to veterans' affairs, which I find more satisfying.

In fact, I've handed over so much of my workload to her, I have more time on my hands than I've ever had before.

Not once, has she flinched at the projects that I've tasked her with. So, to see her stressed out today, for the first time since she came to work for me, gives me pause.

"I should be asking you that question." She glances at my phone, then back at me.

The fact that she doesn't answer my question right away confirms to me that she's under some kind of strain.

"I had to make it clear to the woman I went out on a date with last night that I'm not interested in seeing her again." I raise a shoulder.

She firms her lips. "You were on a date last night."

"How else am I going to find someone to marry?"

Her shoulders stiffen. *Interesting.*

"I've been on a date every night since we met Arthur."

"You have?" She recoils, then seems to find her composure again. "I mean, of course, you have. You're single and, as you say, you need to find a wife."

She spins around, but not before I see a flash of what I swear is jealousy cross her features. Unable to stop myself, I rise to my feet.

I am around the desk in a flash, but by the time I grab her wrist, she's already opening the door between our offices.

"What?" She turns on me with such anger in her voice that I stare.

I'm also aware of the electricity zipping up my arm. The air between us buzzes with that awareness which has only grown since the day we met, and my groin hardens with pure lust. While my heart... My heart stutters. *Fuck.* This is getting bloody complicated.

Especially when I spot the naked agony in her eyes before she blanks it. I wasn't imagining it. She's definitely upset that I was out with a different woman every night this week.

She looks down at where my fingers are wrapped around her wrist. Instantly, I release her.

"Did you want something?" Her voice is cool.

I lower my chin. "I have a question for you, actually."

"Well, what is it?"

"Why do you look so tired?"

14

Lark

Why is he so concerned about me? What does he care? When he's spent all week going out on dates with different women. Jealousy stabs my chest. Anger squeezes my guts. I bat away the confusing emotions.

It makes no difference to me what he does outside the office. He could have slept with a different woman each night, for all I care. He probably did. I can't see Mr. Virility taking a woman out and not fucking her.

I curl my fingers into fists. Nope. Not going there. Don't care for the images of his naked body moving with single-minded focus as he thrusts up and into some other pussy.

I gulp a few deep breaths, trying to ground myself.

His grandfather wants him to get married before the end of the year. Of course, he had to go on dates.

Then, there's me. I *am* getting married before the end of the year.

I should marry him.

Gah. No. What? That's such a stupid thought.

I shake my hair back from my face and notice the mistletoe tacked above us.

Brody made it clear his office was out of bounds for the festive décor.

The mistletoe at the threshold to his domain was as far as I could push it. I asked for it to hang there as an ironical gesture.

It hadn't crossed my mind that we'd both be standing under it at the same time.

"You're standing under the mistletoe." The words are out before I can stop them.

He raises his gaze and notices it. When he looks at me again, the flash of awareness in his eyes, followed by how he fixes them on my lips, tells me exactly the directions his thoughts have taken.

The hair rises on the nape of my neck.

He's so close, the heat from his body rolls over me in waves, engulfing me like a furnace that knows my name. The air between us crackles, charged and volatile.

His sheer size, the strength coiled beneath his tailored shirt, radiates a raw, masculine power that pulls at something deep inside me. It's primal. Magnetic.

My breath hitches. My skin tightens. Every inch of me is aware of him. Of how solid he feels. How safe. How dangerous.

I want to rise up on my toes and press my mouth to his like it's instinct. Like it's oxygen. The need hits me like a freight train. Sudden, intense, undeniable.

I've never felt this overwhelming desire to be close to another person like this before.

No, not with my fiancé either.

That thought gives me pause. I can't kiss my boss. I can't 'cheat' on my fiancé. Even if he has been absentee.

Brody must read my thoughts on my face, for his features close. He steps back. Instantly, I miss the heat of his body.

"You didn't answer my earlier question."

"What's that?" I frown.

"Why do you look so tired?"

I look away, then back at him. "I've been staying up nights reviewing the information for the board meeting. I've been prepping the slides, working through the numbers, and putting the finishing touches on the pitch."

"But it's nothing you can't handle."

The certainty in his voice gives me pause. "You have that much confidence in me?"

"I wouldn't have asked you to run it in my place if I didn't."

My heart blooms in my chest. A flush of happiness unfurls under my skin. Praise from him means so much to me. It feels so good to be acknowledged and appreciated by him. And that he believes in me means everything.

"But that's not what's bothering you."

I gape at him. How did he guess? Has he gotten to know me so well in such little time?

"Is it the dress?" He slips his hand inside the pocket of his pants.

I strive hard not to notice how his gesture tightens the fabric of his pants around his powerful thighs. Not that I haven't sneaked a look in the past. There's only so much I can resist when I'm faced with his hotness on a daily basis.

I'm so distracted, I don't reply right away.

"I mean, the wedding dress," he prompts me.

I frown. How does he know I've been eyeing the gorgeous wedding dresses on the site of one of the foremost designers in the country.

"The screen of your device was open on the website of Karma West Sovrano's atelier," he replies in answer to my unspoken question.

He must have noticed it during one of our meetings when I placed my device on the desk between us.

"I'm not searching for my dress on company time, if that's what you're implying." I cross my arms across my chest.

He sighs. "I wasn't implying that."

I flush at the sincerity in his words. "Of course, not. And I can't afford a Karma West Sovrano dress anyway."

"But you would have liked to have worn one of them to your wedding?"

"Who wouldn't?" I wave a hand in the air. "But I've found a dress at an alternate High Street Label." *Not as good, but it'll have to do.*

"So, what is it then? What's bothering you?"

He narrows his gaze, and it's as if he can see right through to the knot of worries in my chest.

I instinctively realize that I can't lie to him. He'll spot it right away. I blow out a breath. "Do you really want to hear this?"

"I assure you, I do." His body settles into a waiting stance to punctuate the patience behind his words.

He can be an annoying jerkface. But as our working relationship has developed, he's beginning to trust me more. Otherwise, he wouldn't have delegated so much of his workload to me. Maybe, it's time for me to trust him.

I rub at my forehead. "It's the wedding planning." I sigh. "It's been stressful."

"And isn't your…fiancé"—he bites off the word like it's a hunk of plastic clogging his mouth—"helping you?"

I start to laugh, then realize, he's serious. "He's, ah… He's busy traveling for work."

His nostrils flare. A look of anger flashes across his features, followed by something like steely resolve.

He lowers his voice. "If you were mine, I would be with you, planning our wedding every step of the way."

Oh my God. He said 'mine' in that growly voice of his, and I swear, my ovaries quivered. And my core clenched. And I'm pretty sure my panties are wet.

"If you were mine, I'd never let you out of my sight." His eyes flash. "I'd make sure you never felt unsupported during this entire process.

"If you were mine—"

"But I'm not." I say it to remind him *and me* that our relationship is strictly professional.

He stiffens. His shoulders bunch. There's a moment of desolation on his face. Only, it's replaced quickly by a mask which feels impenetrable.

"I hope the wedding planning goes smoothly." He pivots and walks back to his desk.

I want to apologize for what I said. But it's the truth. I'm not his. He's not mine. I work for him; that's the only thing that binds us. So why do I feel so bereft? Like I did something wrong?

He snatches up his phone. When he looks at me again, his features are more composed. "The board meeting is in two days. Are you ready for it?"

The oak table gleams under the lights, so polished I can see my own reflection in its surface. The length stretches from one end of the room to the other. It's designed to make you look small. Forgettable. If I give into it, that is. *Which I'm not going to do.*

I haven't had the chance to exchange more than a few words with Brody since our last conversation. Our encounters have been professional. He hasn't given any hint of being pissed off by our last conversation either.

Now that he's handed over the lead on many of the meetings he chairs with the team, I spend most of my day in video conferences and meetings.

Brody, on the other hand, spends more time out of the office. The change in his daily schedule and mine, is astonishing.

I take in the tinsel strung across the conference-room ceiling, the bowls of candy canes I asked the team to set at intervals along the table, and the soft glow from the string of warm fairy lights draped across the windowsills.

Little things, but they put my mark on this meeting.

I asked the team to add them, a splash of warmth in a room that usually feels like an ice bath. Somehow, it steadies me. Pushes back the doubts gathering like storm clouds in my chest. Gives me the courage to sit up straighter.

On my first day, Brody made me reschedule this board meeting and then told me I'd be leading it.

Here I am, two weeks into the job, stepping into the role of CEO to chair the meeting. My heart is jittery, my palms damp, but I am ready to crush it.

My love life might be a spectacular mess, but at least here, in this room, I get a chance to shine. I look out at the ring of skeptical faces, inhale once, and welcome them to the table.

"We'll begin with the earnings projections for Q4." I keep my voice calm.

"Earnings?" Edgar Kingston, co-chair of the board, a man old enough to be my grandfather, with a full head of silver, sniffs from near the end of the table. "Brody's the one most familiar with the figures. No need to trouble yourself with this."

The laughter that follows scrapes across my skin. I breathe in and out slowly, reminding myself I am the queen of business dynamics. That this boardroom bullying doesn't bother me. That Brody believes in me. Which further helps calm my nerves.

That's when the door to the room opens, and the man himself walks in as if I conjured him. Brody takes a seat halfway down the table. He glances around the table, exchanging pleasantries with a few of the members. Even seated, he's taller and broader than the others at the table.

There's a magnetism to him which draws the eye. An energy around him that's both dynamic and appealing. Also, God help me, he's wearing his spectacles.

How am I supposed to focus on the darn numbers in front of me when he's sitting there looking like a brooding, sexier, more lethal version of Clark Kent?

He nods in my direction, and I take it as a signal to continue.

"I'll walk you through the briefing I circulated yesterday." I school my expression into a cool I-don't-care mask. "If you've read it, you'll find the results familiar. If you haven't… Then perhaps, take notes this time."

Their smirks falter.

In the silence that follows, I can feel a hiss of approval ripple through the air. And his gaze, hot and heavy, lingers on me like a touch. I drink it in. God, how I crave it. Being the sole focus of Brody Davenport's attention is a high I'd do anything to feel.

It coils heat low in my belly. It's intoxicating. Erotic. Addictive. I didn't realize how much I missed being seen like this. And now that I have it, I don't ever want to stop being the center of his world

I keep going, flipping through slides, reciting numbers, countering their interruptions with crisp answers.

Each barb makes my pulse skitter, but I refuse to let it get to me. I meet every question thrown my way with clear, cogent answers. A strange thrill runs through me. A pulse of kinetic energy that keeps me focused and my thoughts fluid. I feel calm, collected, eerily composed. Like I'm where I'm supposed to be. In this chair. Facing off against those around the table. Showing them how good I am at this. I can do this. I am good at this.

"And that's my plan to grow profits by ten percent for next year." I glance around the table.

"Impressive." The only other woman in the room smiles.

That would be Ursula Dalton, the treasurer to the board. She's around fifty, not a hair out of place, flawless makeup, and a designer suit that makes me aware of my High Street purchased jacket and skirt. "I'm sure you'll understand when I wonder if you had help preparing those projections."

Silence descends on the table. All eyes are turned toward me. Brody leans forward in his seat but doesn't jump to my defense. Thank God. If he'd done that, it would've shown I can't steer the meeting without his help. It would've negated all the impact I've made so far. It also shows he has confidence in me.

I take my time gathering my thoughts.

I can't be rude. But I also can't take this insult without responding to it. "I can assure you, the financials in this statement were put together by me." I let the silence stretch, then tilt my head, cool and deliberate. "If you have any questions related to the numbers, I'd be more than happy to clarify."

15

Brody

"These revenue projections for Q4 look optimistic. What assumptions are you making about portfolio performance and market expansion?"

I tense. That's a tricky question. Ursula is whip-smart and her knowledge of the business is legendary. She doesn't suffer fools gladly.

"Thank you for the question." Lark dips her chin. "The projections assume a twelve percent increase in portfolio returns, driven by strong performance in our technology and renewable energy holdings, along with gains from the launch of our new venture fund. We have also factored in a conservative two percent headwind from interest rate fluctuations and broader market uncertainty. Even if some exits underperform, we will meet our growth target. I have built in downside sensitivity, so this is not wishful thinking. It is realistic and achievable."

Ursula looks at my EA with respect in her eyes. "I don't have any further queries."

I couldn't have answered it better myself. I want to pound the table and acknowledge her brilliant response. I want to jump up to my feet, round the table, take her into my arms and kiss her deeply. Goddamn, this woman is not only gorgeous, but she's also bloody astute, and a fast thinker, and so intelligent. She's my dream woman.

I find myself smiling and shut it down right away.

Fuck, I can't afford to think like this. I can't afford to give in to my attraction to her. I can't.

Julian Reed, the Corporate Secretary, looks up from the stack of reports in front of him. "Can you walk us through how the investment budget is being allocated across sectors? And why the reduced exposure to traditional assets this year?"

Lark nods. "Of course. Sixty-two percent of our allocation is in growth sectors: thirty percent in technology and renewable energy, eighteen percent in private equity and venture capital, and fourteen percent in strategic partnerships and co-investments. Traditional assets make up twelve percent, down from last year, because returns there have flattened while newer markets continue to outperform. We are not reducing traditional exposure out of sentiment; we are doing it because the numbers justify the shift."

Julian looks at her with something like admiration. I allow my lips to curl. I don't feel the need to hide my satisfaction anymore.

I had no doubt my woman could hold her own in this meeting. But to have her fulfill my expectations in such sterling fashion is so bloody satisfying. My chest swells. I am so fucking proud of her. I knew she could lead the board meeting in my place. And she's done so admirably.

News flash: She's not your woman. She's your employee.

She continues with her presentation.

When another member interrupts her with yet another question, I watch in admiration as she answers his query with a smile. By the time she's done speaking, another board member is completely mesmerized by her.

When there's yet another question from the table, it's Kingly who interrupts. "Ms. Monroe has the floor. I suggest we save our questions for the end."

Lark acknowledges his support with a warm smile. She can do with all the allies she makes in this room. However, I have a burning need to discourage any other kind of relationship with her. I resolve to do so later. He needs to understand that she's off-limits. After all, she's engaged.

She's also off-limits to me. After that almost-kiss under the mistletoe, I need to remind myself of that again.

She gets through the rest of the presentation without further interruptions. There are a few questions, which she's able to field easily.

All her preparation, and the long nights when I saw her working in her office, have paid off.

"By jove, well done." Edgar nods at her. "That was one of the most comprehensive briefs I've read in a board meeting."

Lark's face lights up. "Thank you."

"The Christmas decorations in the boardroom didn't hurt either. In fact, it facilitated a more pleasant environment and helped with the thinking process," another board member chimes in. "Especially the candy canes." He eyes them with open longing.

"Please, help yourself." She nods at the bowl in front of him.

"Don't mind if I do." He plucks one out, unwraps it, and crunches down.

The person beside him shrugs and grabs one too. Then another director reaches. And another.

Within seconds, the room sounds like a candy cane factory. Crinkling wrappers. Sharp little crunches. Not exactly the soundtrack you expect in a board meeting.

A few of those around the table smile at her. Real smiles. *Warm ones.* Not the usual expressions board members wear during one of these meetings either.

Who would've guessed her insistence on holiday decorations and putting out treats would soften even the iciest temperaments?

It also shows that she recognizes how the holidays tap into the inner child within everyone. Which impresses me.

As if by magic, the tension in the room dissolves, replaced by something that feels suspiciously like contentment.

Color me shocked. A flicker of awe squeezes my chest.

Hayes notices too. "I assume that wasn't your idea, Davenport?"

"The credit goes to Ms. Monroe." I nod in Lark's direction without looking at her. "She convinced me that imparting the festive touch to the office can only help with productivity overall."

"Soft persuasion. This woman is your secret weapon." Hayes sends me a shrewd glance.

"She is a core part of my team. She's made my working life a lot easier." *Now, if only I could find a way to have her feature more prominently in my personal life, too.* I don't say that aloud though.

"Ms. Monroe will take on more of a leadership role in the coming days and weeks," I declare to the table.

"Hmm." Hayes nods slowly. "What are your plans?"

"Plans?" I arch an eyebrow.

"Does this mean she's to feature more significantly in your succession planning?"

Board members normally don't discuss succession planning so openly. Especially when it's a topic fraught with internal politics and lobbying. But then, asking Lark to lead the board meeting in my place was unusual too.

He's right though. After that noteworthy and very successful performance with leading the board meeting, I *have* decided to make her CEO. But that's not something I'm ready to share with anyone yet. Not until I've had a chance to discuss it with her. I also need to inform my grandfather of my decision and make sure he backs her.

Excitement fills me. Lark is the perfect candidate to take over my role. I couldn't have planned this better.

Things are progressing at a pace I hadn't quite expected them to. But I'm not complaining. Not when work has not given me the kind of buzz it used to. Not when delivering on profit goals had begun to feel hollow.

Once I make Lark CEO, I can devote time to pursuing the stuff that seems meaningful.

But would it feel as purposeful without Lark by my side? I know the answer to that.

Outwardly, I keep my tone casual. "And if I were?"

Hayes surveys me with a glint in his eyes. "Then, I think you have a viable candidate there."

He rises to his feet, shakes my hand, then Lark's, before heading out the door.

The others, too, begin to depart. Some of them stop to catch up. By the time I'm free of them, I find Kingly is deep in conversation with Lark.

"You did good, kid." He pats her shoulder.

How patronizing. I narrow my gaze on Kingly, but he doesn't seem to notice. Lark looks vaguely uncomfortable and shifts about a half-step away.

"Thank you. I appreciate your support."

"Any time. Brains and beauty. That's a lethal combination." He flashes her a smile.

A burning sensation fills my chest. Is he flirting with her? I close the distance to them.

Kingly's features turn serious. "I was wondering if you'd like to join me for a—"

"Ms. Monroe"—I step between them, forcing them to move apart —"I have an urgent issue I need to discuss with you."

Lark scowls at me. "I was talking to Kingly."

"Who was on his way out." I glare at Kingly, indicating to him without words that he'd better fuck off.

Kingly must get the message for he clears his throat. "I, ah, guess I need to be getting along." He heads out.

The door shuts behind him.

In the silence that follows, I scan her features. She raises one eyebrow, as if to say: *What was that all about?* Something I'm *not* going to study too closely.

I have the distinct impression she's trying to keep a straight face, but her eyes glint with excitement.

Her lips twitch, then she gives in to a big smile.

I can't stop myself from grinning back. "You killed it." I'm not sure who moves first, but suddenly, she's in my arms. "That was bloody exceptional. You were mesmerizing."

"Oh my God, did you see their faces?" She leans back in the circle of my arms.

"They were bowled over by your intelligence. Your charm. Your beauty. They couldn't get enough of you. I couldn't get enough off you." I tuck a strand of hair that's come loose from the sleek coil she'd twisted it up into. "I gave you the chance to prove you belong at this table. And you seized it. You did me proud, Lark."

She flushes at my praise. Her pupils dilate. And when her lips part, I lower my gaze to her mouth. Damn, those luscious lips of hers are a siren call. As is that jasmine scent of hers; with a hint of coconut, it makes my mouth water.

I want to kiss her so fucking much. It's a physical ache that turns my muscles to rock and lights fire in my veins.

"Thank you." The husky note in her voice only ramps up my desire.

The air between us spikes with desire.

A part of me, that possessive, animalistic part that wanted her the moment I saw her insists I throw her down on the conference room table and ravish her.

As if she senses my unspoken question, she raises her chin. My heart begins to race. The blood pounds at my temples. I want her so fucking much. And holding myself back because she belongs to someone else is pure torture. Surely, I could kiss her? Just one teeny tiny kiss?

And if someone were to walk in here to find us in this compromising position? I would probably walk away unscathed. But she'd have to try doubly hard to prove herself. And even then, something like this would dog her footsteps for a long time. I cannot put her in a situation where that's even a possibility.

So, with a superhuman effort, where I tell my dick to calm down and order my brain to take over, I force myself to let go of her. It's the hardest thing I've ever done.

Surprise filters into her eyes, then understanding. She looks stricken at the kiss that did not happen and takes another step back.

"So… What are your plans for the rest of the day? After that stupendous performance, is your fiancé taking you for a celebratory dinner?"

Her face falls. I curse myself for bringing him up. But I had to do it to remind myself of her engaged status. I'm grasping at straws here to keep my distance from her.

"Uh, he's out of the country." She turns away, but not before I see the sadness in her eyes. "Guess I'd better return to my desk and get through my agenda for the rest of the day."

She gathers up her various devices and papers, then begins to head toward the doorway. I get the feeling she's embarrassed. Which she shouldn't be. It's that wanker of a fiancé who needs to be taught a lesson for treating this goddess like she doesn't matter at all.

"It's good that you're going to be here. I need your help with one of the proposals related to driving company culture and leadership development."

She pauses halfway to the door. "You do?" She turns to me.

I nod, relieved that she seems cheerier at the prospect. "Also, I was wondering if you'd have dinner with me?"

"Dinner?" She frowns.

"At my desk. Call it a combined celebratory dinner and working meeting. In fact, I'm so thrilled at the outcome of today's board meeting, I'll order the dinner."

———

Half an hour later, she knocks on the door and enters, carrying the food that I ordered.

I stretch my arms up in the air, then roll my shoulders. "Just in time. My hunger was beginning to eat into my concentration."

I look up in time to find her staring at my biceps. The interest in her features, the parting of her delicate lips… All of it sets my blood on fire. I must be mistaking my hunger for food for hunger for something else. I wrench my attention back to my desk and push my papers aside.

She places the paper bags on the desk. Then, as if unable to stop herself, she jerks her chin toward my face. "You're wearing your spectacles."

"I need them for reading, especially when my eyes are tired."

She continues to scan my features with a look I can only describe as…lust-filled. Damn, it makes me wonder if it was a good idea to ask her to have dinner with me. But no way, could I have let her spend the rest of the evening on her own. Not when her performance at the board meeting was celebration worthy.

I lean back in my chair. "You like my glasses?"

"What?" She seems to rouse herself. "Oh yeah, they suit you." As if uncomfortable by what she's revealed, she looks away, then seats herself.

I rise to my feet, grab some plates, glasses, cutlery and napkins from the kitchenette in my office, and set them in front of me and the seat across from me at my desk.

I plate out the food, dividing it between hers and mine. Turkey Ballotine stuffed with chestnut, sage, and cranberry, sliced into medallions.

She sniffs the food. "Smells divine."

I grab the bottle of mulled wine that came with the delivery and pour some out into our glasses.

"Bon appétit."

We dig into the food. I inhale most of what's on my plate before I pause to take a drink of the mulled wine. The flavors of cinnamon, cloves, star anise and nutmeg explode on my palate.

"So good. It tastes both elegant and Christmassy." She takes another bite of the turkey.

"I figured you'd like it, since you're a Christmas junkie."

She looks at me with a weird look on her face. Her big eyes glitter at me.

"You're not going to cry, are you?" I only half-joke.

"Of course, not." She sniffs. "But that was a nice thing to do. You're a good man, Brody Davenport."

I stare at her. I don't want her to see me as a good man. Well, not *only* a good man. If she knew the things I want to do to her, she wouldn't see me that way.

"What?" She frowns.

I shake my head and take another sip of wine to wet my suddenly parched throat.

She brings a forkful of the medallion to her mouth. I can't look away from the spectacle of her lips curling around the tines of her fork. And I can't stop myself from imagining how it'd feel to have her mouth wrapped round my cock, either. Said appendage instantly perks up.

The arousal I somehow managed to smother into submission tightens my pants again. Good thing I have the desk between us. Her fiancé. Yes, that's it. Focus on the man who treats her so fucking badly, it makes me want to tear him from limb to limb.

I spend a few seconds relishing the thought before fixing my attention on her face.

"Will you spend Christmas with your fiancé?" The words are out before I can stop them.

Bloody hell, why did I have to bring up that tosser now? When I'm having dinner with her, when I know how much the mention of him seems to blight her mood.

Sure, enough her forehead creases. Then she smooths out the expression on her face. "Who else?"

I tighten my hold on my wineglass. The thought of her being with any man other than me...twists my guts and turns my blood to lava. I draw in a few breaths until I find my composure.

"What about your parents?" I manage to ask.

"They're in California."

"And do you have any other family? Any siblings?"

She gives me a funny look. "You're awfully chatty."

"You know a lot about me. You've met my grandfather, and I'm sure you've heard about my brothers who work here." I shrug lightly. "I want to know a little more about you."

She purses her lips. "Didn't you have me investigated? I'm sure whatever you want to know is in there."

I pause. "I read the file, yes. But that's paper. I'd rather hear it from you."

The truth is, I want to understand her—what drives her, what she hides behind that calm exterior. I want the version of her no report can capture.

She frowns, guarded.

"Only if you're comfortable," I add. "It'll help us work together better."

She toys with the food on her plate. Then seems to come to a decision. "I have a younger sister." She looks up at me. "She got a scholarship to study at the Royal Drawing School."

"That's impressive."

She smiles. "Raya *is* very smart and talented."

"She takes after her sister then."

She narrows her gaze. "Are you blowing smoke up my arse, Mr. Davenport?"

I chuckle. I'm delighted that she's mirroring the same words I once used with her. "Touché." I raise my wineglass.

She clinks her glass with mine.

"You're going to need time off after the wedding, aren't you?" *Can't leave it alone, can you?* It's something that, clearly, isn't a favorite topic of hers. But I really want to understand how this smart, beautiful, gorgeous woman got involved with a knobhead like her fiancé.

"Time off?" She blinks.

"You're going on a honeymoon, aren't you?"

Saying it aloud turns my stomach to stone and my muscles to granite. The thought of her on holiday with another man, makes me want to throw something at the wall.

"Uh, hmm, not really." She stares into her wineglass.

"You're not going on a honeymoon?"

"This role is new to me; I didn't think it was prudent to take time off."

She lowers her chin.

"Also, Keith and I decided that it would be best to use the money we'd have spent on the trip toward a down payment for our mortgage."

Her words say one thing. But the hurt in her eyes says otherwise.

Keith, huh? What a fucking loser of a name. And I can't believe he wouldn't take her on a honeymoon. Why the hell is she marrying this man?

To stop myself from saying something I might regret, which is only bound to upset her more, I finish off the contents of my plate.

Then because I'm sure it'll cheer her up, and because I'm genuinely curious, I ask, "Why do you love Christmas so much?"

"I love this time of year." Her gaze drifts, a faraway look in her eyes. "The lights, the crisp air, the way carols float through the streets like everyone's sharing the same memory. There's this hush, like the world is holding its breath. For a few weeks, people soften. They let themselves hope. Believe. It's like the season gives us permission to believe in something good again."

Her phone buzzes. She picks it up, her eyes widen, then she jumps to her feet. "Uh, I have to go."

16

Lark

Remember to buy batteries. For everything. Especially the twinkly lights. And also, for my vibrator.

—From Lark's Christmas to-do list

Oh God, oh no. No, no, no. What is my fiancé doing here?

I pivot and head for the connecting door between our offices.

Thanks to the glass wall between our offices, my boss can see everything unfolding, but there's nothing I can do about it.

I shut the door between our offices and try to ignore the fact that my boss is watching my reunion with my fiancé. Which is easier said than done.

Because this is Brody we're talking about. I'm only too keenly aware of his gaze following me.

Keith is standing at the window looking out.

He turns as I approach. His dirty blond hair is artfully mussed. He's tall enough to look down on my five feet four inches. Not as tall as Brody. Or as broad. And his eyes aren't as piercing. And… Argh. Stop it. This is not a competition.

"Larkie." He half smiles. "There you are."

I've told him so many times not to call me Larkie. I really don't like it. But he keeps forgetting.

I move toward him with determination.

What does he want? Except for that short phone call and the flowers he sent, I haven't heard from him at all. And now he turns up, without any advance notice?

"Where have you been? Why haven't you been in touch? And you left all the planning to me."

"Whoa, whoa, slow down, will ya?" He half-laughs.

"I will not." I come to a stop, leaving enough distance between us that it's clear how upset I am with him.

"Do you even take any of this seriously? You've missed every appointment and haven't even given me your guest list? What is going on?" I fume.

Keith doesn't seem too bothered by my tirade. He stands with his arms loose at his sides, almost at ease.

It's as if we haven't spent a month apart. And that his ignoring my calls and messages, and leaving me to shoulder the burden of the wedding planning don't mean anything.

Because they don't.

Not to him.

I've been so caught up in my new job and preparations for my perfect life as a married woman, I didn't spot it. Or rather, I subconsciously knew it, but didn't want to acknowledge it.

I don't want to accept it.

A shiver ripples through me, an instinctive warning, like my body knows something my mind refuses to see.

I cover up my confusion by aiming another bunch of rapid-fire questions at Keith.

"We have a meeting with the caterer on Monday to finalize details for the lunch at the reception. And now that you're here, you can help me make the place cards."

A strange look comes into his eyes. "Lark, I—"

No, no, no. I don't want him to complete that statement. I don't want to face whatever is coming next.

I don't want to concede how uncomfortable it feels to be anywhere near my fiancé. I definitely don't want to acknowledge how deeply wrong it feels to have my fiancé here in my office with me. With my hot boss watching.

I can't bear to accept that the perfect life I've been planning for myself is about to collapse.

So, I default to what I'm most comfortable with when I'm panicking. My checklist mode.

I push through with the other things on my wedding planning list where I need his input.

"Oh, I need you to share your RSVP list. And did you get your tux fitted yet? Also, can we go see the Christmas tree lighting at Trafalgar Square? It's something I do every year."

I attempt a smile, but my face muscles don't seem to cooperate.

"Lark…" His voice is almost gentle. "I came here because I have something to tell you."

The combination of sadness and determination on his face makes me pause. Also, why is he sweating?

Another chill of unease crawls down my spine.

Out of the corner of my eyes, I notice the door connecting my office with my boss's office open.

My boss steps into the room.

I ignore it because I'm more worried about the weird expression on my fiancé's features. Alarm bells go off in my head. The hair on the nape of my neck rises.

I'm almost not surprised when he looks down at his feet. "I think we should break up."

"What?" My rib cage shrinks in size. I gulp down a few breaths, sure I'm caught up in a nightmare.

He looks up and past me. He must spot my boss, for his forehead wrinkles. "I..." He looks back at me, lowering his voice. "I don't think you and I are good together. I think this marriage is a mistake." He squares his shoulders.

His stance tells me he believes what he's saying.

"What? No. You can't break up with me." I'm aware of my voice rising. And that I'm almost yelling. And my boss is watching. I flush with embarrassment. But the concern about the bomb that has gone off in my life and destroyed all my carefully laid plans takes precedence over anything else.

"I'm sorry." He runs a finger under the collar of his shirt. "Truly, Lark."

I look at him closely, but he doesn't meet my eyes. In fact, there's a guilty expression on his face.

I stiffen. "Is there...someone else?"

He straightens his spine but continues to look away. "What makes you say that?" He risks a glance in my direction, but his gaze skitters away.

The band around my chest tightens. A cold sense of certainty grips me. "There *is* someone else."

Keith opens his mouth. I throw up my hands. "Don't bother trying to deny it; your guilt is written all over your face."

He squeezes his eyes shut, then nods. "I'm so sorry, Lark."

My heart sinks into my stomach.

"Who is she?" I burst out.

"What?" His eyes round in surprise.

"The woman you cheated on me with, who is she?"

"Lark, come on." He laughs nervously. "Surely, you don't want to know that."

"Oh, I very much do." I plant my fists on my hips. "It's the least you owe me, after breaking off the wedding at the last minute."

He sighs, then throws up his hands. "If you must know, it's Tiffany."

I reel back. "T...Tiffany? My bridesmaid, Tiffany?"

He nods.

Oh shit.

"It…just happened. It wasn't intentional," he mumbles.

What the hell? That's his excuse? "So, your penis accidentally fell into her vagina?" I huff.

He reddens. "Lark, come on, don't be a bitch about it."

"I'm being a bitch?" I gape at him. "How did I become the villain in this piece? You're the one cheating on me."

"And that's why I'm breaking up with you. I didn't think it would be fair to go through with the wedding since… You know…" He shrugs.

"Well, thank you so much for being so considerate." I rub at my forehead.

A headache begins to drum behind my eyes.

"How…how long?" I finally ask. I'm not sure why I want to know, but something pushes me to find out.

He looks at the door leading out of my office, then sighs again. "Six months," he blurts out.

"Six. *Months?*" My head spins. "Right after you proposed to me?"

How could I not have known? How could I have missed the signs? Am I such a loser that I couldn't see that my own fiancé was cheating on me?

"How could you do this to me?" I whisper.

"How can you say that, when *you* never wanted to sleep with me," he says in an accusing tone.

I recoil.

"It's why I had to look elsewhere to satisfy my needs."

I gape at him. I can't believe he's blaming *me* for his having cheated on me. I try to speak, but I'm so shocked, the words don't materialize.

He sets his jaw. "I felt constrained. Like I had a noose around my neck. I needed to reclaim my freedom."

I finally find my voice. "Freedom? You wanted to reclaim your freedom?" I shake my head. "You're the one who proposed to me! I'm not the one who suggested we get married!" I feel myself growing hysterical. "No wonder you weren't involved in the wedding preparations. And began to travel even more. And didn't keep in touch. I kept making excuses for you. Thinking it was work."

"It *was* work. All those business trips were real. I closed a real estate deal. One that's going to net me a great bonus."

I set my jaw. "You waited until the last minute before you decided to call off the wedding."

It's only two weeks to the wedding.

My heart sinks as the repercussions dawn on me.

"My friends have confirmed they're coming. My parents are flying out from California to attend the wedding. How could you do this to me?"

I cringe when I hear my words. I sound so desperate.

"Listen, Larkie. I'm sor—"

"Don't call me that," I snap.

He looks like he's about to respond, but I give him a quelling look, and he subsides.

This whole time—while he was away, and while I ignored my misgivings that he wasn't an active participant in our wedding plans—I was holding onto the fact that he loved me. That once we were married, everything would turn out okay.

That I'd have my perfect life: the perfect job, the perfect husband, and the Happily Ever After I've always wanted.

Now, everything has gone wrong.

The blood drains from my face. "Oh God. What am I going to tell them?"

I feel like a living cliché. Instead of the life I planned for myself, I'll forever be known as the woman who was ditched before the wedding. My head spins. My chest hurts. My knees tremble. I wish I could sink through the floor.

That's when my boss closes the distance to me and wraps his arm around my waist.

17

Brody

What am I doing?

I sense the shock ripple through her. Then she stiffens and casts me a confused glance. It's a testament to how upset she is that she doesn't try to pull away.

As for me? I overheard what her fiancé told her; knew it would be mortifying for her that I'd heard it; but I saw the anger and embarrassment on her face and could not stop myself from stepping in.

I knew I had to help her salvage her pride. And if I could do so by embarrassing this sorry excuse for a human standing opposite us, then even better.

I glare at him.

He grows so pale, I wonder if he's going to puke. What a pussy. Seriously, she could do better. Much, much better.

In fact, I can't think of anyone who'd make a good husband for her. She's incomparable. There's no one who'd be good enough for her.

Except me.

I shove the thought aside.

"Wh... Who are you?" The other man swallows.

"I'm her boss."

As if the sound of my voice pulls her out of her reverie, Lark tries to pull away.

I tighten my arm around her and hold her in place. "I'm also the man who's crazily in love with her."

What the—? Where did that come from? I did want to say or do something that'd wipe that smug expression off his face. But love?

"Love?" The other man's jaw drops.

"Love?" She jerks her chin in my direction.

"Yes, baby. I'm sorry if this comes as a surprise. But from the moment I saw you, I knew there was no one else out there for me."

"Wh-what?" she chokes out.

I look into her eyes, willing her to play along.

I know the exact moment recognition dawns on her, and she realizes that I'm doing this for the benefit of her loser ex, for she draws in a breath. "You have feelings for me?"

I take her hand in mine. "I understand how overwhelming this must be for you. But I want you. It was killing me that you were planning to marry this loser. But *I* understand your value in my life. I can't do without you, sweetheart."

Her features soften. "That's a very sweet thing to say."

"I want you to come home with me, so I can introduce you to my family."

She blinks rapidly.

The expression on her face shows she's game to play along, but also, that she's confused. Then she seems to pull herself together. "I'd love to meet your family, honey."

She snuggles in closer.

For a few seconds, I revel in the feel of her body close to mine and the sound of her calling me "honey" in that sweet voice of hers. I used to wince at how couples used such saccharine endearments, but somehow, coming from her, it feels different. It feels right. And with her curvy body melting into mine, I'm in heaven.

Then the douchebag who caused her so much grief clears his throat. "Umm… That's my fiancée."

"No, she's not," I growl.

"Not anymore," she snaps.

He looks between us. "Uh… What… What's the meaning of this. Lark… You, what are you doing? This man —"

"Is going to take care of her the way you never would. You had your opportunity, buster, and you lost it." I jerk my chin in the direction of the doorway. "Get gone."

"B-b-b-ut I —"

"You'd best haul arse before I call security. And *Keith*, aw, that's sweet." I bare my teeth. "Is your middle name mediocre? No wait, I bet it's shitstain."

I have the satisfaction of seeing the twatface turn purple in the face. "Look here, there's no need to get personal," he blusters.

Without taking my arm from around Lark, I swipe out my free hand and grab the other man's collar.

I shove him with enough force that he stumbles. He also seems to get the message, for he makes tracks to the doorway.

Where he pauses. "Good luck, dude. You'll need it with that dead fish. It won't be long before you're looking elsewhere too."

Lark winces and curves into herself.

What. The. Fuck. How dare he talk like that about this gorgeous woman?

When I narrow my gaze, whatever he sees on my face is enough to have him swallow audibly.

"Leave. Now." My voice, like a whip, cracks out in his direction. It seems to catch him with the impact of a body blow, for he shoves the door open and lurches out.

It swings shut behind him.

Lark trembles against me. Tension leaps off her body. When I look down at her face, it's to find that rage has her in its thrall, not disappointment.

"Oh my God, I'm so mad at myself." Her voice quivers with fury as she clenches her fists, stamping her foot like she's trying to drive her anger into the ground.

She's fire. Defiant. Glorious in her fury. And hell, if that doesn't make her even more irresistible.

"I can't believe I was engaged to that…that sorry excuse of a man."

Exactly.

"I don't understand how I missed the signs." She tosses her head, hair flying, eyes flashing.

"It wasn't your fault —" I begin, but she cuts me off.

"You bet, it's not my fault. He made sure he traveled as much as possible. He kept out of my way and made sure I never got a hint of what he was up to."

She squeezes her eyes shut and gulps a few deep breaths. When she opens her eyes, she seems more composed. "Thanks, anyway, for the backup."

She hasn't pulled away from me. Maybe I should feel like a heel for taking advantage of the fact that I have my arm about her, but she's single. And so am I. And I love the feel of her curves against me. So, I don't release her either.

"You're welcome. I'm glad I could be of help," I rumble.

"It did feel good to get my comeuppance against my numbskull of an ex" — she rubs at her forehead — "but I'm not looking forward to what comes next."

"You're not marrying him. End of story." I snort.

She gives me an if-only-that-were-true look. "I have to pick up the pieces."

I heard the last part of her conversation with the douche, so I lower my chin. "You mean, having to tell your friends and family that the wedding is off?"

She hangs her head. "That is going to be agonizing. I'm going to look like such a loser. And my parents are going to be so disappointed. And I'm going to lose my deposit at the Town Hall and at the pub."

"The pub?" I frown.

"That's where we were supposed to have our reception."

At a pub? I let her ex off easy. I should have kicked his arse for how much he let her down.

"This is horrible. And I had everything planned. I really thought—" She swallows. "I thought I was finally getting my dream life."

"With him?" I stare at the door through which the arsehole walked out earlier.

She scowls up at me. Then as if realizing that she's in the circle of my arms, she pulls away.

I miss the feel of her body against mine. Which does not surprise me. I'm realizing, where Ms. Lark Monroe is concerned, the more I have of her, the more I want of her.

"It may not seem like much, but I had the life I wanted all planned out, and now—" She swallows and looks away. "And now, all I'm left with is having to send out emails cancelling the wedding and a stack of unpaid bills."

Her chin wobbles, and fuck if my heart doesn't hurt. And if my chest doesn't tighten. And if every part of me doesn't want to do something… Anything to help her. In fact, I could help her and myself.

An idea forms in my head. One which excites me in its simplicity and its ease to carry out.

"I don't even know why I'm telling you this." She hunches her shoulders. "It's not like this has anything to do with you."

"What if it did?"

Even as I say the words, the idea takes root in my mind.

It's Arthur's suggestion that made me look at her in a new light. And now that the opportunity has presented itself, I can't help but consider that it's perfect timing. *I could marry her.*

The better I've gotten to know her, the more I realize how compatible we are. She's the best match for me.

It's also going to help salvage her dignity, so it'd work for both of us.

Now, I only have to convince her.

She looks around the room, but I know she's not really seeing it. "I'm not sure I follow."

"What if everything I said earlier was real. What if I really was in love with you?"

"Eh?" She stares at me.

"I'm *not* in love with you, of course."

"Okay." She nods slowly.

"But *what if I were*, and what if I asked you to marry me?"

She freezes.

So do I.

The words hang there, shocking with how right they feel. I said I was in love with her to mess with her ex. I wanted to show him what he's missing out on. I wanted him to be sorry for putting her through that ordeal. And now that he's walked, and she's no longer engaged, there's no reason for me not to act on this insane attraction I feel toward her.

I don't love her, of course. I'm not stupid enough to get my emotions involved in this situation. But she's mine to help. Mine to protect. And if I can help ease this situation for her, then why not?

"I—" She coughs. "I thought I heard you ask me to marry you?"

I jerk my chin. "I did."

She stares at me for a second longer, then begins to laugh. There's a touch of hysteria to her laughter which tells me I might have sprung this on her a little too quickly. She's had a huge emotional shock. She needs to digest it.

She needs to understand the ramifications of what I'm proposing. For someone who's known for being strategic, I sure didn't think through how to broach this in a way that would inspire confidence in her. And make her say yes.

When she finally subsides. I walk over to her desk, pick up the bottle of water there and hold it out. "Drink it."

She eyes me with curiosity but does as I ask. Then she places the bottle back on her desk before she rounds it and sinks into her chair. "I'm not sure I can make sense of what you're saying."

"It's simple." I follow her around her desk and lean a hip against it. "Arthur thought you'd make the perfect bride for me. And if I marry you, I'll get access to my inheritance with his blessings. And you"—I cross my arms across my chest—"can go ahead with the wedding as planned. No need to cancel the Town Hall appointment. No need to send out a wedding-is-off email to your friends and family. No need to even cancel the reception at the pub, though frankly, I think we could do better than that—"

"Stop, right there—" She holds up a hand. "You're saying—" She stares at me with intent. "You're saying we should get married." She gestures to the space between us.

"Yes. That's exactly what I'm saying."

She opens and shuts her mouth, then gulps a few breaths. "I think you're crazy."

"I'm not. Think about it. Arthur seems to think we'd make a good couple. Which means, he'd bless this marriage right away. And you get to save face and get your plans back on track."

"I… I…" She seems at a loss for words. "This is completely crazy." She squeezes the bridge of her nose. "I don't think—"

I have a feeling she's going to say no, so I jump in with, "I'm not asking you for an answer right now. Why don't you think about it?"

18

Lark

I glance out the window of my apartment. It's dark and drizzling outside. The weather mirrors my morose mood.

Since that debacle yesterday, I've barely slept.

Last night I tossed and turned, unable to close my eyes for more than a few minutes at a time. When I could, I was besieged by images of Brody comforting me and telling me I was smart and beautiful.

At work today, Brody was all business. We sat through meetings together, but he was completely professional. No glance or gesture from him hinted that he'd sprung that insane proposal on me.

Worse, he looked even more devastating than usual. In that form-fitting suit, and with that sharp, focused gaze, he was every inch the billionaire CEO. Meanwhile, I felt like a wilted piece of lettuce.

I stayed late at the office, and by the time I packed up, even Brody had left. When I got back to my flat, I showered, too tired to even pour myself a glass of wine or think about food, and crawled into bed.

After an hour of tossing and turning, I gave up. I can't put it off any longer. People need to know the wedding's off.

I'm not getting married in a week.

Except...I could.

*If...*I agreed to my boss's proposal. Nah, that's not happening.

His suggestion took me completely by surprise. No way, can I swap out my cheating ex as the bridegroom with my smokin' hot, sex-on-a-stick boss, right?

He's insane for suggesting it. I'm delusional for even entertaining it. It makes no sense. None. Zero.

But...what if I did? I swallow.

What if I said yes, married my boss, and somehow, pulled off the most ridiculous plot twist of my life? Then what?

Could I live happily ever after, with a man I barely know? Then again, I thought I knew my ex. Turns out, I was dead wrong.

As for Brody...I can't deny I'm attracted to him. Violently, embarrassingly so. Way more than I ever was to my douche of a fiancé. But marrying him instead of my ex? That's soap-opera-level far-fetched.

Nope. It's not happening. I have to face reality. The wedding's off. I need to start damage control. I must email my friends, tell my parents, cancel everything. Ugh. The thought of it feels like trying to untangle a mess of tinsel. Painful. Frustrating.

But the sooner I start, the sooner I can pretend my life isn't a glittery disaster zone.

Fine. Fine.

I pick up my phone, pull up my mother's number on the screen, poise my finger over the call button... But I can't bring myself to press dial. Damn.

My mother will be so disappointed. They think I'm doing so well in life. That all their hard work in bringing me up is paying off. They're looking forward to visiting London too.

It's not even midnight yet, so I decide to call Raya instead.

"Hey, Sis." Her face appears on the screen.

In the background, I hear the beat of techno music and see the flash of strobe lights.

"Are you at a club?"

"What?" she yells back. "I can't hear you."

I raise my voice. "Where are you?"

"Hold on." There's a muffled conversation as she talks to someone, some giggling, then the image goes wonky, as she walks through the club.

The sound of music fades. When she holds up the phone again, the light is dimmer. She must have stepped out.

"Sorry the music inside the club was too loud." She sounds breathless. "Why did you call? Is everything okay?"

"Of course, why wouldn't it be?" The lie comes out so easily, I don't have to think about it twice.

I have to tell her the wedding is off.

I steel myself, open my mouth, but no words come out. Damn, why is this so difficult? Tell her already. The words remain stuck in my throat like it's coated with glue.

"How are the wedding preparations? Hopefully, Keith finally called you back and you've sorted the last-minute details?"

Yep. All sorted. I was jilted by my cheating loser ex. Ugh. That should be the name of a rom-com. Only, it's too pathetic for it to ever be the title of one.

Why is this so difficult?

I open my mouth again, but what comes out is: "Uh, yes, I did connect with him. And everything worked out."

Not really. But it might. If I could make up my mind.

"O-k-a-y." She searches my features. "So why do you seem so stressed?"

She's too perceptive. Maybe it wasn't a good idea to call her.

I paste on a smile. "Uh, you know, it's coming up to the wedding. And I'm realizing it's going to be such a big life change. And our parents are flying down. I love that, of course, but —"

"Mom can be a handful. I know. But don't worry. I'll be there to manage them and take the heat off you."

I feel terrible for not being able to tell Raya the truth. And when she's being so sweet.

"You're an amazing sister," I say softly.

"Of course. I need to make up for all the times I was an annoying brat and made your life hell, right?" She sticks her tongue out at me.

I roll my eyes. "Why do you constantly act like you're five when we speak?"

"Because you constantly sound so grown-up. Someone has to lighten the tone, otherwise I worry it'll catch, and I'll be forced to grow up before my time."

I chuckle. "Brat."

She grins. "So, you're good, right?" She peers into the screen.

I can hear the concern in her voice.

"Of course. I'm good." I flash her a more genuine smile. "Are you coming for the bridesmaid's dress fittings later this week? Harper will be there too."

"Wouldn't miss it for the world."

Someone calls her off screen.

"Gotta go, Sis." She disconnects the call.

I lower my phone. That was difficult. And I didn't even tell her the real reason why I called.

And no way, can I dial my mom's phone number to give her the news.

As for Harper, well... She's my BFF, but I'm not ready to be emotionally vulnerable with her either.

Or maybe, I'm too proud to admit I'm flailing?

Why is it so much easier to resolve someone else's mess than face my own?

If I continue to portray the illusion that I have my life together, then I won't have to face the fact that it's currently held together by caffeine, spreadsheets, and sheer denial.

I've built an entire persona around looking like I know what I'm doing, that I know where I'm going, and that I have everything under control. Can't drop the act now, can I?

Thank God for the extreme busyness of my job. At least, I'm in control there. Unlike in my personal life.

'Course, I could email everyone.

The thought of it makes my skin shrivel. And my stomach lurch. And bile coats my tongue.

I stare at my phone like it's going to turn into a monster and swallow me up. Oh God. This is horrible.

I toss the device aside, and switch on the TV. I click through different viewing options; nothing holds my attention.

I switch it off and stare at the blank screen.

It's official. I'm not getting married within the week. And I don't have the guts to break the news to anyone.

Every day I don't call off the wedding, it's going to get harder to do so. And I'll be giving less notice that it's off.

So, what are you going to do?

M-a-y-b-e... I could consider Brody's proposal?

The thought makes my stomach twist. I freeze, my heart pounding so hard it drowns out reason. Am I seriously entertaining this? Have I completely lost it? But then again, can I really afford not to? I'm out of options. Completely cornered.

It sounds absurd, but the date is set. The invitations have gone out. Everyone's expecting a wedding. *My wedding.* And if I don't go through with it, I don't even know who I am anymore.

So much of my pride and sense of control is tied to walking down that aisle, it makes me dizzy to think it might not happen.

It feels vital to my happiness, my identity, my very life, that I get married on the date and time everyone's expecting.

What if I go to the wedding and act surprised when Keith doesn't show up?

No! That's worse. The thought of standing there, all eyes on me, whispers spreading through the crowd, is unbearable. I need a bridegroom. *Any* bridegroom would be better than no bridegroom.

And how do I explain that I'm not marrying that loser ex of mine, but my hot, brooding, growly, alpha male of a boss instead?

I'll think something up. It'll be easier explaining that to my friends and family than breaking the news that there's no wedding. Right?

And love? I swallow around the ball of emotion in my throat. What about love? How do I reconcile my wanting to be in love and have the perfect marriage versus this arrangement I'm contemplating with my boss?

And when I agreed to marry Keith. Was that love? Well, I thought I was in love. But I'm not exactly heartbroken that I'm not marrying him.

I'm kinda relieved, if I'm being honest. Aside from the fact that I'll be at the receiving end of people's pitying glances, and the knowledge that my life plan will be knocked askew if the marriage doesn't go ahead.

Maybe, I could get my life plan back on track first, and then think about love?

Without giving myself time to think, I message Brody.

Me: Can we talk?

He replies, almost instantly.

Bossman: Tomorrow, 6 p.m.

19

Brody

"I've given some thought to what you said and—" She swallows. "I want to know how it would work."

"You want to know how our marriage would work?" I lean back in my chair.

All day, she's been a model of efficiency. She's taken on most of my day-to-day work. And led on two important sales calls with offices in the US and Asia. A couple of times, I glanced up to see her frowning at me. She averted her gaze and went back to her work.

At precisely six p.m., she walked in and perched herself in the seat opposite me at the desk.

Finally, fuck.

I didn't get much sleep last night. I haven't been able to get thoughts of my executive assistant out of my head.

My executive assistant who is now single.

When she texted me and said she wanted to see me, I had to stop myself from pumping my fist in victory. She's coming around to my suggestion. I can feel it.

I wanted to ask her to meet me first thing in the morning, but that would've shown how eager I was.

Instead, I asked her to meet me at six p.m.

And I paid the price for it. On the surface, I was industrious...or tried to be. Given I'd delegated a lot of my everyday stuff to her, I was left with a lot of time to build up scenarios in my head. Scenarios in which she'd become my wife, and I'd spend all my nights buried in her pussy.

Enough for me to have to retreat to the en suite bathroom and rub one out. I managed to compose myself after.

But now that she's here, I need to play it casual. I can't act like I can't wait to put my ring on her finger and marry her... And... *Christ*. I'm only doing it to fulfill Arthur's condition that I get married before I inherit. And, to make him happy by marrying the woman he chose for me.

She grips her digital pad so hard that the skin across her knuckles turns white. "Yes. I want to know how this...*arrangement* would pan out."

I knit my eyebrows. It's interesting that she doesn't want to use the word marriage. She's not yet comfortable with the idea. But that's where I come in.

I've exchanged fire with enemy troops across borders, and with business rivals across boardroom tables, but I am keenly aware that what I have riding on the discussion today with her is far more personal.

There's much more at stake here. My future, for one.

It so happens that my EA is the smartest, most fascinating, most beautiful woman I've ever met.

Being married to her wouldn't be a burden; it would be dangerously easy. We click in ways I don't want to examine too closely.

Arthur choosing her only confirms what part of me already knows. We fit. And apparently, my grandfather had an inkling of that.

He'll be satisfied, and even if there are no feelings involved—no real entanglements—I'm certain Lark and I could build something solid. Something that lasts.

I could do worse than marry her, but I don't think I can do better. As long as she doesn't get too hung up on the whole issue of love, I think we'll make a great partnership.

I reach for the strip of rope on my desk and begin to unknot it. It's more to buy myself time while I formulate my response, but her gaze is fixed on my fingers. She watches, fascinated, as I deftly unknot the strip of silken rope, then smoothen it out, before I tie the first knot.

I show it to her. "It's a figure eight knot. Common in climbing and sailing."

"It looks clean and simple."

"And the symmetry is satisfying. It symbolizes control."

I tie another knot, then another.

Her forehead creases. "Why do you do that?" she asks abruptly. "I assume, it helps you focus?"

She's stalling. But that's okay. I'm the one who opened this particular line of conversation. And it's good for her to get to know me better, since we're going to get married. Something I will make her agree to by the end of this discussion.

I tie another knot. "It's a stress reliever. Helps me keep in touch with my past."

"Past?" She raises her gaze to mine.

"I was in the Royal Marines. In fact, all my brothers except, except Connor, served in the forces."

"How did I miss that?" She looks taken aback.

I shrug. "It's not a secret. Arthur makes it a point to bring it up whenever he gets the chance. It's something he's proud of. As am I. But it wasn't the easiest part of my life either."

Her shoulders relax a little. The conversation is doing its job. It's bringing down her barriers. Putting her at ease. Helping her become more receptive to what's coming next.

"That explains the watch." She nods toward my wrist.

I glance at the sturdy watch with the titanium casing and weathered faceplate. "It belonged to Gramps. He gave it to me when I was headed to the Marines. It saved my life."

She stares closely at it. "How?"

"You really want to know?"

"Of course." She sends me a reproachful look.

"I was on a night op with my team when we got hit by an IED. Something sharp sliced across my ribs. It would've gone straight through my heart if I hadn't been carrying this same watch in my chest pocket."

I touch the space over my heart to demonstrate.

"I took off the watch because my wrist was hurt. I owe my life to the watch. I got it repaired and wear it all the time."

"Wow." Her face pales. "That's scary." Her voice is dazed. Distress filters into her eyes. "You almost died."

"Except, I didn't." I half smile. "Others on my team weren't so lucky."

I remember the feelings of relief and euphoria, followed by sinking disappointment when I found out I'd lost friends.

"I'm so sorry." Her voice is soft. Soothing. It calms some of the guilt I've carried inside. Typical survivor's remorse. I'm aware of it. Doesn't stop me from treading there.

"Do you regret joining the Marines?" she asks softly.

I hesitate. It's not something I've mentioned to anyone else before. But it feels right to share it with her. "Yes. And no."

"How so?"

I complete the final knot on the rope. "It's not that I wasn't physically up to the job."

"Clearly." She nods in my direction.

I dip my head in acknowledgement.

"I joined because I wanted to make a difference. But I wasn't great at taking orders. I hated acting without seeing the bigger picture. And the loss of life... It got to me. I had to keep reminding myself I was protecting my country."

"Is that where you picked up your love for tying knots?" She nods at the length of rope now tied up in knots.

I run my knuckles down the silken surface, and she shivers.

I survey her from below my eyelashes. Rub my thumb over the knotted surface. This time, she visibly shudders. Then folds her arms across her chest, but it doesn't stop me from noticing that her nipples are peaked and outlined against the silk of her blouse.

She's so responsive. My cock twitches. Would she let me tie her up before I fuck her?

Images of her sweet body bound in rope fill my head. I'd wind it around her curves to frame her breasts. Then slip it between her legs to lift the soft flesh there.

Blood drains to my groin.

It's all I can do to not lean over, pull her to her feet, press her into the desk, and take her from behind. Goddamn. I need to slow down. This is not how I'm going to convince her to marry me, then allow me to fuck her.

I clear my throat, release my hold on the rope and lean back. "Tying knots is a core skill across the Royal Marines. I had a particular aptitude for it. It's why I became an assault specialist."

Seeing the confusion on her face, I clarify.

"That's someone trained in construction and explosives. I'm the one who set off controlled explosives to breach obstacles, and who builds defensive positions like trenches, or rope bridges."

"You help the teams survive in the field."

"Exactly." I nod, pleased she caught on so quickly.

"So why did you leave?"

"The usual. The first two missions I was on went without a hitch. On the third"—I push aside the emotions which squeeze my chest —"we were ambushed. We were very lucky to be able to retreat with minimum casualties. All of us got out."

"But you didn't go back."

"Almost having lost my life put things in perspective. I wasn't afraid of dying. But there was more I wanted to accomplish before I did. I knew I could make a bigger difference from the outside."

She leans forward. "How did you do that?"

"I took the discipline and the training from the Marines and poured it into work."

Realization dawns in her eyes. "You certainly have a veteran's thoroughness in how you approach your job."

I tilt my head in acknowledgement. "I prioritize giving jobs to those who'd have otherwise been discarded when they came home."

Realization dawns in her eyes. "Your employees—"

I nod. "I draw from troops and those with military experience, as well as veterans who're floundering. I pay for their retraining so their skills can be transferred to the corporate world. I also work closely with my uncle, who's a former Marine, to expand into corporate security and risk management. We provide extraction and evacuation in unstable parts of the world. And employ those with relevant experiences from the armed forces."

"The companies that you want to fund—"

"—are startups who're researching technology that could provide better intel for our troops."

"Wow." Her eyes grow wide. She thinks over what I said. I know the exact moment she pieces everything together, for she leans forward. "Wait, does this mean that the money you get from your inheritance—"

"I plan on using the bulk of it to set up Davenport Foundation."

"That sounds like a non-profit organization."

"It is." I nod. "The focus will be to retrain vets when they leave the military so they can find jobs in civilian life. I also want to provide them with mental health services to help them adjust to daily life."

"Wait, that's why you want to inherit? So, you can help military vets?" Her features wear an expression of surprise.

"I have more than enough for my needs. If I can make a difference to others, it'll satisfy me more."

She scans my features and must realize how sincere I am about this, for she nods.

"Just when I think you're coldhearted, you say something like this and make me reevaluate my opinion of you."

"Oh?"

She taps her fingers on the arm of her chair. "Your actions are selfless in a way that surprises me."

"Oh, it isn't all selfless. I'll make sure the money also earns me profits."

"But you'll also create employment opportunities and try to make missions safer for future Marines. And you want to use your inheritance to train veterans so they can find jobs and fit back into civilian life."

"Glad your opinion of me is improving." I allow myself a smirk.

She reddens. "Not completely. I find you arrogant, high-handed, and bossy."

"Bossy?" I lean in, lowering my voice. "That's the best you've got?"

Her chin tips up. "I'll keep adding to the list."

"Go on." I let the smirk deepen. "I'd like to hear it. Especially if it means you're thinking about me when you should be working."

Her lips part. Then snap shut. Color flushes her cheeks.

Yes! I have her. She understands my motivations in accessing my inheritance and she's appreciative of it. That's a huge step forward.

"Of course, to gain my inheritance, I need to marry." I narrow my gaze on her. "I was serious when I said you should become my wife."

Her breath stutters. But she doesn't protest. Which tells me, I've come a long way since she almost turned me down outright when I last suggested this.

"And you need a husband, so you can go through with your wedding and avoid embarrassing yourself in front of your family and your friends."

She purses her lips.

"Surely, you've arrived at the same conclusion. Isn't that why you texted and asked to meet me?"

She looks away. Her chest rises and falls. She seems to be gathering her thoughts, and when she finally turns back to me, her face is composed. "You're right. Having thought over your proposition, I must admit, there are certain advantages I see in going ahead with it."

Finally, fuck. If she'd told me she wasn't interested in this arrangement, then I'd have found another way to get her to marry me. You'd better believe it.

Victory tastes sharp and sweet, before I rein in my emotions. No complications, remember? Get married. Get access to my trust fund. Move on with my life.

I compose myself. "But?" I tilt my head.

She blinks.

"I sense a but coming on." I rest my elbows on the arms of my chair, then touch my fingers together.

"But I have some questions."

I force myself to relax my shoulders. Almost there. All you need to do is answer her satisfactorily, and then this gorgeous woman will be your wife. Of course, I'll never let myself fall for her. That's the one emotion I will not let myself indulge in. But in every other way, she will be mine.

"Go on." I jerk my chin. "What do you want to ask?"

20

Lark

"Is this going to be a real marriage?"

He regards me steadily. "It's not going to be a pretend marriage."

Right. Maybe some part of me had held onto the hope that us marrying each other would be in name only?

On the other hand, I've been fantasizing about him, and now, I don't have to feel guilty about it.

He leans forward in his seat. "Don't look so terrified. Marrying me can't be such a horrible prospect?"

Heat flushes my cheeks. "Of course not. But it's all very confusing."

"It needn't be. I'm suggesting we marry each other, and that our marriage is for real."

O-k-a-y. "So, it'll be a real marriage. Between—" I point between us.

He nods. "I'd be your husband. You'd be my wife. And while we may not have started out in the traditional sense of the word, we've gotten to know each other. And this way, we'd get to know one another better."

He raises one eyebrow, and my skin prickles.

"After we get married." For some reason, it seems important to emphasize that.

He nods. "Who knows, you might even begin to like me." He half smiles, but his expression is serious.

I worry that I like him already.

He's demonstrated there are layers to him. He's not the hard-nosed, CEO he likes to portray himself as.

He staked his life for his country. He carries the weight of the teammates he lost on mission. And he wears the watch his grandfather gifted him. The same watch which saved his life. It reveals loyalty, and a depth of sentimentality, even romanticism, I would have not expected from him.

He's pushed me to grow and encouraged me to take on more in my role. He's indicated that he sees me as his successor. *It's very rare that someone does that.*

Oh, and also, he wants to use his inheritance to do good. *And* he's ridiculously attractive.

The man's a freakin' unicorn.

Not to mention, he came to my rescue when my ex dumped me. He helped me salvage my dignity.

So no, it won't be a problem liking him. If anything, I'm sure the more I get to know him, the more I'm going to fall for him.

"And would we share the same bed?" I manage to keep my tone even, but my body betrays me. My nerves coil. I squeeze my thighs together.

The thought of lying beside him, feeling his warmth, his breath, his scent. Of us making love. Of him fucking me? Oh my God. It's the most erotic thought ever.

"You'll be my wife. You'll share of everything I have. Including my bed."

My insides melt. My brain cells might have dissolved. When Brody Davenport growls 'my wife,' it's the height of possessiveness.

It makes my pussy throb, tightens my nipples, and ignites the blood that runs through me veins.

I shove aside the X-rated images in my head and manage to bring my attention back to the present.

"What about love?" I throw that out because, surely, he can't have a glib answer to that? "You said you don't believe in love, and that you'd rather keep your life clear of such entanglements."

The light in his eyes dims. "I did and I stand by it."

"Oh." I lower my chin. My stomach bottoms out, and I feel a strange disappointment in my chest. It's what I expected him to say. And it's not like I'm marrying him for love either.

So why did I hope that he'd say that he wants to marry me because he wants me?

"But—" He narrows his gaze on me. "We can have a good marriage. I'll take care of you. I'll make sure you never lack for anything. I'll put your happiness and that of any children we have before anything else. Surely, that should count for something."

"Children?" I squeak.

I've thought of having children, but at some point in the distant future. I didn't think I'd be discussing it with my boss...who proposed that I marry him.

"I understand you'll need to think about that, and that's okay. I'm not in any hurry there. And if you decide you don't want them, I'll understand."

"Hold on, you're going too fast for me." I rub my temple.

"Your wedding date is less than two weeks away, so we don't have much time left."

"Don't remind me." I hunch my shoulders.

"I'm sorry, I didn't mean to upset you."

I peek up at his face and find his expression is one of genuine contrition.

"But we do need to get the planning for the wedding underway, if we want to make this happen."

My head spins. I've been planning my wedding on my own. And now my boss, who I might be marrying, is offering to plan it with me?

"But... What if we're not compatible?"

He stares, apparently not comprehending what I'm saying.

"In bed. What if we're not good together?"

He chuckles, then bursts out laughing. It's a full-bodied, deep laugh that rolls up his belly. It lightens his features and makes his eyes sparkle, and he looks so fucking handsome. My heart trembles. My thighs quiver. My whole body feels like it's been caught in a tidal wave of some kind of attraction, which threatens to topple me over. It's so unfair that everything this man does, I find attractive.

"It's a real concern."

"Okay." He straightens his face. "But I don't think we have anything to worry about there."

"Why is that?"

"Because —" An intense look comes into his eyes. "The chemistry between us is off the charts, and I'm so fucking aware of you all the time we're together. And when we're not together, I can't stop thinking of you. The only thing stopping me from leaning over this desk and kissing the hell out of you is that it might frighten you off."

"It won't." I gasp. Oh, no! I said that out aloud And now, I can't take it back. And I'm not going to blush that I said that. I won't.

"It. Won't?" He seems to digest that for a second.

The next, he reaches for his phone. His fingers fly across the screen. He must pull up an app, for the walls turn opaque. All four walls of his office. So, no one can see inside.

"Neat trick." I manage to keep my voice casual.

"You ain't seen anything yet." He rises to his feet, rounds his desk and holds out his hand.

Automatically, and probably because my brain is too over-whelmed, I place my palm in his. His skin is rough with calluses on the fingers that drag at mine. Little pinpricks of pleasure whisper over my nerve endings. He pulls me up to my feet.

He's going to kiss me.

He's going to kiss me.

He *is* kissing me.

My hot boss is kissing me.

He has his arm around my waist and is holding me close to

his big, broad, manly chest. The chest I've peeked glances at because I'd have to be blind not to notice how he fills out his jacket. How his sculpted torso is outlined against that white shirt, the bricked layers of his pecs threatening to pop the buttons.

The powerful thighs which I brush up against, which leave me with a sense of coiled muscles and unleashed energy, like the turbocharged vibrations which swell from a rocket about to blast off into space. Then the sensation of his lips on mine takes over.

Softness.

How could his mouth be this soft when the rest of him is like leaning into a brick wall? He holds me with such care. Like I'm the most precious thing in this world. Like I'm a jewel, and he's the velvet casing which encloses me.

The protectiveness in his stance as he cradles my head with a big hand at the back of my head, the other grasping my waist like we're one of those entwined figures in a music box... And the song playing in my head is, surely, brought on by how tenderly his mouth brushes over mine.

Once.

Twice. Then his grasp on my head slides to the back of my neck. A shiver squeezes my spine. The possessiveness is unmistakable. As is how he squeezes the curve of my hip. He pulls me into the cradle of his thighs.

My knees grow weak. I sway forward, and he tightens his hold on the nape of my neck. A full body shudder rolls over me. My stomach seems to bottom out.

It's as if I've boarded a roller coaster and am being pulled up that first incline, knowing what's coming up, knowing it's going to swoop down, and being unable to stop that rush of adrenaline and excitement which fills me.

He flattens his fingers so I can feel each individual fingerprint like a brand through the fabric of my dress. Then he bites down on my lower lip. I feel it all the way to my toes.

I gasp, and he licks into my mouth, the touch of his tongue against mine an explosion of emotions. Taste. Dark and complex.

Sensations like sparks left in the wake of a shooting star. A sweetness which is so unexpected, it's mind-blowing.

I rise up on my tiptoes. When I part my lips, he slants his face, slashes his lips over mine, and then the kiss is everything I thought it would be from the meeting of our lips. Hard, insistent, demanding, and so very hot.

The kiss seems to go on and on, and at the same time, it's so short because suddenly...I'm free.

I sway and am aware that he's stepped back. The cool fluidity of the air, instead of the solidness of his body, is a shock. My world has tilted, my points of reference changed. My expectations from a kiss dramatically elevated. I know I'll never be satisfied by meeting my lips with anyone else's.

My heart feels like it's in free fall, my emotions swooping over mountains and dipping down into the valley between them like an eagle riding the air currents. I stare at him, lips imprinted with the shape of his.

Heat sears my cheeks.

I try to move back, but his hold on my neck tightens...for a second. Then he releases me, stuffs his hands into his pockets and stares into my face.

"You, okay?"

I shake my head.

I have never been kissed like that. Certainly not by my ex. In fact, I've never had such a powerful reaction like this with anyone else.

I thought I wasn't a passionate person. That's what Keith told me. I thought I was someone who didn't like kissing and being held and being intimate with a man.

But fuck Keith.

Clearly, it took the right man to press the right buttons and make me feel like I was going to combust when he touched me.

"Why don't you sit down?"

He places a hand at the small of my back, the touch like a thousand little fireflies fluttering against my skin. He presses gently, and I move forward. He pulls out my chair, turns it, then urges me to take a seat.

Then, he picks up the glass of water on the desk and hands it to me. "Drink it."

I do.

I don't stop until it's empty. Then hand it back to him.

"What was that?" I whisper.

"That was us, kissing." His blue-gray eyes have turned almost indigo. My lips throb in response to his words.

"Wow," I whisper.

"Yeah." He turns the chair next to mine and sits down facing me.

"Now that I've established, we're more than compatible when it comes to sex, what other questions do you have?"

I open my mouth, but my mind is blank. That kiss overwhelmed me. Also, if I'm being honest, I don't have any other questions. I'm so filled with happy hormones, I can't remember what I was so anxious about.

"You think we can pull this off?"

"Absolutely."

He seems so confident.

It makes me want to believe him. "And when my friends and my parents find out you're not the man I originally intended to marry? What then?"

He raises a shoulder. "You can't live your life by what the world thinks of you. You need to stay focused on yourself. And what you want."

I nod slowly. It's reassuring, hearing his words. And somehow, it calms the churning in my stomach. It gives me the confidence to accept what he's suggesting.

When I stay quiet, he nods as if I answered an unspoken query from him. "So, what do you say, about my proposal?"

I pretend to think. And because I sense I'll never have this opportunity again, and because I want to somehow put my mark on this occasion, I tip up my chin.

"Where's the ring?"

Maybe, I'm testing him. Or perhaps, I'm compelled to ask because he ridiculed the fact that my ex-fiancé never bought me one. Or maybe, this time… I'm not compromising on what I want from this marriage.

"A ring." His eyes flash. "Are you saying yes?"

I chew on my lower lip. His gaze, instantly, is caught by my mouth and stays there. His chest rises and falls. When he swallows, I know he's turned on.

From the way he kissed me, I know he finds me attractive. But to see this visible reaction to my unconscious action is the confidence boost I needed. I jerk my chin.

Something like relief filters into his features. "I need you to say that aloud, Siren."

Sweet baby Jesus in a manger. That nickname makes me feel all fuzzy and also overheated at the same time. I shove it aside and nod again.

"Yes." I sniff. "Also, the ring needs to be vintage Art Deco with an emerald in a rose gold setting."

So, I might have a secret Pinterest board where I have images of the kind of ring I want. And this might be on the top of the list.

"Okay." He rises to his feet.

I tip my head back as he towers over me.

"Come on." He holds out his hand.

This time I stare at it suspiciously. "Where?"

"You want a ring, don't you?"

21

Brody

"This is too much." She squirms around in her chair.

"Nothing's too much for my wife-to-be." I put an arm around her shoulders.

She darts a look at the man behind the counter of the most prestigious jeweler in the city. The Davenports invested in this business when they first started out a hundred years ago. It took only one call for the current CEO to arrange for a private viewing at their St. James' showroom.

Of course, it's because we have company that I'm coming across as all possessive. Never too early to start the pretense.

Which is why I agreed to the ring right away.

It has nothing to do with wanting to be sure she doesn't confuse our arrangement with the engagement she had with that turd ex-fiancé of hers.

"And now, for the pièce de résistance." The salesperson behind the counter pulls out a key and, with great ceremony, unlocks a cabinet under the glass case. He pulls out a black velvet tray and places it on the countertop.

Nestled among the folds of velvet is a vintage Art Deco ring in rose gold. In the center sits a breathtaking emerald.

It's rich, vivid, and so dark, it borders on dangerous. The stone catches the light like a secret being revealed. It *glows*. Bold. Uncompromising. Impossible to ignore.

It's framed by slender diamond baguettes that only make the green blaze brighter, like a forest on fire at dusk. Like the sparks in her eyes.

The band is understated, but impossibly elegant, with filigree so fine it looks like spun lace. It's not flashy. It doesn't scream. It commands.

Lark freezes. Her lips part, her gaze riveted by the ring.

And I'm riveted by her. I can't breathe. Can't say a word. I am captured by the hushed surprise, delight, and awe in her eyes.

This isn't a ring. This is a reckoning. Something powerful. Unexpected. Unapologetically her.

She reaches out, fingers trembling slightly. "That's..."

"Yours." I pick up the ring and hold out my other hand.

She stares at the ring, and when she slowly places her palm in mine, her fingers tremble. I slip the ring onto her left ring finger.

"Perfect!" The salesperson claps his hands.

"She is." I'm barely aware I've said the words aloud.

Lark jerks her chin up. Whatever she sees on my face makes her flush. She pulls her hand from mine.

"I can't accept this." She tries to take off the ring which, thankfully, refuses to slip off.

I place my hand over both of hers. "It's yours."

"But... But... It's so expensive."

"It's what you deserve."

She opens her mouth to protest again, but I cut in. "We need to do this right to convince my grandfather, my family, and yours. You're engaged to a Davenport. You're expected to have a ring that reflects the union."

"Right." She subsides a little.

"Besides, it looks perfect on you." I take in the ring on her finger, and the possessiveness I felt earlier multiplies. Woven in with it is satisfaction. That I can proclaim to the world she's mine. *All unfamiliar.* Which also feels, weirdly, right. Was it always about the woman? Is it the fact that it's her I'm marrying that makes it different?

She blushes harder. "Thanks." She lowers her head, so her hair falls over her face. I let her hide her expression from me, for now.

I nod at the salesperson, who seems delighted. No doubt, it's the biggest sale he's made this year. "Congratulations, Mr. Davenport and Ms. Monroe. I hope you will be very happy."

She rises to her feet. "Thank you for your kind wishes." She slips out from behind the chair.

I take her arm and lead her out.

The bill will be debited to my account directly. Nothing so crass as paying with my credit card here.

When we reach the door, I hold it open. Then I wave off the valet and pull open the passenger door to my car. Shutting it after her, I round the front and slip into the driver's seat.

I ease the car onto the road. We drive in silence for a while. When I take the turn off from the main road, she frowns. "You know the way to my home?"

"You did fill out your address on the HR forms."

"And you remember what it is?"

I keep my tone casual. "I have a good memory."

And I made sure to read her HR form thoroughly, greedy for any detail it afforded about her.

Silence falls between us. I glance sideways to find a thoughtful expression on her features.

We pull up in front of the building which houses her flat. I'm out of the car and opening her door before she can.

"I can see myself inside." She slides out, then walks past me and up the path leading to the front door of the apartment block. It's a quiet neighborhood. Firmly middle class. She keys in the code that lets her in the main door. And has security.

Which I approve of.

She turns, holding the door open with her hip. "I really can take it from here."

I read the determination on her features and decide not to push it. I take in her lips and want so badly to kiss her.

But if I do, I won't be able to leave her. And I need to give her a little time to come to terms with all the changes in her life.

I bend my head, kiss her on her cheek instead, then step back. "See you tomorrow at work?"

22

Brody

Tiny trots beside me as I walk up the path to Arthur's door. His tail sways like a metronome, completely unfazed. Meanwhile, there's a knot in my chest that has been sitting there since I asked Lark to marry me.

Otis opens the door before I knock.

Tiny launches himself forward, and the butler smiles. A turning up of the lips which is such a rarity, I blink.

He scratches Tiny's ears while the dog wriggles with his entire massive body, like he's a puppy instead of a grown Great Dane.

"Good boy, we missed you."

Otis grabs his collar. "Mr. Davenport is in the conservatory, Mr. Davenport."

I chuckle. Trust Otis to call every male in this family "Mr. Davenport," and never confuse us. He changes his tone by a fraction, and we all, somehow, know who he's talking about.

Otis leads Tiny in the direction of the kitchen. No doubt, to fuss over him and give him his favorite treats. The mutt's spoiled by all of us. Including me. I'm going to miss him.

I confess, I've gotten used to having company at my place. And having a warm body beside me in bed. Tiny, unfortunately, snores. Also waking up to his doggy breath is not something I'd recommend.

I've learned to shove him with my foot until he changes position and stops snoring.

If I have my way, the next person in my bed will be a beautiful siren who I'm going to keep awake by doing various wicked things to her body. Images of lush curves, creamy skin, soft moans and cries as I take her cunt fill my head. My cock perks up with great interest. Fuck, I can't exactly sport a chub for this conversation with Gramps. I manage to get myself together.

By the time I step into the conservatory, I feel confident I look composed.

It's warm; sunlight pours in through the domed glass ceiling. The heat of the rays is magnified by the glass. Combined with the heating that's on inside, it's sweltering in here.

There are rows of flowering shrubs and towering plants, each one carefully tended. Pots of azaleas, hydrangeas, and fragrant jasmine line the edges, while tall fiddle-leaf figs and palms rise like a miniature indoor forest.

My feet make no noise on the terracotta tiles, yet he looks up from where he's tending to the orchids.

"Aha, if it isn't my non-prodigal grandson." He goes back to watering the plant.

I walk over and watch him with curiosity.

"Didn't know you were into gardening."

"I'm not." He sets down the watering can. "Imelda insists I spend time taking care of the plants as some kind of therapy."

"Right." Arthur and therapy? Not what I'd normally associate together.

"She insists it'll help with my blood pressure, and even out my temper. And help me get less crotchety. Her words, not mine. Figured I might as well indulge the woman. After all, she puts up with me." He touches the petals of the orchid. His features soften. He almost looks like a kind old grandfather there for a second. Almost. Maybe Imelda's onto something?

Then, as if catching himself, he straightens. "Right then, enough of this nonsense." He walks toward one of the two comfortable, faded armchairs facing a marble-topped iron table in the center of the space.

I take my seat opposite him.

He studies me from under his busy eyebrows. "So, you're going through with it?"

I blink. "How did you guess?"

"You think I don't know what my grandsons get up to in this city?"

Likely, he heard about it from the owner of the jewelry store where I purchased the ring. He's a friend of Arthur's, as well as being our family jeweler.

Trust Gramps to be one step ahead. It's no use pretending I don't know what he's talking about. I decide to not bullshit him.

"I'm marrying her."

"Good."

To his credit, he doesn't give me the I-told-you-so bullshit routine.

When he stays silent, I can't help but ask. "You're not going to ask me why?"

"Does it matter?" He raises a shoulder.

"No," I concede.

"You're here to speak to me about something else?" He levels an assessing look at me. The one I grew up under. I used to hate it. Now, I recognize it for what it is. Concern, dressed up as scrutiny. Gramps hates being seen as weak.

As much as I do.

Maybe, he's influenced me more than I realized.

The silence stretches. He doesn't prompt me. For which I'm grateful. I take my time gathering my thoughts.

"Lark's the smartest person in my orbit. She's steady. Reliable. Focused. And a very hard worker. She's proven herself in a very short time. I trust her." My jaw tightens.

"Good," he says, waiting for me to go on.

I let out a slow breath. "We have a good dynamic. We understand each other. We bounce off each other's ideas. She's...wonderful to be around."

I look out the glass walls and over the rolling expanse of Primrose Hill with the London skyline shimmering in the distance.

"But it's more than that. She sees the whole picture. She's strategic yet also detailed. She spots problems before they become fires. She handles people with a gentleness that somehow carries more authority than most men's shouting. She reads a room in seconds. And she's steady. Calm under pressure. And she cares about the employees. She wants them to be happy at their jobs. She seeks efficiency, but not at the cost of employee turnover. She's invested in the future of Davenport Capital. It's like she was built for leadership."

I shift in my seat.

"She doesn't just keep me organized. She tempers me. Sharpens me. Makes me better at what I do."

"Excellent." Arthur's eyes light up. "That certainly makes for a good basis to build a marriage on."

"I want her to be more than my wife."

He stills. His gaze narrows, a calculating expression seeps into his face. I wonder if he knows where I'm going with this. Likely, he does. But he gives no indication.

"I also see her as my successor."

"You want her to take over as CEO?"

I nod. "She's operating at CEO level, and in a stunningly short period of time."

He places the tips of his fingers together. "From what I heard of her performance at the board meeting, she certainly seems capable of leading the team."

I'm not surprised. Edgar and Arthur go way back. He'd have updated Gramps.

"Lark sees people. She understands how the pieces fit together. She listens. And she uses her intuition, along with her talent to make decisions about systems, relationships, and pressure points. She knows how to pull the best out of a room without forcing it. She's the future of this company."

"You don't have to sell me on her abilities. I was the one who spotted how right she was for you. Turns out, it's in more ways than one."

"That may be so. I hired her. I was the one who first took a bet on her."

He chuckles. "And it paid off."

"Absolutely." I nod. "So, you'll understand why I want her stepping up, and soon."

"How soon?"

"As soon as she accepts the role."

"So, you haven't spoken to her yet."

"I wanted your blessings first, of course."

"Bull-fucking-shit." He snorts.

"Excuse me?"

"You'd have made her CEO, even if I decided she wasn't right for the role."

"But you *don't* think that," I say with confidence.

"I think she'll be perfect for the role. She's smart, astute, and courageous. Enough to marry you. And you trust her."

"I do. Implicitly."

"It's time the Davenport Group welcomed its first female CEO," he agrees.

"Wow, I didn't expect it to be that easy." I run my fingers through my hair.

"You knew I approved of her, so I'm sure you didn't expect me to put up too much of a fight."

"That's true." I allow my shoulders to relax for the first time since I entered Arthur's place.

Arthur drums his fingers on the arm of his chair. "The board won't accept a sudden handover. They don't like changes, as you're well aware."

"With your backing, anything is possible." I smile.

"You bet it is. Which is why you brought it to me. You want me to smoothen Lark's path."

"I'm sure, you'd have done it anyway. But I didn't want to leave anything to chance."

"Wise." He searches my features. "And what will you focus on?"

"What gives me the most satisfaction. I want to set up the Davenport Foundation to help with veterans' causes. And startups which fit my vision."

Arthur leans back in his seat. An inscrutable expression in his eyes. "I'm proud of you."

Heat crawls up the back of my neck. Praise from the old man is as rare as a Christmas anthem that doesn't drive me batshit.

"Thanks." I tilt my head.

"There are only two questions left, in my opinion."

"Two?" I frown, not sure what he's getting at.

"When are you going to tell her? And—" He holds my gaze. "Will she go for it?"

23

Lark

Send Christmas cards before they become a New Year's apology.

—From Lark's Christmas to-do list

Is this an alternate reality? That's the only explanation for why my boss and I are meeting with a wedding planner in her plush offices.

I wasn't sure that was needed, but he reminded me this is a Davenport wedding. And Arthur will likely attend the ceremony. As will his brothers and their wives. And his friends.

I've updated Rachel, the wedding planner, on my plans and bookings made so far, and she seemed very appreciative of how much I'd accomplished on my own, and with such a tiny budget. She also reassured me that she'd be respectful of the planning I'd done so far.

She looks up from the device she was tapping on. "You mentioned you chose your wedding dress?"

I purse my lips. I did choose a dress I'd found at the outlet section of a well-known High Street Label. But it's not *the* dress, by any means.

"I took the liberty of arranging for you to have a fitting for your wedding dress at Karma West Sovrano's atelier," Brody interjects.

"Karma West Sovrano's atelier?" I recall our conversation around my wedding dress. He must have made note of the designer's name.

"Her sister Summer is a friend of the family. Through her, I contacted the manager of the atelier. They were happy to fit you in and can have the dress ready in time for the wedding."

"Oh—" I want to say something, but the words stick in my throat. Once again, the contrast between how I struggled through the wedding preparations on my own versus the support I'm getting from Brody screws with my emotions.

When I stay silent, a groove forms between his eyebrows.

"If you'd rather wear the dress you chose—"

I shake my head. "No, that's not it. I mean, the dress I chose is something I can wear for other occasions too. It's just—" I swallow. "That you remembered I wanted to get my dress from this designer."

It's unexpected.

"Told you I have a good memory." His voice is casual, but the intent in his eyes signals his actions are no coincidence.

Which is confusing. Because didn't he tell me he doesn't believe in getting emotionally involved with anyone? And isn't our arrangement one of convenience? Yet, he's acting like there's something more between us. It's confusing.

He must see the disbelief in my eyes, for his features shutter. "If that's not what you want, then of course, it's not a problem."

I hesitate. Am I going to turn down a Karma West Sovrano designer bridal gown for my wedding?

I've picked out the exact wedding dress I want from one of her collections, too.

Surely, I'm not going to let my ego stand in the way of getting the dress of my dreams?

"And the cost?" I venture.

"Nothing's too expensive for my bride."

Rachel sighs.

I flush. There it is. That possessiveness in his tone which makes my blood heat, and my nipples harden, and causes my pussy to melt. Goddamn. When he acts so solicitous, it makes me feel like we're getting married for real. Which is what he said this is. A real wedding. Except, it's not for love.

That sobers me up.

"Thank you," I say stiffly.

His gaze narrows at my tone. "Of course. Your appointment with the atelier is for tomorrow afternoon."

He turns to Rachel. "If you can ensure they have her measurements beforehand?"

I sit up. "I can't make that. I have a meeting with the legal team on the compliance matters, then."

He stares at me steadily. "Your fitting is more important. You can push back the meeting."

"But—"

"That's an order." The softness of his tone takes the sting out of it.

I take in the resolve in his gaze and nod.

"Fine." The ever-efficient Rachel turns to me. "Lark, about the bridesmaids'—"

"That's Raya and Harper." I need to call and update them. Something I've been putting off.

They *are* sharp. They won't stop until they weasel the entire story of how I came to be marrying Brody Davenport from me. It's a grilling I'm not looking forward to. "I told them they could choose their dresses. I didn't want to have too many rules. It felt too cookie-cutter for them to all, I mean, both of them, to wear the same color and style."

"That's smart." Rachel smiles. "It makes for a more relaxed feel when they're not all dressed uniformly. Is that what you were going for?"

Her face holds genuine warmth.

"You could say that." Truth is, I hadn't given thought to what vibe I wanted. I'd been too busy trying to keep everything in the budget I had worked out. Which had come down to spending as little as possible. Going from that to having an almost unlimited budget, *and* a wedding planner to take the load off me, makes my head spin.

As if sensing my discomfort, Tiny whines. I'm so happy Brody brought him along. I scratch him behind his ears. "Aww, you're being such a good boy."

He places his shaggy head on my thigh and sighs.

Yeah, I know how you feel.

Some of my consternation must show on my face, for Brody leans forward in his seat. "Are you uncomfortable with how things are shaping up?"

"No. Of course not. It's just—" I choose my words carefully. "It's more people than I expected…"

"Whether I invite them or not, my family is going to turn up." He chuckles. "But if you want me to tell them to keep away—"

"Not at all. The reason I mention it, is that they won't all fit in the space I booked in the pub for the reception." I purse my lips. "I think we should move the reception."

"You sure?" He searches my features.

"Positive." I shoot him a half smile.

I'm grateful he's trying to make me feel comfortable with the arrangements.

And he's been so involved with the planning. His stern façade at work has given way to something more understanding. If I insisted on having the reception at the pub, I bet he'd find a way to squeeze his family in there after the actual wedding ceremony.

But I don't see the point in that. And it's not like I'm attached to the idea of having our reception at that pub.

"It's only practical that we move the reception to a venue that accommodates everyone. Also, I don't think this entire London tradition of going to the pub after a Town Hall wedding is quite the style of the Davenports." I allow myself a small snicker.

London is split into boroughs, and each has its own Town Hall. It's something else I'm getting used to.

"Are you calling my family snobs?" he drawls.

I widen my gaze, striving for an innocent look. "Nope. But I do want to make sure your family is comfortable."

He frowns, then turns to Rachel. "Can you give us a few minutes?"

"Of course. Call me when you're ready to speak." She walks out of the meeting space and closes the door behind her.

I watch him with curiosity.

"I wanted to make sure you're not doing anything that's out of your comfort zone."

"Okay?"

"This wedding should be exactly how you visualized it. You don't have to cater to anyone else's needs."

I squirm around in my seat. "They are our guests. I want to make sure they feel at ease."

"As long as *you* and *I* are at ease, they will be too."

That's a generous thing to say. Some of the tension fades from my shoulders. "For the record, I only chose the pub because it was close to the Town Hall. Also, it was within my budget."

"You sure?"

"I am."

He searches my features and must be satisfied with what he sees, for he nods. "Arthur suggested we have it as his place in Primrose Hill. He has a beautiful garden with views of London."

I smile. "I think it's a great idea."

His features soften. "Arthur will be pleased. I am the last of his grandsons to get married. He'd love to host us."

He reaches over and takes my hand in his. "Thank you."

Goosebumps snake up my skin. His every touch seems to ignite this fierce desire in me. And this handsome hunk of manliness is going to be my husband. I swoon a little. Then recover long enough to croak, "For what?"

"For suggesting that we move the reception. This entire sequence of events can't have been easy. Yet, you've handled it with a lot of grace."

His voice is soft, but his blue-gray eyes flare with something like heat. His gaze drops to my lips, and I know he's remembering that very hot kiss from yesterday.

And when he leans in. So, do I. Our breaths mingle. Our lips almost touch.

"I want to taste your mouth again, but if we do, we'll be side-tracked, and I want to make sure this wedding is planned exactly how you want."

His chest seems to swell.

With a grimace, he straightens. Disappointed in a way that leaves a hollow feeling at the bottom of my stomach I slowly mirror his movements.

Without breaking the connection between our eyes, he calls out to the wedding planner, "We're ready for you."

24

Brody

The cards whisper against the felt as James deals. He has that usual smug look on his face. The one which indicates he thinks he's in control. Typical chef.

After dropping Lark at her home yesterday I was unable to switch off my mind. I ended up working from my home office. Then decided to work from home today so I could put some distance between us. I need to think through the idea that came to me while talking with Lark yesterday. Timing is everything. Like in poker.

I keep my face blank, eyes on my hand. I can't reveal my cards yet.

James tosses a chip into the pot like he's seasoning a bloody steak. "Call," he says, then fans his cards out with a grin. "Full house."

Toren Whittington, a close friend and CEO of the Whittington Group of companies, groans and throws his hand down. "You've got to be kidding me."

James' grin widens. "Still think I was bluffing?"

"Yeah," Toren mutters. "Right up until you weren't."

Adrian Sovrano, another friend, stacks his remaining chips with precision. "You never learn, Toren. He plays you every time."

I glance at Toren. "He's right. You read James wrong every damn round."

"Don't start, Davenport." Toren cracks his neck. "Not everyone's got ice in their veins."

James nurses his whiskey. "Some of us know how to read a room. Or a table."

I study him for a moment and let him enjoy his win. Let him think he's got it.

Adrian's gaze sharpens, cutting through James's bravado. "Over-confidence gets men gutted."

Perfect cue. I set my hand down slowly, deliberately. Straight flush. The silence that follows is sweet.

James whistles under his breath. "Bastard."

"That's why you don't talk before the hand's finished." I gather the pot toward me. The weight of the chips feels good in my palm.

"Arrogant sod." Toren's lips twitch. He seems to be fighting a smile.

Adrian lifts his glass in my direction. No words. Only respect.

James reaches for the bottle with a groan. "Next round's mine. And if one of you bastards thinks you're walking away tonight with my money, think again."

I let a smile curve my mouth. "You don't make it easy, Hamilton. But I'll keep trying."

The air thrums with competition, with brotherhood. The kind I miss from my stint with the Marines. I'm lucky to have found it here.

"Now that I have your attention..." I glance around the table. "What are you guys doing next week, same time?"

James leans back in his seat. "Attending your wedding?"

The others chuckle.

I raise my glass of whiskey in his direction. "You're right."

"What?" His jaw drops.

The others exchange a look.

Toren, cool customer, merely takes another pull of his whiskey. "You're getting married?"

"To whom?" Adrian scowls.

"Not to your executive assistant?" James takes in the look on my face, and chuckles. "No way. It *is* your EA."

"Next, you'll tell me it's Gramps who chose her," Toren drawls.

I wince.

"He did choose her?" Adrian stares.

I scowl at my cards. "In a matter of speaking."

"Gramps must be over the moon. The last of his grandkids settling down. His life's work is finally realized." James watches me with shrewd eyes.

"He seemed to be strangely philosophical when I told him about it. It's almost as if he was coming to grips with the fact that he doesn't have any more lives to manipulate." I take another sip of my whiskey. "He may have hinted that he has the three of you in his sights."

"I hope not." Adrian shudders. "I'm happy with my life as is."

"Besides, he doesn't have any control over our inheritances." Toren shrugs.

"Unlike you tossers, I'm a self-made man. I have no interest in my parents' inheritance." James drums his fingers on his chair.

"The classic response of the man who has it all." I smirk.

"I didn't start out that way," he reminds me.

James and his siblings are adopted. The Hamiltons made sure to give them the best education and access to contacts within the upper echelons of London society. But there are shadows in James' eyes which can't all be attributed to having seen action.

"You're really doing this?" Toren cuts off the end of his cigar and lights it.

"It would seem that way."

"And are you happy about it?" Adrian places his whiskey glass on the table. "You seem...preoccupied?"

"Not about the wedding. That's a done deal. No, it's about my fiancée." I top up my whiskey glass, then survey the golden liquid. "She's my choice to take over from me as CEO."

Toren and Adrian exchange glances.

"Must make things awkward at work," Adrian offers.

"It might have, except she's so damn good at her job, no one can question her talent. And she's so hardworking that no one can question her commitment."

Toren moves his cigar to the other side of his mouth. "Looks like she made an impression on you and the board."

"More than." I chuckle. "Lark chaired the last board of directors meeting on my behalf. A few weeks in her role, and she's conversant with the numbers, the past performance, future goals, challenges, upcoming initiatives, all of it. You should have seen her go toe-to-toe with the rest of the board. She's badass. And resilient. She has a zest for the business that I haven't had in a while. She also has a natural empathy. It helps her pay attention to employees' welfare." *Something my pride didn't allow room for. She, on the other hand, did not worry about it being mistaken for weakness.*

James gives me a shrewd look. "So, you're finally doing it?"

I nod. "The first two years, when I took over as CEO, I poured my heart and soul into the job. Turned the business around. Hit the revenue goals. Lined up acquisitions to meet growth goals. Along the way, I hired teammates who're former military for as many roles as they were qualified for. But I want to do more."

"You mean, you want to work more closely with veterans?" Adrian blows out a puff of smoke.

I nod. "Lark's taken over a lot of my day-to-day duties in a very short time. Once she's CEO, I can take on more of an advisory role. I can focus on finding startups which fit my vision while continuing to be there for her as a guiding hand. The rest of the time, I would work directly with veterans."

"Very honorable. In fact, you make me feel like a right bastard for not having an outreach goal at my restaurant, you twat," James scoffs.

Toren rolls his shoulders back. "You're going to have to sell Arthur on it."

"I've spoken to him. And he's agreed to back Lark for the CEO position. After all, he's the one who pointed out she'd be the perfect match for me." *In more than one way, as it turns out.*

As if reading my thoughts. James reaches over and slaps my back. "Sounds like it's all falling into place. But I do have one question."

I incline my head.

"Are you going to ask me to be your best man?"

25

Lark

"Wait, you changed the groom?" Raya gasps.

She's seated in one of the velvet chairs lining the lounge outside the fitting room.

We're at Karma West Sovrano's flagship boutique, which is basically holy ground for anyone who worships couture. Her protégé runs the place now, ever since she, well, 'passed.'

Except, there are all these whispers, like mafia-movie-level whispers, that she's actually in a coma somewhere in Sicily, hidden away by her husband, Michael Sovrano, the former Cosa Nostra Capo.

I love her designs so much that a big part of me hopes it's all true.

The space smells faintly of roses and pressed satin. Rachel glides around with a clipboard, conferring with the seamstress.

The wedding is a week away.

I invited my sister and Harper over to choose their bridesmaid dresses from the collection. I'm also going to choose a dress for my mother.

Brody insisted on covering the cost for all of them.

I hope to use the dresses to distract them from the many questions they'll have, now that I've spilled the tea. I told them about what went down with my ex. They know he cheated on me with my bridesmaid. And that I'm marrying Brody.

I step out of the mirrored fitting room in a column of crepe with a plunging neckline. The seamstress tugs the hem into place.

"I'm all for your not marrying Keith, especially after he cheated on you, and then dumped you," Raya says slowly.

"Better he shows his colors now than after the wedding." Harper nods.

"But Brody Davenport? Your boss?" Raya sighs. "You're marrying a man you've known for a few weeks?"

"Two and a half weeks, actually," I say slowly.

I'm marrying a man I've just met. I can only imagine how it looks from the outside.

I'm going to have to sell her and Harper on why Brody is the one for me.

I study my reflection. The dress is elegant, but it's not me. Too severe. I decided to try on a few backups before *the* dress because, let's be honest, once I wear *that one*, nothing else will compare.

And where's the fun in ending the search so soon?

Rachel appears, bright and brisk. "This one isn't you, Lark. Too sharp for your frame. Let's try the off-the-shoulder silk organza."

The next dress is softer, with layered skirts that shimmer as I step out.

Harper sets her cappuccino on the gilt table, eyes scanning me critically. "Not bad. What do you think about it?"

I shake my head. "Not sure it's me." I survey myself in the mirror.

"I've seen, firsthand, how magnetic the Davenport men are." Harper folds one leg over the other. "I've seen friends get swept up in their charm. Their suits should come with fine print warning women to beware."

Her tone is only half joking.

Raya flicks a glance at me in the mirror. "I'm all for falling in love and making spontaneous decisions, but you?" She shakes her head. "I didn't think you'd be the kind to do so."

I frown. "What do you mean?"

"You're so careful. You plan; you never rush. And now? From Keith to your boss in less than a month? It's not like you." Raya lifts a shoulder.

She's not wrong. I've always been so cautious, always prioritizing my career. It's why I took a scholarship from the London School of Economics and traveled to another continent to study, even though it terrified me.

Now, here I am, in an upscale boutique, pretending this wedding is about love and happily ever after, when really, it's a marriage of convenience. *Maybe, deep down, it's also about the thrill of sleeping with my very hot boss.* I shut the thought down.

Rachel circles me, tugging at the waistline. "Better. But not the one. Let's try the lace."

Harper leans back in her seat. "I'm happy for you. But the change in bridegrooms is… You must admit, not a normal occurrence. And I say it as someone who's seen others fold under the charm of a Davenport man."

"You're right about the effect of the Davenport charm." I flash her what I hope is a dreamy smile. "It was love at first sight. I saw him and knew he was the one."

Raya's eyes widen. "I'm happy you're living in the moment, Sis, but this is big." As I step back behind the curtain, she adds, "Are you sure this is not a rebound?"

Back behind the curtain, the seamstress zips me into another gown. The fabric sighs against my skin, soft, fluid, and shamelessly flattering, the kind that remembers every curve it touches.

Delicate lace hugs my arms all the way to my wrists, the modest neckline hints at my cleavage, yet it's high enough to lend an air of grace that contrasts beautifully with the shape of the skirt.

The mermaid cut hugs my hips and thighs before flaring out around my legs in a sweep of silk, elegant and dramatic, as if the dress itself was made to celebrate me.

I look at myself in the mirror and my breath catches.

I look good. I look different. *I look like a bride.* But inside, I feel uncertain.

Am I doing the right thing?

I remind myself that I've gone over the options, and this is the best way forward. I gulp a few breaths, steeling myself. I look at myself one last time, then square my shoulders and step out.

"It's not a rebound." I meet her gaze. On this, I'm telling her the truth. "Brody and I had a connection from the moment we met."

Also, true.

"It's what made me wonder if I was making a mistake with my absentee ex. I didn't want to admit it. I kept clinging to the idea of the perfect life I thought I was close to having. But every moment I spent getting to know Brody showed me how wrong I was. How right he felt. I've never had this kind of chemistry with anyone. He makes me feel desired. He sees my talent. He's given me opportunities at work I used to only dream about. And when he asked me to marry him, something inside me clicked. I knew it was the right choice. And when I said yes, he bought me a ring right away."

I hold up my left hand, flashing them with the diamond.

"That's some rock." Raya sighs.

"I've never heard you speak so passionately about your loser ex, either," Harper adds.

I turn to survey my reflection in the mirror again. "Besides, Mom and Dad have booked their tickets."

Raya's gaze narrows. "That's no reason to rush to marry your boss instead of your ex."

"Of course, not." I scoff. "I'm doing it because Brody and I don't want to wait a minute more to be married. And since I had a date set at Town Hall, it was a matter of him reaching out to the concerned officials to have them make the necessary changes."

"You mean, they simply had to switch around the name of the bridegroom." Harper chuckles, half-disbelieving, half-admiring.

"Brody took care of it." I nod. Another point in his favor. He's been so involved in the wedding planning. A far cry from my having to carry the load of it with my ex.

Rachel gestures for the assistant, who floats the half veil over my face. The lace catches the light. For a moment, even I can't look away.

Rachel tilts her head, studying me in the mirror. "This dress — "

"Is the one." I stare at my reflection in awe.

Prior to today, I only saw the dress on the website but wearing it...is a completely different experience. It feels perfect. Like it was tailored for me.

"Oh, my goodness." Raya clasps her hands. "*This* is your dress."

Rachel beams.

Harper sniffs and wipes a tear from her eyes. "You look beautiful."

I turn this way, then that, taking in my reflection. Who is this ethereal creature? This woman, clad in silk and lace, with a curvy figure that looks like an hourglass? Wow.

Finally. The perfect dress.

My heart feels so full. The backs of my eyes burn. This wedding is going to be perfect.

I need to get my friends to understand why Brody is the perfect man for me.

I get control of my emotions, then turn to Rachel and the shop assistant. "Can you give us a few minutes?"

"Of course." Rachel nods to the assistant, and they both leave.

When the door closes behind them, I turn to my sister and my best friend. "I'm marrying Brody because I have feelings for him." Not a lie, I do. I am powerfully attracted to him. And so is he, to me. "And he...he needs to marry in order to inherit."

Harper and Raya exchange a worried glance.

"But does he love you?" Harper frowns.

"I want to be with him. And he wants to be with me too." *Isn't that why he proposed to me and not someone else?*

When Raya opens her mouth, I raise my hand. "I know you're concerned. And I appreciate it. But really, I know this is right for me. Brody... He and I... Well, there's a lot of chemistry between us. It's not a bad basis for a marriage at all."

I'm using Brody's words to convince my friend and my sister. But by the looks on their faces, they're buying it.

And the truth? I can hear myself talking and I know I'm trying to convince myself too.

If I repeat the lines enough times, maybe I'll start believing I'm not sprinting into chaos wearing a veil and high heels.

"Are you sure, Lark?" Raya takes my hand in hers. "Are you really sure?"

God, am I?

My stomach swoops. My pulse flutters. I keep telling myself I'm making a grown-up decision, not having a very glamorous meltdown in a bridal boutique surrounded by tulle.

"I know my actions might look strange from the outside, but I promise you, I'm doing this because it's right for me." My voice trembles, but I push through. "I'm doing this because I want to be with him. When he looks at me, it's like I'm the only woman on this earth, and when he touches me"—I shiver—"it's like nothing I have ever experienced."

And it's true.

It's so much more than anything I felt with my ex. What I feel for Brody is a thousand times stronger. More potent. More passionate. More everything.

I do want to be with him. *I do.*

My heart is almost caught up with the words coming out of my mouth.

"Okay, TMI." Harper closes the distance to us. "I've never met Keith, but if you feel he's not the right person for you, then I respect that. As for Brody... Well, from what I know of the Davenport men, they are loyal to their wives."

I nod. To be honest, it never occurred to me that he wouldn't be.

She continues. "Arranged marriages run in the family, and my friends who've married the other Davenport brothers are very happy." She weaves her fingers through my other hand. "I can see that you're determined to go through with this. And it's clear there's enough chemistry between the two of you to, at least, make a basis for this marriage."

I squeeze her hand, then turn to my sister.

She studies me with soft eyes. "You don't have to justify your actions. I'm happy you're following your heart."

"I hope the two of you find love," Harper says softly.

I hope so too. I have a feeling I'm half in love with him. I can only hope that he falls for me too.

"There's one thing I agree with a hundred percent." Raya sniffs.

"Oh?"

She gives me a wicked smile. "Cutting that energy-vampy-Tiffany from the bridesmaid role."

26

Lark

Create a spreadsheet that ranks Christmas ornaments and bridesmaids'
dresses on the same 'vibe scale.'
—From Lark's Christmas to-do list

Clearly, I have not given this enough thought. My heart refuses to slow down. I clutch at my wedding bouquet.

I'm in the waiting room next to the Town Hall chamber where the wedding will take place.

Harper bursts in, wearing the bridesmaid's dress Rachel helped her choose. Her cheeks are flushed. She heads straight for the table in the corner, pours herself some water and downs it. Seeming to compose herself she turns to me with a bright smile: "How are you doing?"

"I'm fine. How are you doing?" I ask because Harper seems distracted. Maybe also, to distract myself from what I'm about to do.

"Good. I'm good." She fans herself.

"You seem flustered."

"Probably because I ran into my asshole boss out there."

"You mean—"

"James Hamilton." She turns on me. "Did you realize he's the best man?"

"I've been too distracted to ask Brody who his best man is," I confess.

She firms her lips. "I'm sure *he* won't even notice me. James has a stick up his ass anyway. The way he treats me and the rest of his staff, it's a wonder we don't walk out en masse."

"So, *why* don't you?"

"Because he's a freakin' genius. Every hour I spend working with him, I learn something new. As his sous chef, I have the most hotly contested job in restaurant circles. I learn so much from him. If I stick it out for another year, I'll have enough experience to finally start my own restaurant." She pours more water, this time, into two glasses, then offers me one.

I shake my head. "The last thing I want to do is pee in this dress."

"Well, that's what you have bridesmaids for." She laughs. "If you need to use the bathroom, one or both of us can help you." She takes me in, and her gaze softens. "You look incredible."

"Thanks." I look at the chair longingly. "I'd love to sit down and take the weight off my feet."

"Come on then." She walks over and takes the bouquet from me. She places it on the center table carefully, then holds up my short train. I walk over to the chair. She places the train carefully over the back of the chair and I sink down with a sigh. For good measure I slip off my heels. Their red soles give away the fact that they're from a world-renowned brand. *I couldn't resist.*

The door opens, and Raya enters with a warning look on her face.

"What—" I begin, then stop when my mother walks in after her.

She rushes over to hug me, and I rise to my feet. "Oh, my baby. I can't believe you're getting married."

I hug her back. "Mom, it's so good to see you."

It's been five years since I last saw my mother in person. I call her often, out of a sense of duty, but I've kept my distance, worried that if I let her in, she'd be disappointed in my achievements.

Leaving home gave me the perspective to understand that my obsession with wanting to have the perfect life was less about what I wanted and more about being the kind of daughter I *thought* my mother could be proud of.

Cancelling the wedding was unthinkable because the idea of letting her down terrified me more than standing at that altar with a replacement for my ex.

But seeing her now, I realize, I'm getting married for myself. Because somewhere deep inside, it feels right to marry Brody. I want to be his wife because I'm in love with him. I fell for him the very first time I saw him.

Only, he's never going to reciprocate my feelings. Because he doesn't believe in love.

Unless I convince him otherwise. And I'm not one to back down from a challenge.

In trying to come up with the perfect solution to help me save face and keep my life on track, is it possible, I've hit upon what's right for me?

My mom looks me up and down and claps her hands together. "You look beautiful!"

"So do you." I take in her blush pink dress.

"Thanks to you." She beams at me. "This dress is beautiful. And it fits perfectly."

I wanted to get her a mother-of-the-bride dress that looked nothing like the usual, frumpy mother-of-the-bride dresses you always see. I think I succeeded.

"I don't want to kiss you and spoil your makeup." She settles for blowing me a kiss instead.

"How was your flight?" Raya asks brightly.

"It was comfortable. First time I've flown in a private jet." My mother's eyes light up.

"Private jet?" *What does she mean?*

My father walks through the doorway.

"Dad!" My face lights up.

All the times he dropped me off at school or stayed up to make sure I was home from a date before he fell asleep, flash before my eyes.

He was crushed when he learned I was going to university in London, but he didn't try to stop me. He worked hard to make sure we had everything growing up. And while he couldn't stop my mother from being exacting with us, he, himself, never wanted anything from us. He often told us that he only wanted us to be happy.

My mother, too, was nothing but encouraging when I told them of my plan to go abroad to study.

It's because I didn't want to let her down that I'm so driven. I owe my need to succeed to her.

I am very grateful to both of them. I am who I am because of them.

And now, I can make their life more comfortable by paying off their debts. A surge of relief fills me. I made the right decision in agreeing to marry Brody. I'm setting my parents up for a more comfortable life.

My father walks over and hugs me. "It's so good to see you, honey." He releases me, takes a few steps back, and surveys me with pride.

"You look beautiful."

He puts his arm around my mother's shoulder.

"Can you believe this? Our daughter is getting married, Sheila."

My mom dabs at her eyes. "We did good."

"We sure did." My father's eyes shine. "I have to admit, your man sending us a private jet to fly here was a surprise. But I'm not going to complain about it."

Raya gasps. "You think I could borrow the jet the next time I want to go on holiday?"

I ignore her and focus my attention on my mother.

"Brody sent you his private jet?"

"He must love you very much if he's taking such good care of your parents." My mother's eyes turn dreamy. "Can't say I'm unhappy about you not marrying Keith. I wasn't impressed when he cancelled on our family call at the last minute."

"It's not that I don't trust your judgment, but marrying a man called Keith—?" My dad shakes his head. "Afraid I wasn't too impressed."

Not my dad, too? Gah! I fight for composure.

"Wait a minute! Are you both saying you didn't want me to marry Keith? Why didn't you say anything?" I huff.

"We want you to be happy, sweetheart," my father says softly.

"And you seemed happy to be marrying him, so we didn't say anything." My mother's gaze is soft.

Seems I dodged a bullet in more ways than one by not marrying Keith. And my parents seem to be taking this change in bridegrooms in their stride.

I could have called them in advance to warn them, but really, it seemed easier to let them arrive and then tell them about it. Besides, I calculated that seeing me in my wedding dress, about to get married, would temper their reaction.

Of course, I didn't realize that Brody was contacting them ahead of time. And being picked up by private jet would make a big impact on anyone. They seem positively approving of Brody.

"I take it the two of you aren't upset that I changed bride-grooms?" I look between them.

The two of them exchange a glance.

"What?" I frown.

My father half smiles. "We *were* surprised that you were marrying someone who is almost a stranger—"

"—except he's not a stranger. Not anymore," my mother adds.

I begin to rub at my temple, then stop myself. I don't want to mess up my makeup, or my hair. "Can you please spell it out for me? I'm a little on edge, seeing as I'm about to get married and all?"

"Your fiancé called us and told us how much he loves you. And how he convinced you to break it off with Keith and marry him instead." My father beams.

I sink back in my chair. "Brody called you?" I shake my head to clear it.

And he didn't even let on to my parents that it was my ex who dumped me. That's a level of thoughtfulness I hadn't expected. My heart stutters. Warmth fills my chest. Then a thought strikes me.

"But...I never gave him your contact details."

"I did," Raya pipes up.

"What?" I jerk my chin in her direction. "You...met Brody?"

"I, uh...called him up after the dress fitting and insisted on seeing him to make sure his intentions toward you were right. Imagine my surprise when he dropped everything to meet me the same day. He explained that he loves you and can't wait to marry you."

He told her he loves me. Clearly, he said that to justify why we're getting married. And she believed him? Sweet sleigh bells. He must be a convincing actor.

My head spins. "Uh... I think I need some water."

Harper snatches up the glass of water and offers it to me. I take a few sips and hand it back to her. When I feel a little more composed, I turn on Raya.

"Why didn't you tell me?"

She flushes. "I figured you wouldn't be happy."

"I'm not."

She hangs her head. "I wanted to make sure you weren't committing another mistake. You went from breaking things off with Keith to marrying your boss so quickly." She hunches her shoulders. "I was looking out for you."

"Right." Some of my anger melts away.

"Of course, meeting Brody made me realize, you're doing the right thing."

"Oh?" I try to take in everything she's saying.

"Oh, yeah." She nods eagerly. "The two of you are in love. And Brody insisted he didn't see the point in waiting longer. Most of the arrangements had been made anyway. It makes sense you're getting married. And this time, it's to the right man."

Damn. Brody's done a number on them. He's gotten on their good side. They believe this marriage is genuine. And they're looking at me with happiness and pride. Like this is the perfect wedding for the perfect bride.

Wow. He really did pull it off.

I should be grateful to him. And I am, *in a way*. I don't have to pull out the half-baked explanations I was ready to pull out when I saw my parents.

On the other hand, why didn't he tell me he did this?

"You sure you're okay?" My mother squeezes my arm. "You can talk to us."

"I'm fine, Mom, I promise."

My father puts his arm around her shoulders. "Leave the girl alone. It's natural for her to be jittery on her wedding day. Let's give her some alone time with her bridesmaids so she can compose herself."

27

Brody

The chamber doors open.

Raya and Harper walk up the aisle. Dressed in satin, their smiles are too bright, as if they don't quite believe this is happening. Once they reach the altar, they move to stand on the bride's side, opposite James, my best man.

The doors open again.

Tiny strides down the aisle between the chairs. He's wearing a black velvet harness trimmed with holly and silver ribbon.

The rings are secured at his chest like medals of honor.

Sighs and laughter ripples through the crowds.

When Lark proposed Tiny as ring bearer at our wedding. I agreed right away. She, of course, couldn't resist dressing him up in festive fashion.

"Go, Tiny." James chuckles from next to me.

The Great Dane ambles forward with calm authority. He makes it to me without getting distracted.

I kneel, pocket the rings, then pat him. "You did good, partner."

He woofs, then parks his butt down and thumps his tail.

I straighten as the doors swing open a third time, and the world stops.

She's there. *Lark.*

A shaft of sunlight slants through the arched windows, catching in her hair, turning the pale silk of her dress into something almost luminous. For a moment, my lungs forget how to work. I've spent years commanding boardrooms, entire companies, entire futures. Yet, one woman in white brings me to my knees without lifting a finger.

James leans slightly toward me. "You're a lucky bastard." I don't look away from her long enough to answer.

Lark's gaze never leaves mine as she moves up the aisle. Her mother sniffles from the front row. Her father beams. It feels symbolic that he's not giving her away. She's choosing. Choosing me.

And God help me, the weight of that nearly undoes me.

The rows are filled: Nathan and Skylar are glowing. Arthur looks smug with Imelda at his arm.

Tiny is next to me.

Quentin and Vivian, composed as ever, Knox with June, warm and smiling. Also, Tyler and Priscilla, as well as Connor and his wife Phoenix. Sinclair Sterling, our family friend, and his wife Summer are in attendance with their son.

Adrian and Toren, are here. Ryot can't attend as he's on a tour with his wife, the Princess Aurelia. Though her brother, the crown prince Viktor Verenza is in attendance.

There's a woof, then Tiny ambles over to Lark, his claws tapping on the floor.

"Aww, Tiny." Lark scratches behind his ear. Tiny waves his flagstaff tail. When she straightens and begins to walk, Tiny is by her side. Laughter rolls through the assembled people.

She comes to a halt in front of me. Through her mini veil, her eyes shine up at me. With her lush lips, the radiant column of her neck, and her proud curves shown off to perfection by the lace and satin, she's a dream come true.

My heart begins to beat fast. My pulse rate is unsteady. I hadn't realized until this moment how significant this moment is for me.

The registrar begins to speak, his voice echoing through the chamber. I stand rooted, fists clenching and unclenching at my sides, as if that will keep me steady.

When I say, "I do," the words leave me raw, rough-edged. They don't sound romantic. They sound like an oath. A contract I'll bleed before I break. How strange. It's just a ceremony. These are only words. They shouldn't affect me so much.

When it's her turn, her voice trembles, but her eyes never waver. When she whispers, "I do," I feel the ground shift under me.

I slide the wedding ring onto her ring finger. It's a rose gold band which forms a set with the engagement ring.

I hand her a coordinating platinum band, and she slips it onto mine.

It should feel constricting to have that ring on my finger. Like it's holding me back. Weighing me down, perhaps. Instead, it feels like it connects me to her. To a possible life I could have with her. To a future I never could have imagined before. One I can't stomach right now. Nope, this is not for me. This is not why I married her.

The registrar pronounces us husband and wife. Applause ripples across the chamber, too loud, too intrusive. James whistles, until I shoot him a glare. Nathan claps with gusto. Arthur inclines his head, satisfied that he's orchestrated the whole damn thing. Which he has, in a way.

I should be pissed off at him, but for the first time in years, I don't see a deal being signed, an empire being cemented, or Arthur's approval being won.

My attention is riveted by Lark, standing in front of me. Her lips part. Her chest rises and falls.

I hear the registrar say, as if from a distance, "You may kiss the bride."

As if in a dream, I raise the half veil so I can look into her sparkling eyes. And when I take her hands in mine, my pulse steadies, and my heartbeat settles. I anchor myself in the warmth of her skin, then lower my head.

"My wife," I breathe against her lips.

A full-bodied shudder has her melting into me. I wrap my arm around her waist and hold up her weight, then lick into her mouth. She moans. I tilt my head, deepening the kiss.

The taste of her goes to my head. My heart rate seems to go off the charts. Sweat pools in my armpits. Kissing her feels like a religious experience. I wouldn't have believed the act of marrying her would make me feel this possessive.

Apparently, I'm more sentimental than I realized. It's that thought which makes me release her and step back.

Around me the applause swells again. I notice Arthur wiping a tear. Damn, never thought I'd see the old man get emotional. My brothers and their wives clap. Her sister grins widely. Harper dabs at the corners of her eyes with a handkerchief. Next to me, I sense James glowering at her. I'm aware Harper works for James, but this animosity he feels for her seems more personal. I shove that thought aside, knowing I'll ask him about it another time.

I want to take my wife's hand in mine, but I resist.

I can't let myself fall for her. My attraction for her, combined with the fact that we're now legally bound together, intensifies the sense of inevitability that has gripped me since I put the ring on her finger.

I step forward, following Rachel as she ushers us toward the tall double doors at the end of the chamber. I sense Lark stiffen, sense the hurt that radiates from her.

My guts churn. Anger knocks against my rib cage. Instead of turning to her, I stalk forward. Alone. Through the throng of friends and relatives congratulating us. My tie feels too tight around my neck. Air. I need air.

I burst out of the double doors, and look wildly up and down the corridor, wondering which way to go. James appears at my shoulder.

One look at my face, and his jaw stiffens. "Come on."

I follow him up a flight of stairs, then down a corridor, until we reach a door. He pushes it open to reveal a covered balcony. I slip outside.

The cool air surrounds me. I draw in lungfuls.

I loosen my tie and, pulling it off, stuff it into my pocket. Then I walk to the railing and hold on.

I take in the rooftops of the neighboring Victorian homes. Many have Christmas decorations in the windows and outside their doors. The main street below boasts festive lights. The sound of carol singing reaches me from somewhere down the street. Christmas is two days away. I've never paid much attention to the celebratory spirit.

Except for briefing a shopper to buy the requisite Christmas presents so I could hand them over on Christmas Eve when I made the rounds of my brother's homes.

James walks over to join me.

He scans my features, then with a sigh, pulls out two cigarettes. He lights both, passing me one.

"Thanks mate." I haven't smoked in years. Not since leaving the Marines. But the situation today seems to warrant one. I'll try anything to try to come to grips with the emotions swirling around inside me.

We smoke in companionable silence for a few seconds. Then he blows out smoke and turns to me. "Want to talk about it?"

"Not particularly."

"Alrighty then." He turns back to contemplating the scene in front of us. The cold slides in through my jacket. I stamp my feet and sink deeper into it. The sunshine from earlier has been hidden by clouds which hang heavy over the city.

"Supposed to snow," James murmurs.

As if on cue, snowflakes drift down from the skies.

The cold seems to deepen. James shuffles his feet. "Guess we'd better—"

"I might be falling for her," I growl.

He stiffens. "You're talking about your wife, I assume."

"Who else would it be?"

He turns to face me, shoving a hand in his pocket. "Isn't that why you married her?"

"As you well know, I married her to save my inheritance."

"Right."

"You don't believe me?"

He surveys me with that shrewd look—the one which warns me that he's about to give me the unvarnished truth. My brothers might have done the same, but I've been closer to James than them.

"Hey, I'm not trying to convince you otherwise." James raises a hand. "I can only tell you what I see from the outside."

"Which is?"

"The way you look at her, the way you watch her when she's in the same room as you, the way you kissed her earlier... There was nothing fake about it."

"Hmm." I take a puff of my cigarette, and contemplate the tip. My head spins a little. I'm not used to the nicotine anymore.

My life is changing in front of my eyes.

"You know you can't control life?" James drawls. "We think we make the decisions, but fate sometimes has other plans."

"Are you speaking from experience?"

He smiles grimly. "I'm an adopted kid who's never forgotten that life might have gone another way for me. But it didn't. My parents took me out of the foster care system. They gave me an identity. A purpose. And every day, I try to live up to this second chance I got."

I frown. "You've never spoken about it before."

"Never had to. But if it gives you, perspective—"

The door to the balcony opens. Both of us turn to find Arthur framed in the doorway.

28

Brody

"I need a word with my grandson." Arthur addresses James without taking his gaze off me.

"Of course." James stubs out his cigarette. "I'll be waiting downstairs." He squeezes my shoulder, brushes past Arthur and shuts the door behind him.

Arthur walks toward me. His gait is slow. He's using a cane for support. It makes him appear more frail than usual. His back, though, is ramrod stiff. His shoulders erect. But his cheeks are gaunt. If I ask him if he wants to sit down he'll refuse.

Instead, I head toward one of the two chairs set between the outdoor heaters and fold my length into one of them.

After a moment's hesitation, he seats himself in the other one. His forehead furrows. "You needn't have done that."

I know what he's referring to. "If I hadn't, you'd have insisted on standing. It would have worn you out, but you wouldn't have backed down."

He shoots me a contemplative look from under his bushy eyebrows. "You always were more thoughtful than the others."

"Because despite your bluster, I know you mean well. As do my brothers. Your methods, though, leave much to be desired."

"Hmm." He places his one hand over the one clasping the head of his cane. "Are you trying to tell me you regret my forcing the issue? It's the only reason you moved fast and married your wife."

I firm my lips. "A decision I'm questioning."

"You mean, you're running scared." His tone is casual. I sense he's trying to wind me up, but that doesn't stop me from stiffening.

"Scared? I'm not scared."

"Why else would you be hiding here, instead of being with your wife?" A satisfied light gleams in his eyes.

"Look Gramps, I know you think you know best—"

"I do."

I rub at my temples. This man. He's so sure of himself. How can I make him understand that sometimes you need things to unfold in their own time?

"How can you be so sure?"

"How can you not be sure?" He looks at me like I'm crazy.

"Because I'm not going to let myself be vulnerable enough to fall for someone." The words burst out.

It must be the fact that I'm emotionally vulnerable which has allowed me to lower my barriers... Enough to share this aloud.

I expect Arthur to cast aside my words, instead his gaze turns sympathetic. "It's my fault."

"What do you mean?"

"You don't get to be my age and not look back on your life and wonder about your choices." His shoulders sag.

He looks every one of his eighty-three years.

"I'm not sure I follow." I frown.

"I kept, first my sons, then my grandsons, at arm's length. I ignored my sons. Wasn't around for them much. Yet expected them to deliver on my ambitions. When my oldest son left, I was too caught up in my work to stop him. I was barely on speaking terms with my second son, your father. I ignored and belittled him. I never gave him the love and security of a father. And when I realized he wouldn't be strong enough to take over the company after me, I ignored him completely."

He tightens his jaw.

"Luckily, Quentin left home at eighteen, so he could develop his personality and find himself. When you and your brothers came along, I treated you all as assets."

He squeezes the arm of his chair.

"You were only five when your father passed and six when your mother died. You were also the most sensitive of all your brothers. You withdrew into yourself when you lost your parents. I should have given you more space to mourn. I should have found you the right support to help to process your feelings. Instead, I pushed you and your brothers to excel at school. Unable to handle the responsibility of taking care of you boys, I pushed the lot of you away from me."

The skin stretches white across his knuckles.

"And when you became adults, I saw the future of my company in you boys. I expected you to carry the Davenport name forward. So, I badgered the lot of you to settle down. I thought I knew what was best. I wanted to see my great grandkids before I passed."

"And you have." I nod.

Nathan and Skylar have a son, Tyler and Priscilla have a daughter and Knox and June are about to give birth any day.

"Indeed." His lips quirk. "And sure, I may have manipulated the lot of them to get married."

"*May* have?"

He half smiles. "I admit, I coerced the lot of you into matrimony, but it was for your own good."

I groan. "Personally, I could have done with a little more time in getting my thoughts into some semblance of order before getting hitched."

He chuckles. "Ah, youth and thinking you have time for everything. You need to seize each moment, make the most of it. Make the most of this opportunity you've been given."

"You're talking about my marriage?" I place the tips of my fingers together.

"I understand, it must seem like a big step forward. A leap into the unknown."

"You think?" I scoff.

"It's life changing. And it can be daunting. I remember when I got married. Your grandmother was the most beautiful woman I'd ever seen. I pursued her. I beat off my competitors and married her. I couldn't wait for her to be my wife. All through the ceremony, all I could see was her. We were blissfully happy."

He looks into the distance.

"And then, I threw myself into building an empire so I could keep her in style. Only, that took me further away from her and our children. I realized what was happening but felt powerless to stop it. At some point it became not about the money but the thrill of playing out business gambles and winning." He swallows. "By the time I realized the fallacy of my actions, it was too late. She was gone. So was your father. And I was estranged from my other two sons. You and your brothers were coming into adulthood. That's when I seized my chance. I wanted to make sure the lot of you were settled in life. It would have made her happy. I went at it the wrong way, though."

I've never heard him sound this sincere. That he's owning up to his mistakes is unexpected. Besides, he's right. But given his tortured features, I don't have the heart to tell him so.

Instead, I watch the snowflakes begin to drift down.

We're sheltered, and the heaters on either side of us provide warmth, but the temperature has dropped considerably.

I hunch into my jacket. "Why are you telling me this?"

"Because I want you to think about what you're going to do next."

I slide my finger around the rim of my collar. I needed a little space from her; that's why I ran.

Because I'm falling for her. It's why I asked her to marry me. I'm terrified at how vulnerable that makes me feel. In fact, I can barely admit this to myself, let alone have the courage to share my feelings with her.

"It was tough losing first Dad, then Mom so soon afterward. And you're right, I was too young to process it in a healthy way. Thankfully, I had my brothers. Uncle Quentin, too, filled in as a male role model."

He pales further, then seems to get a hold of himself. "You're right. I wasn't there for you boys the way I should have been. I'm asking you not to punish yourself for my faults."

I shoot him a curious glance. "What do you mean?"

"I'm afraid the lack of love and security in your childhood means that you and your brothers have a hard time accepting it in your life. My insisting that the lot of you serve in the military..." He lowers his chin. "What I'm trying to say is that you shouldn't run from your feelings."

I struggle to hide my surprise and fail. This is Arthur. The cantankerous head of the Davenport family who's spent his life getting all up into the lives of his family. The man who treated his family with the same cutthroat machinations as his group of companies. You could be forgiven for thinking that the man was an automaton. Yet here he is, confessing first, to having been in love with my grandmother, and then, talking to me about feelings, in the breath of a few seconds.

"I see you're taken aback." He arches an eyebrow.

"Can you blame me? You don't exactly fit the image of a cuddly ol' grandpa."

"God forbid," he huffs. "And no, I'm not the kind to talk about my feelings, but then...Imelda happened."

"Oh?" I ask, curious.

"I loved your grandmother. But I was a different person then. I was so lost in power plays and growing the business, I couldn't find the time to tell her enough that she meant the world to me. Her death broke me. It pushed me further into bitterness. But Imelda's forthrightness was exactly what I needed to give me a rude wake-up call. She made me realize I couldn't live the rest of my life hiding from the stuff that really matters."

"Which is?"

"Which is telling you how I really feel. I love you, Brody. I love *all* of you. And I want the best for you."

My heart squeezes in my chest. A strange tightness grips my rib cage. Damn, I do believe Gramps is sincere. And somehow hearing him confess his feelings seems to break a dam somewhere inside of me. "I love you, too, Grandad."

He blinks rapidly. Something suspiciously like tears shimmers in his eyes.

Then, he grins. "Good. Then you'll do exactly as I tell you."

29

Lark

Resist the urge to alphabetize the ornaments by color again.

— From Lark's Christmas to-do list

"Are you okay?" Harper asks in a low voice.

No, I'm not.

My groom literally bolted from my side, minutes after we exchanged vows.

And it's not like this is some fairy-tale love match. We married for reasons that have nothing to do with romance and everything to do with our own agendas. This is far from the perfect wedding I envisaged for myself.

I should be mortified. But for the first time in my life, appearances don't matter. I don't really care how disastrous it looks from the outside. I'm too busy worrying about my husband.

Is he alright?

I saw his expression as he walked away, and it gutted me. He looked tortured. What's happening in his head? How do I reach him? How do I help?

But I can't share my concerns with her. And I don't want to lie to her. So, I avoid answering her.

Instead, I clear my throat. "Can you get me a glass of water, please?"

Harper's forehead creases. She looks like she's going to push for an answer, so I send her a half smile. "Please?"

Her lips turn down. She doesn't look happy, but she nods. Then turns and heads to the counter with drinks which has been set up against the far wall of the anteroom.

It's adjacent to the main chambers where we married. I'm waiting with the rest of the Davenports, including Imelda. And for Brody and Arthur to rejoin us so we can head to Arthur's place for the reception.

Outside the window, flecks of snow drift down from the sky. It looks like it's going to be a white Christmas. My favorite. But I can't find any joy in it.

I play with my engagement and wedding rings, casting another glance toward the door.

What's taking them so long? James reassured me that Brody would be along shortly. That he and Arthur were catching up. What could have happened for Brody to stalk off like that? Was he having second thoughts? This was his idea, after all. So, what set him off?

Tyler's daughter Serene screams as she runs past me with Sinclair and Summer's son Matty in hot pursuit.

Then Serene trips and falls, and bursts out crying.

Before I can think twice, I race toward her, pick her up and examine her knees, then her hands. She's unhurt. But the shock must have gotten to her.

"It's okay, honey." I sit down and pull her into my lap. "You're good."

Matty appears next to me, followed by Serene's mother Priscilla, who I met earlier.

"Is she okay?" Priscilla sinks down next to me.

"She's fine. Just shaken." I rock the little girl in my arms, imagining what it would be like to have my own child. Perhaps, with Brody's dark hair and my green eyes...

Her crying lessens, and she looks up at me with luminous eyes.

She sniffles. "You look like a princess."

I smile. "Thank you."

She touches the fabric of my new dress. "It's so soft."

"I'm so sorry, it's crumpled." Priscilla holds out her arms, and I hand over Serene.

"Oh, don't worry about it at all. I'm glad I was close by and could comfort her."

"Why are you crying?" Matty sniffs. "You're such a baby."

"I'm not a baby." Serene's chin trembles. "I'm crying because I fell."

"But you're not hurt," Matty points out.

She sniffles. "Well..." For a few seconds, she looks confused. "I thought I was."

"But you're not. So come and play." Matty holds out his hand.

Serene looks at Priscilla.

"You can play, but please, no more running," Priscilla admonishes.

"I won't." Serene flashes us a smile, places her hand in Matty's, and the two skip off.

"If only we adults were as resilient, eh?" Priscilla rises to her feet.

So do I. Some of the tension from my shoulders fades.

Around me, the group resumes chatting with each other. Raya gestures at something while talking with Skylar.

My mother turns back to her conversation with Imelda and June.

That's when the door is pushed open, and Brody walks in.

Oh, thank God. My first instinct is to rush to him. But on the heels of that is confusion. Why did he leave me like that? And right after the wedding ceremony.

He stalks toward me with that lithe grace of his which I've always found so very unusual for a man his size.

He comes to a stop about a foot in front of me. I realize he's keeping enough space between us, so I don't have to crane my head to see his face. Somehow, his consideration only pisses me off further. If he were really being considerate, he wouldn't have left me and walked out without an explanation.

In the silence that follows, he says, without looking away from me. "Imelda, Arthur's waiting for you at the balcony on the second floor. As for the rest of you, could I ask you to leave so I can talk to my wife?"

Instantly, the crowd begins to move. Imelda walks toward the door with Tiny in tow. The mutt pauses to butt his head against my arm. I scratch behind his ear and half smile. "Good boy."

He makes a purring sound at the back of his throat and allows Imelda to lead him out. Behind me, there's the sound of clinking as the group set down glasses. There's a rustle of fabric as they begin to move. I hear someone call Matty's name, probably Sinclair.

Harper hands me a glass of water on the way out. I nod my thanks, and she gives me a small smile.

Within seconds, they've left. The door shuts softly behind them.

Some of the tension seems to leave Brody's shoulders.

"Are you okay?" I take a sip of the water, then walk back to the bar counter and set the glass aside.

"I will be." He closes the distance to me. "I'm sorry. It was wrong of me to leave you the way I did."

I raise one eyebrow, but stay silent.

"I never meant to embarrass you like that in front of our families. I'll never forgive myself for doing that. I needed to get my thoughts in order and couldn't do that, not when I was so close to you."

"You didn't want to be close to me?" I tip up my chin in his direction.

What I see in his eyes makes me falter. There's true apology and regret, and it's underlined by something soft and sharp at the same time. Something which feels like a combination of lust and an emotion I can't quite place.

"I wanted to be close to you. *Very* close to you. Too close to you. It's why I had to leave."

"Oh." I swallow. "I'm not sure what you mean."

He drags his fingers though his hair. "I mean, I want you. Too much. Enough to make me realize I calculated wrong."

"Calculated?"

He nods. "I hoped to keep some semblance of sanity, some shred of common sense when I married you. Something that would help me put distance between us. I didn't want my heart involved in this arrangement."

My chest hurts. My throat closes. He wants to keep me at arm's length.

"It might be best if I leave."

I begin to walk past him, but he curls his fingers around my wrist. Instantly, goosebumps creep up my thigh. My heart seems to drop to the space between my legs. One touch... That's all it takes for him to command me.

"Didn't you hear what I said?"

Sensations vibrate out from the point of contact. "I did. And it sounded very much like you don't want to be drawn into whatever it is that's between us."

He half smiles, then explains, "I'm already drawn into what's between us. So much so, I can't stop thinking of you. I wake up with images of you in my head. I fall asleep thinking of your smile. I dream of touching you, holding you, kissing you, making love to you"—his voice drops—"fucking you."

The heat between my thighs turns nuclear. Sweat beads my brow. His words are a spark, and there're explosives running through my veins.

"Y-you...mean—"

"That I want you very much. So much, it screwed up my thinking. Made me want to put distance between us, rather than confront what I'm feeling."

"What...are you feeling?" I breathe.

In reply, he leans in and presses his lips to mine. Instantly, I detonate. Heat screeches through my veins. Fire zips out from the point of contact of our mouths and lights up all my nerve endings.

I feel like a Christmas tree whose lights have been turned on. Dazzling from head to toe. Like a live wire which has been ignited.

I part my mouth on a gasp, and he sweeps his tongue in. The taste of him is an aphrodisiac. The scent of him sinks into my skin, clings to my pores. Makes me desperate for more. I cling to his shoulders, parting my legs. He moves in.

He wraps his big arms around me, enveloping me in his heady masculinity, which makes my head spine. I groan into his mouth. He swallows the sound, deepening the kiss further. He sucks on my mouth, consuming me completely.

I melt into him. I am but a raindrop who's merged with the ocean. I am lost. In him. He makes a growling noise at the back of his throat. The vibrations rumble up his chest and ignite pinpricks of sensations over my skin.

"I want you. So much," he murmurs against my mouth. I stare into those mesmerizing eyes and feel any anger I might harbor against him, any reluctance, any hesitation… All of it fades.

"I want you, too," I admit.

"Be patient with me. Until I figure out my thoughts." He frames my face with his big hands. "Please?"

His beautiful eyes are filled with a pleading which melts my heart. I'm spiraling down a hole from which I can't climb out. I find myself nodding. "Okay."

"Okay." He kisses me again, and it feels like he's drawing my very essence into his mouth. Unable to bear the intensity of what I see in his eyes, my own close. The next second, the world tilts. With an impressive display of strength, he rises to his feet with me in his arms.

I cling to him, unable to take my gaze off his strong, gorgeous profile. He strides across the floor; shoulders open the doors, and steps out.

There's silence for a few seconds, then applause breaks out, along with a few whistles and catcalls.

"Go Brody," James calls out.

I flush. Brody smirks. Confetti rains down on us. Some of the glittering particles stick to his hair. He looks so handsome. My heart flutters. My pussy clenches. I want this man so much.

I want *my husband* so much.

It's a perfect moment. Closer to the kind of wedding I envisioned for myself. But now that it's here, all I care about is that *he's* my husband. *Mine.*

When the noise dies down, Brody grins at the assembled crowd. "Change of plans, folks. My wife and I are leaving on our honeymoon right away."

30

Brody

"You chartered a helicopter?" Lark stares down at the passing countryside covered in white. Luckily, the snow had stopped by the time we reached the helipad. Visibility was good so our pilot had clearance to take off.

We're in the passenger cabin, separated from the cockpit and insulated against the engine and rotor noise.

We changed our clothes into something more suitable for traveling in a side room at the Town Hall. We're also wearing noise-cancelling headsets with voice-activated microphones, so we can talk easily.

"It was my conversation with Arthur that gave me the idea," I admit.

"Oh?" She looks at me with curiosity.

"He told me to not waste any more time."

His exact words were, '*If you want to spend time alone with your wife, then you should follow your heart.'* I took him at his word and ordered the chopper.

I also asked for our bags to be unloaded from the car and moved to the helicopter.

I intended to take her on our honeymoon after the reception. But I couldn't wait to be alone with her. With snow falling, and a blizzard on the way, it made sense to leave early and fly out before it hit.

"He was okay with us skipping the reception at his place?" She leans back in her seat.

"He didn't protest." I reach out to take her hand in mine. "I'm sorry I didn't check in with you first. I figured you wouldn't mind getting out of there without having to attend the reception."

She purses her lips. "It would have been good to spend more time with my parents."

When I stiffen, she throws me a sideways glance. "Kidding. No, I didn't want to be quizzed further by my parents. They met you. They got to attend the wedding. As did my friends. And your grandfather. As far as they're concerned, we're married. No one can refute that."

I rub my thumb over her knuckles. She shivers. And that pleases me enormously. I want her to be aware of me.

I want her to feel as affected by my nearness as I am by hers. "I'm sorry I put you in that spot. I'd have wanted a little more time for us to get to know each other before the wedding. But the invitations had gone out, and your parents were planning to come, and since Arthur was pressuring me too, it made sense to do it now."

She nods, a fold between her eyebrows hinting that her mind is preoccupied.

"What are you thinking?"

She hesitates. "Thanks for not telling my parents about my ex cheating on me. I—"

"I will always be in your corner." I squeeze her hand.

She swallows. "Thank you."

"You're welcome."

Our gazes catch. The air between us sparks with awareness. Her eyes are shadowed.

"You can share anything with me, Siren."

Her lips part. She glances to the side. "I married you because I wanted my ex to feel like he was losing out. And because I didn't want my parents and my friends to think of me as a loser."

"And *I* married you so I could inherit." I twist my lips. "It seems to me that I win this challenge."

She chuckles, some of the tension going out of her shoulders.

I lean in, my voice rough. "I'm serious. When I imagine waking up next to you every morning—your hair a mess, your skin warm from sleep—it doesn't feel wrong. It feels…like home."

Her throat moves as she swallows, and I continue.

"I also married you because I'm very attracted to you. In a way I haven't been to anyone else before. Because when I see you, I can't stop myself from touching you, holding you, and kissing you. Because my body yearns for you in a way that takes me by surprise. Because I want you, Lark. I want to make love to you. More than that, I want to possess you. I want to make you mine. Completely."

Her cheeks turn pink.

"But you know that already."

"Five minutes to landing." The pilot's voice cuts in on a different channel through the headphones.

I hold her gaze as the helicopter begins to descend. Within minutes, we're landing in the garden behind the homestead my family has owned for generations.

The rotors slow until they come to a stop. Then the pilot turns and gives us a thumbs-up through the glass wall separating the cabins.

"Safe to disembark."

He steps out of the cockpit and walks past us to pull the door open and lower the steps. I'm up and moving toward it immediately.

"Thanks, man." I shake the pilot's hand.

"Need help with the bags?" He gestures toward our suitcases, stored in the compartment behind the cockpit.

"I got this. You'd better head back before the weather gets worse." I grab both suitcases and walk down the retractable steps. I place the luggage on the grass, turn and help my wife down the steps.

I wave at the pilot, then grab the bags and head toward the stately Victorian building. Behind us, the chopper starts up again.

I walk up the path that curves into shadow, tall trees pressing in close, dusted with snow. There's a hush in the woods you get after snowfall, like the land itself is holding its breath.

A few hundred yards in, we pass rows of firs like soldiers under starlight, tips frosted.

I glance at Lark.

She's stopped walking. And stares. Mouth parted. "Is that"—she shakes her head—"are those Christmas trees?"

"My great-grandmother planted them."

"They're beautiful." Her voice is hushed.

She didn't get to do any Christmas things because I was a Grinch. Then her ex cheated on her, and she ended up marrying a guy with no use for Christmas. But I don't want her to miss out on her favorite part of the year. The least I can do is give her Christmas, in my own way.

"We can pick one tomorrow if you want to decorate. There's a box of ornaments inside," I say without taking my gaze off her flushed features.

"That would be amazing." Her eyes shine.

Behind us, the helicopter takes off. The downwash stirs pine needles and lifts the hair on my head.

The whup-whup-whup of its blades fades as it recedes into the distance.

Now it's just us. Peace envelops me. Tension I didn't realize I'd been carrying fades from my shoulders. We keep walking.

The path opens up into a clearing, and there it is: the chalet that's been in my family for generations. Glass and timber, pale stone and golden light glowing from inside. The lake stretches out behind it like a sheet of obsidian, the late afternoon light reflecting off the surface. There's steam curling from the outdoor hot tub on the deck. And through the window, I catch sight of the fire, already lit.

"Jesus," she breathes.

It was worth having the caretaker go that extra mile. I make a note to transfer a hefty tip into his account.

"I wanted you to feel like you've stepped out of the world," I murmur. "Just for a while."

We reach the steps of the chalet.

She tucks her hair behind one ear and looks up at the house. "It's beautiful." Her eyes are wide with disbelief.

"It belonged to my great-great-grandfather. Been in my family for generations."

I key in the password on the panel next to the door. The door clicks open. The caretaker should have stocked the refrigerator and the pantry, lit the fires in the living and bedroom, and made sure there's a supply of wood to last us through the stay.

I drop the bags inside the house, then straighten and step back outside.

"Hold on." I scoop her up in my arms and step over the threshold.

"Ohmigod," she squeaks. "That's so romantic."

"I aim to please." I hook my ankle around the door to swing it shut behind me. *Can't risk the cold getting in.* Then head for the staircase.

"This is beautiful." She takes in the spacious hallway.

Through the doorway on the left is the sitting room with its cozy furniture and the dancing flames throwing light over the walls.

Warmth envelops us. Along with the scent of cedar, smoke, and pine. Lark's eyes search mine. "You did all this for me?"

"I did it for us."

Her throat moves as she swallows. Her breath hitches. "That is the sweetest thing anyone has ever said to me."

"And I'm only starting." I hold her gaze, wanting to bend and capture her mouth. But if I did, I'd be sidetracked. Once I kiss her, I won't be able to stop. And I don't want that to happen...yet. I want to make sure I get her settled in first.

I force myself to look away and focus on my steps.

Reaching the first-floor landing, I head past the guest bedroom and toward the main bedroom. I shoulder open the doors and, walking halfway to the bed, stop and lower her to her feet.

"This is amazing." She clasps her fingers together and takes in the room. A large bed faces the fireplace. To one side, a wall of windows overlooks the lake, the view framed by thick curtains.

The fire crackles warmly, surrounded by a seating area with a couch and two armchairs.

A shelf of books lines the wall beside the fireplace, with a small table and chair beside it forming a cozy workspace.

The décor is masculine yet warm. There are deep carpets underfoot, and soft light spills in from the windows and from the lamps switched on around the room.

Then her brow wrinkles. "We're sharing a bedroom?"

"Did you think we wouldn't?"

I slide a hand inside my pocket, watching her gaze bounce around the space. Then she steps toward the window and peers outside. The chalet is in Lechlade, bordering the Cotswolds Hills, which can be seen in the distance. The clouds are heavy with the promise of more snow. She wraps her arms around her waist and shivers. It's both beautiful and cold out there.

"There's a storm coming." I walk over to stand next to her.

"Is that why you hustled us onto the helicopter?"

"I wanted to get here before it broke." I wrap my arm about her shoulders and pull her to me.

She instantly melts into my side.

Her jasmine and coconut scent teases my nostrils and tightens my balls. It feels like there are little sparks of fire flickering through my bloodstream. Damn. This woman drives me crazy. As if she senses how close I am to throwing her down on the bed and making love to her, she looks up at me from under her heavy eyelids. "I can't believe we're married."

"Believe it." I bend and take her lips, tasting her, sharing her breath, squeezing my arms around her and pulling her close, so every inch of her is plastered to me. By the time I step back, she's flushed and panting. There's a dazed look in her eyes which makes my lips twitch. A sense of satisfaction fills my chest. She's my wife. *Mine.*

I release her and step away, because to not do so would mean giving into the basest of my urges.

"You'll find swimsuits and bathrobes in the closet. Why don't you get changed and meet me at the hot tub?"

31

Lark

I step onto the deck and shuffle my feet in the fluffy slippers I found in the closet. By the time I'd changed my clothes and freshened up, not only had Brody brought up our luggage but he'd also managed to change his clothes and head down.

The steam rising from the hot tub is enticing. Though the man whose face and shoulders I can see above the bubbles is even more so. He's spread his sculpted arms over the rim of the hot tub. The bulges of his biceps and the length of his thick fingers do funny things to my insides. His thick hair ruffles in the breeze.

Goosebumps pepper my skin. It must be because I'm cold. It has nothing to do with how turned on I am by the sight of my gorgeous and very handsome husband waiting for me in the hot tub.

"You coming in? Or are you going to stand there staring at me?" He smirks.

The sight of his naked torso disappearing into the water affects me.

I bet I can affect him, too.

Chin up in the air, I head toward the opposite side from him. Then, placing my phone down on the deck chair, I untie the belt of my robe. It gapes at the lapels revealing my cleavage.

He stills. Arrested by the sight of my skin, his gaze rapt.

I raise one shoulder, and it slips down my arm. Then I straighten both arms, and it slithers down first one arm, then the other. The robe stops, arrested by my elbows.

He swallows. I swear, I can see the pulse at the base of his throat beat harder.

Then, with a whisper, the robe slides to the floor and pools around my ankles.

His fingers tighten around the raised lip of the hot tub. Good. And when I kick aside my fluffy slippers and step forward, his chest rises and falls. Yes! He's told me that he finds me attractive. But to see him as affected by the sight of my body as I am by his feels inevitable.

He watches me with a predatory gaze that turns my blood to lava. My heart feels like a hummingbird trapped inside my rib cage. I approach the hot tub and step inside. The hot water instantly pulses heat under my skin, and when I sink down under the bubbles, my entire being feels light. My muscles unwind. Even as I'm so conscious that his gaze is fixed on my chest.

"Take off your bikini top."

"Excuse me?"

"You heard me." He leans back with that lazy stance of a lion watching his prey.

He's going to strike, but only after he's played with me a while.

"Off. With. It."

His voice brooks instant compliance. Which is why I find myself reaching up to undo the knot around my neck. The straps fall to the sides, held up by the curves of my breasts.

"Don't stop." His voice is gritty and strained, revealing how turned on he is. It also gives me the courage to reach behind myself with trembling fingers and flick the hooks holding the top up.

My bikini top falls into the water.

I'm bared. My breasts exposed and, likely, bobbing on the surface.

"Squeeze your nipples," he growls.

Oh my God. That's so hot. Why do I find it hot?

His biceps bulge. The tendons on his neck stand out in relief. Sweat pops on my brow. It's not just the heat of the water but also that being generated between us. As if in a dream, I reach for my nipple and pluck on it. A moan spills from my lips. It feels filthy to my ears.

"Now the other one." His jaw tightens.

I raise my other hand, tending to my other nipple. Electric currents shoot out from the point of contact. I stretch my neck, leaning my head back against the edge of the hot tub. Closing my eyes, I continue to squeeze and massage my breasts. The pinpricks of pleasure build into waves which lap against my subconscious mind. I'm sinking into a quagmire of need. Of want. The emptiness yawns between my legs. I begin to squeeze my thighs together; only thick, callused fingers wrap themselves about the tops of my thighs. I snap my eyelids open and find he's right in front of me.

His hold on me stops me from pressing my legs together.

"Fuck, you're beautiful." His gravelly voice pinches my nerve endings. The way he drags his gaze over my features and down my breasts makes me feel like the most desired woman in the world.

He slides his hands over the curves of my butt cheeks and squeezes. I tremble. The heat from his palms burns through the material of my bathing suit. It feels like it's branding me.

With a flick of his wrist, he loosens the ties of my bikini bottoms. They float away.

He hitches me up, pressing me into the side of the tub. I lock my ankles behind his waist, very aware that my core is nestled against the tent at his crotch.

"Feel what you do to me, baby?"

I swallow and squirm against him. The heat of his body, and the steam from the hot tub clashing with the cool air that hits my bare shoulders, is a tapestry of opposing sensations which makes me feel like I'm high on an aphrodisiac.

He seems to grow bigger, his length stabbing against my core. He fits me over that thick column so I can feel him throb.

"I want to be inside of you, Lark." He holds my gaze. "Tell me you want me inside of you."

"I want you inside of me," I pant.

"Tell me you want me to fuck you."

"I want you to fuck me," I groan.

"Tell me you want me to kiss you."

"Yes!" I writhe in his grasp. "Yes. I want you. Please. I want you to kiss me. Now will you shut up and—"

He closes his mouth over mine. He kisses me so deeply, I feel the sensations all the way to the tips of my toes. My eyelids flutter shut. He squeezes my hips and begins to rub me up against his length. Jesus. The heat generated by the friction oozes through my bloodstream. My clit throbs. My pussy trembles. Oh God, this feels so good. How can he feel this amazing, this right, this everything as he leans his weight further into mine?

"Open your eyes," he commands.

I flicker my heavy eyelids open and stare into those glorious, piercing eyes of his. And when he continues to slide me up and down the ridge of his cock, through his swimming trunks, it feels like I'm going to explode. My belly clenches. My scalp tingles. I dig my fingers into his shoulders. "Brody, I'm so close."

"Good." He takes a deep breath and drops under the water.

"What the—" I cry out as he fixes his mouth on my pussy. I grab at his hair, and moan, feeling him flick his tongue in and out of my channel. He squeezes my butt cheeks, forcing me to push my pussy up further into his mouth. He licks up my pussy lips, curling his tongue around my clit. My entire body shudders. "Brody, please," I cry out.

He continues to eat me out, and when he slides his fingers between my butt cheeks to play with my forbidden entrance, I'm so shocked and turned on, I instantly climax. A low keening cry emerges from my lips. That tension at the base of my spine releases. It feels like rockets shooting up my spine to shatter into tiny pieces behind my eyes. And still, he doesn't stop.

He continues to lick and suck on my pussy until, when I finally slump, he rises up, draws a deep breath, then kisses me again. I taste myself on his mouth, and it's so erotic and intimate. My entire body feels like it's turned to a puddle of satisfaction.

Then, he rises to his feet with me in his arms. Without a flinch. Without any straining. And this is the second time he's done it.

Of course, when I feel the ungiving strength of his biceps under my neck, the sculpted musculature of his abs, and the brick-like formation of his pecs, it tells me I shouldn't be surprised. Man's a freakin' tower of strength.

He cradles me in his arms like I weigh nothing. It makes me feel small and delicate, and very feminine.

I reach up to cup his cheek. He turns his head and kisses my palm. My heart melts a little. It's such a romantic gesture. As is him carrying me bridal style again.

"I shouldn't like this so much," I murmur.

"Shouldn't like what?" He walks across the patio and shoulders open the door to the house.

"You. Me. You, carrying me."

He smirks. "I'm strong enough to take your weight."

"Are you calling me fat?" I huff.

He pauses inside the house, then eyes me, with an are-you-crazy? expression on his face. "I love your curves. They've haunted my dreams from the moment I saw you. Besides, I'm not missing the opportunity to have you in my arms."

My cheeks heat. His words make me feel like the most beautiful woman in the entire world. They confirm to me that I'm desirable.

As confident as I am in my professional life, I'm as insecure in my personal. My ex's cheating hurt me. His telling Brody that I wasn't good in bed eroded my shaky confidence in myself.

And my husband's words praising me seem to quieten the churning emotions in me. They make me feel seen in a way that's almost overwhelming.

Hoping to conceal my emotions from him, I dip my chin. "We're tracking water all over the house."

"It'll dry." He reaches the landing and walks down the hallway.

Entering the bedroom, he makes for the bed. "Oh no, we need to dry off first." I struggle in his grasp. "Please, we can't make the bed wet."

"You're right, I'd rather make you wet."

I flush. And chuckle. "Your dirty talking might be one of your more standout traits."

"What are the others?" He lowers me to my feet but keeps a hold of my hips.

More like, what aren't? "It might be the orgasm you gave me. Or how you agreed to Christmas decorations in the office. Or how you trusted me enough to chair the board meeting."

He eyes me with curiosity. "You want to talk about work now?" He cups my breast, then squeezes my nipple.

I shiver.

"Not particularly."

"Good. Because I need to taste you again." He picks me up bodily and throws me on the bed.

I bounce once. And when he grabs my ankles and pulls me to the edge of the bed, I yelp. "We didn't dry... Oh!" All thoughts empty from my head. For he's on his knees, between my legs, with his hands holding my thighs apart.

"Look at that pretty pussy," he growls.

I look down to find him staring at the triangle of flesh.

Instantly, I flush from my toes to the tips of my hair. My nipples tighten. My core throbs. It's like all my attention is centered on the space he's staring at.

"Brody," I whine.

"You going to be a good girl and come for me again?"

The curl of his lips, the challenge in his eyes, the hard edge in his voice... All of it pushes me to the edge. I ache to reach out and touch him. Ache to do anything to please him.

"Yesss," I hiss.

He stuffs two fingers inside my melting channel, and my eyes roll back in my head. He adds a third finger, stretching me, and the pressure on my inner walls feels so good. Incoherent sounds emerge from my mouth.

He circles my clit with his fingers.

I squirm, pushing up my pelvis, trying to get him to touch me there. Needing more, so much more. That emptiness, once again, yawns in my core. My fingertips twitch.

I dig them into the fabric of the duvet, trying to hold on while he touches me like I'm a blank sheet of paper, and his fingers are the pen he's using to write a poem into my skin.

He inspires me to be creative. He makes me dare to hope that anything is possible. Being with him sets me free in a way I could never have dreamed of.

Sparks shiver up my spine. My entire body seems to be on fire. He continues to relentlessly finger fuck me, curling his fingers inside so they brush up against that hidden part deep inside of me. That's when I stop breathing. *I'm going to come. I'm going to come.*

I only realize I've said it aloud when he suddenly pulls away from me. Cool air flows over my exposed center. *What the —?* I sit up and my gaze clashes with his.

It's like sticking my finger into an electrical socket. As much as his touch arouses me, it's the connection when our eyes meet, when I can't look away, and neither can he. When the very air between us spikes with chemistry, and static buzzes over my skin, lifting the hair at the nape of my neck. It's a euphoric feeling. One that sinks into my blood and ratchets up the anticipation in every cell in my body. I read the intent in the way he tips up one side of his mouth. Then, without any other forewarning, he slaps my pussy.

32

Brody

She falls back into the bed. Her spine curves, she tips up her chin, opens her mouth and cries out as she climaxes. Her entire body is a twisting, writhing mass of release. Fuck. The way she falls apart is the emotion writers have tried to capture with their words over the generations. It's beautiful. And touching. And passionate. And very much her.

When she begins to sob, I throw myself on my back and gather her close. "Hey, Siren, are you okay?"

She only cries harder.

She has been through so much emotionally and has kept it together, but perhaps the orgasm was the tipping point. The thing that pushed her over into sobbing with relief. If so, I'm glad she's letting it all out. I rub her back and run my fingers through her hair in an effort to calm her. She turns her face into my chest and lets the tears flow.

I hold her until she finally calms down.

"You okay?" I tuck her head under my chin.

"Yeah." She looks up at me with swollen eyes. "Sorry about that. Didn't mean to cry all over you."

"You can cry over me anytime."

She half smiles, then her chin trembles. She looks like she's about to break down again.

"Hey, hey. It's okay. I've got you."

Another teardrop rolls down her cheek. God, seeing her cry does strange things to my heart. It's as if she's feeling too much to be able to put it into words. It's as if...she's falling for me.

The way I am for her.

A surge of anticipation floods my body. I want her to want me. I want her to fall for me. Like I have for her.

Though I don't have the courage to confess my feelings for her yet. Does that make me selfish? Maybe. But I'm going to tell her how I feel.

Just as soon as I've got my thoughts together.

"I promise, everything is going to be okay."

She sniffs, then chuckles. "Somehow, hearing those words is very reassuring, though I know no one can guarantee that. Not even you, the big bad CEO."

I wipe the moisture from her cheek. "I'm certainly going to try my best to make sure you're never unhappy again."

She swallows. "You sound like a real husband."

"I *am* your real husband," I remind her.

"Oh?" She reaches up and brushes her lips over mine. "And are you going to fuck me like a real husband too?"

I throw her on her back. She yelps. I plank over her.

"Is that what you want?"

"Very much," she whispers, her eyes filling with lust.

I push off the bed and shuck off my shorts. Then I grab the condom I placed on the side of the bed and sheath myself. Climbing on the bed and planting my knees between hers, I fit the swollen head of my cock to her opening.

I stay poised over her until she meets my gaze again.

"That was, incredible," she whispers.

"Just getting started, baby." I punch my hips forward and, in a fluid motion, impale her.

She gasps and throws up a hand, as if looking for support. I grab it, weave my fingers through hers, and twist her arm over her head. I bring up her other arm and lock my fingers around her wrists holding them there.

She wriggles her hips, and I slip in deeper. She groans, her chest rising and falling. Her beautiful pink nipples beckon me. I dip my head and close my mouth around one of them. I bite down gently and am rewarded by a moan.

"Brody." She shudders.

My name from her lips adds fuel to this fire of possessiveness burning inside me. I pinch her other nipple, and her entire body jolts.

"Oh God. Oh God." She squeezes her eyelids shut.

I lick away the redness on her nipple, then slide my hand down her stomach to tweak her clit. I'm rewarded by an aftershock running through her.

Oh, yeah. *My wife is the most sensitive there.*

Her pussy flutters around my cock, squeezing down. It spikes my desire. Turns my insides to a churning mass of need. My cock lengthens. My balls feel so heavy, I'm sure I'm going to blow any moment.

Fuck, I need to have her right now.

I throw her legs over my shoulders. Then I thrust forward and sink deeper into her. She freezes; a whimper spills from her lips. The sound is a clarion call which causes me to pull back and stay poised at her entrance. "Eyes on me."

She raises her eyelids, and when our gazes meet, a silence grips me.

A peace.

I'm in the right place. This is where I'm supposed to be. Between my wife's thighs. With the snowstorm building up outside. And with my dick inside her pussy. I angle my hips, push down into the bed with my feet, and thrust forward. She pants, and the shivers gripping her tell me she's close. I begin to fuck her in earnest.

I bend over her, making sure to stare deeply into her eyes, keeping her wrists shackled, as I tunnel into her.

She presses her thighs into my shoulders, almost bent in half with how I've draped the lower half of her body over me. I lean in until my lips are positioned over hers, sharing her breath. Watching the light in her eyes scatter with each thrust of my body into hers. I own her. Possess her with each plunge of my dick. I revel in the velvety heat of her pussy sheathing me. Welcoming me inside of her. The melting cum which drips from between her thighs and rends the air with a sugary sweetness makes my mouth water. I lick her mouth, tasting that softness which is uniquely my wife.

Then I plunge inside her again, tilting my body enough to brush up against that secret spot inside her. At the same time, I pinch her clit and order, "Come."

She obliges at once. Mouth open, eyes locked with mine, her body heaves and spasms with the onslaught of her climax. She screams, and I swallow down the sound with my mouth on hers. Absorbing it into my body. The way her pussy locks around my cock and milks me as I empty myself into her.

My arms shudder, and my thighs have turned to stone. I manage to collapse on the side of the bed, our legs entangled, my shoulder brushing hers. Sweat beads my chest and trickles down my temples. I'm breathing so hard, it feels like I've run for miles. My heartbeat thunders in my ears. My blood has surely evaporated in the heat we've generated.

"Holy fuck," I gasp.

"You can say that again." Her voice is dazed.

I lift up, balance my head on my elbow and scan her flushed features. Not that I can stop myself from leaning down and kissing her breast. Instantly, her nipple tightens.

"I can't," she whispers.

"I might give you a short break." I lick the pulse that flutters at her neck, and she shudders. "Of five minutes, maybe."

"What?" She lifts her dazed eyes to my face. "I… I can't."

I chuckle, then pull out of her.

She does a slow perusal of my body, down my chest, my stomach to where my cock stands half-erect. "Damn, did you take those blue pills?" Her eyebrows shoot up.

"It's all natural. It's your nearness, baby. And the fact that all I have to do is reach out and—" I cup her pussy. "Who does this belong to?"

She swallows, a shy smile curving her lips. "You, husband."

Supporting my weight on my elbow, I scoop up some of the moisture from her pussy lips and bring it to my lips. I suck on my finger. "Who does your cum belong to."

"You." Her lips part.

"And these beauties." I bend and kiss, first one nipple, then the other. "Who do they belong to?"

"Only you," she sighs.

I press small kisses up her throat, to her lips, and sip from her mouth. A long, deep, drugging kiss that makes my head spin and has her panting. It urges my cock to full mast. "Fuck." I press my forehead into hers. "I can't get enough of you."

She frames my face with her hands. "Me neither."

"Good thing we're not going anywhere for the next few days."

"What do you mean?"

I turn my head to the window, and she follows my gaze. It's snowing. White powdery flakes are coming down so hard; they obscure the lake and the hills we were able to see earlier.

"Whoa, it's a snowstorm?"

"Didn't think it'd come down quite that thick." I slide from the bed, pull off the condom with care, tie it up, and drop it in the bin.

I hold my hand out to her. She takes it, and I pull her to her feet. "We have enough food to last us for at least a week."

"Aren't we expected back for the new year?"

I shake my head. "Gramps made it clear I should take as long as I need."

"As long as you need for what?"

I allow myself a small smile. "To convince you to become CEO of the company."

33

Lark

Oh my God. Oh my God. My heart is racing so hard, I'm sure it's going to break through my rib cage. He offered me the CEO job.

He offered *me* my dream job. Surely, this can't be happening. Am I dreaming?

But no. Taking in the soft smile on his face and the seriousness in his eyes, I know, he means in.

But why?

"Are you sure? You've been running this company for the past two years. You turned it around. Made it more than profitable. And now you want me to take over?"

After he dropped that bombshell on me, I pulled on one of his sweatshirts and he pulled on a pair of gray sweatpants with a T-shirt before he led me down to the kitchen.

I mourned that he was covering up his physique, but damn, did he fill out a black T-shirt in a way that lit that fire in my veins all over again.

I offered to cook us an early dinner, and he pulled out a bottle of red from the wine collection in the cellar. He pours it into two glasses, walks over and hands me one.

"Remember what you said in your interview?" He looks into my eyes.

"That I wanted to be CEO." I take the glass from him. "And I stand by it. But to do it so soon? I don't feel ready."

He cups my cheek. "I didn't feel ready when Arthur asked me to be CEO either. But that didn't stop me."

"And you did an amazing job too."

"Thank you." He holds my gaze. "It's been two years since I took over the position. The company has a healthy bottom line. It's poised for the next leap of growth."

Needing to put distance between us as I think about what he's saying, I step back, so he has to lower his hand.

Buying some more time, I take a sip of my wine, then place the glass down. "You've done the hard work in growing the company thus far. You should be in charge of the next round of expansion."

"It's precisely because I've brought it this far that I need to step aside," he muses as if he's speaking his thoughts aloud.

I begin to season some chicken thighs with salt, pepper, and oregano. In a large pan, I heat olive oil and place the chicken in it. The delicious smell of frying chicken and the sound that accompanies the searing fills the air.

"It's precisely because you brought the company this far you need to stay on." I sear the chicken until it's golden brown, then remove it and slide it onto a plate.

"It doesn't excite me as much as it used to. The excitement I felt in the early days of leading the growth phase has faded. I don't feel as charged up as I used to."

I mull over his words as I add a knob of butter to the same pan, then the chopped garlic. I stir it, letting the garlic brown before I add the barley grain-shaped pasta, also known as orzo.

The nutty scent of the frying orzo fills the kitchen.

I add the vegetable stock, then the peppers and broccoli I

chopped earlier. I cover it and let the contents cook before I turn to him.

"Are you saying you don't want to be involved with the company, at least, not in a full-time capacity?"

"Exactly." There's a pleased expression on his face.

I feel unreasonably happy that he approves of my question. It's almost euphoric. How weird is that?

"I want to focus on what I love." One side of his mouth tips up.

"Which is working with military vets and, of course, startups?"

I remember the satisfied look on his face when he shared how he employed people from the forces and preferred to fund startups that provide better intel for troops.

"Exactly." His eyes light up. "I want to move away from the day-to-day. Managing Human Resources, employee remuneration and office systems, not to mention tracking sales, finalizing marketing campaigns, etcetera, etcetera." He wrinkles his nose like he's smelled something bad.

"So the stuff that keeps the company running smoothly?" I roll my eyes.

He chuckles. "I prefer the fun stuff."

"Like dealing with high-growth new ventures?" It's not something I enjoy.

He, on the other hand, thrives on the challenge.

"I find these interactions adrenaline-filled." He raises a shoulder. "I love the thrill of finding a new idea that could make a difference to the world, then testing it from all angles and deciding which enterprise to back. It gives me the rush of completing the deal. And the satisfaction of backing a company from the start and building it up. It's almost as good as—" He frowns.

A confused expression enters his eyes.

"You were going to say as good as sex, weren't you?" I scan his features.

"I was"—he lowers his chin—"until I realized, it's not true anymore."

"Oh." I swallow. A sudden heat fills my chest. Is he implying that

—nah, surely not. Not when he said he could never fall in love with me.

"Making love to you is the most sublime feeling in this world. It's as if I've been waiting my entire life to be inside of you." He looks genuinely confused. And I can't help feeling sorry for him. Because my instinct tells me what he can't admit to himself, let alone to the world. That he's falling for me. As I have for him.

I nestle the chicken into the orzo. Then cover and lower the flame so it can simmer.

"You sound like it's not something you expected."

"On the contrary." He guides me to one of the barstools next to the island. Before I can protest, he hoists me onto it.

The way he handles me like I weigh next to nothing makes me feel protected. It gives me the confidence that this man can take care of me. It's the ultimate turn on.

He prowls over to where I've left my glass of wine. Returning with it, he places it on the counter. Then slips onto the stool next to me. Turning, he parts his legs and drags my bar stool forward into the space.

"Whoa." I squeak. Not sure why, but I feel nervous.

He looks deeply into my eyes as if trying to decipher some puzzle, some truth which, perhaps, I haven't admitted to myself yet? I swallow. My stomach flip-flops. To mask my skittishness, I reach for my glass of wine and take a sip.

"You're staring." I savor the wine and set the glass aside again.

"You're beautiful."

I flush deeply. "Thank you." I curse myself for feeling like I'm on a first date. Except, this is my husband. And he's fucked me. And I want more. A lot more.

"And you're distracting me from our earlier discussion."

"That's all you." I scoff.

"So, you'll take on the role of CEO?"

I hesitate. It is what I want. But there's a difference between wanting something and having it handed to you, as I'm finding out. I think I need more experience before I take on that role. Of course, Brody will be there to guide me. But it feels daunting.

When I open my mouth to speak, he must sense what I'm going to say, for he holds up his hand. "At least, think about it."

Holy stocking stuffers! He's persistent. It's one of the things I admire about him. I allow myself a small smile. "Okay."

Some of the tension fades from his shoulders. "Now that we have *that* out of the way." He tucks a strand of hair behind my ear. "You should know that you felt incredible around my cock."

It's a 360-degree change in topic, but I'm not surprised. Not with that current of electricity simmering between us whenever we're together. Still, hearing him say those words aloud makes me flush.

The need to duck my head and hide from his piercing gaze is almost overwhelming. But damn, if I'm going to give in to it. I'm not going to shy away from my sexuality. Or this hunger he's provoked in me. Besides, we *are* on our honeymoon. Which, by its very nature, is meant for exploring carnal desires. So no, I'm not going to turn into a wallflower.

"You felt incredible inside me." I tip up my chin. "I could feel every inch of your hard, ridged shaft."

It feels forbidden to voice how I felt, but also, strangely liberating. And when he drags his hot gaze down to my chest and doesn't move it from there, my nipples tighten. My breasts seem to swell.

"Not complaining about the orgasms, either." I aim what I hope is a cheeky smile at him.

"Oh?" He looks a little taken aback but also recovers quickly. He drags his knuckles down my cheek, then my throat, until he rests them against the neckline of the sweatshirt.

"What else did you like about what I did to you?" He cups my breast, and I feel his touch all the way to the tips of my toes.

"I liked the way you took control. How you carried me to bed. How you threw me down on it, how you pulled me to the edge with my ankles, and how you ate me out."

I confess that I, too, like being in control—at work—which is why I thrive on to-do lists and schedules. I assumed I'd be that way in all of my personal relationships too, but boy, was I wrong. In the bedroom, I want my husband to take charge. I want him to know exactly what turns me on. I want to trust that he'll know exactly how far he can push me without hurting me, so as to draw out my pleasure.

And God, by the way he handles my body, I think he knows exactly what I want.

"Hmm." He pinches my nipple.

I moan, pushing my chest forward, hoping to feel more of his touch.

He clicks his tongue. "Oh, no. You don't tell me what to do."

"But I want more." I scowl.

"More what?" He rubs his thumb over my nipple, and I swear, it throbs.

"More of your touch. More of your mouth on me. Your fingers and your cock inside me." I sway toward him, unable to resist this draw, which seems to have hooked its claws inside me and will never let go. "Brody, please," I whisper.

"Hmm." He places his other hand on my hip. "What do you want, baby?"

I let my gaze roam over his chest, the sculpted ridges of his abs, brick-like and impossibly defined. Every breath he takes draws my attention lower. "I want you," I whisper, the words trembling between hunger and surrender.

"You'll have to be more specific than that."

"I want"—I lower my gaze to the tent which stretches his crotch, and my mouth waters—"I want to taste you."

I never wanted to do this with my ex. But with my husband, I'm so turned on.

He makes me feel wanted in a way that steals my breath. I adore how he's always focused on my pleasure, my release, my unraveling.

I want to return the favor. I want to watch him lose control the way he makes me fall apart.

Something like satisfaction seems to ripple over him. Once more, I have this unreasonable feeling of having done something that earns me his approval. It amps up my pulse rate and pushes up my heartbeat, so I can feel my blood pumping in my ears.

He leans back in his seat and widens the space between his legs. "What are you waiting for?"

I instantly reach over and grasp the ridge outlined at the crotch of his sweatpants.

He hisses. His stomach ripples. And when I squeeze up the column, he grows rigid.

"Fuck," he growls. "Take it out."

I tug on his waistband, and when he raises his hips, I slide it down his thighs. Instantly, his dick stands to attention against his stomach. Large. Long. Swollen. With a purple head and droplets of cum visible.

"You're big." I swallow.

"You knew that already."

Yes, I took him inside me, but noting his girth now, I wonder how he fit. As I stare, he seems to grow bigger. I gulp.

"On your knees," he growls.

His low, hard voice, and the absolute assurance that I'll obey him, turns my insides to putty. My legs seem to fold under me. He pushes the stool backward as I slide down to kneel in front of him. In this position, his crotch is at eye level. Which means, I'm directly facing his cock. He cups the back of my head, his touch gentle. He rubs his thumb into my scalp. It's almost soothing, and gives me the courage to lean forward. I close my fingers around his length and lick up the back of his shaft.

"Bloody hell." His entire body shudders.

And with that, a calm flows through me, infusing me with a sense of power. To have this big, beautiful man become putty under my fingers is the most incredible feeling to envelop me. I squeeze my fingers around the root of his cock, then lick up the column.

He jerks his hips forward as if he's unable to stop himself. His fingers dig into my scalp. He tugs on my hair, and pinching sensations spark in my scalp. My clit throbs. It's as if there's a direct connection between his touch and that part of me. I swirl my tongue over the sensitive head of his shaft. He groans and throws his head back, exposing the strong column of his neck.

A feeling of greed grips me. I want to pleasure him. I want to make him fall apart the way he made me earlier. I begin to lick on his cock in earnest. His body is so rigid his muscles might have turned to stone.

With his other hand he holds onto the edge of the counter, the skin stretched across his knuckles.

A feeling of exultation swoops through me. I half rise, so I'm crouching, giving me the height needed to close my mouth around his cock.

"Lark, fuck." His voice is strained. As are the tendons of his neck. I look up to find an almost agonized expression on his features. His jaw is clenched. A nerve prominent at his temple.

He's looking at me with avarice and helplessness. A combination which draws more moisture from my pussy. My belly trembles.

I reach down to touch myself, but he clicks his tongue. "Stop. Your orgasms are mine."

I pause, unable to disobey his command, then decide to pay him back. I tilt my head and take him down my throat.

34

Brody

"Holy hell." I grit my teeth against the pleasure shooting up my spine. I love her pussy. But the hot wetness of her mouth almost undoes me. I hold onto the counter like I'm drawing strength from it. The way she slurps on my dick tightens the knot of desire behind my balls.

My thighs have turned to stone.

The tension building under my skin is a living, breathing thing threatening to seize up every muscle in my body. I draw in a deep breath, fight for calm, but when she drags her teeth over the sensitive skin of the head, fire ignites in my blood. I tighten my hold on her head and pull her back gently. Enough to stay balanced at the rim of her mouth.

"Breathe through your nose." I wait for her to widen her eyes, acknowledging that she's heard me. Then I move her forward, enough to slide down her throat.

Spit drools down her chin. Her throat is snug enough that I feel the walls press down on my shaft. My balls harden until it feels like I'm carrying a shit ton of weights between my legs. Fucking fuck. I'm going to come.

I pull back, giving myself a little time to recover, and search her features. She draws in a few breaths, then I ease her forward. Farther down than earlier.

I close my fingers around her throat, feeling myself ensconced. And that's so damn intimate. Makes me feel so much closer to her. It leaves me reeling. It's erotic in a way that wrecks me.

It's not only the heat of it. It's the closeness. The connection. Deeper than touch. More personal than breath. It's that over-whelming sense of our souls fusing together which tells me I'm fucked. The realization sinks in. Warning bells clang in my head. But I'm too far gone.

"I'm going to come," I manage to warn her, when my balls draw up tight. I lock eyes with her—and that's when I see it. A single tear slips from the corner of her eye. That's all it takes. I let out a muted cry as I spill my release down her throat.

I don't stop. I keep coming, long and hard, until it overflows her mouth and spills from her lips. Only then do I pull out. I scoop up the mess with my fingers, sliding it back into her mouth.

She swallows.

Her swollen lips are testimony to how intensely she sucked me off. A crackling sensation seems to break through my rib cage. The walls I've built for most of my adult life seem to shake. With my hold around the nape of her neck, I haul her to her feet, lower my chin, and kiss her deeply. I taste my cum in her mouth.

Sweet desire, need, tenderness. A miasma of emotions tightens my throat.

I release her and stare deeply into her eyes. Wanting to tell her how much I love what she did to me. I open my mouth, when she glances at the range and her eyes widen.

"My orzo."

She pulls out of my grasp, races over to the stove and shuts off the flame. Then takes the pan off the hob and sets it on the counter. She pulls off the lid, and her shoulders sag with relief.

"Thank God, it hasn't burned."

She plates out the food, adds a twist of lime to the orzo, along with the fresh tomato and rocket leaf salad she whipped up first.

Then she walks over to slide the plates onto the counter in front of me.

I put myself to rights and drag her stool back beside me, by which time, she's added cutlery next to the plates.

She takes her seat, glances at my plate, then at my face. The anxiety on her features tells me she wants to know what I think of the food.

I scoop up some of it and place it on my tongue. The rich crispy taste of the chicken combined with the earthy taste of the orzo and the sweet-sharp taste of the garlic seeps into my tongue.

I lick the food off the tines of my fork and am rewarded by the flare of her eyes.

I allow a small smile to curve my lips, then go back for another mouthful. This time, I also spear a portion of the salad. The burst of sweetness and acidity from the tomatoes cuts through the creamy starchiness of the orzo.

"Mmm, where did you learn to cook like this?" I chew and swallow.

She blinks as if coming out of a trance, then glances down at her plate. "I moved to this country to study on a scholarship. I didn't have the money to go out shopping or to the night clubs. I learned to look up recipes and buy marked down food at the supermarkets. If you go late enough in the day, they mark down the stuff that's about to expire. I found bargains on the good stuff. Then cooked for myself. It was a great way to unwind after a hard day. It also meant I ate healthy."

I scoop up more of the food, chew and swallow. When I catch her watching again, I smirk.

"Yes, you look sexy when you eat." She tosses her head. "Don't have to look so pleased about it."

"I love you watching me. Love it more that you get turned on when you do."

She allows herself a small smile then eats a few mouthfuls.

When we've both finished what's on our plates she reaches for her glass of wine and takes a sip. "Did you mean it?"

"You mean, you being the CEO?" Without waiting for her nod of acknowledgment, I add, "I wouldn't have said it otherwise."

"I'm not saying I'm not up for the job."

"That's good." Damn, her self-confidence turns me on.

She narrows her gaze. "But I have to ask, why me?"

"Why not you?"

"Because I'm your wife?" Her gaze darts to the rings on her left hand.

"Yes."

She jerks her chin up with something like shock in her eyes. "But that's—"

"And because you're the most qualified for the job. And you have shown that you can take over the running of the company."

"Hmm." Her eyes light up.

She's pleased with my praise.

"You handled the board meeting without much of a briefing. You put in the hours. Studied the issues involved. And had the mettle to hold your own against senior members who have years of experience over me."

"All of that is true. But I have to ask why you chose me over those who have been with the company far longer than me, and who could do the job."

I set down my fork. "They may be more seasoned, but what they lack is the firepower, the freshness, the ability to look at situations and come up with out-of-the-box thinking, which you can."

She rubs at her forehead. "Not that I care particularly, and of course, it's not anything I'm not used to, but there are going to be some very upset people if I take that role."

It pisses me off to think of all the misogyny and ill will she's faced to get this far in her career. And yes, I'll be giving her a leg up when I make her CEO. But she'll bring a fresh perspective to the role. One it will benefit from.

She gives me a look. "You'll be off finalizing funding for startups while I'll be putting out the day-to-day fires."

"And closing deals, *and* overseeing expansions like the one in Asia. You enjoy the adrenaline." I lower my chin. "People who want to be critical will be, no matter what. You've shown you have the courage to hold your own. That will take you far."

Her features soften. But the dip between her eyebrows tells me that she's not completely on board.

I take her hand in mine, wanting to maintain the connection. And missing the feel of her skin, the taste of her mouth, the sweet scent of her body, which is etched into every cell of my body.

"What if I told you that Arthur is supportive of your taking over as CEO?"

She reels back. "You're kidding, right?"

When she tries to pull her hand from mine, I hold on. Then place my other hand over hers, so her palm is caught between mine.

"It's true."

"Oh." Her eyes widen in surprise. "Your grandfather thinks I should be CEO?"

I smile. "News of how well you handled the sharks in the boardroom meeting travelled up to him. He has enough eyes and ears in the organization that stories of your capabilities and astute decision-making reached him almost instantly."

"Oh." Some of the tension goes out of her. "That's huge praise, coming from him. And frankly, a lot to take in."

"I understand." I rub my thumb over her knuckles and am rewarded by her shiver.

Damn, I feel triumphant that she's so responsive to my touch.

"When we spoke before we left on our honeymoon, he told me he'd throw his weight behind my decision. He'll make it clear to the entire Davenport Group how much he respects your astuteness and values your judgment. And if Arthur vouches for you, there'll be no doubt in anyone's mind that you're the right choice for the position."

Her features turn pensive. "Is he doing this because—"

"—because you're my wife?" I laugh. "Can you see Arthur risking his reputation for anyone else, even if they're family?"

Her expression lightens. "No. He's someone who knows himself and who can't be swayed."

"Exactly." I pull her into my arms and am relieved when she comes willingly. "I wasn't surprised he supported me in making you CEO. It first crossed my mind when I saw you at the head of the table handling those men like a badass."

She smiles. "Badass, huh?"

"It was a real turn on." I pull her into my lap.

Her cheeks turn a pretty shade of pink. Her expression is pleased, then she tosses her head like she's trying to hide it.

"I was so proud of you then. I'm even more proud of you now. You're talented, baby. You're good at what you do. We make a good team. And honestly, I'm bored with the CEO role. I want to focus on what excites me, something I'll lead for not only Davenport Capital, but for the entire group."

"So, your role would expand?"

He nods. "It would be a promotion, of sorts. One I can't take on, unless you agreed to be CEO. So, you'd be doing me a favor." I rub my nose against hers. "What do you say?"

35

Lark

Make sure I have enough festive snacks for 'holiday emergencies.'
—From Lark's Christmas to-do list

Maybe it's because he referred to the company as 'our' company. Or because he admitted to being turned on by watching me in action. Or because he seemed genuine when he said he believes I have it in me to be CEO. Or because Arthur made it clear he'll back me, and that's no small thing. Whatever the reason, I find myself considering the possibility seriously.

"I'll think about it." I frame his face with my hands.

"Good." He kisses me firmly.

Then he slides off his stool and, holding me, he begins to walk away from the kitchen.

"Where are we going?"

"To open your Christmas present, of course."

"Oh." I stare at him, stricken. "I didn't get you a Christmas present."

"You're my Christmas present." He smirks.

I want to roll my eyes. But his bravado can't hide the sincerity in his eyes. "You've already given me a Christmas present by asking me to be CEO."

"That's nothing compared to what I'm giving you next." He reaches the bedroom and, after another kiss which makes my head spin, he lowers me to the bed.

He grasps the hem of my sweatshirt and pulls it up and over my head, then rolls my panties down my legs. He slides off the bed and stands at the foot. He sweeps his gaze over me, leaving goosebumps in its wake.

"Stay there." He points at me, before he marches to the closet. As if I'd go anywhere else. He emerges holding several neck ties in his hand.

"You carried neck ties in your luggage? Were you expecting to wear suits?"

"That's not the only reason to use neck ties." He reaches me, then surveys me up and down. His eyes glint. Oh no. I so don't trust that look.

"What are you up to?" I scowl.

He cups his chin, then tilts his head, first this way. Then that. "I want to tie you up."

My jaw drops. "Excuse me?"

He slides one of the ties through his fingers, his movements controlled. Quiet authority clings to his powerful frame in a way that turns my throat dry. I am so transfixed by his actions that when he speaks, I jolt.

"Remember what I told you was my specialty in the Royal Marines?" he murmurs.

"Tying knots," I recall.

"Turns out, a fringe benefit to having that expertise is that I get to use it in the bedroom, too."

"Oh." A shiver of anticipation curls in my belly. "You're really going to tie me up?"

"If you feel ready for it."

I purse my lips. How would it feel to have him practice his exper-tise on me? Not that he needs the additional help the ties would offer him. Just his fingers, his lips, his mouth, and that gorgeous cock of his were enough to bring me to ecstasy. But the thought of him tying me up first? Whoa.

That certainly amps up the need inside me. The curl of anticipa-tion turns into a river of desire which drips from between my legs.

As if he senses my heightened lust, his nostrils flare. "You like the idea, don't you?"

I nod.

"Good girl."

A surge of delight pushes the tension from my shoulders and allows my weight to sink into the bed. I've pleased him. And that makes me happy.

"Stretch your arms over your head," he orders.

Instantly, I oblige. The position thrusts my breasts up into the air. Makes my nipples tighten further. It might be how he devours me with his eyes, but I feel free. Wanton. Rid of whatever reservations may have held me back from giving myself up to this man who's my husband.

Or it might simply be that his complete self-assurance in taking charge, and deciding he wanted to tie me to his bed and have his way with me seems to satisfy some deeply hidden craving inside of me.

Something I've never acknowledged before. Something I didn't think I ached for. But given the hunger unfurling in my belly, I know I want a taste. To experience. To find out how it's going to change me when he finally touches me.

"Part your legs for me," he commands in a smooth, dark voice.

It flows over me like melted chocolate, sinks into my skin, and oozes through my veins like syrup through honeycomb grooves.

And when he fixes his gaze on the melting flesh between my legs, I realize, I've moved them apart without conscious thought.

His throat flexes. And when I look below his waistband, his gray sweatpants are tented at the crotch. His cock outlined through the fabric ramps up my craving.

When I begin to sit up, he clicks his tongue. "Stay where you are."

I freeze.

He walks around the bed to stand next to the headboard.

He pulls off his T-shirt, exposing his ripped chest. Then places one knee on the mattress, leans over, and loops one of the ties—the one he wore at our wedding—around my wrist. Then he knots it around the slats in the headboard.

His thick fingers move gracefully like the legs of a ballerina across the stage. He tugs on the restraint.

The silk slithers against my skin, sending goosebumps scattering from the contact.

"Not too tight?" He glances at me.

I shake my head.

Whatever he sees in my gaze has him lower his head and kiss me. It's a firm meeting of our lips, where he takes charge and plunders my mouth like he's a lion lapping water from an oasis. My head spins. My entire body turns into a stream of longing.

I begin to squeeze my legs together, then gasp, for he straightens, then moves over to grasp my ankle.

He fastens it to the foot of the bed, then circles around and uses another tie to restrain my other ankle.

When he's done, he steps back and surveys me splayed out for his delectation. The touch of his eyes on my body feels physical. Enough to make me flinch yet also bloom with the satisfaction of being at the focus of his attention. It feels right in a way I can't even begin to verbalize. It's a feeling in my guts, which spreads to my extremities. A sensation of being one with the darkest, most hidden parts of me.

He reaches into the bedside drawer and pulls out a vibrator, along with a tube of lube.

My breath hitches. My stomach tightens. "Are you going to use that on me?" I squeak.

"Will you let me use it on you?" He holds my gaze.

The expression in his eyes asks: *Do you trust me?* The question isn't spoken aloud, but I hear it anyway. I nod.

His nostrils flare.

"That's my good girl."

A moan leaves my lips. I realize, I'd do anything to hear him say those two words over and over again.

The bed dips, and he kneels between my legs.

He leans over me and pours a drop of lube on each of my nipples. Then on my clit. I've hardly processed that when he switches on the vibrator. The low buzzing is as if a million bees have fluttered their wings over my nerve endings. I can't stop myself from shivering in anticipation. He hasn't even moved, and my thigh muscles clench. My shoulders tremble. I can't wait to see what he's going to do with the wand. At the same time, I dread it.

I'm so turned on, I'm going to come quickly. I'm embarrassed by how turned on I am.

He touches the toy to my nipple, and I buck my body. "Oh my God," I pant.

He pulls back, giving me time to adjust to the sensations pulsing from the point of contact.

"You're so sensitive," he says with satisfaction. "If I were to touch your clit, how long would you hold out."

"Not long," I admit.

"Hmm." He firms his lips. "You can't come until I give you permission."

"What?" I swallow. "How is that even possible? I'm so close."

"You are." He reaches down, scoops my cum from my inner thigh, and holds up his glistening finger, like it's a trophy. "Which is why you can't come."

I scowl. "How does that make any sense? Also, it's physically impossible for me to wait until you tell me to."

His lips curl. "We'll see, shall we?"

36

Brody

"Your body knows I'm your master."

My statement might sound arrogant, but it's the truth. And she knows it. As evidenced by the doubt that flashes across her features.

She huffs. "We'll see."

In reply, I touch the vibrator to her other nipple.

Her back arches off the bed. "Brody," she cries out.

The sound of my name from my wife's lips is a clarion call to the beast inside me. I lower my head and close my mouth over hers. I draw in her breaths, feast on her taste, and swipe my tongue over the seam of her lips.

When I pull back, she stares at me dazedly. A stunned look on her features. I've pleasured her. And damn, if that doesn't feel incredible. To worship at the altar of her satisfaction is what gives *me* the greatest satisfaction.

I slide down her chest, pressing a kiss to the valley between her breasts, then lower down in the center of her rib cage. I lick into her belly button and am rewarded with a shudder. And when I reach the hallowed pink flesh between her thighs, her entire body shudders.

"Oh, Brody," she moans my name again. And goddamn, I grow even harder.

I blow gently over her clit, and she writhes, then pushes up her pelvis so the sweet scent of her pussy envelops me. My blood drains to my cock. I'm not going to last much longer. Which means, I'd better speed this along and get her off first.

I need her to come at least thrice before I fuck her. I'm too much of a fucking coward to say I love her, but maybe I can show her.

I can make her orgasm until her entire body is a melting mass of desire, and every cell in her body has my name imprinted within.

I sit up, touch the vibrator to her clit, and she cries out. She thrashes her head from side to side and curves her spine. Without giving her time to recover I slip the vibrator inside her. It slips in easily; that's how wet she is.

She spreads her legs wider apart—there's enough stretch to the rope to allow that—and tips up her chin.

"Ohmigod." She huffs. Then shudders again. I pull out the vibrator then slide it back in again. This time, it slides in even deeper.

"Brody that...feels...soooo good."

I watch her features, taking in the flushed skin, the strained tendons of her neck, the bead of sweat sliding down to pool in the hollow at the base of her throat. "You're so fucking gorgeous."

Holding the vibrator steady, I lean over her and suck gently on her nipple. She's so sensitized that instantly goosebumps pepper her chest. She writhes again. "It's too much."

"Good."

"I...I don't know how much more I can take."

"You'll take everything I give you and you'll do so happily," I growl.

She bites down on her lower lip in reply. I release it from her teeth. "Only I get to hurt you, baby."

Her chest rises and falls. She exhales and shivers.

"Your body belongs to me. You feel me? Answer me, Lark."

"Yesss," she hisses back. "Yes."

"Good." I pull out the vibrator and this time when I touch it to her clit, her eyes roll back in her head. The pulse at the base of her throat speeds up further and I know she's close.

I switch off the vibrator and set it aside. Then I part her pussy lips and lick her from the eyelet between her arse cheeks to her clit.

A long low moan emerges from her gorgeous mouth. Her fingers flutter. I feel her touch as if she's carded them through my hair. This is the connection I felt the first time I saw her. This resonance with her is what drew me to her.

I slurp at her pussy lips savoring the sweetness of her arousal. She tastes like every single wet dream come true. Like the elixir of everything sinful. Better than a cold beer at the end of a long hard marathon. She tastes like she's mine. My wife.

The thought jolts longing through my veins. I begin to lick and sip from her pussy. Taking in the strain on her face. The way she tugs at her bindings, wanting to get free. She arches her back, pushing her shoulders into the mattress. And when her mouth opens in a silent cry I know she's about to come.

With timing born of a sixth sense I pull back.

Instantly, she subsides. Her eyelids flutter open. "What are you—?"

I sit back. "You may come now." I slap her pussy.

She orgasms instantly. And so suddenly her entire body freezes for a long few seconds. Then with a shudder she floats back to earth. Her body slumps. But I'm not done yet. I scoop up her cum and smear it on the vibrator. Then I hold it to the entrance of her back channel.

A tremor runs through her. Her thighs quiver. And when I ease the wand through the forbidden opening, her frame quakes. The device slips in through the ring of muscle. She gasps. Her eyelids flutter open, the pupils so blown, there's barely a circle of green around her iris. Our gazes meet, and the air turns electric.

"You're so fucking turned on." Satisfaction drips from my words. Surely, there can't be anything as gratifying as seeing my wife so ready and open and waiting for what I'm going to do next. I hold the wand in place, allowing her to adjust to the girth. When her body begins to relax the vibrator slips in further. I touch that secret space deep inside her, and her breath catches.

Her cheeks deepen in color, the flush spreading to her décolletage. Her entire body seems to vibrate, and she pants loudly.

I pull the vibrator out, then slide it in again, once again rubbing up against her P-spot.

"Come for me," I order.

She cries out and I'm rewarded by seeing her fall apart as she climaxes. Her features scrunch up, her breasts heave, and her nipples are so hard, they could, surely, cut diamonds. Her body is perfectly arched as she shudders and whimpers, then slowly collapses onto the bed.

I slowly ease the vibrator from her and set it on the bedside table.

Then I lean over her and untie first, her arms, and then, her legs. I massage her wrists and ankles, making sure the ties haven't left any marks, and that her blood is circulating properly.

I watch her features until she finally focuses her gaze on me.

"Hi." I brush my lips over hers.

"Hi," she whispers back.

"How are you doing?"

She sighs. "I feel like I'm coming back to earth after flying through the skies wearing wings. You give the best orgasms, Brody."

"That might be the best praise I've received in my life." I chuckle. "And I'm not done yet."

Her eyes widen in horror. "What do you mean?"

"I promised myself I'd make you come one more time before I fuck you."

"One more time?" She begins to inch away. "I can't do that."

"You can. And you will." I flip her over.

She gasps. "Ugh. This is going to kill me." She tries to crawl away this time.

In response, I yank her close, then press my palm into the small of her back. "I won't let you die sweetheart. And I'm going to make sure you enjoy every last second of your climax."

She looks at me over her shoulder. "That sounds like a threat."

"More like a reminder to myself that I can't let you down."

Her features soften. "You're a generous lover."

"That's because I love your body." *Fuck, I used the 'L' word.*

But at least, it was in the right context. I meant, I love her curves. No way, could I have slipped up and used it in a different context. Not possible.

Not when I've known this woman for such a short time. Though I did propose to her within weeks of meeting her. But that was out of necessity.

Besides, if I were in love with her, I wouldn't be able to withstand losing her when she realizes she made a mistake marrying me on a rebound. And those don't usually last.

She's the best executive assistant I could have imagined, and I didn't want her falling apart because some douchebag dumped her. I wanted to help her save face. Not to mention, Arthur insisted I marry, and oddly, he chose her.

Besides, I'm probably so drunk on the power I hold over her orgasms that my brain cells tripped over themselves. Yep, that's all it is.

She frowns. "Brody, you okay?"

"Of course." I smack her butt cheek to prove it.

A full body shiver grips her.

I slap her other butt cheek. This time, she swallows, and a soft sound escapes her.

"Damn, you like that."

She looks like she's going to deny it, then changes her mind. She nods slowly.

"I'm going to spank you baby. Gonna work you over real nice. I'm gonna make you feel real good, sweetheart. Would you like that?"

This time, she can't stop the eagerness in her eyes when she nods.

"Good girl."

She swallows. Her breathing speeds up. Damn, could she be any more perfect?

I grip her hips and tug so she's on her knees, with her butt in the air. Then I push down into the small of her back. I urge her to flatten her cheek into the mattress. She looks up at me with anticipation. That, and the pear-shaped outline of her backside, almost undoes me. I'm so hard, it feels like my balls have turned to stone and weigh me down. *One more time. Get your wife off one more time, and then you can bury your cock in her sweet, tight pussy.*

I grab handfuls of her fleshy butt and squeeze. She moans. And when I bite into one of the luscious cheeks, she whimpers.

I sit back on my haunches, grasping her waist to steady her. Then I spank her butt. One cheek, then the other. Then the first. Each time my palm comes into contact with her curved rear, the sound echoes around the room.

Her gasps and groans fill the air. The sounds are so erotic, they amp up my horniness to fever pitch. When I've counted to ten, I stop. Then slide my fingers down between her pussy lips. She's so wet her cum slides down my palm. I bring my fingers to my mouth and lick it off. "You're so fucking sweet."

She shudders. "Brody, I need you inside me."

"Soon baby." I spank her butt. "Just as soon as you come."

I increase the speed of my ministrations. Alternating her butt cheeks for another five slaps.

"Oh my God," She tries to pull away, but I'm holding her down. So she simply writhes in place. Her back curves and once again I know she's close. I raise my hand and bring it down with enough force on her backside that her entire body moves forward.

"Come. Now," I order.

And with a choking sound she shatters. Her knees give way from under her. I take her weight and gently flip her over. She lays there panting, breathy sounds emerging from her lips. She looks spent, a look of such peace on her features, her eyelids half open, watching me from somewhere in subspace. And it's the fact that I've given her so much pleasure that threatens to send me over the edge.

I lean in, fit my cock to her slit, and in a single fluid motion, impale her.

37

Lark

He buries himself inside me and it's as if I'm forced right back into my body. Like someone shot a syringe loaded with adrenaline into my heart. My pulse rate rockets. My blood begins to flow again. I bring my arms and legs up and wrap them around him, wanting to hold him so very close. He seems to understand my need and stays still, his dick buried in me, his balls flat against my pussy, his gaze holding mine, his lips above mine. We stare at each other. The world seems to slow.

Our breathing, our heart beats, the rise and fall of our chests synchronize. One life. Two bodies. It's the most intimate I've ever been with anyone. More intimate than the times with my ex.

This feels different. More heartfelt.

Maybe it's because of the number of times he made me come, making me feel disjointed. My bones have liquefied. My brain cells have turned to water. But my heart? It beats strongly in my chest. And my skin is very aware of his nearness, and the weight of his body on mine. And I feel him throb inside me. And grow bigger. And push against my inner walls. I feel pinned in place. Caught in his magnetic gaze.

Then he lowers his chin and gently brushes his lips over mine. His touch is so soft. So sweet. So raw. It undoes me. I've never felt this close to someone else. It must be because my emotions are so close to the surface that I feel tears well up. A droplet squeezes out from the corner of my eye.

"Are you okay?" He searches my features. "Tell me, Lark?"

"I'm not." I sniffle.

Alarm whips through his gaze.

I can't let him know how strong my emotions are right now. I'm in love with him, but he might never love me. I can't tell him that. Instead, I use the one thing that will distract him: sex.

"Because you haven't started fucking me properly."

The tension leaves his shoulders. One side of his lips quirk. Then his biceps flex as he shifts his weight. He pulls out of me, then thrusts back inside with enough force that the entire bed moves. He impales me and hits my G-spot. Shock waves of heat whip up my spine. I can feel it all the way to the roots of my hair.

"Wow." I grab hold of his shoulders and hold on.

"I'll take that as an affirmation." He pulls out again, then plunges into me. This time, the headboard slams into the wall.

Once again, he hits my G-spot. I tremble and lock my ankles around his waist. The fact that I can see his eyes, and the look of ecstasy on his features, adds to the feeling that this is special.

He continues to tunnel into me.

The ridge of his pelvis brushes up against my clit, and the shock waves turn into a tsunami of sensations which crowd my mind and shut down any possibility of thinking.

The next time he pushes into me, I tighten my inner walls around him. He falters. "Fuck, Siren, what are you doing to me?"

I love that his jaw is tight. And the nerve that throbs at his temple tells me how affected he is, too.

The tendons of his beautiful throat stand out in relief. And his biceps flex as he holds up the weight of his body. When I run a finger over his shoulder and down the center of that impressive chest, the muscles jump underneath his skin.

Damn, he may hold the control, but I have power, too. I circle his very male nipple, and he makes a growling sound at the back of his throat. It delights me and turns me on further. Enough for my pussy to flutter around his cock.

"Jesus, just when I thought you couldn't feel any better, you prove me wrong." He begins to fuck into me again. And again. The sensations begin to build in my lower belly. Building and folding in on themselves and extending to my thighs, my waist, my entire torso. When he makes a noise at the back of his throat, I realize he's very close as well. And I want to see him come inside me. So much.

I rise up, meeting his every thrust, pushing up my breasts so they're plastered against his chest. I lock my arms around his neck and lift up my chin, trembling as he continues to hit that elusive part inside of me. And when he slides his hand down to squeeze my butt, I whimper and gasp, knowing I'm close. So close. But I can't come until he lets me. He's trained me so well.

He tilts his hips, making sure to hit my clit at a particularly intimate angle. Shock waves screech up and over me. *Please. Please.*

I must say it aloud for he growls, "Come."

A long cry emerges from me. Like a wounded animal. Or one which has found salvation. Maybe that's what this flare of golden light engulfing my vision is about. I hold onto him, keep my eyes open and am rewarded when, with a harsh cry, he empties himself inside me. Only then do I let my eyelids flutter down and my arms release their hold on him as I collapse onto the bed.

He kisses my forehead and pulls out of me gently. Then looks down to where the cum drips out of me.

His forehead crinkles. "I didn't wear a condom." He looks up and searches my features, waiting for my reaction.

"I'm on birth control."

He nods slowly. "I've been tested. I'm clean."

"Likewise." I yawn.

He cups my cheek. "To be clear, I don't intend to sleep with anyone else, but you."

"And I, you." I take in the tenderness in his eyes. His soft expression. How his gaze on my features feels like a caress. His promise of loyalty layered on top of the wedding vows feel achingly close to a declaration of love.

He may not have said it aloud, but I feel positive that he feels something deeper for me.

"You do realize I'm falling for you, right?" I whisper.

The tendons of his throat flex as he swallows.

I'm crushed when he doesn't reciprocate my words.

Heat pricks behind my eyes. I swallow. I really don't want to cry again.

He must sense the emotions welling up in me, for he lowers his chin and kisses me until I'm breathless. Until I've forgotten everything, except how it feels to be in his arms.

Then he flips both of us so I'm on his chest. I place my head against where his heart beats against his rib cage.

Let the *thump-thump-thump* soothe me to sleep.

When I open my eyes a few hours later, it's to find I'm on my side facing him.

He's asleep on his back, one arm bent and under his neck, his head turned to me. I take the opportunity to study him when he's not aware. Long eyelashes curl up in an almost feminine manner that enhances the angles of his cheekbones, the singularity of his straight nose, the square jaw, that stubborn chin, the broad forehead which hints at the intelligence I see in his eyes.

He's handsome, but it's more than that. There's a sense of power clinging to him. A charisma very few people possess. The kind which allows him to lead a company. *Can I do that?*

It's not because I'm a woman that I'm doubting myself. I've never felt being one has ever put me at a disadvantage. It's more that I've never been in such a senior role before. Which is not to say I can't do it. But it's daunting.

I'll need to draw on my reserves of energy and stamina, and my ability to persevere. It's going to be a stretch, but the fact that he believes in me? That's what has made me even consider the possibility of accepting this role.

"You're thinking too hard." He smirks with his eyes closed.

"How did you know I was awake?"

"I can sense everything about you, baby." He turns more fully to face me and opens his eyes. And like the first time when he fixed me with those gunmetal eyes, I'm entranced.

There'll never not be a time when I'm not in thrall of being the focus of his attention. Bewitched. Spellbound by how the touch of his eyes on my face leaves pinpricks of awareness in their wake.

"And what am I thinking now?" I flutter my eyelashes, hoping to distract him.

I don't want him to guess the self-doubt that fills me with this new role he wants me to take. It feels important that he sees me as capable. Is that because I still see him in the role of my boss?

Maybe I haven't transitioned to him being my husband.

Though in bed, with both of us naked, it's difficult to think of anything other than how I can get him to use me for his pleasure.

Maybe my thoughts flicker in my eyes, for his own glint. "You're thinking you want me to make use of your body."

I try and fail to stop my jaw from dropping.

"How did you—" I gasp as he throws me on my back and covers my body with his.

"How did I guess?"

I begin to nod, then shake my head. "I can't say I'm completely surprised you did. I haven't been able to hide my thoughts from you." I frown. "Though I hope I'm not that transparent."

"You're not, except to me," he says in a quietly confident tone. One that has no sign of smugness. It's almost a statement. One that implies he knows me. That he watches me closely. One that gives me immense satisfaction.

"You going to fuck me then?" I sigh.

He chuckles. "You, using the F-word, is strangely arousing."

"Same." I lower my chin.

And when I feel the stab of his cock between my legs, a helpless shudder scrolls through me. "Brody." I cup his cheek. The tenderness I feel for him always takes me by surprise. Because he's the big, bad dominant. And I want him to order me to do his bidding. There's security in it. Home, a sense of belonging which is strangely calming. I don't have to make choices. Or decisions. I trust him to make them for me. And it's that trust, that devotion he inspires in me, which also inspires this absolute loyalty. I'm afraid I'm falling deeper in love with him.

"Brody," I whisper again. I want to give voice to my thoughts, but hold back... Because he doesn't. He's made it clear; something as silly as falling in love is not for him.

Sadly, that's not going to stop me from feeling what I do. Or from taking pleasure in how he draws orgasms from my body. Nothing wrong with that, either. Not when I don't know how things are going to be once we're back in London. This. Here. Now, is what I have with him. I'm going to make the most of it.

I'm sure he's going to breach me with his cock, which has grown bigger, thicker, and more insistent over the last few minutes. Instead, he shoves off me and lays on his back, then pats his chest.

"Get on here."

38

Brody

The surprise on her face gives way to delight. She scrambles up and begins to straddle my face. I squeeze her waist and flip her around. She gasps. I lower her down onto my mouth, swiping my tongue over that luscious flesh between her thighs.

She shudders. I allow myself another lick up her labia. She moans. Then, as if unable to hold herself up, she falls forward and digs her fingernails into my sides. I ease her forward enough that she's able to hover her face over my crotch.

When I lick around her clit, she gives a hoarse cry. Damn, these little noises she makes short-circuits my brain cells.

My cock thickens and twitches. I'm sure I'm dripping cum from the head. "Suck me off, baby," I command through gritted teeth.

Instantly, she lowers her chin and takes me inside her mouth. The feeling of her silken warmth closing in on me reverberates through my body. My dick extends, the blood throbs at my temples. I literally see stars. I groan against her cunt. The vibrations seem to turn her on further for she drips down my chin. I lick up the liquid and come back into myself a little. I squeeze her butt cheeks, then use my thumbs to pry her lower lips apart.

I begin to lick up her pussy, then push my tongue into her slit. She sinks down, impaling herself deeper on my tongue, as if she's unable to hold herself up.

Which also means, she swallows around my cock.

I slide down her throat, the warm wet embrace of the channel closing in on me like it was created for me. The suction is overpowering. I'm going to embarrass myself by coming in record time. But not until she comes with me.

I stab my tongue in and out of her slit, savoring the taste. Drowning in the warmth that coats my palate, and the tightness that squeezes my dick.

I continue to slurp on her, laving her trembling flesh, relishing how she swallows around my shaft, devouring me like I'm her favorite snack. And when I close my mouth around her clit and suckle on it deeply, her entire body freezes, her thighs turn tight with awareness, her mouth locks about my shaft, and when I slide my thumb into the eyelet between her arse cheeks, the tension drains out of her.

She shudders, and with a muffled moan that vibrates around my cock, she shatters. Her orgasm races up her spine, arching her back like she's being pulled heavenward.

A sweet culmination which I can afford her. And then it's my turn to thrust up and into the wet hollow of her mouth. She gags, drawing on my length, and with a muted roar, I empty my balls down her throat.

I can't seem to stop. Not even when my cum overflows her mouth, slides down her chin and pools on my belly. It feels like I'm pouring my very soul into her.

She sinks further onto me, and my cock slips from her mouth.

I lick up the last of the moisture coating her pussy lips, then maneuver her body so she's on my chest, with her face tucked into the hollow under my chin. Her heart is racing, mirroring the speed at which my chest rises and falls.

Sweat turns our skin into a sticky, suction-filled surface. I hold her close, an arm around her waist, the other around her shoulders. Then trail my fingers down the ridges of her spine, to her butt and cup it tenderly.

A shiver rolls down her body. She moans softly. And just like that my dick stirs again. I continue to pet her, running my fingers down the cleavage between her butt cheeks. She stirs restlessly. Resting her chin on my chest.

"I can't." She clears her throat.

"That's what you said last time."

She frowns, then whimpers, when I slip my fingers down to play with the opening to her pussy. And when I slip a finger inside, she huffs in protest, but parts her legs.

"Your cunt feels like home, baby."

She flickers her eyelashes, and sighs. "*You* feel like home."

My heart seems to cleave in my chest. My rib cage turns to putty. The wall I've built around my feelings dissolves, leaving me exposed. Open. Vulnerable. Alarm bells go off in my brain. I need to pull back.

Clearly, the physical act of making love to my wife has brought my emotions too close to the surface. I can't let that happen. I can't. I grasp her hips, ready to set her aside, but then she rises up and peers deeply into my eyes. Her thick blonde hair rains down, entrapping me. Holding me captive.

I'm caught in the crosshairs of an enemy. One I didn't see coming. And now…it's too late.

I'm falling for her. I need to find a way out of this mess. But not now.

Right now, I'm too taken in by the scent of her body, her curves, the seductive slide of my cock against the melting center of her pussy. I squeeze her fleshy hips and position her over my cock. The engorged head teases her opening. I'm rewarded by the growing color on her cheeks.

"So soon?" She shudders. Her mouth opens, her lips glistening and swollen.

"Always for you," I admit.

I tease her legs apart until she's straddling me. I lower her gently onto my cock, and when I breach her entrance, both of us gasp.

Her eyes are large, luminous pools of black. Her desire clings to the curves of her cheeks, the jut of her chin, and the way she digs her fingers into my shoulders like a cat clinging to the side of a boat. Unable to let go for fear of drowning.

But drown, she will. As will I. We're fated on this course. There's no way out. Not for either of us. I piston my hips up and impale her. My balls slap against the cleavage between her arse cheeks.

"Brody," she cries out. And that inflames me further.

I flip us over so she's on her back. I urge her legs up and over my shoulders, then twist her arms up and over her head. I curl her fingers around the slats in the headboard. "Hold on."

39

Lark

He pulls back until he's balanced at my entrance. Then, in one graceful move, he sinks inside me. It's forceful enough that I move up the bed, and hard enough for the headboard to slap against the wall.

"Don't let go," he warns.

Then he begins to fuck me in earnest. Like he's racing to a finish only he can comprehend. Or like he's finalizing a merger that everyone else has decried hostile but which he views as challenging.

His complete focus is on me, his eyes narrowed, his jaw set, a fierceness to his features that lights fires under my skin. I love how his cock fills me up and pushes down against my inner walls. And how his big body dwarfs mine. And how the heat from his skin infuses mine, uniting us in more ways than just his cock impaling me. I love that.

But it's more than physical. More than how he fucks me, like being inside my cunt is the only thing that brings him pleasure. It's all of it, really.

The physical, *and* the way it feels like we've fused our souls together. Plus, it's on a cellular level. And in the meeting of our eyes. He's overpowering me. Overwhelming me. Making me feel like I'm his to command. His to do with as he pleases.

His. I'm his. And he's mine.

He's the bad boy appealing to the wickedness inside me. Giving me permission to unlock the sinful part. The part that wants him to do dirty things to my body. The very things which also appeal to my spirit.

The skin around his eyes tightens. He thrusts inside me again, making sure to hit my G-spot. Vibrations of pleasure sizzle out from my core to my hips, my back, my limbs. He keeps going, making sure to pinch my sensitive nipple, drawing a groan from me. Then slipping his hand between us to pluck at my clit. I'm helpless to stop the climax zipping up my spine, then bouncing down to my feet. It crashes over me with the force of a tsunami. I open my mouth in a soundless cry and gratefully receive his lips on mine, as he absorbs any stray sounds that escape me, before filling my cunt with his seed.

When his biceps tremble and he begins to sag, he makes sure to sink down on the bed on his back and pull me on top of him. I like being draped over him, love how my skin sticks to his, and how my head seems to fit exactly under his chin. I belong here. I flatten my palm over his chest and soak in his presence. If only he'd realize he belongs with me, too...

Almost as if he hears my thought, he stirs. "Did I hurt you?" he asks in a soft voice.

"It was perfect." I look up at him. "*You* are perfect."

"You too." I want to say that sex with him has blown my mind. That he's it for me. But when I open my mouth to speak, I end up yawning.

"Sleep." He settles me in his arms.

I want to ask him questions about his emotions for me. Tell him that the way he made love to me tells me he must feel something, but the events of the last few days catch up with me, and I slide into a deep, dreamless sleep.

When I wake up the next morning, I feel refreshed. Also, it's Christmas Eve. Even better, the world outside is covered in snow.

It's going to be a *white Christmas*.

And I'm stranded in a chalet with my handsome hunk of a husband, who finds me very desirable.

I can't remember the last time I slept more than twelve hours in one go. I stretch, wincing at the soreness between my thighs. Which reminds me of how my husband made love to me. I also realize I'm alone in bed.

I take a quick shower, pull on jeans, a sweatshirt, and soft socks, then pad down to the kitchen.

He's looking out the window with a cup of coffee in hand.

He's wearing a pair of gray sweats, and a T-shirt that hugs his shoulders and pulls across his back. It highlights how built he is.

When he raises his hand to take a sip of the coffee, his biceps stretch the T-shirt sleeve.

The muscles of his forearms ripple, and I feel an answering response in my lower belly. The soreness in my pussy makes itself known, reminding me how my very well-endowed husband fucked me earlier.

But apparently, I haven't had enough of him. I watch him for a little longer, reveling in the fact that I know how it feels to have his weight on top of me. Then, when I can't stop myself any longer, I walk over to stand next to him.

Without missing a beat, he puts his arm around my waist and pulls me close. I melt into his side, looking outside at the world covered in white. It's quiet. Completely quiet. Not a soul stirs anywhere. There's not a breath of wind. Just snow-covered earth and boughs weighted down with white. The surface of the lake has frozen over and reflects the blue of the sky. It feels almost other-worldly.

"It feels like we're the only people alive," I whisper.

"I have you. I don't need anyone else." He turns to me, and the puzzled expression in his eyes tells me he wasn't expecting to say that aloud.

"Is that good?" I ask slowly.

"It's…" He hesitates. "I'm making up my mind about it," he says honestly.

Disappointment clenches my chest. I'm aware of him watching me closely, so I look outside. I nod in the direction of the pine trees. "You did say we could put up a Christmas tree and decorate it?"

He nods. "We have ornaments in the basement."

"Oh good." I blink away my disappointment and flash him a smile. "And I want to bake Christmas cookies."

He groans.

"It's one of my traditions to bake Christmas cookies at least once during the festive season. I haven't had the time this year."

He takes in the excitement on my face and his own softens. "Whatever my wife wants."

That's it. My pussy melted into a puddle because he said, 'my wife.'

"What?" He frowns.

"You're romantic."

He seems taken aback then pretends to look around. "Shh, don't let anyone else hear you say that." He smirks.

I chuckle and pat his massive chest. "Come on, Bossman, let's see if you're as good at wielding an axe as you are a pen."

Turns out, he's *very* good at wielding an axe.

He's also stripped down to a thin white T-shirt which is stuck to his back because he was sweating freely as he chopped down the fir tree, we both agreed upon.

It's a seven-foot-tall Normann fir, which will fit perfectly in a corner of the living room.

Naturally, I've been unable to remove my gaze from my husband as he brings his axe down into the trunk. His biceps flex. His shoulders seem to have swollen to twice their normal proportions. And I can make out the bricks of his abs, and the outline of his male nipples against the fabric of his T-shirt.

He looks good enough to lick up.

I give up any pretense of helping and watch him from the sidelines.

He brings his axe down again, then with a grunt, pulls it out. The tree shudders.

"Take a few more steps back," he warns.

I obey him, without taking my eyes off his intent face. The muscles of his jaw tighten. He buries his axe into the trunk one last time and when he pulls it out, the tree topples over.

"Timber." I cup my palms around my mouth and yell.

He eyes the fallen tree with a very masculine look of pleasure on his face. "Not bad, huh?"

"Why do I get the feeling you've done this before?" I point to the grove of Christmas trees around us.

"Not me, but I did watch Arthur cut down a tree when we were but young boys."

"Oh?" I look at him with interest. "I can't picture your grandfather doing something this physical."

"My brothers and I get our build from him. Our father was slender in physique. We spent many of our Christmases with Arthur in this house."

He thunks the axe down in the tree stump, then walks around the tree. He's figuring out the best way to carry it back.

"And did you enjoy your time here?"

He shrugs. "The gifts were always welcome."

"Wow, don't smother me with your enthusiasm." I chuckle.

He shoots me a quizzical glance. "You know, I'm not big on Christmas."

I nod. "And I can't understand why."

He rolls his shoulders; then his eyes reflect him coming to a decision. "The last time I remember my parents and my brothers and me being together as a family was here at this house, celebrating Christmas. It was one of the few times my mother seemed to be genuinely happy. Or so I thought." He rubs the back of his neck. "My mum and dad had a big fight on Christmas morning. Something about the gift he got her, which she hated. She accused him of never really understanding her. They had a massive fall out. He walked out, met with an accident and died on the spot."

"Oh my God!" The words scrape out of me on a sharp breath. "I'm so sorry."

"Not your fault. Or my mother's fault. I was five when my father died. My last memory of him? He looked haunted... Upset... Hurt. It was also the last time I saw my mother smile. After my father's passing, she became increasingly distant; drowned herself in alcohol. She couldn't get through the next holiday season, so she overdosed on sleeping pills and passed away."

I flinch. No wonder, he hates the holidays. What he went through as a kid would put anyone off Christmas.

"I'm really sorry that happened to you." I close the distance to him and throw my arms around him.

He rests his chin on my head and pulls me close, the hard line of his body softening a little.

"Christmas reminds me of things I'd rather not relive. That's why I hated it. But you changed that."

"I did?" I tilt my face up at him.

"You sailed into my office, demanded Christmas decorations, and called it a workplace morale initiative. After that, I figured the season might deserve another shot."

"Thank you." I cup his cheek. "You won't regret it." Then because I want to lighten the mood, I add. "Your Royal Grinchness."

It has the desired effect, for his lips curve.

He arches an eyebrow. "You being sassy, Siren?"

A thrill runs up my spine when he uses that nickname.

"How can you tell?" I flutter my eyelashes at him.

His eyes flash. His gaze fixes on my lips. "You can show me how grateful you are later."

Heat flushes my cheeks. My panties are suddenly wet. I have no doubt exactly what he means by that. A shiver grips me.

His gaze narrows. "Let's get you and this tree, inside."

"It's looking amazing." I smooth down the tinsel that hangs from one of the branches.

Brody hangs another ornament, then steps down from the ladder he's been using to decorate the tree. "Go on, switch the lights back on."

After testing the lights, we turned them off to up the 'wow factor' once we finished decorating. I skip across to the wall, flip the switch, and the lights come on.

"Oh!" I walk over to stand next to him. "It's beautiful." I gaze at the tiny lights dotting the decorated Christmas tree.

"It is."

Something in his voice makes me turn. He's looking down at me. I flush a little. "I meant, the tree."

"I meant, you." His smile is tender.

"Aww." I go up on tiptoe, and when he dips his head, I brush my lips against his.

Of course, he hauls me against him and licks his lips over my mouth.

When I part my lips with a sigh, he kisses me deeply. My head spins, and I clutch his arms for support. "Thank you," I whisper against his mouth.

"You're welcome." He tries to kiss me again.

I lean back in the circle of his arms. "Oh no, you're not going to distract me."

"Who, me?" He tries to look innocent and fails completely.

"Yes, you. You're not getting out of making Christmas cookies."

40

Brody

"Why is this dough so… Doughy?" I glance up from where I've been waging war on what's supposed to be cookie dough.

I managed to distract her enough to get out of making cookies yesterday.

I also distracted her all night, so we both barely got any shut-eye.

Today, however, there's no escape.

She insisted we spend our first Christmas as a married couple baking cookies. Which, I'm realizing, is more difficult than running a billion-dollar company.

Lark's laughing so hard she's doubled over, hands on her knees, a smear of flour streaking her cheek like war paint.

Christ, she's gorgeous. I fix the image in my mind, something to return to when I need a reminder of what happiness looks like.

Damn, she's making me sentimental.

We'd raided the kitchen and found the ingredients as well as the equipment she needed to bake. Whew! Disaster averted.

She's also making me worry about things other than conference calls and budget projections. It's a whole new world for me.

She takes in my flour-streaked T-shirt. "You're supposed to *mix in* the flour, not bathe in it." She wheezes between giggles.

I drag the back of my hand down my face, which grinds more flour into my jaw. "Next time, don't hand the whisk to a former Marine and say beat it *gently*."

That sets her off again. Her laugh fills the kitchen, bright and contagious, and for a second, I forget this is supposed to be about Christmas cookies. I feel like I've been given my very own Christmas surprise.

She's wiping her eyes when I grab a spoon, dip it into the bowl, and hold it up like a weapon.

"Mock your CO again, and you'll be eating dough straight from the source."

She looks up, eyes wide. "You wouldn't."

"I absolutely would." I launch a dollop of dough at her, and it lands right on her cheek. *Direct hit.*

Her mouth drops open. "You—"

"Careful," I warn, grinning now. "Retaliation is futile."

"Futile, huh?" She snatches a handful of flour and flings it at me. A cloud of white bursts between us.

Now we're both covered. Me, her, the countertop, the floor. Every surface in sight, actually.

She steps closer, brandishing the rolling pin like a sword. "Say sorry."

"Never."

"Say it!"

I catch her wrist mid-swing, and everything stops.

She's so close, I can smell vanilla and cinnamon on her skin, see the fine dusting of flour clinging to her lashes.

Her breathing's fast. So is mine.

There's cookie dough on her chin. I swipe it away with my thumb before I can think better of it.

Her lips part a little, and my brain short-circuits. "You missed a spot," I murmur.

She swallows. "Where?"

I lean in, slow enough that she could move if she wanted. She doesn't. Right before our mouths meet, the oven timer beeps.

We both jump.

She clears her throat, turns and yanks open the door. "Saved by the bell."

Or not.

She pulls out the spiced ginger loaf she put in to bake.

"That smells delicious." My mouth waters.

"It tastes even better."

I reach over and am about to touch it when she slaps my wrist. "Hey, not yet. It needs to rest and then cool before we can eat it."

"Damn." I look at it longingly.

"Patience, Grasshopper." Her eyes shine. "Meanwhile, let's roll out the cookie dough."

I stare at her. "You're going to have to do better than that."

She chuckles, then walks over and bumps me with her hip. "Move."

I step back.

"First, prepare your surface." She wipes down a section of the countertop.

I move back far enough to watch her hips sway as she works. She's wearing a pair of jeans that squeeze her butt, and goddamn, my fingers tingle to squeeze them.

"Then lightly dust it with flour; just enough to prevent sticking, not so much that the dough dries out."

"Mm-hmm."

I soak up the sweetness in her voice and can't take my gaze off her hourglass figure.

"Are you listening?"

"Oh, yeah."

With the smattering of sugar on her cheek and the scent of butter clinging to her, she looks good enough to eat.

"Next, shape the dough." She grabs a portion of the cookie dough and presses it into a flat disc.

Unable to stop myself, I reach over and squeeze her fleshy butt cheeks.

"Hey!" She stares over my shoulder. "What are you doing?"

"Shaping the dough."

She giggles. "I meant, this one." She slides the flattened circle of dough over to me then pats out another. "Now we roll it out." She nods to the space next to her and offers me a wine bottle.

With a sigh, I release her hips and move up next to her to accept it.

She uses a rolling pin. Starting from the center, she rolls it outward in every direction, turning the dough a quarter-turn after every few rolls.

I copy her actions, and to my surprise, end up with a wider circle. "That's good."

"I'm a natural." I smirk.

She dips the cookie cutters in flour, offers me one then uses the other to cut out the shape from the dough.

Within minutes we have a dozen Christmas trees, stars and heart-shaped cookies.

"Ooh, these are adorable." She transfers them to a baking tray, walks over to slide them in the oven.

"That needs to be in for twenty-minutes." She sets the timer.

Then she transfers the spiced gingerbread onto a cooling rack.

She turns and gasps for I'm standing right in front of her. "I know the way to pass the time."

"Ooh." She tips up her chin. "I wonder what you have in mind."

I drop a quick kiss on her nose. "That too, but first I have a present for you."

"You already gave me a Christmas present." I glance at the now smooth skin on her wrist where the marks from the ties have faded.

"Is there a rule that I can give you only one?"

I hold out my hand. When she places her palm in mine, I bring her fingers to my mouth and kiss the tips.

Her breath hitches.

She's so damn responsive. It's the most beautiful thing I've ever seen.

With a small smile, I lead her out of the kitchen and to the living room where the firelight casts a golden glow on the space. The late afternoon sun streams in through the window.

"Sit." I push her onto the sofa, then sit down next to her.

I pick up a slim, bow-wrapped package from the coffee table and hold it out to her.

She eyes it cautiously. "If you'd told me that you planned to give me Christmas gifts, I'd have come prepared."

"I told you, you're my Christmas gift." I curve my lips.

"Aww." She flushes. "You're so sweet."

A warm sensation fills my chest. I feel rather pleased with myself, so I allow myself a small smirk. "I think you're going to find me even sweeter when you open your gift." I wave the package under her nose.

Her expression turns curious. "What is it?"

"Open it. Go on. You know you want to."

She reaches for it, weighs it in her hand.

"What's inside it? Is it a book? No, it feels too light for that."

She tugs on the ribbon, which loosens. She pauses. Then, as if consumed by curiosity, she pulls off the wrapping to reveal an envelope.

"It's a document?" She looks at me from under her eyes, then slides the flap open. She pulls out a sheet of paper and glances through it.

Her eyes widen. "What's this?"

"That is the agreement handing over majority ownership of the shares and confirming you as the CEO of Davenport Capital."

She pales. "You're making it official? So soon?" Her fingers tremble. The papers begin to slip from her grasp, but I catch them. Then place them on the table.

"I did say I want you to be CEO," I remind her.

"And I said I'd think about it."

"Well, this is me showing how serious I am about it." I take her hands in mine. Finding her fingers cold, I begin to rub them. "As part of the arrangement, once we were married, Arthur instructed his legal counsel to hand over the majority shares to me. It seemed right that they were made out to you."

She pulls her hand from mine, then jumps up and begins to pace. "To say that you're making me CEO is one thing. But handing the shares over to me... It's going to take me a minute to absorb that."

I watch her pace the floor in front of the fire. The light teases out the honeyed highlights in her hair and paints her skin in glowing shades of pink. She's so beautiful, my wife. And smart. And gorgeous in every way. And she's a wonderful human being too. I lucked out that she agreed to marry me.

Too bad, I'm not able to commit my love to her. But this... The handover of the shares should make up for it, surely?

She spins on me and slaps her hands on her hips. "This arrangement started out as a way for me to redeem myself in front of my family and friends."

"Which has been done. Your parents came to our wedding. And they were happy that you were marrying me."

"Apparently." She seems a little taken aback by it.

I allow myself a small smirk. "We must have put on such a convincing performance that they bought it."

She purses her lips. "So how did we go from your needing to get married to placate your grandfather to this?" She stares at the sheaf of papers. "It's become so very complicated."

And if I had my way, I'd tie you even more strongly to me, so you'd never let me go. Especially since I can't use my love to bind you to me.

I pat the seat next to me. "Sit down, so we can talk it over."

She hesitates then approaches me and sinks down on the settee, keeping the length of it between us. I'm not happy about that, but I let her for now.

"I told you this marriage was real for me."

She nods.

"But that I could never let myself fall in love with you?"

"Because of some stupid idea you have that you're incapable of love," she huffs.

"It's the truth."

"Why is that?" She leans forward. "Why are you so against the idea of falling in love. You did love your parents, I assume? And you care for your brothers and your friends, don't you?"

"I did and yes, I do." I drum my fingers on my thigh. "I lost...first my father, and then my mother, relatively early. Then saw friends killed in combat."

"That must not have been easy." Sympathy laces her expression. The softness in her features is like a balm to my soul. I shouldn't feel it so keenly. But it's as if another layer has dissolved between me and the world. She's chipping away at my defenses. Bringing me closer to a version of me that can't hide. It makes me feel exposed. And it's not altogether a comfortable feeling.

"It wasn't." I lower my chin. "It made me realize emotions like love don't have a place in my world. It's why, when I left the Royal Marines and focused on building up the company, things finally began to make sense. As long as I didn't get my feelings involved, I'd be safe."

She regards me with something like shrewdness and, also, pity. Discomfort slithers under my skin. I resist the urge to say or do something in response. That'd be a sign of weakness. Only this isn't a game.

It's not one of my corporate power plays. I don't need to put on an act here. This is me and my wife having a conversation. And it's okay to be myself with her. Right?

"You are one of the most astute people I know. It's nothing short of a miracle that you managed a turnaround of your company in such a short period of time. But for someone so smart, you can be really dumb."

I reel back. "Ex-fucking-cuse me?"

"You know what I'm talking about. You're letting the events of your past hold you back. You're using what happened to you as an excuse to not take risks."

"Not take risks?" I snort. "Without taking them, I wouldn't be here. I wouldn't have been on the Forbes forty-under-forty list without taking risks at every stage of my career, both in the board-room and in the war room."

She gazes at me steadily. "I'm not undermining all of your accomplishments in either space. And of course, it would have taken guts to do what you did. But when it comes to your personal life, you've given up before you've even started."

The back of my neck heats. "You'd better explain yourself."

She must hear the edge in my voice and the threat that has the hair on my arms standing on end. She swallows and looks a little shaken, but does she back down? Of course not.

"You've decided you're never going to fall in love because you're too scared of being hurt." She firms her jaw. "You, who've not flinched from an enemy's bullets or from navigating the hostile terrain of corporate takeovers, are unable to come to terms with your own emotions. You don't even want to try because you've decided you're going to get hurt." She throws up her hands. "It's cowardly and so bloody frustrating." She looks about ready to tear her hair out. "On the face of it, you're the most macho man I've come across, but you lack courage."

"I lack courage?" I try hard to keep my voice even, but it emerges as if I have razor blades lining my throat.

She stiffens further. "Facing your internal fears is a sign of true courage. And that, you don't have."

A fine anger pinches the sides of my vision. It's as if a haze of red has descended on my brain. "You have no idea what you're talking about."

She scoffs. "You thought you could buy me with your agreement and handing the shares over to me. You thought you could distract me from the fact that you've decided you can't fall in love with me."

"It's not a distraction."

It *is* a distraction. And my wife is smart enough to have seen through it. And she's right. I did want to, somehow, make up for my inability to fall in love with her. I wanted to give her what she most wants. I recognized the burning ambition in her, that hunger for achievement, backed by the need to be acknowledged for her efforts.

"What else do you call it?" She folds her arms across her chest. Her stance is both belligerent and defensive. There seems to be this wall between us, replacing the defenses which have collapsed around my heart. And I'm finding I don't like it at all. And that confuses the fuck out of me.

"Look, this is how I can show you that I'm dedicated to this marriage. I want you to have the shares in good faith. I see you as my successor. It's why I had the shares made out to you. I believe in you, Lark."

She swallows hard.

"Once you become CEO, I'm free to pursue the things that give me the most joy."

Her eyebrows knit. "Which is focusing on veterans' affairs and startups?"

Not only.

I'm happiest when I focus on you. Why am I not able to say that aloud? Instead, I firm my lips.

"Yes," I manage. "That's what's most important to me."

"I see." A stark expression filters across her face. She draws in a few sharp breaths.

Then seems to come to a decision.

She marches over to the table, grabs the contract. "I'll accept the CEO position." She shoots me a sideways glance. "At least, *I'm* honest about what I want. Unlike you."

"What do you mean?"

She sets her jaw. "I wish you'd be honest about your feelings for me."

41

Lark

Try not to fall asleep watching my fave Christmas movie after the tenth "just one more scene" time.

—From Lark's Christmas to-do list

"What are you talking about?" His features are slack with surprise.

I want the title of CEO. But it strikes me that it's also a diversionary tactic. A way for him to not accept his feelings for me.

Sex with Brody has been stupendous. And emotionally satisfying, in a way I could not have predicted.

The way he looks into my eyes when he takes me? It feels like a kind of claiming. A possessiveness bordering on the side of primitive-ness. So raw in its intensity that, every time he came inside me, it felt like he marked me as his. Which is why I refuse to believe that he has no feelings for me.

Only he's too scared to accept it. Grr!

"Why can't you man up and be truthful about your feelings?" I jut out my chin.

"Man up, huh?"

"I did not expect Brody Davenport, the big bad CEO, to be scared of speaking his mind."

He sets his jaw. The tips of his ears grow white, which is the first warning that he's pissed. "I'm not scared."

"And *I'm* in love with you."

There, it's out there. Take that, *Mr. Broody McBroody.*

Predictably, he pales. "Y...you love me?"

"That's what I said."

He seems taken aback. "You barely know me."

I roll my eyes. But my voice softens. "I know you're brilliant and handsome and trying, in your own stubborn way, to make the world a little better. I know you care about your grandfather so much, you'll bend yourself into knots rather than disappoint him, even when you disagree with him. You let him choose your bride to make him happy."

I swallow.

"You want to pour your inheritance into veterans' programs, and you fund startups that make missions safer for our armed forces. You're one of the most decent men I've ever met."

My heartbeat stumbles.

"I know you put my pleasure first. Always. You pay so much attention to satisfying me, it makes me feel like the most beautiful, most cherished woman in the world."

Heat rises in my cheeks.

"Not to forget, you let me cover the office in Christmas decorations because it mattered to me." I chuckle.

"You act like you're a ruthless, untouchable, grouch-face. But underneath... You're a teddy bear."

His features soften. His eyes fill with a combination of lust and need and a myriad of emotions that I interpret as love. Then he bats them away. A tortured expression fills his features.

"I don't know what to say."

"Why don't you tell me how you feel about me? Why can't you tell me that you love me? Because I see it in your eyes."

"I want to." He curls his fingers into fists. "And I promise, I will. I need a little more time."

I look at him with disappointment. "What are you afraid of, Brody?"

"I'm afraid of losing you!"

I place the document back on the table, then close the distance to him. "I'm not going anywhere."

He rises to his feet, slowly.

"You better believe, you're not. I have you. I'm not letting you go."

The possessiveness in his voice lights tiny fires under my skin. I can feel the intense emotions rolling off of him, and my knees tremble.

I tilt my head back, and further back, to meet his eyes. And the way they burn into me? I flinch.

His muscles vibrate with barely contained emotion, a storm trembling beneath his skin. For the first time since I met him, unease prickles down my spine.

I've always known there were passions simmering beneath that calm, controlled exterior; but provoking him and watching them claw their way to the surface feels like standing at the foot of Mount Vesuvius, hearing the first ominous rumbles before it explodes.

I take a step back, and another. He doesn't move. But he watches me carefully. I get the sense I'm a rabbit, and he's the big bad wolf who's been provoked.

"You're my wife, am I right?"

"Well, duh." I wave my left hand with the rings on my finger, in what I hope is a casual gesture. Too bad, my fingers tremble.

"Excellent." A smile I'd categorize as evil tugs at his lips. "And you liked everything I did to you so far."

"Meaning?"

The animal part of my brain tells me I need to buy time here while I figure out an escape route. Escape from what, I don't know. But whatever he's thinking and planning, it's no good.

Which means, I'm going to love it.

"The tying you to my bed and fucking you... Using the vibrator on you... Taking your virgin back hole... You liked all of it, yes?"

I flush to the roots of my hair. Not because I'm a prude, but because hearing him describe what he did to me in that dark, growly voice recalls all the sensations that coursed through me when he performed those things on me.

A strangled sound escapes me, but it must satisfy him, for he nods.

"Good. And you're open to exploring more of your kinky side?"

God help me, I am. I manage to nod again.

His expression softens. "There's no shame in it."

"I'm not ashamed." I pout.

"Good." He rumbles. "Take off your clothes, wife."

I'm never gonna get used to this man calling me 'wife' either. It shouldn't sound so erotic, but coming from him, it's everything.

"Now," he snaps.

Oops, okay then. I hurry to obey him and strip off my clothes.

Suddenly, I'm naked in the center of the living room, with the world outside bathed in snow. In a chalet, in the middle of the most beautiful part of the country. On Christmas morning. What even is my life?

He prowls forward, then slowly circles around me. I feel his eyes on every dip and curve and hollow of my body. By the time he stops in front of me again, my nipples have pebbled, my thighs tremble, and I'm positive fat drops of cum have slid down my inner thigh. I manage to stay still. I'm not giving him the satisfaction of finding out how turned on I am.

He taps his chin. "I know what I want for my Christmas gift."

"What's that?"

"You." His eyes gleam. "Gift wrapped for me."

A ripple of anticipation unfurls in my belly. The thought being offered up to him for his delectation is the culmination of my every erotic dream.

"Would you like that, wife?"

Even if he hadn't called me wife, I'd have agreed. But add that to the intention he outlined, and I feel almost faint with desire. I want everything he's going to do to me. And more. I want to be at the receiving end of every bit of his desire. Only me.

"Yes." Barely is the word out of my mouth when he scoops me up in his arms. I'm too overcome with lust to be surprised. Too taken aback with the pulsing need coursing through my veins to protest. Why pretend I want anything else than being used by this man in any way he wants?

He stalks into the bedroom and places me on my feet near the bed. Then he walks into the closet.

This time, he emerges with coils of dark ivy in his hands. *No, they're ropes.*

Strands of emerald-green that look silky and soft to touch. My pulse skips. My breath stutters.

"Come here." He gestures.

I step closer. The air between us hums. He reaches for my wrist, tracing his thumb along the inside, where my pulse stutters. His touch is warm, grounding.

"This isn't about restraint." He searches my features. "It's about trust. About letting go. Do you understand? Say yes, if you do."

The words make something inside me loosen and quake all at once. But when I speak my voice is strong. "Yes."

"Good girl." He bends to kiss me firmly.

Then slides the rope over my skin, a whisper-soft glide that sends shivers spiraling down my spine. He moves behind me, his body a wall of throbbing heat I can feel even without touch. Each loop he makes is measured, deliberate. His breath is steady, while mine, in contrast, is ragged.

He crosses the rope over my shoulders, down my back, then around my ribs, a careful cradle that holds me upright. It's not too tight.

Enough to make me aware of every place the fibers kiss my skin.

I can feel the faint press between my breasts, the pattern forming. Each loop painting a line of tension and release on my skin.

I can smell him now: dark, peppery, and so masculine; every cell in my body hums in appreciation. My body sways without permission, my lungs seizing up under the onslaught of his overpowering presence.

"Breathe for me," he whispers.

I inhale; the ropes shift, expanding slightly with my lungs. The sensation is intoxicating. The awareness that even my breath moves at his will makes my head spin and my thighs quiver.

His fingers trace down my sides as he gathers more rope. He threads it around my waist, weaving it through the pattern at my back, the pressure growing firmer.

My skin tingles, alive beneath every pass of the rope.

When he kneels in front of me, the sunlight slanting in through the window carves shadows across his jaw. He loops the strand around my thighs, guiding it with the same care he might use to handle something sacred.

The pattern is simple but beautiful: diagonal lines tracing from my shoulders to my hips, crossing at the center of my chest like the wrapping on a precious gift.

He lifts my arms, guiding them up until my elbows point outward, and my hands rest behind my neck.

"Hold still," he murmurs.

Rope slides over my wrists, the friction sparking goosebumps across my skin. He binds them together, then threads the rope behind my neck, drawing it snug until it keeps my hands resting there.

The result is, I have to push out my chest. The ropes are criss-crossed to expose my nipples. Framing them. Exposing them for his delectation.

I glance down long enough to see how the ropes bear down under my thighs to lift up my pussy lips, with the engorged and very obscene looking button of my clit between them as an offering.

I feel open, exposed, in a pose of surrender that feels both restrained and intimate.

He ties off the final knot low at my stomach. His hands linger there, palms warm, grounding me in his touch.

"Look at you." He swallows. "My Christmas miracle. Wrapped for me."

My breath catches. I should feel exposed, but instead, I feel luminous. I feel seen. An offering for my master. Tied up and at my Sir's mercy. The ropes hold me the way his gaze does: reverent, possessive, protective.

He reaches up and brushes a stray lock of hair behind my ear. "How do you feel?"

"Like I belong to you." I force everything I'm feeling into my eyes, hoping he sees how much deeper I'm falling in love with him every second that we're together.

His eyes flash. His breathing grows rough. He senses how I belong to him completely. Mind. Body. And soul. I challenge him to tell me he loves me with my eyes.

His gaze turns fervent.

But when he opens his mouth, what comes out is, "You do. You belong to me. You always will. And after today, you'll never forget that."

The intent in his voice is a promise, a pledge. A declaration. He may well have carved those words into my soul. The ropes creak softly as he draws me into his arms. My skin hums where the fibers press. The yawning desire in my center is fanned by the flames in his eyes.

He drags his palms down my spine, slow and possessive, until they find my arse. He massages the skin, tender from his earlier ministrations. Electricity zips out from his touch. My nipples harden. My clit throbs.

His fingers dip into my sensitive curves, claiming, testing, worshipping. The ropes cinch across my skin, a perfect lattice that frames the curve of my buttocks, lifting and presenting me to him. The ropes frame me, and offer me up for his pleasure, his control, his indulgence.

In that moment, tied and trembling under the force of his desire and mien, I realize, this isn't about control at all. It's about surrender.

Giving myself up to be used by my master. It's a strangely freeing sensation. To realize, I've submitted myself. Put myself at his mercy. For him to do with me as he wants. That I trust him to ensure I'm thoroughly pleasured. That when it comes to my body, he knows what I want more than I know myself. As if he senses my thoughts, he steps back slightly. "Choose a safe word."

"A safe word?" I frown. "Do I need that?"

"This is your first foray into kink, so it's important that you choose it. That way, you know you're in control. Anytime you want to stop you only have to say so and I will."

Okay then.

I think for a few seconds then say, "Mistletoe."

He absorbs it, then nods. "Don't hesitate to use it." He lifts me up by the backs of my thighs then carries me to the bed. He places me on it, then bears down so I sink down to sit on my heels. He uses more of the silky rope to tie my ankles to my thighs.

Then tips me back gently onto my back. In this position, my knees are bent and spread out.

He continues to work with the rope, looping it gently around my neck once, twice. He's making a collar, I realize. I should be repulsed by it, but I'm not. It feels like the ultimate sign of ownership. But not owning me in the way of an inanimate possession. More like a promise to protect. It feels like some kind of unspoken claim. Like he's asserting his authority over me in a very intimate way.

The surge of endorphins from the thoughts course through me, relaxing my muscles. It feels like he's fully attentive, in command. His movements sure. The brush of his fingers, the slide of the rope over my skin strangely reassuring. Almost rhythmic.

Having him work on me, his focus so fixed on me, his heightened sense of awareness as he tugs on knots and checks to make sure that the ropes don't hurt my skin—not more than he intends, that is— forges a sense of emotional intimacy that's headier than anything I've encountered.

At the same time the feeling of the ropes, the pressure, the texture, the restriction they place on my movements heightens my awareness of my body. I feel myself come into my body fully for the first time ever. My breath. My heartbeat. The tension in my muscles. The rise and fall of my chest. The give of the rope against the physiological movements of my body, all of it is grounding. It's a meditative state that I haven't experienced before.

I'm floating, yet also keenly aware of everything around me. Of his breathing. His scent. The tension coiling his muscles. The elevated beating of his heart, in sync with the rhythm of my own.

He slides his finger under the collar he's fashioned for me and presses against the pulse fluttering at the hollow of my throat. "You good?"

Umm, good is not the word I'd use. More like. Ecstatic. In a kind of floating, happy kind of way. And this is from him tying me. I wonder what's going to happen when he gets around to fucking me.

His features soften. He's so tuned into me it's as if he senses my thoughts. "Answer me, Siren. You good?"

42

Lark

I jerk my chin.

"I can't proceed until you tell me so." He seems so concerned. The waves of emotions bouncing off him touches me to the core.

I swallow. "I'm good."

Some of the tension seems to slide from his shoulders. He bends his head and brushes his lips over mine. I open my mouth, hoping to invite his tongue in, wanting to feel him consume me. But he merely smiles.

"Not yet." He kisses my chin, then my nose, then my cheeks before he steps back. He reaches behind him and pulls off his T-shirt. He shucks off his sweatpants, revealing his erect cock.

It juts up against his stomach, the vein at the bottom of the length throbbing. The head is purple with drops of cum clinging to the slit. He stands there with his arms at his sides and lets me have my fill of looking at him. He's so impressive, every part of him finely sculpted. Every dip and hollow filled with echoes of his masculinity. Every crevasse between the cut muscles a reminder of his mastery over my body.

He prowls forward until he stands next to me on the bed. There's satisfaction on his features as he surveys every inch of my body. I should feel vulnerable tied as I am, with every hole in my body exposed for his inspection. But I feel anticipatory. I feel secure in myself. Knowing he wants me.

He may have not said it aloud, but his actions have made it clear how much he needs me too. It's what gives me the confidence to tip up my chin and meet his gaze.

"Look at you all laid out for my delectation." He reaches over and flicks a nipple.

He may as well have slapped me for the shock waves which radiate out from the point of contact.

A low keening cry spills from my lips. It sounds feral in intonation. Marking me out as someone who's human in form but who's darkest deepest desires have been drawn out in a whirlwind of emotions.

"Damn baby, the sounds you make will be the death of me." He flutters his fingers down the lines of ropes which dig enough into my skin to mark me. They don't hurt me, but every time I shift as much as my restraints allow, they warn me of their presence. Remind me that he's the one who tied me down. That he's the one I obey.

He reaches my belly button and lowers his head and licks into the hollow. It's both a sweet and an erotic touch. He drags his whiskered chin down to the delicate skin bared by the ropes above my pussy. Goosebumps pop on my skin. *Ohgod. Ohgod.*

I writhe in anticipation and in ecstasy.

The desperation inside me builds and spirals into a vortex threatening to draw me under. My fingertips tremble. I want so much to touch him. To dig my fingertips into those rock-hard muscles. To feel the strain of those shoulders, the tightness of his chest planes, the throb of his arousal as I wrap my fingers around his length. He reaches my exposed pussy and when he blows on it, I orgasm.

It's a sharp, straight ride to the top, and then a shattering orgasm that kicks the bottom out from under me. I shudder and shiver and groan as I recover from it.

"You're so incredibly sensitive." His voice is awed.

I look down to find him staring at me with a worshipful look in his eyes. And as if he was waiting for me to meet his gaze, he flicks out his tongue and swipes at the pulsing bud in my center.

Warmth bursts through my veins. My eyes roll back in my head. I don't have the energy to cry out. So I set my jaw and content myself with a violent shudder.

He grips the underside of my thighs and lifts them up, then licks up between my pussy lips. The fact that I'm tied down amplifies the pleasure a hundredfold. I tremble like I'm a leaf caught in the wind. Like the branches of a tree bending under heavy rainfall. The sensations fill me, pour through me, filling up my veins. Turning my blood into gasoline. And he's lighting the spark that zips up my spine. "I can't take this, I can't." I moan.

In answer, he slides two fingers inside me, curving them, touching my G-spot and I come again. This time it's a slow gentle release of the tension that's built inside me. If it weren't for the bindings, I'd dissolve into a pool of melting flesh. He brings his fingers to my mouth, and I suck on them.

"Fuck." He swallows. I take in his flushed features. The sweat that clings to his temples. He seems on the verge of coming undone.

He leans up fitting the blunt head of his cock to my opening, then with one thrust he slides inside of me.

"Fuck," he growls.

"Oh, Brody," I groan.

He stays there balanced on his arms, biceps trembling, massive chest heaving. The sweat clinging to his beautiful shoulders. "You feel so fucking good." The cords of his neck stand out in relief. "Seeing you all wrapped up in my knots, and ready and open to take everything I give you makes me feel like a fucking god."

The emotions in his voice, and the sheen in his eyes are a shock. This is the closest he's come to revealing how he feels for me.

Apparently, kink is the way to get to this man. Declarations of love aside; the physical act of tying me up is his kryptonite.

"Take me. Use me for your pleasure," I gasp.

He seems to stop breathing at that. His gaze turns molten. A mix of fire and water, and all five elements of the universe seem to come alive in his eyes.

"Goddamn, wife, you've made me your slave for life with that declaration." He bends his head and kisses me sweetly. More tenderly than before.

His lips are soft and coaxing and when I part mine willingly, he surges his tongue inside and both of us catch fire. I strain against my bindings wanting to wrap my arms around him. But then in that eerie way he has of reading my mind, he wraps his arms about me and presses more of his body weight on me, almost smothering me.

It's as if he knows how much I love feeling him on me, pinning me down. It's a sense of security. Of being held in a space where I'm no longer tied down by my body. Like I've broken free of earthly constraints and am floating near the ceiling looking down on him.

His gorgeous, beautiful body stretched out, the wings of his shoulder blades flexing, the muscles of his tight buttocks rippling, his thigh muscles coiling as he fucks into me.

Then I'm once more back in my body staring into his eyes.

"Where did you go?" He searches my face. "Thought I lost you there for a few seconds."

"I was having an out-of-body experience," I say honestly.

One side of his lips quirk, and he seems inordinately pleased. "That's what I like to hear."

With that, he pulls out of me, then lunges forward, sinking inside me again.

Once again, his face grows lax. His lips part. He seems like he's about to lose his control. I tighten my inner muscles, feeling the vise-like hold my pussy has on his cock.

"F-u-u-c-k." He pushes his forehead into mine. "I do believe I'm having an out-of-body experience, too." His movements change into long, deep strokes, as he thrust into me. Taking me. Owning me. Possessing me. This is more than fucking. This is mating... A meeting of our souls.

"Brody" I whisper. Wanting to tell him so much more. But

somehow this is all I can muster. And he seems to understand the wealth of meaning in the word for he impales me again, the edge of his pelvic bone connecting with my clit, while he slides his fingers down the cleavage between my butt cheeks to find that pleated hole.

He slides a finger inside and presses his tongue inside my mouth. And that feeling of being stuffed in all three holes with his eyes holding mine and communicating an emotion I haven't seen before whips a climax through me. I clamp down on his cock and orgasm.

Any sound I make is drawn into his mouth, along with my breath. He's consuming me completely. Finally. I feel his cock pulse inside me as he fills me with his release. Only then do I slip into oblivion.

When I open my eyes, it's to find he's undone my knots. He's watching me with a worried look on his face.

"Hi," I whisper.

"Hi." He pats a cool towel on my forehead then on my cheek. "How're you feeling?"

"Good." I smile.

He doesn't smile back.

He tosses the cloth aside, then holds out a glass of water. "Drink."

He helps me sit up, arranging the pillows at my back as I drain the glass and set it aside.

Then he reaches for a tube and squeezes some of the mixture onto his fingers. The scent of mint and something else herbal fills the air. He begins to rub me down.

I take in the patterns left on my skin by the ropes. "They're beautiful." It's as if he's branded me. And I know they're temporary but somehow it also feels like he's changed me from within.

"It's my privilege to adorn your skin with the markings from my rope."

He finishes working on my hands and torso, then rubs it down my thighs and legs, before gesturing me to turn around. By the time he's done with my back and my hamstrings. I'm so relaxed I'm sure it's all I can do to breathe.

He turns me on my back, then caps the tube and places it aside. "You should get some rest."

"Only if you sleep with me."

His features soften. He slides off the bed, pulls the curtains on the darkness outside—*when did the sun go down?*—then slips in next to me and pulls the covers over us. He pulls me close.

I throw my arm and my leg around him, and sigh. "Goodnight."

My eyes begin to flutter shut when something flashes across my mind. "My cookies, I didn't take them out of the oven," I mumble through another yawn.

"I'll do it." He kisses my forehead. "You get some sleep."

My last thought is that they're definitely burned. But that's a small price to pay for that incredible orgasm and the closeness I feel with my new husband.

This time when I wake up it's to find him dressed and watching me with a brooding expression in his eyes. He's freshly showered as evidenced by his wet hair which has been combed back. He's also wearing a button-down and a pair of black slacks. He looks delicious and like the man I first met. Especially the hardness to his features and the lack of any emotion in his eyes.

Gone is the dominant who was moved by the power exchange. The husband who took responsibility for my safety and pleasure.

I'm looking at my boss.

I don't have my dream job anymore. But what bothers me more is that I seem to have lost the one thing which makes me truly content. The attention of this man who's my husband.

Yes, I want an amazing career which fulfills me. But it means little without the man I've fallen head over heels in love with.

His next words confirm that he's not ready to share his feelings with me.

"I need to get back to work."

43

Brody

Yes, it's Boxing Day. The day after Christmas. A public holiday in the country. Not that it matters for the helicopter service I use.

Within an hour of my calling them for a pickup, we're in the air and on our way home.

I saw the surprise then the disappointment on her face when I told her that we were leaving. On the heels of it was understanding. Then sympathy. Followed by anger.

Yes, I acted exactly like the coward she accused me of being. Craven. And unable to tell her how I feel or acknowledging it to myself.

But I'm beginning to realize that self-preservation is a trait that I value more than anything other. And I need to think.

To digest what it was I felt when I saw her covered in welts from the knots I'd placed against her skin. And the marks that were painted on by the ropes I'd slid over her curves. Or the possessiveness that filled me when I looked into her eyes and came inside of her without any barriers between us.

She's the first woman with whom I haven't used a condom. And the symbolism of that isn't lost on me.

The fact that she's my wife makes it feel right. And that gives me more cause for concern.

It shouldn't feel this natural.

This effortless.

This inevitable.

Like this is where she belongs. *With me.* That this is where I belong. *With her.*

The fact that I spent the night watching her sleep and began to dream of tying her up and fucking her every night, and waking up next to her every morning, concerned me greatly.

It's not so much that I'm not committed to her. I married her and I take my vows seriously. This is different. More and more, I find myself needing her. And I can't have that.

Try as I might, I wasn't able to remove the images from my mind. The longer I stared at her, the denser they grew. Until I began dreaming of caring for her, contemplated falling for her, wondered how it would be to have a forever with her that consists of more than a piece of paper.

What if I gave her more than my name? What if I gave her my heart?

To say that sounded the alarm bells is an understatement.

That's when I knew, I had to get back. Enough of this honeymoon bullshit.

The marriage has been consummated.

Gramps is happy that we're legally married. Enough to hand over my portion of the shares in the company. His lawyer reached out about giving me access to my trust fund before the ceremony.

This is why I went through with the marriage, after all. And yes, to help her go through with a wedding to save her the ignominy of being dumped a few days before she walked down the altar.

All of which were delivered. There's no need to pretend anymore. Is there?

Except. I'm in love with my wife, and I don't have the guts to confess my feelings to her.

I've gone on missions where one wrong move meant death.

I've dragged brothers out of danger and stared down enemies without blinking.

I've faced corporate predators who'd sell their own blood for a profit.

But none of it prepared me for this feeling of being torn apart from inside.

There's no need to accept that, for the first time, there's something in my life that feels more important than myself and what I need.

I glance sideways to find her looking out the window. She's wearing jeans and a sweatshirt and has her hair put up in a messy bun with tendrils escaping that frame her face. That familiar lurch of my heart, the one I'm not used to yet, takes me by surprise.

No, what I feel for her is not simple at all.

And I have a sinking feeling that it might be too late to put distance between us. But I have to try.

"Ten minutes to landing," the pilot's voice comes over our earphones.

Suddenly, the chopper pitches to the side, then dips as if the bottom has fallen out of the world.

She gasps and grips the armrests. My heart threatens to leap out of my rib cage, and all I can think to do is grab her and hold her close.

Then the helicopter straightens out. It regains altitude, then levels out. It's flying along now like that brush with turbulence never happened.

"Sorry, folks. Bit of wind shear. Caught us off guard, but all good now," the pilot apologizes.

Some of the tension slides from me, but my muscles refuse to relax completely. My heart feels like it's in my throat. My cheat heaves, and each inhale scrapes against my throat. I have her head pushed into my chest, and for a few seconds, she stays there.

I sense her trembling and run my fingers down her hair.

"It's fine. You heard the pilot. We're okay."

She nods. Takes in a few breaths. She doesn't let go of me, and I don't release her, either.

I tuck her head under my chin and absorb her nearness. It was a patch of rough weather. I've faced much worse on my tours as a Royal Marine. But that had been *me* in the line of fire. That, I can cope with.

The thought of anything happening to her, though, is unbearable. It sets my heart racing and my pulse rate multiplying all over again.

She must feel my agitation for she runs slow circles over my back. Her touch is soothing. The gentleness of her touch a balm for my ragged nerves. Slowly, the rest of the tension fades away. But I don't let go of her. And to my relief, she doesn't try to break free of my embrace either.

Once we land, I help her off the chopper.

Our bags are unloaded, and I thank the pilot, who apologizes again for the rough ride. I wave him off, it's not his fault, and really, it barely lasted a few seconds. But it was enough to turn my world upside down. I can't seem to let go of her hand as I walk her to the waiting car.

Once inside, though, I take refuge in the length of the back seat between us.

Coward.

The fresh burst of confused feelings inside of me doesn't let me start a conversation or look at her.

I sense her shift restlessly in her seat and look at me a few times. But I pretend not to notice. I keep my gaze firmly on the passing scenery. Once we reach home, my manners don't allow me to leave her behind. I make sure to be the first out of the car and wave the chauffeur off to open her door. She doesn't look at me as she gets out of the car and precedes me to the house.

I should carry her over the threshold. This is the first time we're coming home after the wedding. And this is her home as much as mine. I do want her to feel comfortable here. Only I'm unable to get the words out.

The incident on the chopper has revealed the depths of my feelings for her, and that's confused me further.

Surely, I can't have fallen for her so quickly?

But my reaction to thinking I could lose her was pure panic. And the realization that my life would be incomplete without her. The thought of losing her makes it difficult for me to breathe. My world only makes sense with her in it. It was a blinding, and unwelcome, revelation. One which is sinking in. Not surprisingly, it took a perceived brush with death to strip away my bullshit refusal to call it what it is.

Love.

I'm in love with my wife.

And I want to tell her how I feel. But I don't know how.

Which means, I'm thoroughly fucked.

Because, for the first time in my adult life, I'm vulnerable.

Cracked open in a way I swore I never would be again. Not since I stood at my parents' graves, stone-faced and hollow, pretending I didn't care while my insides burned.

When my father died, I turned to my mother for solace. And, when she too was gone, the world felt stripped bare. Like someone had torn away the shield and left me standing naked in the cold.

And this…this thing I feel for my wife…it hits deeper.

It's a hunger that chews through bone. A constant ache that eases when she's near, when her scent is in my lungs, when her voice threads through the chaos in my head. And when she's gone… Christ, it's like a void opens inside me, dragging me under.

If this raw, consuming, brutal thing that turns me inside out and threatens to eviscerate me is love, then I want no part of it.

But it's too late.

Because it's found me.

I'm in love with her. And no matter how hard I fight, I can't shake it off.

I carry our bags into the house, then take the stairs. She follows me. I reach my bedroom, leave my suitcase by the door, and carry hers inside the closet. Then, I grab a couple of suits and ties, along with business shoes, and step out with my arms full.

She turns from where she's standing next to the bed. When she takes in what I'm carrying, her gaze widens. "What are you doing?"

Good question. What the fuck am I doing?

44

Lark

Remember that hot cocoa and Christmas pudding is not a meal replacement.
(What a pity!)

—From Lark's Christmas to-do list

"I'm moving into the guest room."

Ugh. Seriously? How can he do this? My heart sinks. I feel my spirits dip. But I don't show him how upset I am.

Instead, I huff. "I hope you realize how predictable this is?"

He seems to take affront to that. "How so?"

"First, you insist you have no feelings for me. This, despite the fact that when the helicopter ran into a little turbulence, you all but threw me down and covered me with your body."

"It wasn't a little turbulence, it dropped nearly fifty feet, which is serious. And I was doing what any soldier would have done in my position. I wanted to protect my wife."

The way he says 'my wife' has chills clutching at my nerve endings. Only his face is set in tight lines. And his eyes — they have a sheen of cold glass encasing the irises, so I can't really see what he's feeling. But I know.

He's retreated behind those walls I thought, nae hoped, had come down permanently. Apparently, he has reserves of aloofness hidden deep inside that he's able to draw up like bridges across a moat. Once more, he's that island of detachment with signs saying 'keep off' that I noticed when I first met him. And the more I try to prove the error of his ways to him, the more he's going to resist. The more he's going to insist that he has no feelings for me.

Still, I have to try one last time.

"If you don't care about me, why did you tie me up and fuck me?"

He blinks. Clearly, he didn't expect me to ask him that outright. Well, too bad.

I'm not going to shove things under a carpet and pretend I didn't see what I did all those times he made love to me. I'm not a coward. I can name things, even if he can't.

Hiding and pretending the emotions we feel don't exist makes for miscommunication, and I'm keen to avoid it.

"I tied you up…because you were my very own Christmas present to unwrap."

"Oh." My insides quiver. My pussy throbs. My skin tingles with memories of how I felt when he tightened those silken ropes around my limbs.

"And because that's the kind of kink I enjoy — when the woman I'm fucking is tied up and helpless and submits to me. So I can do what I want with her body."

I swallow. It's so erotic, having him talk about his preferences with that emotionless face. The contradiction between the eroticism of his words and the straightlaced features makes me all hot and bothered.

I'm in a lot of trouble if my husband talking has me so turned on.

But there's something he hasn't taken into consideration. Something I can read between the lines. Something I can see in how he rakes his gaze over me. And how his fingers tremble to touch me. How his muscles bunch as he holds himself back. How his body wants to protectively lean over me.

I tip up my chin. "If you'd tied up anyone else, it wouldn't have affected you so much."

He seems to reel back at that. His eyes widen. He firms his lips, but the tendons standing out at his neck tell me my words have hit home.

"It's because I'm your wife that my submitting to you in bed had such an impact on you," I murmur in a steady voice.

Inside, I'm melting, both from the lust that crackles in the air between us, and because it's the first time I've said aloud that I submitted to him. And hearing myself admit it brings home the gravity of what happened between us. He must recognize it too, for his features soften. He takes a few steps forward, until he stands in front of me.

"I'm grateful you trusted me enough to tie you up. I'll never forget that you let me pleasure your body and take from you what I needed to satisfy myself. But you must understand it can't happen again."

His stubbornness is so annoying.

I throw up my hands. "You're kidding right?"

But no. There's no mistaking the resolution in his features. Or the way he holds himself erect. There's a certain finality in his stance that makes my heart sink. Oh no. He's going to brush aside whatever he feels for me. He's going to pretend it doesn't matter. That it's fleeting and doesn't mean anything.

"Don't do this." I swallow.

But before he glances away, I know my appeals are not going to be heard.

Thanks to the incident on the helicopter, when he realized what he feels for me, he's running scared. First despair, then anger grips me.

You know what? Fuck him.

If he can't face his emotions, then there's nothing I can do. I'm not going to spend my time moping. I'm not going to try to convince him otherwise. This is something he has to realize on his own.

Meanwhile, I'm not going to mope around his house. Except, sleeping in his room, in his bed, which smells of him, is going to make it all worse.

I draw myself up to my full height and tip up my chin. "Fine. You do what's best for you."

He seems taken aback then recovers. "I will."

His features are smooth. Every shred of feeling locked away behind that mask. Someone give this man an Oscar. He's perfected this role of someone who's shut down all feelings.

He heads for his suitcase and rolls it down the hall. Then stops. "I'll meet you in the home office in twenty minutes to start the handover for your new position."

The door closes behind him.

That's it? He walked out like it doesn't matter to him that we're not sharing a bed anymore. That he doesn't care I'll no longer be in his arms at night? That he'll no longer do to my body the wicked things which brought me, *and him*, so much pleasure. Like it doesn't matter to him that we'll no longer be husband and wife in the true sense of the word.

I manage to keep the emotions off my face.

No sense in letting him see how much his words have affected me.

Everything in this room reminds me of him, but I can't let that affect me. I need to see this through. I must hope that, at some point, he's going to acknowledge his feelings for me.

Until then, I need to put up a front. And make sure he doesn't realize how much I miss him.

I roll my shoulders, shake out my hands, and take a few deep breaths. It doesn't really help, but it's a relief to keep moving. To keep my thoughts on what I must do next.

Twenty minutes later, I walk into the home office on the first floor.

I haven't yet given up my apartment. But while we were away Brody asked a team to move my clothes, my shoes, and of course, all of my cosmetics and books into his place.

Yep, he had them working through Christmas to do so.

He hasn't given me a tour of the house, but it's not so big that I can get lost in it. It's not tiny either. There are four bedrooms on the second floor, including the master bedroom.

For a few seconds I mourn the loss of my apartment. I took such pains to decorate it too. Not that he'd mind if I changed the décor in this town house to suit my tastes.

In fact, he'd welcome it.

Too bad, he isn't as open with revealing his feelings for me.

On the first floor, an open-plan living room flows into the kitchen, which in turn opens onto a deck that faces Primrose Hill.

There's also a gym and an office/library, which is where I meet him.

He's seated behind the big desk. Wearing his slacks and button-down, his stance is all business.

I notice the bookshelf lining one wall and can't resist walking over. My fingers trail across the spines of the books, until I spot a familiar title.

"No way." I pull it free. "You read romance novels?"

I turn to him, stunned.

He seems uncomfortable, then adjusts his glasses. "I'm terrible at talking about my feelings. I figured I'd try learning from the experts. Hence—" he nods at the book in my hand.

I arch a brow. "And do you think it's helped?"

A faint crease forms between his brows before he smooths it away. "The jury's still out."

At least, he's honest about his inability to speak about his feelings. That's a start, right? I slip the book back onto the shelf, my heart tugging a little, then cross to his desk.

Once I take the seat opposite him, he nods to the device in front of me. "I emailed the CEO Delegation of Authority Document. It formalizes your powers, like spending limits, sign-off rights, hiring/firing, etc. You'll also find the board communications & strategy briefs, annual and quarterly performance reports with the KPI dashboards, operational plans, legal and compliance overviews, and the org chart."

I've been privy to a lot of company information as his EA, but what he's sent me is akin to handing the literal keys to his kingdom. He's sent me everything I need to run the business.

"You sure you want me to take over as CEO?" I feel pulled to ask him again.

He places the tips of his fingers together. "As sure as I was that I wanted to marry you."

His reference to our wedding is like a fist to my solar plexus, and I'm not sure I keep the hurt off my face.

It was only yesterday that he tied me up and fucked me. But with the width of the desk between us, it feels in the past. When his eyes heat, and he sucks his lip inward, I know he's recalling how he made me do his bidding. How I sucked him off. How he took me with such assurance. How he made me his.

Then he blinks, and the possessiveness is replaced by a clinical detachment.

Now he's all CEO. One who's handing over the tools to his successor.

I pull up the documents on my device. He takes me through them. One after the other. Relentless. Projections. P&L. Cash flow forecasts. Payroll and benefits summaries. HR challenges. Vendor & contracts fulfillment. The hours wear on.

Except for a short break, where he serves me coffee from the minibar in the corner of the room, he doesn't stop. His analysis is precise. He outlines foreseen problems in a crisp tone. Astute. Summarizing complex operational objectives and potential conflict zones between department heads. My head spins. My eyes hurt, but I don't complain. I can do this.

I can keep pace with his steel-trap-like mind. I can deliver on the role he's entrusted me with. When my phone buzzes, I welcome the respite. It's on my desk, face up.

His glance is drawn to it, as is mine.

The screen indicates: Keith calling

Huh? Why would he phone me? To be honest, I've forgotten about my ex. Also, maybe I'm exhausted from perusing all the spreadsheets, but my reflexes are slow.

Before I can reach for my phone, my husband snatches it up and answers. "Hello?" He raises his gaze to mine. "If you try to reach my wife again, I'll come over and tear your tongue from your throat." He disconnects, then his fingers fly over the screen.

"What are you doing?"

"Blocking him so he'll never reach you again." He slides the phone across the desk.

A warm rush of sensations pools between my legs. When Brody gets all possessive, it's the sweetest, most erotic, most reassuring feeling ever. He makes me feel owned and claimed and seen, in a way my ex never could.

Still, I feel drawn to put up a token of resistance. "That was an invasion of my privacy."

Not that it's going to make a difference.

Brody's a law unto his own. Also, he's invaded so much of my body, him doing the same to my privacy feels minor by comparison.

When he continues to stare at me from under hooded eyelids, I firm my lips. "You didn't have to go all caveman." Internally though, my heart booms in my chest, my stomach flutters, and my traitorous pussy is swollen with being turned on at how he told Keith off. How he seemed pissed off and upset, and *jealous* that my ex called me.

How can I be so stupidly happy that he asserted his control over me? This, after telling me that he didn't want to share a room with me.

"I beg to disagree." He firms his mouth. "The thought of your ex trying to talk to you, makes my blood boil."

45

Brody

I'm frustrated at the jealousy I feel that her ex called her. And I'm confused about these primitive feelings welling up inside of me. The bitterness that he has her number, that she considered answering his phone call, makes me want to take her across my lap and punish her.

I glare at her, and she pales.

Then, in that spirited response I've come to expect of her, she tips up her chin. "I didn't do anything wrong."

"You still have his number in your phone; that was wrong."

"Maybe, he was calling because he owes me the money for the wedding."

"We don't need it."

"I *did* almost marry him," she points out.

"But you didn't. You married me." I lean forward in my seat. "You're *my* wife."

I don't bother to hide the proprietary tone in my voice. I'm giving away how, despite moving into the guest room and wanting to keep some separation between us, I'm not quite succeeding. Given how she watches me with a speculative look in her eyes, it's clear she's noticed it too.

"You call me your wife, yet you're unable to deal with the emotions that evokes in you." Her voice trembles. "You don't want to share me. You're upset because my ex called, yet you can't name your feelings. You can't own your vulnerabilities." She curls her fingers into fists.

I drag a hand through my hair, frustration tightening in my chest. She's right. I want her. I love her. And yet, the words stay trapped behind my teeth. She looks at me, waiting.

The air between us hums with tension, electric and heavy. It skims over my skin and winds tighter inside me until I can hardly breathe. I open my mouth, ready to finally tell her what she means to me, but all that comes out is, "That's it for today. I'll see you tomorrow at seven. We'll ride to the office together."

Her face falls.

I almost jump to my feet and round the table to gather her in my arms. But I stop myself. I need time to think this through.

Maybe if I sleep on it, things will be clearer?

I rise to my feet. "Goodnight, Lark." *My sweet wife.*

I manage not to look at her as I walk past. Manage not to pause at the doorway and call out to her to come with me. Manage to keep my gaze straight ahead, mount the stairs, and head to the guest room. Once there, I look around the space, a little lost. Just a few nights of making love to her and holding her in my arms in bed, and I'm not sure how I'm going to sleep without her.

Shoving aside thoughts of her and the hard-on I sport at the thought of how I fucked her, I strip off my clothes and head into the en suite bathroom. I turn the shower on cold and step under it. I gasp a little at the contrast with my heated skin.

But long years of showers in the barracks, and wherever we stayed when on tour, means I adjust quickly. It also means, it doesn't do much to bring down my chub. With a sigh, I pour conditioner into my palm, then squeeze my very erect shaft from root to crown. Thoughts of the welts I painted into her skin with the ropes fill my head. Images of Lark's big eyes, swollen lips, trembling tits and thighs, and all that glistening pink flesh between them, crowd my mind. I swell further in my palm. Fuck. This is not going to work.

Not when the reason for my being this turned on is down the hall in my bedroom. I squeeze again from base to tip, and again.

"That looks painful."

The words are spoken low, yet they reach me over the noise made by the shower. I'm not surprised to open my eyes and find her standing at the entrance to the large shower cubicle. She's also naked. *Fuck*. Gloriously. Lushly. Naked. I drink in the sight of her hair cascading around her shoulders, the swollen tits I imagined in my thoughts a few seconds ago, now revealed in front of me. The tiny waist, that slight, sweet roll of her stomach, then those gorgeously flared hips, and fleshy thighs which I swear, I need to mark with my teeth and my nails.

I continue to jerk myself off as I take in my erotic dream come to life. "Come 'ere," I growl.

She swallows, then slowly puts one foot in front of the other. Step by step, she approaches. When she reaches me, I notice she has one hand hidden behind her.

"What do you have there?" I arch an eyebrow.

She looks guilty, then holds up her hand with a sprig of mistletoe suspended from between her fingers.

Her safe word. Which she's now laying out between us as an offering, perhaps? A sign that she's giving in to her innermost desires?

Does my little wife have any idea how transparent she is?

"Where did you get that?" I allow my lips to tilt up slightly on one side.

"I noticed an oak tree in your garden. After you left, I decided to walk out and pick one. Figured it gave me an excuse to come into your room. Then I found you under the shower." She shrugs.

"You don't need an excuse to come to me. You never need an excuse to ask me for what you want."

I hold out my hand, and when she places the mistletoe in it, I carefully place it on the far side of the shower bench, out of the reach of the water. Then I seat myself, part my legs, and nod to the space between my feet.

She willingly folds herself and sinks to her knees. I reach out and shut off the shower. In the silence that follows, the sound of her breathing is audible.

She reaches for my cock, and I click my tongue. "You may only use your mouth, your tongue, and your teeth."

She scowls. "Is that a challenge?"

"Why not?" I lean back against the shower wall. As she stares at my cock, the blood rushes to my groin, extending it further, elongating it, making it bob against my lower belly.

She flicks out her little tongue to lick at her lower lip, a giveaway of how much she's aroused. The thought of my wife locking her gorgeous mouth around my shaft and sucking me off is enough to knot the muscles in my groin. My testicles tighten. I widen my legs to accommodate my erection.

As if it's a sign, she bends and licks around the rim of my shaft. A line of fire zips up my spine. I grit my teeth and focus on tamping down this need to come right away. Instead, I hold her hair away from her face so I can watch my cock disappear inside her mouth. Everything I've said about eroticism before? Forget it. This…right here…my wife swallowing my dick down her throat and gagging around it, and my wrapping my fingers gently around her neck to feel the shape of my dick ensconced in the snug column, is the answer to a prayer I've never voiced aloud.

I tighten my hold on her hair. In response, she looks up at me. A teardrop stays balanced at the tips of her eyelashes. Unable to stop myself, I run my finger over it and scoop it up. She shivers. The walls of her throat tighten around my cock.

"Fucking hell, wife, you're going to be the death of me." I gently pull her back, so my cock stays balanced on her lower lip.

Saliva drools from the edges of her mouth. Combined with the strands of wet hair that stick to her head, and her mascara running down her cheeks, she resembles something forbidden. Something almost innocent. Except, she isn't. Not anymore. Not when I've introduced her to the pleasures of the world I inhabit.

It's a different side from the woman I interviewed for the role of my EA.

I was immediately entranced by her.

She never hesitated to go toe-to-toe with me. She delivered on her promise of being a spitfire. But that guilelessness that marked her out like she was wearing a crown of neon is now tarnished. By me. It's both humbling and a source of pride that I was the one to awaken those hidden cravings in her.

I created this version of her who craves being dominated by me. Who'll yield only to me. Who'll never bend that proud head to anyone else except me. A fierce protectiveness arises in me. I shaped her. Molded her into my fantasy.

A woman who's both fiery and submissive. Who can match my intelligence in the boardroom. Who isn't scared of exploring the kinkier side of herself. Who looks at me like the sun rises and sets with me.

It's hard to miss the adoration in her eyes; it makes me feel twenty feet tall. That yearning with which she now looks at me while swallowing around my cock.

Her features are flushed. The pulse at the base of her neck flutters like the wings of a dragonfly. One who will be imprisoned by me. For I'm never letting her go. The decision sinks into me, and instantly, a sense of utter peace, of rightness, descends on me. Of course, I'm not allowing her to leave me. She's mine. I married her. I'm keeping her.

I'm never letting her go.

She must see some of the emotions flickering across my features, for her gaze widens. She begins to sit back on her heels, but I hold her in place with my grip on her hair. I ease her forward, and my dick slips down her throat. I hold her there once more, allowing her to adjust to my size. Then slide my hand down to cup her swollen tit. I pinch her nipple, and she almost loses her balance. Of course, my hold on her keeps her upright. The flush spreads to her décolletage, then her torso. The rosy hue covering her skin is a delight. I slide my foot between her knees and kick them further apart.

Her shoulders tremble; her pupils are so blown, she might well be on a hallucinogen. A flush of pride fills me. I did this to her. I'm the one to give her so much pleasure, she looks like it might take but a touch before she climaxes.

"Don't you dare come," I warn.

Her gaze narrows. A flash of obstinacy lights up her eyes. I allow a small chuckle to escape.

I've pissed her off. Good. I want her to fight me. Not that it's a fair scenario; I'm going to win. Her body knows who's in charge. Not that it's going to stop her from putting up a spirited defense.

To illustrate my point, I arch my foot so my toe grazes across her slit. She jumps. Her breathing intensifies. The green of her eyes turns almost golden. Fuck, she's beautiful when she's aroused. Tied down by nothing but my words. Which makes her struggle more delicious.

My cock thickens, pushing out on the walls of her mouth. I tighten my hold on her nipple and tweak it. At the same time, I breach her slit with my big toe and begin to fuck her mouth in earnest.

The triple assault on her senses makes her entire body jolt. Her thighs tremble, her shoulders snap back, and I know she's close. I straighten my foot so I can slip my toe inside her channel fully. I ease her head back, then forward. And when I punch my hips, I hit the back of her throat.

She gags. Her inner walls close around my toe. And I realize then, the assault is as much on my senses. For my balls draw up. I release my hold on her and cup both of her breasts, massaging them.

"I'm coming."

46

Lark

That's all the warning I get. I feel his shaft kick back as he empties himself down my throat. I can barely taste him.

He's come inside me so many times the last few days, yet each climax lasts a long time. When he pulls back, I taste the salty, musk of his cum. He paints my lips with the crown of his cock. And when I lick it up, something shifts behind his eyes.

He hauls me up and replaces my tongue with his. He swipes it across my mouth, and when I part my lips, he slides his tongue inside. He lifts me up and onto his lap, so I straddle him. My pussy slides over his heavy shaft.

And even though he's come, he's still erect.

It feels so good to have him throb against my opening.

He'd feel better if he were to stuff the aching hollow inside with it. When I begin to rub myself up against the thick column, I expect him to stop me. Instead, he leans back further, trains his gaze on where my pussy drips all over his cock and drawls, "If you can come, you may."

I almost cry out in relief. I balance my knees on either side of him, gripping the outside of his thighs, then begin to work myself over the ridge of his cock. Oh God. That feels so good.

I let my head fall back, open my mouth, aware I'm making little noises, very explicit noises, as I grind myself on the column of his dick. Again. And again. And again. Until the tightness at the base of my spine expands out, grips my thighs, and rises up my spine. I still don't stop. I'm aware his heavy palms are on my hips, balancing me.

I grip his arms, all of my focus on where I'm pleasuring myself on his cock.

"Such a slut you are, wife. Are you going to come all over my shaft?"

I nod.

"Are you going to drench my dick with your cum?"

"Yesss," I hiss. Helpless to the onslaught of the climax that pours over me, I shudder, and groan, and whimper as my orgasm forces its way out of me. I'm panting and seeing stars. And he holds me, rubs my back, and eases me against his chest.

I lay there, hearing the thundering of my heart in my ears, and the satisfying drumming of his in his chest. His beating as fast as mine, I note.

The next moment, he's rising, holding me in his arms. He steps out the cubicle and sets me down. He rubs the towel over me , then himself.

His biceps bulge, his pecs bunch under his skin. My pussy clenches in response.

The heat, which is never far from the surface, is quick to rise under my skin.

Then he scoops me up once more, walks me to the bed, and lays me down on it. One flick of his hands, and I'm on my front. He grips my hips and pulls me up so I'm on my knees, my cheek flattened to the mattress. The bed dips, and the next thing I know, he's pulling my thighs apart. I feel him between my legs, holding me up with his hands squeezing the outside of my thighs.

Then he licks up my pussy lips, and I whimper. That feels so good. I dig my fingers into the mattress, giving myself over to the sensation of him sucking on my lower lips. And slurping at my slit. And flicking his tongue around my clit. And when he plays with the pleated skin between my ass cheeks, the pinpricks of heat under my skin fan into flames.

"Please." I writhe my hips, trying to squeeze my thighs together to relieve the pressure between them.

"Keep your legs apart." He slaps my butt.

Sweet frosted pinecones. That hurts. It shouldn't take me by surprise, but it does.

The pain rolls up my spine, pushing aside all thoughts in my head.

It's like a sign for me to stop struggling. To relax my muscles. To take the spanking he administers on my alternate butt cheeks.

I count until twenty, and by the time he's done, my backside smarts. I feel the individual palm prints as if burned into my butt. The skin throbs. Alternating hot and cold shivers course through me. He cups my cheeks and rubs in the pain.

I groan loudly.

"The sounds you make. I could come from the need in them alone." His voice is strained.

Then he slides his fingers inside my swollen cunt. Two… No, I count three of them. He twists them, hitting my G-spot, setting off another chain of shudders.

He pulls his fingers out. I look over my shoulder in time to see him licking them clean. His eyes are so dark, they seem almost black. His expression is one of avarice.

"I'm going to fuck you, wife."

He rises on his knees, his strong thighs bunching. He holds my gaze as he fits his swollen cock to my slit.

"Would you like me to come inside you, wife? Would you like me to leave a part of me inside you?"

Oh God. His low, dark voice is tinged with enough malice to let me know that his questions are rhetorical. He knows, as much as I do, how much I love to have him inside me. To feel his cock swell inside me and paint my insides with his cum.

A few months ago, I'd have been horrified if someone had told me I'd be at the receiving end of such explicitness, and that it would be my husband who'd be speaking to me this way. That he'd be tying me up and spanking me, and that I'd enjoy it.

But here we are.

I want him to take me, use me and do to me whatever he wants. I want him to pleasure me. To take pleasure from me. I want him to push my limits because, damn, the orgasms are so much better when he does.

"Yes," I gasp. "Yes, please."

His eyes flash. "You beg so prettily wife. I might just oblige you."

He punches his hips forward and buries himself inside me. And doesn't stop. He doesn't let me catch my breath.

Every time he impales me, the force of it rattles the headboard against the wall. But he holds me pinned with his big hands on my hips. Squeezing me in such a way, I know he's marking me, and that turns me on further. Not to mention, he has this uncanny knack of hitting my G-spot, which turns my insides into a melting, blubbering mess.

And then he reaches down and slaps my cunt, and it's as if my blood has turned into gasoline and his touch is the spark, and I ignite into a fireball of need. I'm aware of him grunting as he fucks me through my climax.

He plants his big hands on either side of my body, curves over me, half protectively, half in a sign that screams possession. Then he digs his teeth into the curve where my shoulder meets my neck.

The pain is a sharp agony that whips through the drugging orgasm. He holds on with his sharp teeth as he releases his cum inside me. I shudder, half mad with the mix of pleasure-pain, which totally confuses the receptors in my brain.

The feral edge to his gesture sends me over the edge, and I come again. He continues to thrust into me, holding me and fucking me through the aftermath. It feels like he's taken over my body, possessed me, marked in some deep way I can't quite give voice too.

And when he finally releases his hold on my shoulder, the blood rushes into the space.

I'm sure I'm bleeding from where he bit me, but as I think that, I know he was careful.

I'm sure he planned the exact pressure to give me maximum pain while leaving the imprints of his teeth in my skin, but he wouldn't have broken the skin.

Then he pulls out of me, and with measured movements, lowers himself to the side. He pulls me into his arms, and I lay there, once more, listening to the bam-bam-bam of his heart as it thunders against his chest.

The slick flesh of his cock, still half-swollen, lazily nestles against my side.

"This is going to be a problem," he rumbles, half to himself.

I look up. "A problem?"

He tucks a strand of hair behind my ear, his expression half-awed, half-frustrated.

"I can't seem to go long without wanting to fuck you."

"Umm, I don't see any problem with that," I say primly.

He smirks. Then grabs a handful of my butt and squeezes. "It does mean that I'm not going to stay too far away from you at any time. What do you think about that?"

47

Brody

Turns out, she wasn't averse to the idea at all.

Over the next few days, she also slipped into the role of the CEO like she was born to do it. I brought her up to speed with the obvious things: briefings on current board dynamics, key department heads she needed to build rapport with, upcoming product launches, media touchpoints.

There was also the less visible layer: understanding the rhythms of the business, the politics woven through every email and offhand comment, the unspoken alliances that shaped every major decision.

The more I gave her, the more I saw how capable she was. I had no doubt that she was going to kill it. The time we spent together worked in my favor.

We spent a lot of time alone in my office. I made full use of my CEO privileges for the time I still had them.

I'd darken the office walls, lock the door, and ask the newly appointed EA to my ex-EA not to disturb us.

Then I'd fuck my wife.

I made sure to keep nipple and clit clamps on hand to heighten her pleasure. My desk was the right height to bend her over it, while the paddle I purchased was perfect for leaving reddened rectangles over the curve of her butt.

It doesn't mean I neglected the handover of my CEO duties, either.

I walked her through investor expectations, reviewed legacy deals she was inheriting, flagged the power players who didn't sit at the table but controlled half the room. We combed through strategy decks, HR restructures, confidential staff issues, and vendor contracts worth millions.

Very soon, all the information I've carried around in my head and in the files is hers.

It's a testament to her astuteness that a handover which should have taken months was accomplished in days. Which is a pity. I'd hoped it would take longer. I was enjoying our workday trysts.

The evenings have been all mine. And I've used the time to take her out to dinners and to the movies, before bringing her home, tying her up, and fucking her.

I've enjoyed every bit of it. Too much. We sleep in the same bed. And I wake up with her in my arms. I enjoy waking up before her and watching her. I've felt my heart move, and a softness has taken over my chest. I'm falling for her more every day. And I'm helpless to stop it.

I'm aware of the repercussions of this. Of making myself vulnerable to her. Giving her a chance to hurt me. Or worse, risking something happening to her and being destroyed. But none of it matters. Not when I tie her up, lower her onto the desk in my home office, and fuck her. Not when I take the wooden ruler to the soles of her feet, and her thighs, and her breasts, leaving my marks on her, and then shag her. And every time, as I edge her and then topple her into subspace, I can't help but follow her. Trapped in a web of my own making.

I can't stop using her body to satisfy my desires. I can't stop *myself* from satisfying her desires, either.

But there's no getting out of the board meeting this morning. The one which she's going to chair for the first time as CEO.

48

Lark

The oak table gleams under the lights, so polished I can see my own reflection in its surface. I take in the faces around the table. It'd be wrong to say I'm not wary. Difference is, I don't feel intimidated by the board. Guess the view looks different when you're seated at the head of the table?

The room smells familiar: of polish and power plays. But unlike the last time I was here, I'm the one setting the tone.

It's New Year's Eve. Yesterday, the board of directors voted to confirm me as CEO of Davenport Capital, taking over from my husband. And today, I wasted no time calling my first board meeting. It's unusual to have one so soon after the last one, but not unheard of.

But these are unusual circumstances, with my taking over as CEO with no warning.

That, combined with the fact that it's the last day of the year, when the city thrums with excitement and everyone's making plans to ring in the new year, means I can catch them with their guard down. Or so, Brody advised me.

"Even the most cynical board member isn't immune to the holiday mood. There's a hum of anticipation in the air, and that means distraction. Distraction means advantage. *Your* advantage," he said.

Once he laid it out like that, I didn't hesitate. I took his advice and called the meeting.

Only Brody won't be attending. He's still a member of the board and perfectly entitled to be here, but he wants me to lead this one on my own.

To establish myself. To make it clear that the title isn't a courtesy. To show them I can lead this company.

"Let's begin." I turn the page on the deck. "The Q4 P&L is ahead of forecast by nine percent. Operating margins are up six percent, and we've reduced discretionary spend by twelve percent without compromising growth."

Gazes lower. Foreheads crinkle as they peruse the contents of the document before them. There's silence. Until Julian Reed clears his throat.

"Impressive numbers, Mrs. Davenport. I imagine the wedding band did wonders for your prospects?"

The words drop like a match on dry kindling.

Ursula Dalton, seated halfway down the table, stiffens. She narrows her gaze on Julian. But I lift my hand before she can open her mouth. I don't need anyone else to fight this battle.

"Mr. Reed." I fold my hands on the table. "You're not suggesting my marriage earned me this role?"

A few uneasy glances bounce around the table. Julian gives a half-smile. "Just observing how…quickly things moved."

And there we have it.

"You're right. It was quick. The board realized I was doing the job without the title. Which is why Arthur Davenport nominated me for the role. And the members of this board, who are in this room, appointed me as CEO."

Brody handing his shares over to me gave me voting power. And

Arthur backing me, as the Chairman of the board, meant my appointment was sealed. But the board still needed to vote for me. And all of them had.

Except for Julian, who curls his lip.

"Now, if we can move to projections for next year." I turn the page on the deck. The rest follow.

"Revenue growth is projected at eleven percent, driven by sustained performance in digital and logistics. Which you will agree, is stellar."

Most of the heads around the table nod.

Except Julian's.

He leans back in his chair, fingers steepled, voice smooth as glass. "Stellar projections," he says. A smirk plays at the corners of his mouth. "Though one might argue, optimism comes easily when your grandfather-in-law chairs the board."

The air thickens. Ursula goes still. Tension ripples around the room.

"An interesting observation, Julian." I flip to the next page of my report. "Though *you*, of all people, should know that projections are approved by the oversight committee and not by marital consensus."

A few quiet chuckles break the silence.

I glance up, meeting his gaze head-on. "Every figure in this report was reviewed by Finance, verified by Audit, and ratified by Strategy. The same committees you sit on. So, if you're questioning my objectivity, you might want to extend that doubt to your own minutes."

A beat. Then Arthur's low chuckle rumbles through the room. "And that's why she got my vote to be CEO."

I turn around to find Arthur walking into the room, with Tiny at his side.

The Great Dane ignores the rest of the board members, and with his head held high and his tail higher, he ambles across the carpet until he reaches me. He bumps me with his big head.

Love bursts inside my chest. I scratch him behind his ear. He huffs, then plants himself on the floor next to me.

It's not that I was nervous facing those around the table—okay, so maybe I was a little—but having Tiny by my side definitely bolsters my courage.

Arthur walks over to one of the two empty seats at the table. One is Brody's; the other belongs to him. He takes the one closest to me, then gestures. "Proceed."

I clear my throat, picking up my train of thought.

"Now, unless there are further personal theories to discuss, I suggest we turn our attention back to performance, which is, after all, the only thing that pays dividends."

"Hear, hear." Ursula claps her hands.

Arthur's features are wreathed in a smile.

Julian's smirk fades. He looks down at his notes.

Tiny shifts beside me, tail thumping once against the floor.

I turn another page. "As I was saying, projected revenue growth for next year is eleven percent, with continued margin expansion from operational efficiencies. And unlike gossip, that's substantiated by data."

"You fucking aced it." My husband strides into my office, which used to be his, and pulls out his phone.

With a quick tap, the walls of the office turn opaque. I may have taken over his office, but he has access to the privacy settings. For moments like this.

He holds out his arms. I break into a run. He catches me and whirls me around.

"I am so proud of you." He grins up at me.

My heart is so full, it feels like it's going to burst out of my chest. To have my husband look at me like I'm the most important thing in the entire world, and to know that he *means* it, is a feeling I never thought I would hold.

"You heard," I say breathlessly.

"Arthur called me on his way home and gave me the low down. He couldn't stop gushing about how you eviscerated Julian Reed."

I wince. "He was asking questions which I'd already asked of myself."

"But you had all the answers," he growls.

"I did." I wrap my arms around his neck. "Not gonna lie. It was difficult, but I held my own."

"I knew you would. I had every confidence that you'd more than hold your own."

"If it weren't for you, I never would have dreamed of coming this far so quickly."

"And if you hadn't faced your fears and agreed to take on the role of CEO, I wouldn't be able to focus on what I love to do." His features grow tender.

"I love you." The words burst out of me. "I love you so much."

His eyes flash. He opens his mouth, and it seems like he's going to respond in kind, but then he simply lowers his mouth and kisses me deeply. There's so much feeling, so much heart, so much love in the kiss, my head spins. By the time we break apart, I'm trembling.

He looks at me with what I can only describe as a love light in his eyes. I know, without a doubt, that he loves me. With the handover, we've spent so much time together the last three days. His focus, his attention to detail, the pains he took to bring me up to speed with the business—that, too, was a kind of love he showed for me.

So why hasn't he told me so yet? Argh, this man is so annoying. But he did ask me for time. And I know, he'll tell me when he's ready.

I push aside all doubt and smile up at him. "Was it a good day for you too?"

"The best." He walks over to sit in my big armchair, placing me on his lap so I'm straddling him.

"I agreed to invest in a startup that provides a digital platform which matches veterans to civilian jobs based on their military skill sets and temperament."

I lean back in his arms and stare in admiration. "That's incredible. You've combined the thrill of funding new ventures with the satisfaction of working for veterans' causes."

"Absolutely." His smile grows wider.

"God, you're so intelligent, it makes me want to kiss your head off." I dip my head and press my lips to his.

He makes a growling sound at the back of his throat.

And when I wriggle closer, so my core is positioned exactly over the tent that's forming at his crotch, he hisses out a breath. "Fuck."

"Yeah." My heartbeat picks up.

"You feel bloody good, exactly there." He squeezes my hips and holds me in place. And when he experimentally punches up his pelvis, he hits my clit with the ridge of his cock, and I gasp.

"Oh."

"That all you have for me, wife?" He begins to rub me up and down the column of his shaft, and though we both have our clothes on, within seconds, we're panting.

"Oh my God." I throw my head back, baring the column of my neck. He obligingly bends his head and runs his nose up my throat, then down again.

When he bites down on where my shoulder meets my neck, I cry out, "Brody!"

"Much better." He picks up speed and pistons his hips upward, bringing me down at the same time. He hits me exactly on my swollen clit. My entire body shudders. Shock waves scream up my spine. "Oh God. Oh God. I'm coming."

He stops. "Not yet."

It takes a few seconds for me to realize he's standing and has placed me on my desk.

He pushes me down with his palm pressed to my chest. Without any resistance, my vibrating body sinks back. I glance up as he steps between my legs. My very tight skirt is gathered around my hips. My jacket is undone. As are the top two buttons of my shirt.

Jeez, when did that happen?

He twists first one arm, then the other, over my head, shackles them together with his long fingers, then reaches for the rope, the same one I first noticed on his desk.

"What are you doing?"

He arches his eyebrows. "I'm gonna tie up my wife and make her orgasm. Any objections to that?"

49

Brody

After I fucked the new CEO of Davenport Capital in her office, on her desk, I kissed her forehead and accompanied her home.

Now, I'm waiting in the living room of our home for my wife to complete dressing, so I can escort her to my grandfather's New Year's Eve party.

It's been half an hour since I came down and poured myself a drink to calm my nerves. Ridiculous. I have nothing to be apprehensive about. Yes, I'm living in a kind of fugue state, where I'm overcome with feelings for my wife, but I'm still in control. *I am.*

Why then, do my thoughts feel strident?

I have a sneaking suspicion that I'm trying to convince myself. I run my fingers over the slender platinum strip in my pocket. It doesn't mean anything that I plan to give this to her today.

Then I hear her footsteps on the stairs. I turn and stare at the vision descending the steps.

She wears a silver dress made of a soft material which seems to pour over her curves. It flows to her ankles, wraps over her arms up to her wrists and ends in a high neckline, which lends a demureness to her figure.

One promptly destroyed by the flash of thigh revealed by the slit that runs up one side. She's the perfect blend of wife and whore. It's why I've fallen for her. She satisfies my urges. Lights up my lust. Challenges me and leaves me wanting more. I've never felt as strongly pulled toward another person as I am to her.

Her thick hair is pulled up, with tendrils floating around her features. Her makeup is light, except for the slash of red lipstick and the winged eyeliner which turns her green eyes into pools of water at the base of rapids. Red-tipped toes peep out from her heels. Then she reaches the bottom of the stairs and glides toward me.

The thrust of her breasts is hypnotizing, as is the cinch of the dress at her waist, and the flare of her hips which highlights her hourglass figure. I place my glass down on the bar counter, and when she reaches me, I can't stop myself from scanning her features. "You look beautiful."

She flushes slightly. The flutter of her eyelashes tells me she's pleased with my compliment.

"Turn around," I order.

She frowns, then does as I ask.

"Good girl." I run my knuckles down her spine. As much as her dress is modest from the front, it's wicked from the back. The neckline plunges almost to the cleavage between her butt cheeks. Goosebumps erupt across the expanse. Her responsiveness never fails to please me.

I pull out the thin chain with braided links and settle it around her neck. I fasten it, then turn her around to look at the overall effect.

"Beautiful," I whisper.

She runs her fingers over the textured pattern. "This feels like a rope."

"It is." I look into her eyes. "I had it made right after I met you."

Her eyes grow wide. "After the first time you met me?"

I nod slowly. "I didn't think I'd give it to you. I wasn't sure why I decided to have it made… Except maybe, subconsciously…*I did* know."

She swallows. Hope flickers across her face. But then she banks it. And there's wariness instead.

I hate that I'm the one responsible for that. I'm responsible for making her doubt how I feel toward her. But I hope my actions will put to rest her apprehension.

"I think I was falling for you, even then. I didn't want to admit it. Arthur picking you as the woman I should marry cemented it further. Then you took on those sharks in the boardroom. Went toe-to-toe with me about the Christmas decorations, until you got your way. You brought light back into my life. For the first time, I looked forward to going to work, because you'd be there.

"When I proposed the marriage arrangement, I told myself it was practical, that it would help us both. But deep down, I knew the truth. I wanted to keep you close."

Her features soften.

"I saw you walking down the aisle, and it hit me. Everything I'd ever wanted was right there in front of me. And I was afraid of losing it. Making love to you felt like coming home. It was…too much, too fast. I needed time to make sense of it."

I take a few breaths and find my composure.

"But when that helicopter hit turbulence, all I could think was— I'd die before I let anything happen to you. And that I had to tell you what you meant to me."

She searches my features. "So why didn't you tell me right away?"

I rub the back of my neck. "Because you were right all along. I am a fucking coward. It took me a little while to get my thoughts in order. And then I knew I had to do something more… Something that would make what I told you special."

A look of comprehension dawns on her face. She touches the chain around her neck. "Is this—"

"A mark of my possession. A token of my love. A sign that you're mine. And for the world to know it too."

I cup her cheek.

"That is, if you'll have it."

Her features flush. Her pupils dilate. "Does this mean that you—"

I nod once, deliberate. "I love you."

Her throat works as she swallows. The silence stretches, weighted and breathless.

"I think I've been in love with you since we first met." I pause, letting the words settle in my chest before I give them breath. "You undo me, wife."

Her eyes snap to mine.

"With you, it's not only about exchanging power. It's about claiming your surrender. About winning your trust. Your devotion. I don't simply want to command you. I want to deserve you. To give you something that carries the weight of everything I feel. You're the first woman I've wanted to claim, and I want the world to know that you're mine."

A sharp breath escapes her like it's been punched from her lungs. "You... You love me?

"I thought that was obvious." I step closer. "But let me make it very, very clear. You, Lark Davenport, are the only woman I've ever wanted to claim. The only woman I've wanted to mark. The only one I've wanted to marry."

50

Lark

Don't accidentally turn decorating the mantel into a project-management exercise.

— From Lark's Christmas to-do list

How he destroys me. How his words cut me to the core and resonate with those deeper, darker, needy instincts inside of me. How he makes me feel wanted. And lusted after. And protected. And loved.

He loves me.

This strong, handsome, cold dominant, who vowed to never fall for anyone, just admitted that he loves me. My heart speeds up. My pulse hums. Every nerve ending in my body seems to fire at the same time. I shiver.

"You love me," I repeat the words aloud to make sure I heard them correctly.

His eyes narrow. The blue crackles with an iciness that burns. He's dropped enough of that mask so I can see the surging emotions under the surface.

"I love you. I want you. I need you. I can't live without you. You're mine, Lark."

The skin stretches across his cheekbones, lending a kind of depth to his expression I've never seen before.

"You're mine to claim, mine to protect, mine to please. And now, the world will know it, too."

His words are both territorial and proprietary, and yet, also speak of something more delicate. Something affectionate. And fragile. They show his vulnerability in a way I've never felt before.

By wearing his ring, I was his wife. But by wearing this chain, I feel closer to him.

It's a sign of the emotions that he's kept in check all his life… The emotions he's unleashed for me.

It makes me feel like I'm his. In every way. My heart stutters. My pulse rate spikes. Every cell in my body seems to fill with a burst of elation.

I'm his.

He's mine.

Truly mine.

Tenderness and awe squeeze my chest. He draws his lower lip inward, and I know that he's as moved as I am by this moment.

That he feels this connection between us. That this is more intimate than when he placed the ring on my finger. That's what tradition dictated. I touch the chain again. This is for us. This is our secret.

One I wear with pride. "I love you so much."

His features light up. His throat moves as he swallows. "Those are the most beautiful words I have ever heard."

My heart stutters. My pulse thrums. This feeling of being so in sync with him is intense. It's perfect. It's everything.

"Kiss me." I lift my chin. "Please."

His eyes flare.

"You don't get to direct what I do. But this once, because you begged for it so prettily..." He grips my jaw to hold my face and presses his thumb into my lower lip, so I open my mouth.

When he feels I'm positioned for maximum pleasure, he swoops down and closes his lips over mine. Hard and soft. The firm press of his mouth against mine, the velvety softness of his tongue, the hard clasp of his fingers on my chin, the gentle rub of his thumb over my cheek, the hardness of his chest molding mine, the firm hold of his other hand on the nape of my neck.

I'm aware of every single place where he's touching me, though my focus is completely on where our mouths and lips and tongue meet.

He must reach some internal breaking point, for he draws me up to my tiptoes, plasters me to his torso so we're smashed together from chest to groin, to thigh. Then, he releases his hold on my jaw to wrap his thick arm around my waist.

He bends me over, so my back is curved, and I'm suspended over his forearm. I'm forced to part my legs for balance. He instantly moves his hips between my thighs. That thick rod at his crotch throbs through the clothes we're wearing, branding my lower belly.

The sensations zip up to my collar and seem to heat the metal.

It feels like he's marking me all over again. Then he sucks on my tongue, and my head spins. All other sensations coalesce into this one touchpoint, spiraling into a vortex that sucks me in. Cinches all my emotions into the feeling of his mouth on mine, his lips crushing mine, the way he seems to swallow my taste, swallow me whole.

I'm but a speck in this universe, and he's the force that powers it.

He groans into my mouth; a shudder rolls over him. Then he slowly gentles the kiss. Millimeter by millimeter, he releases my lips. Until he's barely sharing my breath. Then he straightens me gently, pressing his forehead to mine in that affectionate gesture I love.

His massive chest rises and falls like he's run a mile. He eases his hold on me, so he's holding me in the circle of his arms but without pressing me to his chest. He begins to sway, and me with him. It's gentle. Soft. Heartfelt.

Like we're dancing to our own internal music. I sigh. And melt into him further.

I place my cheek against the crisp material of his shirt, drawing in lungfuls of Brody.

He notches his knuckles under my chin.

I raise my eyes to his. The lust I see in his makes my breath catch. "The party. Won't we be late?"

EPILOGUE

Lark

Keep reminding myself: perfect isn't the goal, magical is.

—From Lark's Christmas to-do list

We are *very* late.

We didn't leave until there were only a few hours left to close out the year.

And not until my husband made me almost orgasm… Twice. He brought me to the edge, only to pull back.

Then he straightened my clothes…still without fucking me.

Argh! I can't believe he left me this needy, but he smirked when he saw the disbelief on my face. "I promise, it's going to be worth it when you finally come. At midnight." He kissed me firmly, then led me out of the house.

When we walk into Arthur's townhouse, Otis half bows. "My congratulations, sir, ma'am." He takes our coats, then seems to melt into the closet near the front door.

"How does he do that?" I ask in awe.

"I have a feeling he was born that way," Brody answers, half in jest.

I chuckle.

He leads me down the hallway into the conservatory. The buzz of noises reaches me. All our friends and his family are here.

Summer sees us and a big smile curves her lips.

"There you are." She walks over to us and leans in. Holding my shoulders, she kisses me on both cheeks. "You look incredible."

"Thanks." I smile. "I feel incredible."

"We were wondering when you newlyweds were going to resurface." Sinclair joins us.

He and Brody half hug, half backslap, in the way that men have.

Brody smirks. "Needed to keep my wife to myself for a little while."

"It must be true love." James walks over to join us. His attention is on Brody's cuff links.

They have tiny Santa's hats on them. I couldn't resist buying them for my husband. I was touched that he wore them right away.

"It is." Brody pulls me close and kisses my forehead.

"How disgustingly sweet the two of you are." James sighs. "I managed not to call or message, so as not to disturb your newly-wedded bliss. I hope you noticed?"

"It was exceptionally peaceful not to see your ugly mug." Brody chuckles.

"Your loss." He turns to me. "Wonderful to see you, Lark, and congratulations on the new position."

"Thank you." I smile at him with genuine fondness.

I understand Brody enough to know that he doesn't let too many people close. Not even his own brothers. Perhaps, to some extent, his grandfather. But it's James who's Brody's true wingman.

"I have to admit, when I heard the news, I was taken aback. But then it made sense." He shoots Brody a sideways glance. "She's smarter than you. More patient. More astute. And you delegated so much to her in such a short period of time, it was logical for you to make her the CEO."

Brody frowns. I wonder if he's going to be pissed off by James' words. But I should know my husband better. Not once has he been anything but secure in his talents. He puts his arm around my shoulder and draws me close. "Best decision I've ever made."

There's genuine pride in his words.

"I'm not lying when I say she's the best person for the job. She's more patient than me. She has the fortitude to not lose her temper with the team. She'll foster better relations with them."

"Women are more empathetic; it often makes them better leaders." Summer winks at me.

"You won't find me arguing that," my husband concedes.

James shrugs. "When it comes to managing a kitchen, I'm not so sure."

All our gazes swivel in his direction.

"Hey, I'm not being sexist. It's simply a fact." He raises his hand. "Being a chef takes long hours, it's grueling, it needs complete commitment. It's physically taxing. Mentally challenging. It's more than leading a team. It's innovating on the spot, thinking on your feet, planning out, having fail safes in place. It takes a one thousand percent commitment, to the exclusion of having a family or a personal life of any kind."

"It's like being a doctor—" Brody begins.

"Exactly." James nods, pleased.

Brody scoffs, "I was being sarcastic."

"I wasn't. Doctors are trained to save a life, but we teach you to indulge it." His phone buzzes, but he ignores it. "It falls to us to stir up emotions, awaken pleasure, and create moments worth living for. And all through the power of food."

He has a point.

"I've never heard you speak this eloquently." Nathan joins us.

"Not even when we served together, and we've been on some tough missions."

That's right, Brody mentioned how he met James through his brother.

"Taking lives to protect your country and your fellow citizens, can have the effect of dampening your enthusiasm for a lot of things in life." James and Nathan exchange a look.

Then Nathan slaps him on the back. "But you found food."

"Now, all he needs is a woman to save his soul." Quentin ambles over, with Vivian in tow.

"Or to crack his façade?" Knox, too, joins the crowd.

James takes in the faces of his friends and holds up his hands. "Why do I sense an intervention?"

"Probably, because it is?" Brody snorts.

"Because we're all married, settled down, and having babies, and now, it's your turn?" Nathan chuckles.

"I can do without you lot butting into my life." James scoffs.

"I don't think it's us you need to worry about." Knox nods over his shoulder.

We follow his gaze to where an older woman, with a sleek bob of hair, dressed in a Chanel suit, is seated next to Arthur and Imelda. The three of them have their heads bent close.

"What's Margot doing here?" James does a double take.

"Who's Margot?" I take in the wary look in James' eyes.

"His grandmother." Brody watches James as if to monitor his reaction. "Thought you didn't get along with her?"

"She's a shark, is what she is." James frowns.

A ripple of surprise runs through the assembled crowd.

"Nothing very grandmotherly about her then?" Nathan lowers his chin.

"If you thought Arthur was manipulative, you haven't met my grandmother."

"Ooh, that sounds not very pleasant," I offer.

"If it's any consolation, Arthur apologized to me." Brody draws me closer to his chest.

Nathan does a double take. "The old coot apologized?"

"He said he had our best interests at heart. And that he realized that he might have been a little overzealous with his meddling and trying to get us married." Brody raises a shoulder.

"And you believe him?" Knox strokes his chin.

"No reason not to."

"He hasn't apologized to the rest of us," Nathan points out.

"Not yet," Brody agrees. "I wouldn't be surprised if he's waiting for the right opportunity to apologize to each of you separately.

"The fact he apologized is out of character." Quentin purses his lips. "No doubt, he hoped you'd convey his sentiments to us."

"He seemed genuine. And he did it right after our wedding ceremony."

"He did?" I glance at my husband in surprise.

He looks down at me, a tenderness filling his gaze, the kind which never fails to send a thrill down my spine. I'll never get used to this strong, proud man, not hiding his emotions when it comes to me.

I feel privileged and cherished and protected and happy. And it must show on my face, for he tucks me closer.

"Let's say, it was when I was filled with self-doubt. When I was riddled with questions about what I was doing. And you should know"—he tightens his hold on me—"it was in another time. When I was someone else. Before I was changed by my love for you."

"Aww." Summer sighs. "That's so romantic."

"He is, isn't he?" I cup his cheek. Then, because I can't help it, I rise up on tiptoe and kiss my husband. It's meant to be a quick peck on his lips, but Brody deepens the kiss, and by the time he releases me, I'm flushed and panting. And applause breaks out from those watching.

"You guys are practically oozing happiness." James' tone is disgusted.

"That's what you could have, too." Quentin nudges him.

"I don't begrudge you guys your contentment." A haunted expression crosses James features, one that crosses over the border to jealousy, perhaps? Is James jealous of his friends' happiness?

It's almost as if he thinks he doesn't deserve it. But nah, that's not possible. James is such a confident man. Surely, he's not the kind to fall prey to such misgivings.

"But?" Brody prompts him.

"But my restaurant is a jealous mistress. It doesn't leave space for any other woman in my life and"—his phone buzzes—"excuse me." He pulls out his phone and takes in the message.

It must not be good news, for he tightens his upper lip. A scowl darkens his features.

"This... This is what I mean. I put a woman in charge of my kitchen, and what I get is disaster."

"Do you mean Harper?" I frown.

"Who else?" He grips his phone like he's about to throw it on the floor and jump on it. For someone who's always so composed, it's a startling revelation to see his features twisted with frustration.

His mouth is set in grim lines. He seems furious.

Whoa, whatever Harper has done, it must be serious. Apparently, she can silence the chef who's well known for speaking his mind.

"First time I've seen anyone get under the skin of Hell's Chef," Brody drawls.

Now, that's a nickname I haven't heard before. But having heard of his legendary temper, I can guess where he gets it from.

James cracks his neck. "For one day, could she hold things together without everything falling apart? Of course, not." His nostrils flare.

"Maybe you're building things up in your head? You know how persnickety you can be," Brody drawls.

"It's because I'm persnickety that I have three Michelin stars." He narrows his gaze on Brody. Anyone else would wilt under James' fierce scowl, but not my husband.

He inclines his head. "And you worked hard to pull that off. It makes me wonder, though, how many you need before you're satisfied?"

"Satisfied?" He snaps it out like it's a dirty word. "I'll rest when I'm six feet under, and not a moment before. Now, I'd better bring this fire under control, otherwise I may not have a restaurant to go back to."

I slip out into the garden.

It's cold. My breath puffs silver in the air, but the sky above is a masterpiece. Stars crowd together like diamonds flung across velvet. Somewhere inside, voices are rising, glasses clinking, someone calling out that there are five minutes left.

Footsteps crunch softly behind me. Then a coat drapes around my shoulders, and two arms slide around my waist.

"Couldn't let you ring in the new year alone," Brody murmurs into my ear.

I lean back into him. "I knew you'd follow me."

We stand like that for a beat. Silent. The house glows behind us, windows spilling golden light over patio. It snowed lightly earlier, and white powder glistens like fairy dust on the leaves of trees and reflects moonlight off the grass. The air is cold enough that the lights of the city in the distance seem to shimmer.

I draw in a breath laced with cedar and pine, and the darker scent of my husband. "It's beautiful."

I stretch my spine and luxuriate in the cut edges of his chest which rise and fall in sync with my breathing.

"You're beautiful." He has his arm about my waist, the other over my shoulders.

"You're biased." I chuckle.

"Always, when it comes to you."

I melt into him more. And as if hearing a distant melody, when he begins to sway slightly, I slide my fingers around his wrist and allow myself to be carried away.

The soft rush of his breath raises the hair on my head. The crunch of the snow underneath our feet as we dance, is like having our own private orchestra accompany us.

Surely, this is what life should be about?

Happiness. Contentment. Poetry in motion. It's a different world. One where time slows. One where it's just us.

"Do you hear that?" he murmurs.

For a few seconds, I listen, then I do. The music in the rustle of the trees, in the occasional burst of laughter from inside.

I turn in his arms and press my palm to his chest. His heartbeat pounds steadily beneath my hand. It's a strong, certain, rhythm that anchors me. The sound of it calms me, each thud a reminder that I'm safe right here, with him.

"I don't want this year to end."

"It's the beginning of the best time of our lives." He brushes his lips across my temple. "I'll do everything in my power to keep you happy. And whatever life throws at us, I promise, we'll face it together." He twirls me out, then draws me in, before turning me over his arm.

I gasp, then laugh when he straightens me up and brings me close.

"I promise, I'll never allow you to want for anything. I promise to always love you. Protect you. To ensure you want for nothing. And when we have children"—he frowns—"you do want children, right?"

"I do." My heart melts.

We've touched on the topic before but never had a chance to discuss it until now.

Unlike couples who had such conversations before they got married, we've done so much backward. But then, our union was not exactly a conventional one. Look how far we've come. There's nowhere else I'd rather be than here in his arms, dancing under the stars.

"Good." He cups my cheek. "I want to make sure you're settled in your career and have fulfilled your ambitions, and feel ready to be a mother, before we go down that route."

I gaze up at him, certain adoration is written in every dip and valley of my features. He gazes deeply into my eyes, a softness tugging at those stern lips, and turning his eyes into pools of fierce need.

"How did I think you were unfeeling, when you're such a softie at heart?"

One side of his lips quirks in a comma, and it's both sheepish and wicked and helpless. "Only for you, baby."

Our steps slow.

"I'd burn down the world, if it meant keeping you safe."

There's a fervent note to his voice that leaves me in no doubt of the seriousness of his intent. A thrill runs through me. "You always know how to say the right things." I wrap my arms around his neck.

"You make it easy."

We stare deeply into each other's eyes. I love it when he fucks me. Relish feeling him throb inside me. Adore it when he holds my gaze as he sinks inside of me. And yet, this is more romantic. This, when he's holding me close enough for our bodies to touch from torso to thigh, and his arms are a steel band around me, promising me that he'll never let me go.

When the expression on his face is one of reverence, and devotion, and also, captivation.

When every line of his body, every angle of his face insists that I'm his. And he's mine.

Only mine

I melt into him further. "I love you."

"I love you." His reply is instant. The moonlight illuminates his glittering eyes, picks out the hollows under his cheekbones, and turns him into a dashing god. Equal parts angel and devil. Who can make me orgasm until I'm faint. Who can make me feel so special, until it feels my heart is going to burst.

"Only you. My entire life has led up to this moment. Has led to you. It was always you, Lark. Always."

People begin to trickle out of the house.

"Ready to welcome in the new year?" Nathan calls out to us.

"You bet." My husband nods back.

Then he twines his fingers through mine, moving us away from the house and into the shadows.

We reach the tree line that borders the property.

"Where are we going?"

"You'll see." He leads me down a path between the trees, and away from the house.

A few minutes later, we enter a clearing. We're shielded from being seen by those at the house and in the garden. There's a bench in the center, facing the slope of Primrose Hill. Beyond that, the city lights shimmer in the distance.

He leads me toward the bench.

We sink down, and he wraps his arm around me and pulls me close. For a few seconds, we enjoy the view.

Then, as one, we turn to each other. He lowers his head as I raise mine. His jacket slides off my shoulders. Our mouths meet. Our lips cling. Our tongues marry.

The kiss is soft and deep. Sweet and sexy. Arrogant and affectionate. It's everything I've ever wanted. It's my sun and moon, and the stars. It's him. I'm surrounded by him, and it feels right. Like I've come home. Like this is the start of my life.

All the heartaches and uncertainty, and the woman I was, so very different from who I'm going to be. With him. There's a completeness. A rightness. A springboard to where I want to go. Our future stretching out before us.

Him and me. And our love. And the life we'll build together.

I feel so happy, I think I'm going to burst.

And when he finally ends the kiss and presses his forehead into mine, his breath brushes my cheek, and I can feel his heart thudding as fast as mine.

"Wow," I whisper.

"Wow, indeed." He chuckles.

Then I chuckle too, and we hold each other, laughing.

If our joy had a color, it would be a fuchsia pink.

The air between us sparks, heat simmering between the molecules. This...shift from love to joy to lust. It's the complete spectrum of feelings that characterizes our relationship.

"It's almost midnight." His eyes gleam.

"It is." I swallow.

"Remember what I promised you?"

I nod. "My orgasm."

"Indeed." He urges me to stand then step between his thighs. "Lift your dress."

"What?" My gaze widens.

"Don't you want your orgasm?"

Of course, I do. What kind of question is that? It no longer surprises me that the question spikes my lust and tightens a knot of desire in my lower belly.

His touch sparks a raw ache behind my pussy and turns me into a mass of molten need.

"Answer me, wife."

Well, hell, when he calls me that, it touches something deep inside of me. No way, can I resist him.

"Yes." My voice emerges strong and sure.

He nods as if it's confirmed something to him. "Then do as I say."

The edge of dominance to his tone is sharper than the lash of a whip. It spurs me on to take handfuls of the silky material of my dress and pull it up. Slowly. Slowly. The whisper of the fabric against my thighs sends goosebumps trembling over my skin. I pause when the hem brushes against my upper thighs.

He's at eye level with my cunt. He leans in and nuzzles the shadowed place between my legs. Oh God. Liquid heat licks up my veins. My knees threaten to buckle from under me.

He steadies me with a hand on my hip. When he's confident I can stand on my own, he lowers his arm and leans back as if settling in for a show.

"Keep going," he orders.

I lift my dress up, then further up. Until my pussy is bare.

He makes a noise at the back of his throat. "No panties."

I allow myself a small smile of triumph. *The dress wouldn't allow for it.*

"Of course, not." I hear the smirk in his voice.

He urges me to take a step back. "Widen your legs."

The dark desire in his words, the sin which drips from his tone, lights a fuse in my blood.

I shuffle my feet apart as much as my position will allow.

The red-soled heels I wear lend extra height to my legs. It makes me feel strong and proud and powerful. That, and the fact that my husband is staring at my cunt, and his elevated breathing, as well as the growing tent between his legs, tell me he's very aroused.

He snakes out his arm and slaps my pussy.

I cry out. I should have expected him to do this. It's his favorite way to greet that intimate part of me. Yet it takes me by surprise.

Shock waves pulse out from my clit to my nipples, which tighten, and to my brain cells, which turn into oscillating pendulums of desire.

"Keep it down, we don't want to alert my family," he drawls.

Oh my God. That's so forbidden, not to mention, embarrassing. And of course, that ratchets up my desire.

Still, I put up a token resistance. "If anyone walks in on us, they'll see me like this."

"In which case, you'd better come quickly."

Brody

I pry her pussy lips apart like they're two halves of a peach.

But when I lick up her slit, she tastes so much sweeter.

"Brody," she groans.

My name from her lips drains the blood to my groin.

My balls turn so hard, it feels like they're dragging me down. I'm no longer surprised that she has this effect on me. I knew I was a goner the first time I saw her. I tried to resist my feelings for her, while knowing it was futile. And then, as I got to know her. As I saw who she was.

The fiery, sassy woman who could hold her own against me. The woman who put her trust in me. The woman who drew out the protective part of me in a way no other submissive ever did. I want to take care of her. Shield her. Hide her from the world, but I can't be that selfish with her. Not when she has so much to offer.

But I can ensure that I'll be by her side. So, when... *If* she needs my help, I'll be there for her.

She's the only woman I've ever wanted to keep close. The only partner who could satisfy my desires and who could be my successor. She complements me in so many ways. It's a perfect fit. The kind I never dreamed I could have.

And now I know, I can never let her go. My wife. My soulmate. *Mine.*

I slip two fingers inside her soaking wet pussy and curve them, brushing up against her inner walls. Her knees threaten to give way. She grabs at my hair for support. The tug on my scalp lengthens my cock further. Fuck. She's not the only one who's going to come quickly, at this rate. I increase the to-and-fro action of my wrist, adding a third finger to stretch her. She shudders, and moans. And a stream of words spills from her lips.

"That feels so good." She gasps as I lick around her swollen clit, sliding a finger back to play with the velvety eyelet of her forbidden opening.

Her thighs tremble. "I need to come. Please."

I bite gently on the nub of her clitoris and growl, "Come then. Show me what an obedient slut you are."

I glance up in time to see the jolt that pistons through her. Then she throws her neck back, and with a low sound, she gives in to the orgasm. Fat drops of cum slide down her inner thigh. I lower my chin, licking them up.

When she sways, I pull her down into my lap and arrange her, so she straddles me. Then I kiss her deeply. I taste her sweetness, mixed with that umami taste that is her cum.

She buries her head in my chest.

Reaching between us, I loosen my belt and lower my zipper and briefs. When my cock juts up, I position her over it.

Then I apply pressure on her shoulders. At the same time, I piston my hips up so I breach her.

She gasps.

A low groan wells up my throat. "You feel incredible, wife."

She stares at me from under hooded eyelids. Swollen lips, flushed cheeks. Thick strands of hair have fallen from her French twist. I reach up and pull out the pins, so the rest of it rains down around her face.

"You are beautiful." I reach up and slide my thumb inside her mouth. She sucks on it, and my cock jerks in response.

"I'll never get enough of you." I pull my thumb out and use both of my hands to hold up her hips, until I almost slip free. Stopping before I do, I thrust up, lowering her simultaneously, until I'm buried inside her again.

Her mouth opens; a moan escapes her. The agonized expression on her features tells me everything.

"I feel it too." I squeeze her hips. "I feel all of you. You're so tight. So hot. So wet. Such a good girl, taking her master's cock."

A whimper this time, and she shudders.

"You like it when I praise you, don't you?" She nods.

"But you love it when I spank you." I slap the top of her butt.

She throws her head back and pants loudly. "Oh. My. God."

"You're welcome." I slap her other arse cheek, then the first again. I keep alternating until she's moaning and whimpering and squirming to get away. But I hold her in place, so she ends up impaling herself further on my cock. I rub up against the secret spot inside of her.

Both of us inhale sharply.

Her body jerks and twitches. Sweat beads on her forehead. The moonlight reflecting off her hair forms a halo around her head. I could well be holding an angel in my arms. A beautiful whore in my lap. My wife. My everything. Only mine.

From the direction of the house, the faint sound of counting reaches us. *Ten. Nine. Eight.*

She digs her fingers into my forearms. And when I lock my fingers around her wrists, holding both of her hands in place with one of mine, her pupils dilate further.

Seven. Six.

The submissive stance I've twisted her into seems to push her to the edge. She flutters around my cock, and I know, she's so very close.

Five.

I twine her hair around my palm to pin her in place. The tug of the hair on her scalp amps up her desire which, in turn, adds fuel to mine.

Four.

I pump up and into her with rhythmic precision. Sweat clings to my shoulders. I'm impossibly hard, pushing against her inner walls.

Three.

Two.

One.

Stars burst overhead. Silent. Almost otherworldly, as the design joins, then pulls apart, then forms a convoluted zigzag of starlight overhead.

It's the New Year's Eve drone show Arthur arranged, to celebrate his grandsons being married.

Faint squeals of delight, then clapping, reach us.

High in the night sky, the drones come together in a pattern that resembles a snowflake. As unique as the woman who's impaled on my cock.

The light flickers over us, illuminating her features, picking out the copper strands in her hair and turning her skin into a stream of soft delight.

And when I growl, "Come," as if in response, the drones above us pulse out a starburst of rays lighting up the night skies, and she shatters with a low cry.

I close my mouth over hers and partly absorb the sound, so we don't attract the attention of my family, and because I'm greedy enough to absorb the sound into my body.

Her pussy suctions around my cock, milking it, and with a groan, I pour my seed into her.

Above us, the drones continue their aerial display. Coming together. Parting. They scatter light like stars, then burst into intricate patterns that dispel the darkness.

Each shifting pattern seems to reflect the emotions tangled within my chest.

I feel breathless, suspended, in a way where the only thing that matters is her. And me. *Us.*

In that way lovers have, where a glance means a thousand words, and our bodies lean into each other, communicating in a way that's heady and potent.

I come and come, like it isn't less than twelve hours since I last made love to my wife. But each time feels like the first. Each time her pussy quivers, it feels like the first time I sank into her.

Each time I look into her eyes, it feels like the first day of our lives together. She's so full of my cum, it slides out of her. I push it back inside.

"That's so filthy. I shouldn't find it hot, but damn, if I don't get turned on when you do that." She wraps her arms around my neck.

Overhead, there's a final burst of light that sparkles across the skies then fades away.

I slide my fingers into her mouth, and she licks them clean. Which, in turn, makes my cock twitch.

"Again?" She looks at me in shock.

"And again. And again. Though unfortunately, not now." I help her off my lap, then pull out my handkerchief.

I wipe her clean between her legs. "If it weren't my family back there, I'd have loved for you to walk around with my cum dripping from your cunt." I straighten her clothes.

The tremor that overtakes her draws a groan from me. "You like the thought of that too."

"What's not to like?" She bites her lower lip. "My husband's cum overflowing my pussy. That feels forbidden, which makes it more carnal."

I observe her flushed features thoughtfully. "I might have created a monster."

"You *have* created a monster." She chuckles, then bends and tucks me inside my pants, before zipping me up efficiently. She begins to straighten, but I clamp my fingers around the base of her neck. "Complete the job."

She blinks. "I did."

I nod toward the wet patches from cum — hers and mine — which blot the fabric over my thighs. "Did you?"

Her gaze widens. She seems like she's about to refuse me.

"Are you going to safe out, baby?"

She purses her lips. A stubborn look filters into her eyes. No, she won't. My wife has a spine of steel. And a streak of determination which will never let her back down.

I slide my feet together, and she drops down, using my dress shoes to support her knees.

Without taking her gaze off mine, she proceeds to lick up the moisture from my slacks. They're dark enough that the wet patches won't be visible from a distance.

When she's done, she nuzzles her cheek against my thigh. Contentment washes over me. With her, I can be myself, and she loves it. I ruffle my fingers through her hair, and she sighs. I cup her cheek, and she turns her face into my palm to kiss it. My shoulders relax. We stay that way for a few seconds, until she shivers.

"You're getting cold; we should go inside."

I help her to her feet, and onto the bench.

I pick up my jacket, which had dropped to the ground earlier, dust it off and place it around her shoulders. "I love you in my clothes."

I smoothen down her hair and sit beside her on the bench.

"I love myself in your clothes." She smiles.

I grin back.

We laugh, holding each other, that oneness, that sense of harmony, completeness, togetherness, convergence… Every single word in the dictionary which signifies a merging of two people into one being, comes to mind. Yeah, I've become like my brothers. Overcome with love for my wife. And happy in my marriage. Once again, Arthur has won. He's the one who picked out Lark to be my bride. Turns out, he was right. I can't imagine myself with anyone else by my side.

A soft bark reaches us. Then Tiny pads over to us. He tries to sniff my crotch. Damn, Tiny knows what we've been up to.

"Sit, Tiny."

He wags his tail and parks his butt on the ground.

"Tiny, what are you doing here, boy?" Lark places her hand under his chin and lifts it to look into his eyes..

"Good boy, Tiny." I scratch the Great Dane behind his ears "If it weren't for you, I wouldn't have met my soulmate."

Tiny makes that purring sound which indicates he agrees.

Footsteps approach, then James steps out of the shadows. "I was taking Tiny for a walk, and he headed straight over to you guys."

As he enters the clearing, he adds, "Hope he didn't bother you?"

"Not at all, we're heading in." I nod in his direction.

Facing the view, he pulls out a cigarette from his pocket. He hesitates, then, with a sigh, tucks it behind his ear.

"Are you going to smoke that?" Lark tilts her head.

"I'm trying not to," he confesses.

"Didn't know you were trying to quit." I pull my wife into my side.

She melts into me willingly. Once again, that feeling of everything being as it should be envelops me. Once more, I must grudgingly admit that my grandfather was right in insisting that we settle down.

"I wasn't." James shifts his weight from foot to foot. "At least, I didn't think I was. But now, every time I light up"—he slides the cigarette out from behind his ear and looks at it longingly—"I realize I might be taking off years from my life. And I don't want that happening."

"Hmm." I exchange a glance with my wife. The gleam in her eyes tells me the same thought occurred to her.

"You in love, ol' chap?" I ask gently.

"What?" He reels back like I punched him in the face. "Of course, not."

The way the blood drains from his face tells another story. I begin to chuckle, then turn it into a cough.

"It's okay if you are." I rub circles over my wife's arm. "I used to react with as much horror as you at the thought of opening myself up to someone. But now, I realize, it's more about meeting the right woman."

His mouth tilts to one side. "I'd say you crossed over to the dark side, but I have too much respect for Lark here. Anyone can see the two of you are made for each other. You guys got lucky. That doesn't mean I will."

"By that logic, each of my brothers got lucky. As did my uncle Quentin. And our friends, Sinclair and the rest of the seven. Seems we've struck a rare vein of good fortune. There's no reason it can't extend to you."

He rubs his chin. "Given the amount of time Margot has spent with Arthur in there…" He nods over his shoulder. "It's more likely going to be her manipulating events, so my siblings and I tie the knot. I'm going to do everything possible to avoid the traps she sets for me."

"You sound like there's someone special in your life. Someone you're trying your best to avoid falling for," Lark says with that flash of insight I find particularly appealing about her.

He looks like he's going to deny it. Instead, he nods.

"Oh, there is someone. Someone who occupies my mind and drives me a little crazy. Someone I'm going to do my best to make sure she doesn't screw up my life."

"You're talking about Harper, I take it." Her tone is cautious.

He scoffs. "Who else? Since I took her on as my sous chef, it's been one incident after another. If I hadn't been badly in need of someone as my second-in-command, and if my first and second and third choices hadn't turned out to be too busy to take on the role, I'd never have offered it to her."

"But you did." I nod.

"And here I am." He cracks his neck. His phone buzzes. He pulls it out, looks at it, and groans. "And I thought I resolved the earlier flash point, but of course, there has to be another."

"Harper again?" My lips twitch.

"Harper, I assume?" Lark bursts out at the same time.

I glance at her sideways to find she's trying her best not to giggle.

It feels like poetic justice to see the unflappable James Hamilton getting his panties in a twist.

"Of-fucking-course, it's Harper!" He stabs at the phone like it personally offended him, then jams it to his ear. "This had better be good."

To find out what happens next, read James and Harper's best-friend's-brother, marriage-of-convenience romance, in *The Unwilling Bride* by L. Steele.

Here's an excerpt

Harper

"This steak's so rare, it tried to moo at me."

Don't chuckle. Don't giggle. Don't even breathe. Don't. A tickle niggles the back of my throat.

Don't you dare! I try hard to swallow down the giggle bubbling up. I end up choking and wheezing, then turn it into a snort.

"Is that funny, Ms. Richie?" My boss glowers at me. His gray eyes, which resemble the icy expanse of the tundra, grow so stony, it feels like the temperature drops by a few degrees. I shiver.

His jaw hardens. His thick eyebrows knit.

That thin upper lip of his firms. His pouty lower lip, so plush it should look out of place on his austere face, juts out in a way that sends a weird tremor up my spine. It's hate. That's what it is. I have never hated anyone in my life as much as I hate this man. So what, if he's my best friend's brother? He never gives me any concessions because of this. He has never once acknowledged that we know someone in common. In *The Edge*, he's the owner and the chef. I'm his slave. Sorry, sous chef.

"No, sir." I resist the urge to snap to attention and toss off a mock salute.

His eyes gleam. Apparently, he likes it when I call him sir. What a surprise! *Not.*

When I got the chance to work here, I was over the moon. Years of hard work and climbing my way up through the ranks was finally paying off. Not only did I get to work with the Michelin-starred, world-renowned Chef James Hamilton, but I was also getting a substantial raise in my earnings. Enough to help my sister take care of her daughter. Jenny means the world to me.

My ten-year-old niece is the love of my life, and I'll do anything to ensure her future is assured. Including putting up with the whims, notorious mood swings, and mercurial temper of my brilliant but volatile boss. Thoughts of my niece sober me, and I wipe the mirth from my features. But I know he caught it.

Nothing slips past James Hamilton. He didn't get to be at the pinnacle of the culinary world by allowing people around him to get away with anything that he doesn't deem as fitting his standard. Which, sadly, includes my finding his comment funny. Which it was, to be fair. Also, I have a sense of humor, which flares up at the most inappropriate moments.

"Your demeanor indicates otherwise." He stares down his hooked nose from his superior six-foot, three-inch height of brooding surliness.

"Five times."

"What?"

"You will cook this steak at least five more times before you leave today."

"We're in the middle of service." As if to punctuate my point, there's a crash from somewhere behind me. I recognize the swearing as coming from our line cook, Leo.

My boss's gaze doesn't flicker. It's too much to hope he'll let this pass. His next words confirm, he noticed the transgression.

"If you can't keep the team under control then, perhaps, you shouldn't be sous chef."

The blood drains from my face. What an absolute knobhead. How dare he hold my job over me like this? How dare he threaten to fire me? How dare he use every little mistake I, and the rest of the staff, make against us? Grr!

I hate that I'm at this twat's mercy. That I have to depend on him for my job. And since the day I joined, he's been relentless.

He's found fault with me, put me down, and made sure to rub in the fact that my fate depends on satisfying his demands—his very unreasonable, outrageous, unrealistic, over-the-top demands, I might add. This man has pushed me, and prodded at me, and tried to diminish me and belittle me, and make me feel like I'm the most stupid person in the world and... No more. Perhaps, it's the fact that I'm sick with apprehension about paying my debts.

About how I'm going to find the money for my niece's ballet classes—something she's amazing at. About how I'm going to pay the rent on my place.

Or it might be the late nights I've had this entire week which have left me feeling lightheaded for lack of sleep. Or maybe, I'm sick of this man's superior attitude and the fact that he wears his condescension like it's his birthright. Or that I'm tired of being so aware of him, I can pick out the spicy notes of his burnt sugar and sea salt scent. It's raw and masculine. Unadulterated. It's not from a bottle.

Like most chefs, he doesn't wear a cologne, to protect his sense of smell. Yet, I have learned to recognize the unique scent of his body from the plethora of food smells in the kitchen. Must be survival instinct. The way an animal in the forest knows when a predator is nearby so it can protect itself.

And I'm exhausted from the effort of putting up a front. Keeping my emotions in check. And being civil. Because he's my boss. And I need this job. But there's a limit to how much I can be pushed.

I might be only five feet, four inches, and he might think, because I don't answer back, I'm some kind of docile person, but he doesn't realize I have a mind of my own. That he's pushed me too far. And that my patience has run out.

I square my shoulders and thrust my forefinger into that massive chest of his which—gulp—doesn't give. Is he made of steel? Or granite? Or some material that crashed to Earth on a comet. That's how unforgiving he feels. Almost as forbidding as the expression on his face. *Mistake. Mistake.* My senses blare. I ignore them.

"Don't you dare hold the threat of my job over me. I've earned my title here, and you know it. I've worked eighteen-hour days since I joined this restaurant. I've barely slept four hours each night. I'm the first in here and the last out. I've given my life to this job."

Around me, I'm aware people have stopped what they're doing and are watching. In fact, I see the junior chef pull out a phone and aim it at us. It's against the rules to have a phone in the kitchen. But it's not like I can talk about rules, considering I've broken the most cardinal of them all: don't talk back the boss. I've started now. Best to keep going.

"I forfeited holidays." I stick out my chin. "Missed seeing my family. I've dedicated myself to perfecting the dishes. I've accommodated all your"—I wave my hand in the air—"ridiculously over-the-top changes to the menu. And listened as you've constantly berated me and never provided a single word of praise."

There's a gasp from somewhere in the room. I don't dare look at the source. If I do, I'll lose my nerve to allow the groundswell of complaints that I've held inside me all these months. Now that I've allowed them to pour out though, there's no stopping me. It feels like I've pulled the pin on a grenade, and there's no turning back.

"The only time you talk to me is to complain. In fact, I'm sure you only know how to find faults. And it's not like you are perfect, by the way."

There's silence now, and my words echo hollowly around the room. As for my boss, he's gone rigid. Muscles bunched, shoulders rounded, biceps stretching the sleeves of his chef's coat. He's so annoyingly fit. For someone who spends most of his day in here cooking, perfecting the menu, and schmoozing the guests, he's in annoyingly good shape. He must work out at night.

Maybe he's like a vampire who never sleeps, but instead, sucks the spirit from his employees and thrives on them.

I begin to chuckle, then swallow it down. Only, he must catch the gleam of amusement in my eyes.

He tilts his head, a look of interest on his features.

It's the first reaction I've seen since I embarked on this one-way ticket to getting fired. So, what the hell? I have nothing to lose. He's certainly going to ask me to walk after this appalling breakdown. Might as well not hold back.

"You have a temper that clouds your judgment. And an ego that prevents you from admitting when you're wrong." I toss my head. "And you surround yourself with people who say yes to you because they're too afraid to tell you where you're lacking."

Damn, that came out better than I expected.

His gaze widens.

Yep, that was impressive. Enough to have surprised this jerk. I should rejoice; except, with every moment, my spirit plummets. My adrenaline, which had spiked, now begins to recede. In place of that galloping sense of euphoria is a sinking hole... One that tells me how much I've screwed up.

Then he glances down to where I have my finger pushed into his chest. I've been deeply conscious of it and enjoying the feel of those brick-like planes shift. Too much, perhaps. I lower my arm. Take a step back.

It's a first sign of capitulation, which he instantly seizes upon.

"Are you done?" he asks in a low voice.

One thing about my boss? When he gets upset, he becomes calmer, and his tone grows more casual. But the atmosphere seems to grow electric. I swear, I can hear rolling thunder, and dark clouds, and crackling lightning. Also, I can almost imagine the horns on his head lighting up. In fact, I'm sure I can smell sulphur in the air.

Those gray eyes are now colorless, like the ashes left behind after a fire. A fire that has consumed me and burned me to a husk. The hair on the back of my neck rises. Oh no.

No. No. No. I'm in so much trouble.

"I—" I look around the kitchen. Take in Leo, staring at me with his mouth open. One of the other line chefs stands over an open pot with a dripping spoon. The grill chef looks at me like I've lost my mind. Which, admittedly, I think I have.

The junior chef continues to film us. When I scowl at her, she hastily lowers the phone and slips it into her pocket.

"I— Um— I'm—" *Not going to apologize.*

I didn't say anything wrong. If anything, I've only outlined how full of himself he is. How horribly he's treated me and the rest of his team.

I set my jaw. "I'm not sorry for what I said."

His eyes widen. A flash of something—very much like lightning—flashes in his eyes. Those luscious lips part slightly. I do believe, I've managed to surprise my boss again. I should celebrate... Except, it feels like this is my funeral. My stomach drops to my feet. Best to get out while I still have some pride intact. I pivot and race toward the exit that leads to the alleyway. I pull open the back door, and only when I enter, do I realize I'm in the walk-in fridge.

Harper

The door shuts after me. The noise from the restaurant fades. The light from the kitchen cuts off. The motion sensor kicks in, and the overhead fluorescent lights turn on. I should head out again and find my way out, but really, it feels so much safer in here. Maybe I'll stay here and freeze to death? At least, I won't have to face Lucifer out there.

Slowly, I move to a far corner where there's a sturdy delivery box. I wipe off the frost on it, then sink down. The chill begins to penetrate my skin. Damn. Maybe this wasn't such a good idea?

I pull my knees up to my chest, cross my arms over them, and rest my head on my folded arms.

That was so, so stupid. Why did I have to lose my temper? Why couldn't I have nodded along to whatever he said, then gone back to my life? Why did I give in to the bone deep exhaustion and allow my emotions to overtake me? I don't have enough control over my feelings.

I take things to heart. And I have never been good at hiding my thoughts either. Ugh. And I thought I'd been doing so well. I lasted six months—six hellish months—as sous chef to the most infuriating boss in the world. I should get a medal. And a pay rise. And he should be thanking me for keeping things going whenever he's had to leave the restaurant suddenly for a few days.

Instead, he comes back twice as grumpy and with more of a ferocious temper. He seems determined to make me slip up so he can gloat at my mistakes. In fact, sometimes it feels like he's angling for a reason to fire me. And I handed it to him on a silver platter.

At least, I stood up to him. If only I hadn't spoiled my grand exit by going through the wrong door.

A few more minutes pass. The overhead lights switch off, leaving me in complete darkness. I'm not scared though. It's comforting to be able to take the weight off my feet and sit here, surrounded by boxes of food and meat and vegetables, and that curious scent which is a mishmash of many things and smells like nothing. My heartbeat slowly settles. The adrenaline fades. I yawn and close my eyes. I'm so tired that, despite the chill wrapping around my shoulders like a cloak, I fall asleep.

When the door to the freezer opens again, I'm so startled, I fall off the crate and onto the floor. I hit my tailbone and whimper before looking up from where I'm sprawled on the floor. The fluorescent lights flicker on, bathing the figure silhouetted in the doorway in a bluish light. It picks out blue tints in his dark hair which I don't think I noticed before.

I take in the breadth of his shoulders. He's so tall, the top of his head seems to brush the ceiling. My boss is a handsome mofo, no question. And he has the bad attitude to go with it. He's a Grade-A arse. A bloody crumblehead. A Count Crankula. A pickled in self-importance meatball. *Ha.* I swallow down my chuckle.

At least, I haven't lost the ability to see the lighter side of things.

He stalks toward me, pulls up another overturned crate and sits on it. Then he jerks his head toward my seat. I rise to my feet, resist the urge to rub at my smarting backside, and sink onto my box.

"How long have I been in here?" I clear my throat.

"Almost half an hour."

Damn, it felt like two hours. My back feels stiff. And my legs seem to have gone to sleep.

"Were you planning to come out any time soon?" His voice is husky and rumbly and sets off little sparks in my belly. I have got to stop noticing my boss's obvious physical attributes. Besides, he's my friend Phe's brother. So, I definitely can't objectify him. And let's not forget, I hate this man.

"I'm good," I belie my words with a shiver. My feet are so cold, I can barely feel them. I shove my hands under my armpits in an attempt to warm them. Hunch in my shoulders to contain my body heat. Despite my best efforts, another tremor overtakes my body.

He frowns. Then unbuttons his chef's jacket and shrugs it off his powerful shoulders. I did not look at how it caught on his massive biceps or how he had to peel it off. I did not notice how thick his fingers are or how broad his hands are.

"Here." He hands me his jacket.

"I d-don't n-n-need th-that." Of course, my attempt at being firm is spoiled by my chattering teeth.

He merely drops it around my shoulders, then tugs the front over my arms.

Instantly, it feels like I'm being enveloped in his body heat. And that scent of his, like burnt sugar and the clean heat of sea salt, over-powers me.

I fill my lungs with the heady scent. Then realize what I've done. Thankfully, he doesn't seem to notice it. Maybe, it's because I feel a little vulnerable after that outburst. That's why I'm so aware of him.

"So, what was that about?" He nods in the direction of the kitchen.

I look away. I'm not going to pretend I don't know what he means.

"I didn't mean to lose my temper," I finally say.

"Sure, you did."

There's so much conviction in his voice, I jerk my chin in his direction. He's watching me from under hooded eyelids, an assessing quality about his gaze.

He's surveying me like he does the ingredients of a dish he's going to put together. Measuring, planning, tracing the different steps in the process. Imagining how the final result will look.

It's clinical and focused. Like he's seeing through the walls I've put up between me and the world.

"What?" I scowl, forgetting I resolved not to challenge this man again. Though it doesn't matter, considering he's probably not going to be my boss anymore.

"What got you so riled up that you snapped?"

My jaw drops. I cough. "You don't hold back do you?

"Life's too short to not say what you're thinking."

"Is that your personal philosophy? Is that why you're always so unfiltered?" At least, I got to ask him one of the questions I've always had about him.

The light shifts in his eyes. He stares at me steadily. I shift my weight, trying to find a more comfortable position. Even my arse is cold. I tug his jacket closer, glad for its cover.

"I was a Marine. I had many near-death experiences. Each time, I took it as a sign that I'd been given a new lease on life and that I shouldn't waste it."

"Makes sense." I'm surprised he's sharing so much of himself. In the months I've known him, he's barely grunted at me. Except for the time he hired me, when he laid out the unwritten rules of his kitchen, which were basically:

The chef is always right.
The chef is always right.
The chef is always right.

Okay, not exactly. But close:

Speak less.
No excuses. Only results.
Don't let the door hit you on the way out.

The last, because so many sous chefs before me had quit. None lasted more than three months. I'm positively a unicorn at six months on the job. You'd think he'd want to find a way to keep me as a result? But apparently, not. Despite his reputation as a nightmare taskmaster—or perhaps, because of it—there's a queue of people lining up to work with him. I'll be replaced in hours, if not minutes. And neither he nor the kitchen—not even the friends I made here—will miss me.

"When I left the Marines, I had one goal in mind. To cook so well, I could not be ignored. I set my mind, not on becoming the best—"

"No?"

He shakes his head. "I wanted... Still want to be the only one doing what I do. I knew I had to break the rules to create something new. To reinterpret the old classics. To redefine what fine dining meant."

"It's why you never let a dish leave the kitchen unless it's flawless."

"I also know that what I'm making here is my legacy. This is the way I will pass something on. An identity. A philosophy. A mindset, perhaps."

I nod, entranced. All of which makes sense. The Michelin stars are like winning gold in Olympics—in the culinary world. You have to be beyond exceptional to have gained three like James has.

"You live by discipline, hierarchy and precision. You have to account for every detail in the kitchen. Orchestrate each dish like a symphony. So each one is a masterpiece."

"You're as good as your last dish," he agrees.

It's true. "I don't disagree, but—"

His gaze widens. He hadn't expected me to interject that, huh?

Well, surprise. "When you're so obsessed with control—"

His eyebrows rise, probably because I used the word 'obsessed,' but I push on. "—when you're so obsessed with control that any deviation feels like a failure, then it's that very control that stifles your creativity."

He goes still. His shoulders seem to turn into boulders. His massive chest stills. He stares, unblinking. Those gray eyes of his turn into pools of glass. Colorless and fathomless. If the last time our eyes met it felt like a breeze had blown in from the Tundra, now it feels like we're on the moon without any protective gear. That's how stark and cold it feels. And it has nothing to do with the fact that we're in a freezer.

My heart seems to stop beating. *Did I go too far?* Ice seems to bite the space between us.

A fresh wave of goosebumps dots my skin. Without conscious command, my legs seem to move of their own accord, and I to rise to my feet.

I sidle toward the doorway, not daring to look over my shoulder. He hasn't spoken a word, which is good… Right?

I reach the door and grab the handle when his voice stops me.

"Come here," he orders.

I freeze. The command in his voice snaps at my nerve endings and vibrates to my core. I'm suddenly so turned on. Liquid heat pools between my legs. My nipples tighten. *No, no, no.* I cannot admit to being so attracted to this man that I'll do anything he asks of me. Though, if I'm being honest, that's one of the reasons I've stayed on in my job. It's why I put up with his bossiness. Because it secretly turns me on. And that's so very unprofessional. Because I'm a sous chef with five years of experience.

My last job was with a very well-known restaurant in London. I know what I'm doing. But he treats me like I'm a novice. Still, the absolute authority in his voice, and the fact that he's my boss, stops me. I pivot, then make my way to him. Coming to a stop in front of him, it feels like I've been called to the principal's office. Or for an audience with the devil himself.

"I came in to show you something."

"You did?" Had not been expecting him to say that.

He pulls out his phone, swipes it, then turns it around and shows it to me. For a few seconds, I don't understand what I'm seeing, then my jaw drops. "Is that... Is that—" I'm unable to complete my sentence.

"It is."

"But how—?" I look on in horror as our earlier interaction in the kitchen plays out on his phone. "Who uploaded it to social media?" Then I remember the person filming us. "Was it Tilda, the junior chef?"

"Whoever did it is gone."

Right. Okay. I can't take my gaze off the video clip which has amassed... "A million views?" I gasp.

"And counting." He navigates out of the screen, sliding the phone back into the pocket of his pants.

"That's... That's terrible." I swallow.

"Or an opportunity."

"I look like I'm having a meltdown, and the comments... I haven't seen them yet, but I can guess what they're saying."

"They haven't been complimentary...completely," he admits.

"I bet none of them criticize you," I say bitterly. Typically, it's the woman who gets the short end of the shrift in these cases.

"There might have been a few which marveled that the normally bad-mouthed chef seemed to be stunned into silence."

"That doesn't seem like a compliment to me, somehow."

"They seemed to think it was a lovers' quarrel."

"What?" My jaw drops. In fact, my knees give way, and I sit back down on my upturned carton heavily. "That's it, I'm definitely not leaving this...this...walk-in fridge." I look around the blue-light lit space. "I guess there's enough here to eat for me to survive. Not the fresh meat, but I could eat the tomatoes and the edible fruits and vegetables. And I can manage with this set of clothes and—"

"Stop," he commands.

I firm my lips, feeling the words bubble up my throat, but not giving voice to them. Instead, I content myself with scowling at him. "Easy for you to say. I bet you're not the one being painted the villain of the piece."

"On the contrary. My phone has been ringing off the hook. The investors of my restaurant are very upset."

Oh no. "That doesn't sound good."

"It isn't." His voice grows hard.

A prickling of discomfort crawls up my spine. I shove it aside. "Bet you can convince them otherwise."

"I did."

"Okay?" That prickle of discomfort turns into a volley of agitation. I squirm around on my carton, trying to find a better position. "What does that have to do with me?"

"Everything." He drums his fingers on his thigh. "I assume you want to keep your job?"

I straighten. *No way. He's going to let me keep my job?* After what I said? And after having insulted him in front of the staff? Not to mention, the negative PR from that little viral video clip? "You're kidding, right?" I snort.

He stays unmoved. His expression turns to stone.

"Guess not." I hunch my shoulders. This entire conversation is getting very weird. I can't put my finger on it, but there's something behind these questions he's asking me.

"I convinced my investors there was a reason behind that clip. A

very good reason, which convinced them not to pull their invest-
ments, and also to put more money into a PR campaign in the same
vein."

I'm relieved. "If the investors don't pull out, then the restaurant
can keep running. Which means, I have a job?"

"You do."

Some of the tension fades from my shoulders. "And to be clear, I
do want the job. Definitely. And I promise never to challenge you
again. Well, not unless it's something you say which is so obnoxious
that I don't have a choice." I cringe hearing my own words, but it's
best to be upfront. Best to be truthful. I wouldn't be truthful if I said
I'd stay silent no matter what, right?

His eyes flash. A nerve throbs at his temple. "Obnoxious?"

Yeah, not the best adjective to have used. "You're the one who
said it's best to say what you're thinking right?"

He nods slowly.

"You have to admit, some of the things you say are not conducive
to the workplace."

He curls his fingers into a fist. The veins on his arm stand out in
relief. The cords of his throat are so pronounced, I'm sure he's going
to have a coronary. He draws in a deep breath. Another. Seems to
get himself under control. Then nods. "You may have a point." He
bites out the words through gritted teeth.

That's unexpected. I look at him with suspicion. It's not like him
to agree to what I've said. Unless—a bulb seems to go off in my
head. "There are conditions attached to your investors not pulling the
money."

He jerks his chin. "As I said, many of the viewers are convinced
what they saw was a lovers' quarrel. Enough that my investors
thought the same."

"You dissuaded them from that misconception, I assume."

His face grows closed. "Unfortunately, not."

That feeling of discomfort under my skin is now full-grown
dread. And agitation. And a strange apprehension. Oh my God, I'm
not going to like what he's going to say. I'm not. I manage to tamp
down my thoughts. "What..." I clear my throat. "What are you trying

to say?" I say through lips gone numb. This time, not just from the cold.

He squeezes the bridge of his nose, and when he opens his eyes there's a look of fatalism in them. "Nothing I said could convince them that we—" He frowns. "That we aren't in a relationship. Ultimately, I had no choice but to agree to their condition."

"Wh-what condition?" I whisper.

He cracks his neck, then rolls his shoulders like he's preparing for a fight. When he looks at me next, his expression is twisted, like he's finding what he's going to say deeply unpleasant. "My investors will not pull their money from the restaurant, provided we get married."

To find out what happens next, read James and Harper's best-friend's-brother, marriage-of-convenience romance, in *The Unwilling Bride* by L. Steele.

BONUS SCENE

Lark

"Mom, I promise I'm not working too hard." I glance around my office. This used to be my husband's office at Davenport Capital, but he insisted I take it over since he prefers to either work from home or on the road with outreach activities related to Davenport Foundation. He's also busy finding and backing new startups who can revolutionize the way we provide intel to our troops.

"You are CEO of a multi-billion-dollar company. That's no small change." She wags a finger at me from my phone screen.

My jaw drops. "How did you find out what Davenport Capital makes?"

"I know how to use the internet," she scoffs.

"But you've never previously been interested in my career." I can't keep the surprise out of my voice.

Her features soften. "I haven't been very supportive of your career, I'm aware."

"It's fine—" I begin.

She shakes her head. "It's not fine, Lark. You've worked so hard to get to where you are. And I've never appreciated it."

"You and Dad made sure Raya and I never lacked for anything. That's why you went into debt."

"We did what we had to do." Her features soften. "We love you. The two of you are the most important things in our lives."

A warm sensation fills my chest. I never doubted that my parents loved me, but to hear her say it aloud is everything.

"Oh, Mom." Warmth pricks the backs of my eyes.

Since I got married, something has shifted between my mother and me. It's like the moment she saw that ring on my finger, she finally exhaled. For the first time, she isn't holding her breath over my unmarried state. She can actually see *me*. My career, my choices, the life I've built.

"Now, now, no tears." She sniffs and dabs at her cheek. "Where's that handsome husband of yours?"

The door to my office opens. My husband stands framed in the entrance, his wide shoulders taking up the space in a way that makes my breath catch.

He swaggers in, wearing a sweatshirt that stretches across his massive chest, with a leather jacket that's seen better days. And those ripped jeans. Damn, they mold to his powerful thighs and lovingly outline every muscle rippling under his skin as he prowls toward me.

His spine is erect. It reminds me of the Marine he once was. The shadow on his face, and the hair on his head cut so close to the scalp, give him a dangerous edge. My heart stutters. My thighs quiver. Every cell in my body seems to hum with appreciation and anticipation at seeing him.

"He just got here," I say to Mom without looking away from my husband's gorgeous face.

He walks over to put his arm around me.

"Sheila." He nods at her.

"Brody, lovely to see you." My mother beams. "How was your business trip?"

"Good. Productive. But not as satisfying as coming home to my wife." He pulls me close and kisses my forehead.

"Aww." My mother sniffs again. "That's so sweet. You two are adorable. You take care of my daughter, you hear me now?"

"Yes, ma'am." He touches his fingers to his forehead in a mock salute.

"I have to go now, but it was lovely talking to both of you." She disconnects.

I place the phone down and turn fully into my husband's embrace. I wrap my arms around his broad torso, trying to embrace as much of him as I can reach.

Then bury my nose in his chest. The scent of pine and sandalwood with dark peppery overtones fills my sense. My body finally relaxes. It's as if, on some primitive level, I finally register that he's home. "I missed you."

"Me too." He tips up my chin. "I'm going to have to find a way to spend more time at home. I can't bear to be away from you."

"But your work—"

"Is important. But not as much as being with you." He releases me long enough to pull out his phone. He slides his finger across the screen. Instantly the glass walls of the office turn opaque. I catch sight of my EA surreptitiously watching us before her face cuts out. She's great at her role, and is not a gossip, but I can sense the curiosity in her eyes whenever Brody comes into my office.

Especially because I've made it clear to her that she needs to hold my calls and cancel meetings for as long as Brody is with me.

No doubt, she knows exactly what we're up to in here, but honestly, I couldn't care less.

The title and the power I wield has come with a confidence in my own actions. That, and the fact that I'm secure in my husband's love. And that I'm hungry for every bit of attention he bestows on me. Enough to focus on my needs and not pay attention to the speculation of the world around me.

I can't control what people decide to say about me. But I can control how I feel about myself. About how I make the most of every second I have with my very handsome, very hot husband.

He boosts me up and onto the desk.

I wrap my legs around his waist and hold onto his shoulders.

"You feel so good." I reach up to try and kiss him. But he grabs my wrists and twists my arms behind my back.

He takes in my flushed features and the thrust of my breasts against my blouse and the jacket I'm wearing over it.

"Mrs. CEO, at my mercy." He smirks.

I wriggle a little, and his hold around my wrists tightens. A thrill of anticipation scrolls up my spine. I love it when he holds me down. When I can test my strength against his and realize how powerful he is. When it feels like I'm here to do his bidding. And the flex of his biceps, and the swell of his shoulders, and the tent at his crotch tell me how much he wants me. And the tenderness in his eyes reveals the love he feels for me.

"Mr. CEO, my husband." I smile up at him.

"No longer CEO," he reminds me.

"You'll always be the CEO of my life."

"Oh?" He rakes his gaze down my face to the hint of cleavage exposed by my jacket. "So, you'll do everything I ask of you."

"Always," I say without hesitation.

"Good." He releases me and steps back. He walks across the floor to the armchair in the sitting area of the office. He sprawls in it, thighs spread apart. The shape of his cock is visible against the zipper of his jeans. My mouth waters. He looks so big. So brawny. So utterly male. And with that smirk playing around his lips, and that intent look in his lust-filled eyes, he's a far cry from the Grinch I labelled him as.

I take a leisurely tour of his gorgeous body. The way the jacket stretches across his shoulders. His trim waist. His muscle-bound thighs, the very masculine scuffed boots he has on his big feet. Confidence oozes from his pores. The assurance he carries around his shoulders like a cloak hums in the air between us.

"Take the rope on your desk and put it between your teeth."

He's referring to the braided rope he had on his desk and which I insisted he leave behind as it makes me feel close to him.

"What?" I frown.

"Is that you picking a fight, Siren?" His unhurried drawl carries an edge of menace that hits me like a spark. My body tightens.

Hungry anticipation squeezes my guts and turns my pussy into a quivering mess.

"N...no." I reach for the knotted rope on my desk and place it between my lips.

"Good girl."

Happiness blooms in my chest at his praise. Need pours through my blood with such force, my knees almost give way.

Of course, my husband knows exactly what he's doing to my body, for he crooks his finger. "Crawl to me."

Brody

Without hesitation, she folds to the floor, onto her hands and knees. She's wearing a designer suit, with red-soled heels. She earns enough to afford the best to wear. She runs a company worth billions. Can hold down a boardroom filled with corporate sharks who wouldn't hesitate to cut her down if she got one nuance wrong. Yet, she bends to me.

It's a heady sensation. One which drains the blood to my groin. My cock extends further, pushing up against my jeans. My erection is almost painful. My skin feels like it's on fire with longing for this beautiful, gorgeous woman who's my wife.

She keeps her eyes lowered, as she slowly crawls the breadth of the office. Each move forward makes the rounded shape of her arse sway. The neckline of her blouse dips, affording me a view of the peaks of her tits. I'm almost impossibly hard now. But I make no move to relieve myself. Why should I, when my wife's mouth will soon enough afford me that particular pleasure.

She reaches me, coming to a stop between my thighs.

I pat her head. "Very good."

A visible shudder rolls up her spine.

I take the rope from her and tease out the knots while she waits obediently.

I shake it out with a swish.

She shivers.

I hook it over the arm of the seat, then slide my legs further apart. She crawls into the space.

"Take it out." I nod toward my crotch.

Instantly, she sits up on her knees. She lowers my zipper, and my cock bounces free.

"Oh." She draws in a sharp breath.

Yep, I'm not wearing boxers. Did I come here, hoping for this scene? Maybe. Subconsciously. I planned to make the most of it if the opportunity presented itself to me.

"Suck me off," I order.

She leans in, wraps her fingers around the base of my shaft. Then licks up my length to my crown.

"Fuck." I jerk my pelvis forward in reflex. Goosebumps pepper my skin. My thigh muscles tighten into tempered steel.

She looks up at me from under her eyelids. Then closes her mouth around my cock.

I groan, "Siren, your mouth."

I slide my fingers through the hair she's twisted into an intricate coil at the nape of her neck. The clip she used falls to the floor. Her hair rains around her face. Damn. I love stripping her of that professional façade she wears. Love seeing her give up that carefully fought for control she needs to lead. Love that she trusts me enough to give up her decision-making to me. With me, she can relax. She can allow me to lead, knowing I'd never do anything to ever hurt her. She carries a lot of stress during the day, but when she comes to me, I know exactly how to relieve her of that tension. How to take her mind off everything else but pleasuring me.

I hold her gaze as she licks and sucks, and when she takes me down her throat, it feels like I'm being held in a vise.

"Jesus." I grit my teeth, trying to stop myself from coming so quickly. Sweat beads my forehead. My stomach muscles lock tight. I tighten my hold in her hair, easing her back until my cock is balanced between her lips.

Then I slide her forward, watching as my dick disappears down her throat again.

Saliva drools from the corners of her mouth, and down her chin.

Her chest rises and falls. The pulse at the base of her neck flutters in sync with the beats of my heart.

"You're so gorgeous," I praise her.

Her pupils dilate further. Her cheeks flush. She swallows around my shaft, and fuck me, but I know I can't hold back further. The pressure at the base of my spine tightens. "I'm going to come, and you're going to swallow every drop."

She nods.

Then the tension unfurls and zips out to my extremities, and I'm pouring my cum down her throat.

I can't seem to stop coming, a testament to how much my wife turns me on.

When she swallows, I'm filled with this affection overflowing my chest. With my heart racing, and my pulse rate high enough for me to see black spots at the corners of my vision, I ease her back, until my dick slips out of her mouth.

Then I pull her up, until she's seated on my thigh, and kiss her deeply.

The taste of her, combined with that of my cum, goes straight to my head. "You drive me crazy," I murmur against her mouth. I want to tie you up and fuck you until you can't walk straight, but I don't want to mess you up so much that you can't go back to work either.

She moans against my mouth. "I do want you to tie me up too. Please?" Her tone is pleading. The look in her eyes still hungry.

I find myself giving in. It could be something fast and simple. Something that won't mess with her clothes.

But also give her the release she needs.

I guide her arms up and fold them loosely across the front of her jacket, arranging her exactly where I want her.

Then I take up the rope and draw it around her chest in two slow, unhurried passes. Each wrap settles against her skin like a stroke of my own hands, framing her curves with deliberate care. The rope molds to her, soft yet certain, marking the place where my touch would stay if I could hold her forever.

I slide the rope between the bands, tightening it enough for her to feel the shift, the claim, the quiet pull of intention running through both of us.

A breath escapes her. Not quite a sigh, not quite a moan. Something in between. I tie off the final knot, the harness settling against her like a whispered promise.

Her body melts, her muscles loosening under my hands as if she's sinking into the moment. Into me.

I finish the harness with a final pull and knot, the rope resting against her like a promise she can feel.

I kiss her, and she melts into me completely. Holding her around the waist, I stand up with her.

Walking her over to her desk, I lower her until her feet touch the floor. I lift up her skirt, so it's bunched around her waist. Then I pull off her panties. I plant her on the desk, easing her onto her back.

Then pull up one of the chairs and sit. The width of my shoulders forces her to spread her legs. I urge her to throw her legs over my shoulders, then bend and run my nose up her slit.

"Brody," she moans.

Unable to touch me, given her restrained arms, she writhes about. I slide my hands around her upper thighs and squeeze. "Hold still."

She freezes.

"Now, don't take your eyes off of me," I order.

Without waiting for her acknowledgement, I hold her pussy lips open, then lick her from the pleated skin between her butt cheeks up to her slit. I stab my tongue inside her pussy, and she cries out.

She squeezes her thighs around my face, and I welcome the pressure. I glide my tongue up her pussy again, then lap at her clit.

"Ohgod. Ohgod," she gasps.

Not letting up, I slide two fingers inside her weeping slit, then bite down gently on her clit.

"Brody." She arches her back.

"Come in my mouth, Siren," I order.

With a long low moan, she explodes. Her climax sweeps through her. And she shudders and whimpers. Her cum bathes my tongue. I lap it up. Lick up the moisture that drips from her slit. Then I rise up.

I bend over her and fit my very erect shaft to her opening.

"I'm going to fuck you, Siren."

Lark

My mind has barely registered his words when he thrusts his hips forward and impales me. I cry out. I'll never get used to his size. I'm so very wet, and yet, he's too big to slip in completely. He pulls back, looking deeply into my eyes. "Open for me, wife."

As always, his calling me wife does something to my insides. My heart melts. My pussy softens further. And this time, when he pistons forward, he slides inside all the way. His balls slap against my inner thighs. The crown of his shaft brushes up against my innermost secret spot.

A tingling shoots out from the point of contact. My pores pop. My scalp tingles. Unable to dig my fingers into his scalp, I curl my fingers into fists, gulp in air, and hold on for the ride. And what a ride it is.

He plants his arms on either side of me, holding up his weight. His biceps stretch the sleeves of his jacket.

He holds my gaze, like he's peering into my soul. It's the intimacy of it which always touches me in places deep inside. And then physically, he tunnels into me, again and again. Putting the power of his body behind each long, deep stroke.

It's so intense. So intimate. I'm the focus of his attention, the recipient of his ministrations. And it's the most incredibly erotic feeling in this world.

Sweat beads his forehead. His lips are slightly parted, his eyelids hooded. His shoulders seem to swell. I sense him gathering the energy within himself. And then he tilts his hips at the right angle that when he plunges forward this time, he rubs up against my clit.

Then his cock stretches me in that way that's half pain and half pleasure, and the crown rams into my G-spot. Oh my God, the sensations swell my skin and zip up my spine. My entire body shudders. My toes curl.

"Come," he orders.

And my climax crashes over me. The vibrations shoot out to my extremities. A scream of pleasure wells up my throat. I'm half aware that, from my office, it might be heard outside, but am unable to stop myself. Then he closes his mouth around mine and swallows down the sound. I jolt and shudder and give myself up to the waves of ecstasy enveloping me.

And then I feel more than hear him grunt as he follows me over the edge.

Aftershocks ripple through my body. And his. He lowers more of his weight on me, his dick throbbing inside me. Then raises his head. I flutter my eyes open, to see him gazing at me with tenderness and awe.

"That was incredible. You were incredible." He kisses my forehead, then straightens.

When his dick slips out of me, it leaves a trail of wetness against my inner thigh. He helps me to sit up. With quick, efficient moves, he unknots, then unwinds the rope from around me. He places it aside.

"Stay there." He points to me.

He puts himself to order and heads for the en suite bathroom. Then emerges a few seconds later with a wet hand towel. He wipes up between my legs. I'm floating high on the endorphins, the sensations creeping back into my limbs.

He helps me into my panties, urges me to stand, then smooths down my skirt.

"Wow." I look up into his beloved face. "That was one heck of a way to get my mind off the meeting with the finance team."

"I bet you're going to do a great job."

I continue to beam up at him.

He laughs. "You look like you've been thoroughly fucked, Mrs. Davenport."

"It's your magic dick, Mr. Davenport."

"Come on, you need to fix your makeup." He grabs the soiled hand towel, then my handbag and leads me to the bathroom.

By the time I emerge, the walls of the office are, once more, transparent. And he's on the couch, scrolling through his phone.

There's a buzzing sound. I reach my desk and see the message from Harper.

Harper: Help, we need to speak.

Then Brody's phone buzzes, too. He picks it up. "James. Hello, mate." He listens, frowning. "Slow down. I can't understand what you're talking about."

I raise my eyebrows in query.

Brody shrugs.

"What do you mean? You're following in my footsteps?"

Intrigued, I walk over to sit next to Brody

"You're thinking of getting married?" He looks at me. "Oh, you *are* getting married?" He rubs the back of his neck. Amazement is writ large in his eyes. "To whom?"

His gaze widens.

"To Harper?"

To find out what happens next, read *James and Harper's story*

Read an excerpt from Summer *&* Sinclair Sterling's *fake relationship romance in* The Billionaire's Fake Wife

Summer

"Slap, slap, kiss, kiss."

"Huh?" I stare up at the bartender.

"Aka, there's a thin line between love and hate." He shakes out the crimson liquid into my glass.

"Nah." I snort. "Why would she allow him to control her, and after he insulted her?"

"It's the chemistry between them." He lowers his head, "You have to admit that when the man is arrogant and the woman resists, it's a challenge to both of them, to see who blinks first, huh?"

"Why?" I wave my hand in the air, "Because they hate each other?"

"Because," he chuckles, "the girl in school whose braids I pulled and teased mercilessly, is the one who I—"

"Proposed to?" I huff.

His face lights up. "You get it now?"

Yeah. No. A headache begins to pound at my temples. This crash course in pop psychology is not why I came to my favorite bar in Islington, to meet my best friend, who is—I glance at the face of my phone—thirty minutes late.

I inhale the drink, and his eyebrows rise.

"What?" I glower up at the bartender. "I can barely taste the alcohol. Besides, it's free drinks at happy hour for women, right?"

"Which ends in precisely" he holds up five fingers, "minutes."

"Oh! Yay!" I mock fist pump. "Time enough for one more, at least."

A hiccough swells my throat and I swallow it back, nod.

One has to do what one has to do… when everything else in the world is going to shit.

A hot sensation stabs behind my eyes; my chest tightens. Is this what people call growing up?

The bartender tips his mixing flask, strains out a fresh batch of the ruby red liquid onto the glass in front of me.

"Salut." I nod my thanks, then toss it back. It hits my stomach and tendrils of fire crawl up my spine, I cough.

My head spins. Warmth sears my chest, spreads to my extremities. I can't feel my fingers or toes. Good. Almost there. "Top me up."

"You sure?"

"Yes." I square my shoulders and reach for the drink.

"No. She's had enough."

"What the—?" I pivot on the bar stool.

Indigo eyes bore into me.

Fathomless. Black at the bottom, the intensity in their depths grips me. He swoops out his arm, grabs the glass and holds it up.

Thick fingers dwarf the glass. Tapered at the edges. The nails short and buff. *All the better to grab you with*. I gulp.

"Like what you see?"

I flush, peer up into his face.

Hard cheekbones, hollows under them, and a tiny scar that slashes at his left eyebrow. *How did he get that?* Not that I care. My gaze slides to his mouth. Thin upper lip, a lower lip that is full and cushioned. Pouty with a hint of bad boy. *Oh!* My toes curl. My thighs clench.

The corner of his mouth kicks up. *Asshole.*

Bet he thinks life is one big smug-fest. I glower, reach for my glass, and he holds it up and out of my reach.

I scowl. "Gimme that."

He shakes his head.

"That's my drink."

"Not anymore." He shoves my glass at the bartender. "Water for her. Get me a whiskey, neat."

I splutter, then reach for my drink again. The barstool tips in his direction. This is when I fall against him, and my breasts slam into his hard chest, sculpted planes with layers upon layers of muscle that ripple and writhe as he turns aside, flattens himself against the bar. The floor rises up to meet me.

What the actual hell?

I twist my torso at the last second and my butt connects with the surface. *Ow!*

The breath rushes out of me. My hair swirls around my face. I scramble for purchase, and my knee connects with his leg.

"Watch it." He steps around, stands in front of me.

"You stepped aside?" I splutter. "You let me fall?"

"Hmph."

I tilt my chin back, all the way back, look up the expanse of muscled thigh that stretches the silken material of his suit. *What is he wearing? Could any suit fit a man with such precision?* Hand crafted on Saville Row, no doubt. I glance at the bulge that tents the fabric between his legs. *Oh!* I blink.

Look away, look away. I hold out my arm. He'll help me up at least, won't he?

He glances at my palm, then turns away. *No, he didn't do that, no way.*

A glass of amber liquid appears in front of him. He lifts the tumbler to his sculpted mouth.

His throat moves, strong tendons flexing. He tilts his head back, and the column of his neck moves as he swallows. Dark hair covers his chin—it's a discordant chord in that clean-cut profile, I shiver. He would scrape that rough skin down my core. He'd mark my inner thighs, lick my core, thrust his tongue inside my melting channel and drink from my pussy. *Oh! God.* Goosebumps rise on my skin.

No one has the right to look this beautiful, this achingly gorgeous. Too magnificent for his own good. Anger coils in my chest.

"Arrogant wanker."

"I'll take that under advisement."

"You're a jerk, you know that?"

He presses his lips together. The grooves on either side of his mouth deepen. Jesus, clearly the man has never laughed a single day in his life. Bet that stick up his arse is uncomfortable. I chuckle.

He runs his gaze down my features, my chest, down to my toes, then yawns.

The hell! I will not let him provoke me. Will not. "Like what you see?" I jut out my chin.

"Sorry, you're not my type." He slides a hand into the pocket of those perfectly cut pants, stretching it across that heavy bulge.

Heat curls low in my belly.

Not fair, that he could afford a wardrobe that clearly shouts his status and what amounts to the economy of a small third-world country. A hot feeling stabs in my chest.

He reeks of privilege, of taking his status in life for granted.

While I've had to fight every inch of the way. Hell, I am still battling to hold onto the last of my equilibrium.

"Last chance—" I wiggle my fingers from where I am sprawled out on the floor at his feet, "—to redeem yourself..."

"You have me there." He places the glass on the counter, then bends and holds out his hand. The hint of discolored steel at his wrist catches my attention. Huh?

He wears a cheap-ass watch?

That's got to bring down the net worth of his presence by more than 1000% percent. Weird.

I reach up and he straightens.

I lurch back.

"Oops, I changed my mind." His lips curl.

A hot burning sensation claws at my stomach. I am not a violent person, honestly. But Smirky Pants here, he needs to be taught a lesson.

I swipe out my legs, kicking his out from under him.

Sinclair

My knees give way, and I hurtle toward the ground.

What the—? I twist around, thrust out my arms. My palms hit the floor. The impact jostles up my elbows. I firm my biceps and come to a halt planked above her.

A huffing sound fills my ear.

I turn to find my whippet, Max, panting with his mouth open. I scowl and he flattens his ears.

All of my businesses are dog-friendly. Before you draw conclusions about me being the caring sort or some such shit—it attracts footfall.

Max scrutinizes the girl, then glances at me. *Huh?* He hates women, but not her, apparently.

I straighten and my nose grazes hers.

My arms are on either side of her head. Her chest heaves. The fabric of her dress stretches across her gorgeous breasts. My fingers tingle; my palms ache to cup those tits, squeeze those hard nipples outlined against the—hold on, what is she wearing? A tunic shirt in a sparkly pink... and are those shoulder pads she has on?

I glance up, and a squeak escapes her lips.

Pink hair surrounds her face. *Pink? Who dyes their hair that color past the age of eighteen?*

I stare at her face. *How old is she?* Un-furrowed forehead, dark eyelashes that flutter against pale cheeks. Tiny nose, and that mouth —luscious, tempting. A whiff of her scent, cherries and caramel, assails my senses. My mouth waters. *What the hell?*

She opens her eyes and our eyelashes brush. Her gaze widens. Green, like the leaves of the evergreens, flickers of gold sparkling in their depths. "What?" She glowers. "You're demonstrating the plank position?"

"Actually," I lower my weight onto her, the ridge of my hardness thrusting into the softness between her legs, "I was thinking of something else, altogether."

She gulps and her pupils dilate. *Ah, so she feels it, too?*

I drop my head toward her, closer, closer.

Color floods the creamy expanse of her neck. Her eyelids flutter down. She tilts her chin up.

I push up and off of her.

"That... Sweetheart, is an emphatic 'no thank you' to whatever you are offering."

Her eyelids spring open and pink stains her cheeks. Adorable. Such a range of emotions across those gorgeous features in a few seconds. What else is hidden under that exquisite exterior of hers?

She scrambles up, eyes blazing.

Ah! The little bird is trying to spread her wings? My dick twitches. My groin hardens, *Why does her anger turn me on so, huh?*

She steps forward, thrusts a finger in my chest.

My heart begins to thud.

She peers up from under those hooded eyelashes. "Wake up and taste the wasabi, asshole."

"What does that even mean?"

She makes a sound deep in her throat. My dick twitches. My pulse speeds up.

She pivots, grabs a half-full beer mug sitting on the bar counter.

I growl, "Oh, no, you don't."

She turns, swings it at me. The smell of hops envelops the space.

I stare down at the beer-splattered shirt, the lapels of my camel colored jacket deepening to a dull brown. Anger squeezes my guts.

I fist my fingers at my side, broaden my stance.

She snickers.

I tip my chin up. "You're going to regret that."

The smile fades from her face. "Umm." She places the now empty mug on the bar.

I take a step forward and she skitters back. "It's only clothes." She gulps. "They'll wash."

I glare at her and she swallows, wiggles her fingers in the air. "I should have known that you wouldn't have a sense of humor."

I thrust out my jaw. "That's a ten-thousand-pound suit you destroyed."

She blanches, then straightens her shoulders. "Must have been some hot date you were trying to impress, huh?"

"Actually," I flick some of the offending liquid from my lapels, "it's you I was after."

"Me?" She frowns.

"We need to speak."

She glances toward the bartender who's on the other side of the bar. "I don't know you." She chews on her lower lip, biting off some of the hot pink. How would she look, with that pouty mouth fastened on my cock?

The blood rushes to my groin so quickly that my head spins. My pulse rate ratchets up. Focus, focus on the task you came here for.

"This will take only a few seconds." I take a step forward.

She moves aside.

I frown. "You want to hear this, I promise."

"Go to hell." She pivots and darts forward.

I let her go, a step, another, because... I can? Besides it's fun to create the illusion of freedom first; makes the hunt so much more entertaining, huh?

I swoop forward, loop an arm around her waist, and yank her toward me.

She yelps. "Release me."

Good thing the bar is not yet full. It's too early for the usual officegoers to stop by. And the staff...? Well they are well aware of who cuts their paychecks.

I spin her around and against the bar, then release her. "You will listen to me."

She swallows; she glances left to right.

Not letting you go yet, little Bird. I move into her space, crowd her.

She tips her chin up. "Whatever you're selling, I'm not interested."

I allow my lips to curl. "You don't fool me."

A flush steals up her throat, sears her cheeks. So tiny, so innocent. Such a good little liar. I narrow my gaze. "Every action has its consequences."

"Are you daft?" She blinks.

"This pretense of yours?" I thrust my face into hers, growling, "It's not working."

She blinks, then color suffuses her cheeks. "You're certifiably mad—"

"Getting tired of your insults."

"It's true, everything I said." She scrapes back the hair from her face.

Her fingernails are painted... You guessed it, pink.

"And here's something else. You are a selfish, egotistical jackass."

I smirk. "You're beginning to repeat your insults and I haven't even kissed you yet."

"Don't you dare." She gulps.

I tilt my head. "Is that a challenge?"

"It's a..." she scans the crowded space, then turns to me. Her lips firm, "...a warning. You're delusional, you jackass." She inhales a deep breath before she speaks, "Your ego is bigger than the size of a black hole." She snickers. "Bet it's to compensate for your lack of balls."

A-n-d, that's it. I've had enough of her mouth that threatens to never stop spewing words. How many insults can one tiny woman hurl my way? Answer: too many to count.

"You—"

I lower my chin, touch my lips to hers.

Heat, sweetness, the honey of her essence explodes on my palate. My dick twitches. I tilt my head, deepen the kiss, reaching for that something more... more... of whatever scent she's wearing on her skin, infused with that breath of hers that crowds my senses, rushes down my spine. My groin hardens; my cock lengthens. I thrust my tongue between those infuriating lips.

She makes a sound deep in her throat and my heart begins to pound.

So innocent, yet so crafty. Beautiful and feisty. The kind of complication I don't need in my life.

I prefer the straight and narrow. Gray and black, that's how I choose to define my world. She, with her flashes of color—pink hair and lips that threaten to drive me to the edge of distraction—is exactly what I hate.

Give me a female who has her priorities set in life. To pleasure me, get me off, then walk away before her emotions engage. Yeah. That's what I prefer.

Not this... this bundle of craziness who flings her arms around my shoulders, thrusts her breasts up and into my chest, tips up her chin, opens her mouth, and invites me to take and take.

Does she have no self-preservation? Does she think I am going to fall for her wide-eyed appeal? She has another thing coming.

I tear my mouth away and she protests.

She twines her leg with mine, pushes up her hips, so that melting softness between her thighs cradles my aching hardness.

I glare into her face and she holds my gaze.

Trains her green eyes on me. Her cheeks flush a bright red. Her lips fall open and a moan bleeds into the air. The blood rushes to my dick, which instantly thickens. *Fuck.*

Time to put distance between myself and the situation.

It's how I prefer to manage things. Stay in control, always. Cut out anything that threatens to impinge on my equilibrium. Shut it down or buy them off. Reduce it to a transaction. That I understand.

The power of money, to be able to buy and sell—numbers, logic. That's what's worked for me so far.

"How much?"

Her forehead furrows.

"Whatever it is, I can afford it."

Her jaw slackens. "You think… you —"

"A million?"

"What?"

"Pounds, dollars… You name the currency, and it will be in your account."

Her jaw slackens. "You're offering me money?"

"For your time, and for you to fall in line with my plan."

She reddens. "You think I am for sale?"

"Everyone is."

"Not me."

Here we go again. "Is that a challenge?"

Color fades from her face. "Get away from me."

"Are you shy, is that what this is?" I frown. "You can write your price down on a piece of paper if you prefer." I glance up, notice the bartender watching us. I jerk my chin toward the napkins. He grabs one, then offers it to her.

She glowers at him. "Did you buy him, too?"

"What do you think?"

She glances around. "I think everyone here is ignoring us."

"It's what I'd expect."

"Why is that?"

I wave the tissue in front of her face. "Why do you think?"

"You own the place?"

"As I am going to own you."

She sets her jaw. "Let me leave and you won't regret this."

A chuckle bubbles up. I swallow it away. This is no laughing matter. I never smile during a transaction. Especially not when I am negotiating a new acquisition. And that's all she is. The final piece in the puzzle I am building.

"No one threatens me."

"You're right."

"Huh?"

"I'd rather act on my instinct."

Her lips twist, her gaze narrows. All of my senses scream a warning.

No, she wouldn't, no way—pain slices through my middle and sparks explode behind my eyes.

TO FIND OUT WHAT HAPPENS NEXT READ SUMMER & SINCLAIR STERLING'S FAKE RELATIONSHIP ROMANCE IN THE BILLIONAIRE'S FAKE WIFE

ABOUT THE AUTHOR

Hello, I'm L. Steele.

I write romance stories with strong powerful men who meet their match in sassy, curvy, spitfire women.

I love to push myself with each book on both the spice and the angst so I can deliver well rounded, multidimensional characters.

I enjoy trading trivia with my husband, watching lots and lots of movies, and walking nature trails. I live in London.

Made in United States
North Haven, CT
28 December 2025